Hush Hush Honeysuckle

Katherine Black

Nightsgale Books

Message from Katherine

The Silas Nash series has character evolvement throughout the books; but each novel has a contained central story that stands-alone and can be read out of sequence.
I hope you enjoy my books.

Best Book Editions

1 3 5 7 9 10 8 6 4 2

First published in 2023 by Nightsgale Books, Suite 97320, PO Box 1213, Belfast, BT1 9JY

Paperback ISBN 979 8 3670486 1 2

Cover by Nightsgale Press

A CIP catalogue record of this book is available from the British Library

Contents

Chapter One

Chapter One

He would feel like killing himself again today.

He was a man without a purpose and therefore didn't make sense. Life had lost its meaning. In a fit of unaccustomed rage, Nash picked up his clock and threw it at the wall. He didn't understand what was happening to him, and a temper like this didn't fit his personality.

So what did?

He'd forgotten. The echoes of a violent dream swam around his head as he sat up in bed drenched in sweat.

Detective Chief Inspector Silas Nash was bored out of his mind. He didn't see the point of getting out of bed—but he did because that's what he'd done for almost half a century.

Five thirty. Get up, pee, and let the cat out.

Five forty. He would take his pyjamas off, fold and put them under his pillow. Shiver summer or winter, and shuffle into the ensuite shower.

And so his day progressed up to seven-thirty in the morning when he used to leave for work. Now he didn't, but the routine was still the same. Sometimes he'd go wild and put the coffee pot on instead of the kettle.

He'd never been a drinker, but since jumping at early retirement, he'd taken to having a pint in the evenings, sometimes he had several. Monday to Friday, a glass sat alongside his dinner—something on toast or a TV dinner.

At the weekend, Nash would stare at his whiteboard and have his second beer in his office with cheese and biscuits for supper. It was an established routine: crackers and a wedge of cheese. Nash was a man of structure and habit.

After eating and washing the things he'd used, he'd watch a police drama. There were plenty of them—and if all else failed, there were the boring ones, Broadchurch, Midsomer and Poirot. He looked forward to his weekends, especially if he was seeing Sandy, but more often than not, he was on his own these days, and TV was what separated Friday and Saturday from the rest of the week.

Nash was terrified of losing his edge. he couldn't lose what he called his blade—the part of his brain with the razor-sharp reason. In the afternoons, he'd do *The Times* crossword and watch general knowledge quizzes. However, that didn't sharpen the blade. Only detective work could do that.

He'd stop the show near the end when the story had developed, but no resolution had been reached. He'd take his supper into the office. This was where the programme came to life for Nash. At the centre of his whiteboard, he'd write the victim's name. Using spider graph lines, he'd add details about the victim. Gender and age first. Then their personality and character. Were they kind or unkind? He'd add more branches with the suspect's names and smaller twigs for each one's details. And then he came to the motive. What was the motive behind every suspect? Who had the most to gain? The final branch of the tree contained the clues. What had been dropped into the show in conversation? What was hidden in drawers?

Nash would work through the TV programme to solve the crime. Using his skill as a detective, he'd work out the perpetrator, murder weapon and motive. Most of the time, there was no challenge. The TV show was light entertainment and had to be dumbed down to cater to the masses.

Woman. Fifty-two. Suspects: spouse, colleague, jealous sister, and neighbour. The motive in order of suspects: Spouse—money. Colleague—after her job. Sister—money and infatuation with the spouse. They could be in it together. Neighbour—ownership of the property-line boundary. He added a branch, took it through all of his notes to the corner of the board, and wrote *Where does the son come into it?* He added the missing clues that had been drip-fed into the show.

This one was too easy. Her son got married. The mother commented on the flowers in the marital bed being toxic at night and warned the son to take them out before they went to sleep. They were indeed dangerous because, as far as the son knew, the victim had never seen the bedroom part of their bridal suite. Conclusion: the son murdered his mother in a jealous rage after she slept with his new husband on their wedding day. Too predictable.

Once he'd determined the outcome, he watched the final episode and was right. Always right.

This morning he'd thrown his clock at the wall, but that's all that set it apart from any other morning. Ensuite bathrooms and coffee machines, what a world we live in. He wasn't old but just about remembered the days of the toilet at the bottom of the yard. It was a clichéd story that people told their grandkids about the olden days, but he lived those times and remembered being four and standing with his pee-pee out in the middle of the night through the dead of winter. Monsters coming at you while you were peeing was unthinkable. He remembered candlewick blankets and a frosted Enigma Code on the inside of his window pane every morning.

It was a different world—too violent— and the reason he'd hung up his hat. He liked the old ways of policing, and sometimes he still wore a trilby, but only for funerals these days after ten years of ribbing by the young PCs.

The day was so damned long. He was at the peak of physical fitness and went to the gym five times a week. People said he was like an older David Beckham—Beckham's dad. the gym killed a few hours in the morning. Nash liked circuit training. He'd think back over his cases—the few unsolved ones—and pondered anything he might have missed. In Barrow-in-Furness, the crime rate was high, but the misdeeds were usually petty.

He'd left the force and by the time he'd accepted his golden hand-shake—very nice, thank you very much—he was putting away the kids of the people he'd sent down years earlier. They started young.

After weight training, he'd take a bracing cold shower and do a hundred lengths of the pool. His reward was a sauna. He'd have lunch at The Round House Hub and Café and discuss the decline of the town or at The Meeting Place bar, which was modern, but the food was good. Eight hours into his day, and he still had at least another eight to get through.

When he got home, he'd clean his house. It was pristine, spotless, and he didn't do it to be obsessive but just because there was nothing else to do. On the days when the cupboards and fridge groaned under the weight of food, he couldn't go shopping again, so he'd go for a brisk walk. He even did a couple of bouts of running. He was fitter than he'd been for years but stepped down to make way for the modern method of policing. You can't put solid old-way policy into a spread-sheet, for Christ's sake.

They have a database for how to be a policeman now.

When the house was more sterile than an operating theatre, and he'd talked to the cat until even she'd had enough of him—there was nothing left but the television. God, please save him from daytime television.

Far too much of his day was taken up by thinking about Sandy. After spending most of his adult life in one relationship he was dating again. But he felt ridiculous calling himself somebody's boyfriend. Things had been difficult between them lately, and there were only so many delicious moussaka and steak dishes he could make. When Sandy came over, it was the only opportunity he had to cook. There was no point in cooking for one. Sandy detested anything healthy and lived on junk food. Left to choice, their main meal would be McDonald's, and then bacon sandwiches for supper. Nash couldn't imagine anything worse.

Today he was making stuffed aubergine with a pork chop, couscous and a creamed mushroom sauce. He hoped Sandy would come to eat it with him. But Sandy and kept promises were words not used in the same sentence. Their nights were getting less regular. It might be the right time to progress to the next step and live together—but the thought of the mess Sandy made was unbearable.

It was late afternoon when his phone rang.

'Nash. It's Bronwyn Lewis.' She didn't give him a chance to respond with the usual pleasantries. 'How do you feel about coming back to work? We've got a case.'

Chapter Two

Chapter Two

Maxwell Jones was invincible. Nothing could touch him. He couldn't be killed because, at twenty-eight, he was already dead. He had a brain tumour, and it was terminal.

That morning, he'd worked two hours at his youth group for refugees and was humbled by how little the children and young people had. After everything they'd been through, they still smiled. Their homes had been bombed, and their relatives killed. And then, they'd risked their own lives by sailing to England—the land of plenty—in a sardine can. When they got here, they were housed in a concrete hell. They were spat on in the street, and wherever they went, the good British public abused them and told them, 'Go home. Scum.'

Max taught them to read, and he helped with their English. He taught them interview techniques and showed them how to find work. He'd even brought many of them into his own business, often having to create an opening for them, to the consternation of, Henry Watson, his business partner. Some of them robbed him blind, and some were doing well. Like every walk of life, there were good people and not-so-good people—and these were desperate people, which heightened the results of these extremes. Most of all, he taught them three words to help them through every brick wall. 'Sod you. Arsehole.' That got him into trouble with the organisers, but he wanted these good people—part of our country's future—to walk with dignity.

'Right, you motley rabble. Repeat after me Mot-ley rabble.'

There were thirty attempts with varying degrees of coherence. 'I'm going to the store cupboard. You know, that place where some of you find all kinds of goodies to flog outside Barrow Market? Keep practising, and when I come back, you're going to give me your opening gambits in an interview.'

As usual, in the store cupboard, supplies were low, and it wasn't, as he'd suggested in a joke, that the students were stealing them. He grabbed two of the last three reams of A4 paper and made a mental note to come back after class and place an order on his own company credit card. He'd done this at least once a month for six months, and Henry had gone from turning himself varying shades of purple to accepting that what couldn't be changed had to be endured. 'Henry, you old penny counter. You can't change how people treat you or what they say about you. All you can do is change how you react to it.' At this point, Henry would go into a rant about accountants and end-of-year bookkeeping. 'Blah, blah, blah,' Max would say before stealing chocolates from the dish Henry kept on his desk for clients.

Max grinned at the thought of another Henry tirade as he looked up. One of the refugees had come in, and he was almost nose-to-nose with him. Max jumped out of his skin. He was a big lad over six foot, with a shock of black hair and intense steel blue eyes. Max hadn't seen him before, but these frantic people came over in boats every week. Max was going to say hi, and guide him to the classroom but didn't get the chance.

'Me Kami. I am Iran.'

'Hi Kami, let me show you where you should be, mate.'

'You find, man. Hurt me.'

'Somebody hurt you?'

'I Kami Hakimi. You find Man.'

'Okay, dude, let's talk about it, and I'll see what I can do.'

The man had done some form of martial arts training, probably after being enlisted in the Iranian army, where they were still forced into National Conscription. Every young man from eighteen had to go into the army for two years. The refugee pushed Max in the chest, but he never saw it. The movement was so fast that one minute he was on his feet, and the next, he was hurtling backwards into a rack of shelves and looked up, sitting amid a pile of stationary on the floor.

Kami was gone.

Chapter Three

Chapter Three

Max came out of the hospital entrance, sat on a bench and sobbed. People stared at him as they passed, and one old lady said, 'Oh, dear,' but didn't stop, thank god. He cried until he was dry and then determined that he wouldn't cry anymore if he could help it because it was a waste of time. And time was so very precious.

He had a funeral to go to the next day. Nanny Clare was dead. Tomorrow they were putting her into the ground—and soon, he'd be there too. He didn't know how he was going to face all that hurt, so he'd live in every moment. He wouldn't think about anything but what was happening right now.

To him, the word terminal had always been a holiday departure lounge, the gateway to sun, sand and lots of casual sex, but today, he'd joined the other club. He was 28 and had just missed the 27 Club. It was a shame he'd missed it. He could have had fun with that. However, he was still in the 18-30's holiday bracket, and he hoped the trip was wild where he was going. He'd been a good guy all this life. He was bolshy sometimes, a bit of a twat, and despite his business being a success, he was always accused of being childish. But what now? He'd been good, said the right things, toed the line and had still been abandoned in the end. His mother, father, every lover he'd ever enjoyed and even his beautiful wife had all left him. He hadn't done anything to make his parents leave him—they just did. The only permanent relationship in his life had been with his childhood nanny. And she'd chosen this week to leave him too. He was going to be different. From this moment, he was going to say what he wanted, do what he felt like, and to hell with anybody that got in his way. This was his death, and he'd damn well live it.

A child coming out of the hospital stared at him; Max smiled because that's what you do to sick children in wheelchairs.

'Piss off, knobhead,' the kid said.

He needed to be taught some manners. Max took his chair and ran with it down the steep hill while the kid screamed his head off like a girl on helium.

'Get off me. Get off me, you dickhead. Put me down. Mum.'

'Kid, you're looking at this all wrong,' Max bellowed. 'See it as fun. Get your arms in the air and scream to the heavens how great it is to be alive.'

'Put me back.'

'Careful. One more negative word and this chair tips. You aren't frightened, not if you don't want to be. It's all down to the way you look at it. Come on. Arms up and yell for joy, we're coming up to the steep bit.'

The boy put his arms in the air, and as Max ran, he heard him giggle. Soon they were both screaming their heads off. 'Hey, sick people on the top floor, can you hear us? Wake up,' Max yelled.

'Yeah, wake up and scream for joy. You're alive,' the kid shouted in his high-pitched, reedy voice.

Neither of them had as much puff coming back up the hill, and it seemed no manners had been imparted because the child came out with some profanities that even Max had never heard of. He parked him back in position, unharmed and grinning. His mother was shouting something about calling the police, but Max didn't stop to listen.

'That was awesome. But you're nuts, mister.'

'Have a great day, kid.'

Max felt the growth expanding in his head by the second. He was post-diagnosis, post-drugs, post-operable and post-caring. They'd given him six months. It wasn't a death sentence—he was a free man for the first time in his commendable life. Nothing had a consequence.

He could do crack cocaine without it harming him. Die if you do, die if you don't—easy peasy lemon squeezy. A list of crimes ran through his head, and he was surprised at how many he came up with. Everything from arsenic poisoning to zoophilia—although he didn't fancy diddling a donkey just yet. Who knew where his tumour would take him? He could have a new bucket list of all the crimes he could commit before he died. It was unlikely he'd be brought to trial. Max could join an orgy party. He had no harmful gifts to give in that respect—except a nasty pramful of twins—and if he caught something green with exploding pus, it didn't matter.

Maxwell Edward Bartholomew Tyler Jones had it all. Born with a silver spoon rounding his vowels, everything he wanted to have and make of himself fell into his lap at his command. He excelled in property development and nurtured his successful company, from business plans to multi-millions. It meant he could take as many foreign holidays as you could slather coconut lotion over.

Through choice—his choice—he didn't have kids. His wife wanted them, but the time never felt right. They waited too long, and the marriage fell apart. He could line up half a dozen babies now if his little Michael Flatleys were still dancing. He'd never live to see the brats, but they'd be his legacy—his love heart drawn in the sand with a stick before the tide washed him away.

A sweet finality grounded him as he left the Grim Consultant's office. They couldn't do anything for him, and their only offer was palliative care to ease his passing.

Sod that.

Outside, Max took the steps two at a time and wanted to whistle a Pharell Williams tune. He used to be able to, but his whistle had abandoned him. He had the same number of teeth, but no sound came when he pursed his lips. He needed to whistle again.

This was his life, and he'd never felt freer—unlike most people, he knew when death was coming. Forewarned was forearmed and all that jazz. It was September, and he'd be dead by the fifteenth of February. It was more liberating than being at Old Trafford on match day or the time he'd pissed in the Trevi fountain.

He might pay to change his name. He realised he wasn't the most creative bloke on the planet, but he'd go for a name like Vlad the Impaler, Maximus the Shagger or maybe just Deathwish. He'd been lumbered with his five-word monstrosity of a name since the day he was born, and enough was enough. He didn't want Maxwell Edward Bartholomew Tyler Jones on his death certificate.

His plan was coming together. He'd relearn to whistle, change his name to something shocking, and travel to the halls of Valhalla with a drinking horn and Odin for company. He'd seen some foreign lands, but he wanted to visit lots of places before death took him. He wanted to fly in a hot air balloon over the Nile at sunrise and take a gondola ride on the Grand Canal while being serenaded—because that wouldn't be weird at all. He needed to see diamonds of sun shards bouncing off the Taj Mahal as he smiled at the pretty girls passing by. It was imperative.

But first on the agenda—even before masturbating himself into blindness—was shoplifting. Max could honestly say that he'd never stolen anything in his life, not even a young girl's heart. But, there was no time like the present.

He drove to the local shop and parked his Beamer in plain view of anybody inside. He wore Armani and drew as much attention as the old lady dragging her wheeled shopping bag behind her. This wasn't going to be as easy as he expected. He didn't even know what he wanted. Beer? No, there was a camera above the shelving unit. He could always throw his jacket over it or spray paint the camera as they did in the movies. But he didn't want to steal paint as well as beer. Not being seasoned, it might draw attention. He'd blame the young tearaway with his head in the fridge. Max resisted the urge to shut the door on him. A man stinking of urine shuffled up beside him. He heard the old man sniff, and they smelled each other—though not like dogs.

As with stealing, he'd never smoked a cigarette, but he fancied one now. He wanted to steal and smoke a whole pack of fags, but they were kept behind the counter under close guard by the lady serving. He realised he might have to hone his gentleman thief persona first.

Deciding between a Twix or Snickers was akin to choosing which of your children to save from drowning. If he'd been paying for it, he'd have bought them both and a Mars too. This stealing endeavour vastly reduced his options.

He looked at the cashier, who was talking to the stinky man. She was oblivious. He had a vision of walking out with the shop on his back, and she wouldn't have noticed. She didn't own the business, then—she was an employee, probably on the minimum sixteen hours a week—the tarnished wedding ring, been married awhile. The marriage was stale. Her roots had two inches of growth. She'd stopped making an effort a long time ago. Max could read people and situations. He was what they called astute. His hand slid out, and he grabbed a chocolate bar without a rustle. He put it in his jacket pocket and waited for the coat to set on fire. It didn't, and there was no lightning bolt either.

'Yes, love. What can I get you?'

He didn't want anything. He already had it.

'I'd like a packet of your finest cigarettes, please.'

'Eh?'

'A packet of cigarettes, please?'

'What kind?'

'They come in kinds? Well, that's thrown me. Those brown ones, please.'

'Marlboro Red? Are you sure you don't want Silver Blue?'

'Are they better?'

'Couldn't tell you, love, I don't smoke.'

'Yes, okay, Blue, please. And a lighter.'

'Kings or Superkings?'

'Well, if you're going to be a king, you might as well be a super one.'

'Look, love. There's a queue. Do you want them or not?'

There was one smelly old man who still hadn't decided what he wanted.

'Yes, please.'

He paid for the cigarettes, stole a 70p *The Sun* newspaper from the rack by the door and walked out of the shop without alarm bells going off.

Stealing was so fricking easy.

He got in his car, opened the wrapper and ate the best chocolate in the world because it was free. He took his first-ever drag of a dirty cigarette, coughed, wondered what all the fuss was about and called to a lad of about twelve who was getting off his bike.

'You, kid. Come here.'

'What? I ain't done nothing wrong.'

'Do you smoke?'

'No.'

'Oh, I was going to give you some cigarettes.'

'Well, I do a bit. Now and again, like.'

Max threw him the packet and wound up his window.

'Oh. Wow, thanks, Mister.' The kid had a fag lit before he'd made it around the corner into an alley and out of sight.

Max turned the radio on, and it irritated him. The presenter talked about a rockstar dying yesterday and said they'd have some great music and time for quiet reflection. They all said, 'Time for quiet reflection.' It was wholly inaccurate when they were blasting music at you. It was hardly reflective and anything but quiet.

It was a day of revelation. He left his car in the nearest car park and rode a bus. He hadn't been on public transport since he left school, and even then, it was a rarity.

As the doors opened, he joined the three people ahead of him and climbed to the driver behind a Perspex window with a gap at the bottom.

'Where to, Bud?'

'A day return, please.'

It was as though the driver had done him a massive favour by letting him on the bus, and Max ought to be grateful. He didn't know if he should tip him. Max took his card out and looked for the payment device.

'We don't take cards. Cash only.'

Luckily he had a twenty-pound note in the back of his wallet.

'I can't change that. Have you got anything smaller?'

He hadn't, and the driver took his money and said he'd have some change by Ulverston and would give it to him at the end of the route.

'It's okay. Keep the change.'

The man looked at him as though he was insane. 'More than my job's worth, mate. I'll give it to you when I get some change.'

Life was more confusing than Max had ever realised. There were rules and ways of doing normal things that he didn't understand and was no part of. He took a seat two rows down from the driver. It was pleasant. Even the wet anorak smell was new, and he enjoyed himself and wondered why he'd never tried something like this before. He had no idea if there was any other bus etiquette he should know about or a way to behave. He would have done the opposite anyway.

Max listened to several conversations at once and felt as if he knew these people within five minutes. He even found out where one of them lived.

He wanted to break wind and looked around. There was nothing to stop him. He could do whatever the hell he liked. He let rip and even lifted one buttock off the seat for maximum effect. He smiled and enjoyed the piquant aroma. The sound bounced around in the confines of the bus and rattled off the walls. People looked shocked. The lady closest to him covered her lower face with her hand, and two boys collapsed in gales of laughter. Max was proud it reached them.

Of course, people would say his behaviour was down to shock—but Max was having a tremendous time dying.

His days consisted of work. He went to the office, poured over designs, skipped lunch, argued with tradesmen and never left until after eight. Today was an adventure, and he wasn't going to die with his face in a schematic. It was hot on the bus, and he took his jacket off, enjoying the bounce of the suspension and the wealth of conversations as the vehicle filled with passengers. It was a busy service—who knew?

Max got off the bus earlier than intended. It pleased him to be contrary. As a workaholic, and despite his prognosis, he had a two o'clock meeting with the planning committee, but to hell with them. He should ring the office and ask his secretary to make an excuse on his behalf but sod them. He'd heard that The Farmers Arms was very good for lunch.

He draped his jacket over his shoulder and helped a lady down the steps with her pram. The two boys who laughed at his flatulence got off behind him.

'Hey, farty arse. Have you shit your pants?'

'Not yet, but the day is still young. Have you?'

They held onto each other as they bent in gales of laughter. When they straightened, one nudged the other and then grabbed Max's jacket. He waved it in front of him like a matador to a bull and set off running.

'Hey, come back, you little bastards. Have you any idea what this suit cost? I could sell you into child trafficking for less.' Max thought it was fun being inappropriate.

He ran after them and realised he hadn't run for years. He was twenty-eight, and other than a tennis tournament at a barbeque the year before, he hadn't done much physical exercise. This may well give him a heart attack, but what the hell.

The kids took a left after St Mary's Church, and he followed them. He was stiff at first, but his legs loosened, and he felt the lactic acid in his limbs, giving him a burn that hurt but, damn, it felt good. He laughed. As he ran, he pumped his arms like a lunatic. He hadn't belly laughed in a long time, and it hampered his speed, but he was flooded with joy.

As they pounded down the back road towards the old police station, the boys looked over their shoulders. Max wasn't giving up. They threw his jacket into a garden where it caught on a laburnum bush, but Max didn't stop chasing them. They were like three thirteen-year-olds playing tag. He realised he couldn't care less about his jacket. It was just clothing. This was more fun than he'd had in a long time.

The boys hit the bottom road, came out at the Stan Laurel pub and ran up towards the roundabout. They were yelling.

'You're nuts, you are. Bonkers. Pervert. Kiddy Fiddler. You're mad.'

The slight incline was enough for Max. He'd tired. He wanted to keep chasing—and the mind was willing, but the body wasn't playing. He stopped and put his hands on his knees.

'Cheeky sods.'

He retrieved his jacket, saw it had a rip in the lining, and rather than take it to a shop to be repaired. He stuffed it in a waste bin. The chase had been about having fun and had nothing to do with his expensive suit. He had lunch and enjoyed a walk around town. Ulverston was lovely, and he saw that not one shopfront was boarded up. Maybe he could do something about the state of Barrow. It was every second business there. He'd look into it. He thought about the regeneration on the bus ride back.

When he returned to his car in Barrow. It was scratched and missing a wing mirror. It was one more sign of the times and the way people had no pride in their town. With nowhere else to go except home, he wanted to drive but didn't know where until one road led to the next, and an hour later, he arrived in Morecambe—another shithole but as good a place as any. He went for a drink in a run-down side street café. However, the coffee was good. The girl did some kind of art on the top, and he couldn't tell if it was a feather, a branch or a dripping dick. Then decided he didn't care. Gone were the days of complaining about trivial matters and demanding refunds. She was pretty and had a great smile, the kind that lit up a dreary seafront café. Her voice was as soft as the trickle of a stream, and as she chatted to the pensioners, he was jealous. He wanted her to talk to him.

He sat in a window seat, and instead of looking outside, he watched her. Every time she looked his way, he turned to the window and felt his face colouring. He wasn't the shy type, and he had no idea what the hell had just happened to him. In the last five minutes, one pretty girl had turned him into a bumbling mess. He slopped his coffee onto the table, and she was there in an instant with a cloth to wipe it up.

'My mother says that if you spill your coffee, you get to make a wish.'

'Really? I've never heard that.'

'No, I just made it up. But you look like a man that could do with the magic of a wish or two. Go on, try it anyway.'

And that was it. In three sentences, Max was smitten.

Her name badge said that she was called Paige, one of those fluffy popular names that rose in the early noughties. Max would prefer her to be called Elizabeth. It was a name that suited her demeanour. He saw that she was five foot five, maybe six. Her hair fell straight down her back and had that modern two-tone hairstyle of blonde on top and brown at the bottom. He liked the fact that she was a barista and didn't just slap some Nescafe into a mug. She may have been a kid out of college taking any minimum wage job she could get, but to him, she oozed class. She wasn't wearing a wedding ring, and her left breast was ever so slightly smaller than the right.

She interested him. He liked her.

Chapter Four

Chapter Four

The next day coffee shop-girl—Paige—was still on his mind. Thinking about a pretty girl was easier than thinking about a dead nanny.

Despite that, he went back to the first memory he could drum up and tried to go back further. There wasn't a single day in his life when Nanny Clare wasn't there for him and his sister Melissa. They were wealthy, and people who haven't got money have a misconception that being rich automatically means being happy. It doesn't matter how many songs tell you that money don't buy you love, other people—the ones without a platinum card—expect you to be delirious. If you aren't a Happy Joe, it's as though you're letting the side down.

Mel was all right. She was one of those people that didn't mind being on her own. Max didn't know how Laurence put up with her. When he bothered to think about it deeper, he realised it was because Laurence was a doormat. He knew his place and kept it.

Max wasn't like his sister. He wanted his parent's love. He'd go so far as to say he had an unhappy childhood. Poor little rich boy and all that. His parents had children and then realised that life was more fun without them. They sailed around the world doing their thing, and somehow—though Max never understood how— spending money made money, and they grew richer every second.

They had enough money for themselves, the staff, and their various affairs. Though that was mostly to pay the gigolos and mistresses off when it turned ugly. They didn't skimp on their children, and there was always a trust fund for every time they felt lonely.

When Max was nine, and it came to the divorce, the money wasn't enough for either parent they each wanted more than they could ever spend. They'd lived in a huge townhouse, long since sold now, but Max could hear them screaming at each other wherever he was. And Nanny Clare would come to him in the playroom and pass him his PlayStation controller. Grand Theft Auto III made everything better.

And she'd sing Rhianna songs to him until the shouting was over. She was a Geordie born and bred, and he was her sensitive bairn.

There was always Nanny Clare. And now there wasn't. How did that work?

He was shocked to walk into the tiny wooden church and see that he was the only mourner. There was Max, a priest and one bored-looking altar boy who was swinging incense about as if he was passing a ganja pipe around.

Max laughed at the irony of the pomp. As well as paying for this farce of a funeral, he'd booked an events room and paid for a buffet for fifty. Clare would love that. He wondered how long the staff at the wake would leave the sandwiches to curl before they realised that nobody was coming. He'd put out a sombre message for the occasion on social media, welcoming everybody, and he'd put the standard obituary in the newspaper—figuring she was of that age. But nobody was there. Not one person. Shame on them all.

As an adult, Max had never stopped visiting her. She was involved in every major decision of his life. She'd even advised on some of his business ventures. Max owned her cottage, but she lived there alone. He couldn't give it to her—she was too proud. But he'd spent ages finding just the right place for Nanny. He said he needed a caretaker to look after it for him, so she'd spent the last ten years there rent-free under the guise of being a hostess, even though she'd never had a single visitor other than Max. She didn't like the word caretaker, and she said she was happy.

He took his phone out while he was on his knees in that moment of quiet reflection. He texted Mel. *Where the hell are you?*

I can't make it. Sebastian's sick.

Your seventeen-year-old, Sebastian. That Sebastian? 'Piss off, Melissa,' he hissed.

The priest coughed and crossed himself, and the altar boy opened his eyes properly for the first time.

'Sorry, Father.'

Every few months, they went out for one of those fancy cream teas that cost a fortune, particularly on the day given over to thanking your mother for having you. He told her, 'You brought me up. You're the only one that deserves the fuss on Mother's Day.' He'd pour her some tea out of a teapot with honeysuckle painted on the side. He loved watching her choose her tiny sandwich and cake. These outings reminded him of Mel's tea parties with all of her stuffed toys and dolls lined up and the tiny plastic tea set that she loved. Then one day, in a fit of spite, he'd filled the teapot with Das modelling clay, and it set like concrete, and that was that. Poor Mr Sniffles, the stuffed dog nightdress case, had to do without his cup of tea.

Nanny Clare would only have one of each, a little sandwich—usually salmon—cut into a rectangle with no crusts, and that charmed her. 'I do hope they give the crusts to the birds. They won't waste them, will they, Barty?' she'd say, using the pet name that infuriated him as a child. Her fingers would float over every cake, and her rheumy eyes would sparkle like pale emeralds as she made her choice.

She always went for the miniature strawberry tart, which she ate with a knife and fork. She tried to be very posh, and Max would suppress a laugh as the Geordie in her tripped her up at the first piece of cutlery.

Max would eat more, but it wasn't his kind of food. He'd rather have a juicy steak, so most of the tiny food items would sit on the three-tiered cake stand to be returned to the kitchen. He had to tell her that the waitresses would enjoy them during their break to stop her worrying.

'Barty, you're spoiling me. You naughty boy,' she'd say. And as he sat on the hard wooden pew, he felt the tears as he remembered her. He didn't mind when she called him Barty anymore, even when they were eating out, and a business associate came to say hello. He loved being told off by her, even at twenty-eight. It was the only time she ever called him Maxwell. 'Maxwell Jones, I'm warning you, if you don't get your hair cut, you'll never meet a nice girl. And stop calling it Barra. You live in Barrow, dear. Didn't that fancy boarding school teach you nothing? You'd better be kind to your sister. She won't always be around, you know.' And here they were. Mel was going to live a long and miserable life, and he would be gone. Until today when she was laid in satin, not one swear word had ever left his lips in Nanny Clare's presence. He respected her too much for that and was going to miss her—bloody he ll.

They wanted him to go up to the coffin. He just saw a fancy box. For all he knew, Nanny Clare might not even be in there. They might have sold her to make ancient Eastern medicine. She was ancient. Nanny Clare would mix well with a couple of snakeheads and a bit of rhinoceros horn.

'See you very soon, Nanny. Coming ready or not,' he whispered, kissing his fingertips and dropping them onto the lid of the coffin. He felt that's what was expected.

The funeral curtain came across, and the priest said another load of meaningless prayers, presumably to give the gravediggers-cum-pall-bearers the chance to carry old Nanny to her grave. He smiled when he heard one of them grunt as they took the weight of the casket off the gurney. Nanny would have tutted.

Father Murphy Sang *Lord of the Dance* and Max mumbled the odd word out of tune. The altar boy seemed to manage the last word of every second line until the chorus, and then he still didn't sing, but he jigged side-to-side a bit to show willing. It was a rousing number. If he'd had more time, he'd like to have made the funeral grander for her, maybe hired a hundred mourners from an agency. And he'd like to have made the altar boy smile. He remembered what it was like when your parents forced you to be one. They had no idea the ribbing Max took for wearing that white dress. His best friend, Bobby, wasn't Catholic, and the other one, Jon, had a mother that listened to him when he said he'd rather die than go to church. Which was probably an exaggeration, but Max was still in awe when she didn't force him.

They left the chapel and made a sad parade, the three of them walking down the path to the cemetery. The altar boy had swapped his thurible for a huge black umbrella that he held over the priest's head in the drizzling rain. 'The kind that gets you wet,' Nanny would have said. Father Murphy was dry, but pathetic little Tommy Tucker, or whatever he was called, was sodden.

Father Murphy strayed off the cinder path to the grass verge and stepped in some dog dirt. Max and the altar boy could tell how much he wanted to swear as he wiped the side of his shoe. He didn't swear, but he did mutter under his breath. Max nudged the boy from behind, and they both snorted. The boy, more used to the priest's lack of humour, hid his laughter better.

'Yes, quite,' Father Murphy said, and neither one of them could hold it in any longer.

'Please. Respect.'

'Sorry, Father,' Max said and blessed himself for good measure.

At the graveside, the priest stood at the head of the grave.

The old man was cold, and Max saw him shiver. The boy held the big umbrella over his head, but the wind kept taking it, and the lad was only short. It clunked the priest on his head. He didn't look pleased in the grace of God, and Max didn't think the prayers were supposed to be said as fast as they were.

He lowered his head and clasped his hands together. For the first time ever at a funeral, he didn't think about how fast he could get to the pub—not the one with the buffet, any other—for his first pint. He remembered Nanny Clare—his Clare and all the good times and bad times. And all the ones when she'd changed the course of his life for the better.

'We, therefore, commit this body to the ground. Earth to earth, ashes to ashes, dust to dust.'

Max felt the priest's hand on his shoulder, and he cried quietly. When he raised his head, they were gone, and he was alone at the open graveside.

'It's just you and me, Nanny. I'm not happy with you for leaving me, you know. But guess what? I get the strawberry tart from now on.' He sat down in his eight hundred-pound suit and let the rain wash over his face. It wasn't raining when he came out, so he didn't wear his ash-grey overcoat, bought especially for funerals. He went to a lot of funerals for his aged business contacts.

He dangled his legs over the hole of Nanny's grave. She wouldn't mind, or maybe she would. She was always one for proprietary, but what could she do about it now? He smiled at the memory of her face of disapproval. He glanced at the sky to see if she was pointing down at him through the clouds and then grinned because he'd imagined her telling him off again. Just like always.

'I've met a girl, Nanny. She's really pretty. I might bring her to meet you one day.'

He stood up and dusted down his wet trousers. They were ruined—just like his life.

'I'm going to get her, Nanny.'

Chapter Five

Nash pulled himself up the last flight of stairs to the room allocated to the task force. Who was he kidding? He loved it. He'd tried retirement—pruning roses and baking cakes. He even went on a few dire cruises full of old people with bunions and arthritis—but it wasn't for him.

When the call came in from Chief Superintendent Bronwyn Lewis, he couldn't get away from the cackling *Loose Women* fast enough.

It was the first time anybody on the force had decided to come out of retirement, but Nash couldn't put up with the loneliness. This case had fallen into his lap at just the right time. He said he worked on intuition, but some of the team believed he had psychic powers when it came to tracking down the bad guys. Nash laughed. The puppies coming up these days didn't train in the Old Ways. He paid attention, that's all. He listened, he looked, and observation was key to finding out what you wanted.

He knew every leggy spider in this place, and most of the cobwebs were there from the last time he'd worked. He'd been stationed in Barrow-in-Furness pretty much from boy to man, and the city squad weren't going to take this one away from them—not if he could help it. This was his home and his work. Right on the southern tip of the beautiful Lake District, he always bragged that he was within five minutes of ocean, river, lake and mountain. Barrow was a blue-collar town with none of the neighbouring town's tourism to rely on, but the shipyard kept the place in employment, and the people were good. Most of the crime was petty—but not today.

This wasn't his first murder case. Back then, he was a sergeant stationed for a few months at Morecambe nick, forty miles away, or five minutes if you swam across the bay. A little girl had been murdered. She was five years old, and the bastard drowned her in a puddle of mud while he raped her. She was a gipsy girl, so nobody in authority cared. Except for Nash and the team, both above and below him in rank. They cared. They worked through the nights to find her killer and bring him to justice.

He remembered the day when the little girl's cousin was caught. He was seventeen and old enough to know what he was doing. They booked the Broadway Hotel for a policeman's piss-up to release all that post-case tension—but it was a bitter-sweet affair. They'd got the bastard off the streets—but there was still a five-year-old dead girl at the heart of it.

He's out now, John Johnston, walking the streets as a free man with a new identity. Little Marga was still dead. Lest we forget, Nash thought. Lest we forget.

This time he was on his own stomping ground in Barrow-in-Furness. The team had been set up, a task force of forty people initially. They didn't even know if their hunch was correct yet. And the term serial killer was only spoken in hushed whispers. Three bodies. Three.

They didn't know, but Nash did. Nobody else had connected the dots between the crime scenes yet, and at this stage, he was keeping the flowers and the music between him and the spiders. He wouldn't reveal his cards too early and wanted to see what the rest of the guys had come up with. Showing his hand at such an impressionable stage of the investigation would be to send the team out blinkered. Going down a single lane might mean that they'd miss other possibilities.

It was up to Nash to prove there was a serial killer on his streets.

He walked into the incident room, and in a five-second scrutiny, he checked everything was in order and that he had what he needed.

The whiteboard was empty apart from one statement. Now it was up to him to build a case.

The big dick is back.

'Right, guys, settle down. Thank you for the vote of appreciation. If only my name was Richard, eh?'

They laughed at the reference.

'What is your name, sir? We had a book running on it before you retired.'

'Should you ever be my superior officer, Lawson, I'm sure you will find out. Until then, let's move on to the matter at hand.'

'Welcome back, sir.'

A round of applause rippled through the room.

'Right, we have another body. That's three in eight weeks.'

'I think it's a serial killer, sir,' PC Bowes said

The rest of the room laughed at him, stating the obvious, and Nash held his hand up for silence.

'Technically, if it's all been committed by the same perpetrator, you could be right. Three is the classification, Bowes. However, here's the crux. Until we know otherwise, we will be treating this as three unrelated incidents. There's nothing, not one shred of evidence or even a good hunch, to connect these murders. We're in a county that, by the grace of God, isn't generally crawling with killers. We likely have one of two scenarios. Either three killers have each killed one person.

Or we have one who has murdered three people but made them look like separate killers. Before we can catch him, that's what we need to find out. Three murders in Barrow makes my nose twitch.' He didn't feel guilty for lying to them and withholding vital evidence. There was a connection. They just hadn't spotted it yet. It was as plain to them as it had been to him, but to see things, you had to know how to look.

'Do we know it's a man, sir?'

'No, we don't, Molly. However, there may be indicators. It depends on how you define sexual abuse. In post-mortem positioning and planting, we have had some unusual indicators—but more for effect than sexual gratification, I suspect.'

'You have to be non-binary, sir. You can't call him a him unless you know the perp is male.'

'And yet, you just did. Molly, honey, I'm a misogynistic old bastard, and that isn't going to change. I'll always open the door for a lady and always feel that a woman's place is not at the gristly end of a murder investigation. That's just me. If I get kicked in the balls for it, so be it. Right. Focus, team. Here's what we've got.'

His hands moved like lightning as he refamiliarised himself with an incident board. It felt bloody good to swap a TV remote for a marker.

'Three vics. The first is William Armstrong, known in the community as Billy. Sixty-eight, a private piano tutor. He was killed at home. Stabbed with a tuning fork. The killer attached sharp compasses to the tines This wasn't pretty, and it looked like a frenzied attack, but the positioning of the body, the blood spatter, and the arrangement and staging say anything but. His was the first body found, but until the post-mortem, it didn't have to follow that it was the first murder. Bill Robinson, our esteemed coroner, has since confirmed it was. However, we also think it's the first time this person has killed somebody. It lacks strength and conviction. We have evidence of practice cuts. The killer underestimated how difficult it is and how much pressure it takes to kill somebody this way. The victim was stabbed sixty-eight times. Keep in mind that's how old he is, but we haven't found a correlation to that yet. Any questions about William?'

'What was the staging?' Bowes said.

'We'll get to that.'

'Sir.'

'Victim number two. Chelsea Green, interior designer. She was thirty-three and killed in a client's home. They found her swinging from a crystal chandelier with music playing on a loop. Interesting fact, he didn't go for mock-frenzy this time. He wanted us to know that he'd gone to a lot of trouble with this one and had worked on it. A mechanical device was used to keep the chandelier moving, and he'd set Spotify to repeat the same piece of classical music. In this one, he was going for artistry, and he was fixated on the detail. We'll get to more of that as well.'

'How did the chandelier take her weight, sir?'

'Good question, Lawson. He reinforced the fixings. It took time, and he constructed some kind of pulley to get the body up there. Otherwise, he'd have had to be a weight lifter to get her in place and hold her in position. Okay, the residence was unoccupied, but he made more than one visit to the home to complete his work. He wasn't averse to taking risks.'

The room was silent apart from the scream of the marker as he added information to the board. Nash saw Molly Brown shudder as if he had dragged his nails down a chalkboard.

'Victim three. The most interesting and the one that I think will give us valuable information about our killer. Robert Dean, thirty-three and unemployed. The lad had hit rock bottom and was no stranger to a can of strong lager. This killing was personal. It meant more to the perp. Dean was killed off-site and taken post-mortem to the bridal suite of The Abbey House Hotel.'

Molly Brown stood up and addressed the room. 'No clues from the hotel booking. It was under the victim's name, and payment was made by direct transfer from his bank account. His benefits went in, and the perp made sure the payment was taken before Dean had the chance to empty his account as was his custom by ten AM on the day it cleared.'

'What is it about this one that separates it from the others?' Bowes asked.

'This wasn't random. The others are ambiguous, but with this one, we know that the perp knew Bobby Dean.'

'How, ma'am?'

'Because he cared about him.'

'Yeah, enough to bump him off.'

A ripple of laughter went around the room.

Molly sat down, and Nash stopped scribbling on the board. 'Somehow, he got into that room and evaded the cameras. He was in there long enough to bathe the body. It's a big risk in a busy hotel. He bathed the victim, dried and shaved him, and then rubbed baby lotion on every inch of his body. He dressed him in white silk pyjamas and positioned him comfortably in bed before calling room service for a mug of hot chocolate. He recorded Dean's voice giving instructions for the waiter to walk in and put the chocolate on the bedside cabinet. The perp had a window of six minutes to get out undetected. The phone call was time-stamped, and the waiter's key card was recorded from the moment he opened the door.'

'Brazen. How was number three killed?' Lawson asked.

'Cyanide poisoning—sodium cyanide, to be exact. His death was fast, and we believe Dean died elsewhere and before he had the chance to vomit. It was orchestrated to the smallest detail. The perp didn't want a mess. All three of these scenes were staged. He wanted a tableau to show off to the world. If this is one guy, he wants to be seen.'

'Do you think it's a serial killer, sir?' Bowes leaned forward, eager to hear the answer and almost overbalanced his chair.

'There's not a single thing to connect these murders. But three in eight weeks, when we don't get many murders around here, makes that a connection in itself. It's either that or the world's gone mad. We have to keep an open mind. It could be three unconnected perps. However, off the record, I'd bet my kidneys on it being one person.'

'Spooky, sir. Did you check your crystal ball before coming out?'

'No, just my waters.'

***

Nash left his car and walked home from work for a change. It was a couple of miles from the station to the island where he lived and it was connected to the mainland by a single bridge. He walked a long way to find a bar where he was unlikely to run into another police officer or anybody else he knew. Nash was torn between being alone and being with somebody special. He walked past the hotel where Sandy worked and almost went in for a drink, but they had an agreement that workplaces were strictly out of bounds. He enjoyed the stiff breeze and tang of the sea on Walney Island where he owned the biggest house. It was a large white building, with a balcony and two round towers, and it stood like a sentinel looking out towards the ocean. Until his thirst, and the evening chill, got the better of him, he carried on walking past his house and the Round House at Biggar Bank. His home was too empty tonight. The streets were quiet, and he called into the Castle

House pub for a drink. Nothing was waiting for him at home apart from the cat and without a couple of pints he'd be too wired to sleep.

He wasn't a big drinker, but he sought company in his isolation. Nobody would bother him, and he could sit on his own, thinking about the case, and yet still feel part of something. He asked for a Guinness and told the bartender not to draw a shamrock on it. The thought of somebody putting their finger in his beer appalled him.

He'd stayed behind at the station to go over the files again, hoping that some fact they'd missed would jump out at him. He liked it there at night. The incident room was far enough away from the drunk tank that the roaring and banging of the guests was only a dull background accompaniment to his thoughts. Shift changeover had come and gone, and the hum from the lower floors settled down. It was slow through the week, and nothing had disturbed him. He felt more at home there than here in a pub alone.

They rang the bell, and a lanky bartender shouted the last orders. Sandy's shift would be finishing. They'd been dating for eight months, and this Plenty of Fish scene was a foreign field to him with very little no-man's-land in the middle. He knew in his heart that Sandy was slipping away, and he didn't know how to hang on to their relationship before it crumbled. He was a very different man in his private life from the person he was when he wore his badge. The roses at home had a different smell from the ones that gave him hay fever in the office. He took roses home every Thursday night, but recently he'd been the one to arrange them in a vase when Sandy left the gift unwrapped on the kitchen counter. He felt like a drowning man, and his partner held the life vest. Nash was terrified of losing the only relationship he'd had in years and overcompensated for his ineptitude with an unaccustomed clinginess that the guys at work would never recognise in him. He needed to call.

'Hey, Sandy.'

'Si, hi. I wasn't expecting to hear from you tonight.'

'I'm in a bar, on my own.'

'Boo for you, babe.'

'I'll be home soon. Do you want to come over?'

'What? Now?'

'No, in three weeks time on a Monday. Yes, now. I miss you, Sandy.'

'Oh, honey. You know what it's like. I've just finished my shift, and my feet are killing me.'

'It was just a thought. See you on Friday.'

'I'll have to let you know about that, honey. It's Becky's birthday, and the girls are going to Blackpool. I could always miss it, though, if you want me to?'

'No, you go. Just let me know when you're free.'

They made kissy noises down the phone, and Nash heard somebody in the background behind Sandy as he hung up. The cocktails were there, apparently. Somebody always needed attention, and there were always cocktails, or drama or Blackpool. Sandy was younger than him but acted like a twenty-year-old. The vitality was one of the things Nash loved. He hoped they might settle down together. He didn't expect marriage and all that hoo-ha—but his house was more than big enough for two. His double-fronted home fronted the Irish sea. It was big enough for ten people, and he rattled around in it on his own. Sandy said they had a long time ahead of them to grow old, and no way was it coming any time soon. Most of the hotel staff were kids in their twenties. Nash didn't get it.

He wished he hadn't called Sandy. It just depressed him more. A woman at the bar smiled at him and tipped her glass. She was drunk and no doubt saw him as the gateway to another drink or two. It was time to leave.

He contemplated walking along the beach to the headland. It was invigorating, and the path walkway was only about a mile long from here. A picnic table at the end was put there as a reward for weary walkers who had come much further than Nash. He did his best thinking when he walked. But he had a seven AM start. It was already close to midnight, and he wouldn't get in until the sun was up. On a clear morning, the sunrise painted the Isle of Man glinting on the horizon, and if he turned to the right, he'd see the town of Millom waking for the day. It was tempting to take his aloneness to the headland, where it stopped being lonely and turned into quiet solitude. His house was the emptiest place on earth.

He got in, and Lola wrapped around his legs. At least somebody loved him. Her dish was empty, so he fed her. That explained her greeting then—cupboard love. Nash took a tot of Glenfiddich to help him sleep and got into bed.

'Alexa, play Enya.'

'Finding Enya.'

Chapter Six

Chapter Six

Max had been in her company for less than five minutes, and she was nagging him already. 'Have you been to see Mum?'

Max's sister, Melissa Jones-Whitehouse, was two years older and behaved as though she had the birthright to nag him at every opportunity.

'No, Melissa, I haven't seen her.'

'Don't you think you should?'

'No.'

'Are you going to keep being this childish? I didn't have to come, you know.'

'First, your question. Hell, yes, I'm loving the childish. Your statement, so go back to where you came from. I don't care. And lastly, the guilt trip. Mother has probably forgotten my name by now. She'll be on a yacht with that rich bastard of hers. Which is this husband, number three? Four? Twenty-seven?'

'Maxwell Jones, you're impossible.'

'And you, my dear sister, could do with getting laid by somebody other than Laurence. Get a toyboy, and you might just be in time to save yourself. But it's not my business to run your life, so what the hell makes you think you can run mine?'

'I wanted to tell you how sorry I am about your illness. Why do you have to be so negative?'

'Because it's fun. Why do you have to be so self-righteous?'

'Because it's fun.'

Melissa gathered her things and picked up her calfskin gloves and keys.

Max wasn't done. 'Oh, yeah, because you ran the PTA and sit on the school's board of directors. Aren't you just something? But some of us remember that you got yourself knocked up at thirteen. And now the world's lumbered with the teen messiah Sebastian, the incredible static knob job. And that makes you the font of all knowledge and, for some reason, puts you way above us mere mortals. Old Laurence's willy must be the only part of him that isn't limp.'

'Have you finished?'

'No, don't slam the door on your way out.'

On a roll, he dressed down for the meeting with his partner, Henry Watson.

***

He was late and didn't care. It was the first time since he'd formed the company that he attended a business meeting in Sliders and trackie bottoms. Even if this had been the norm, his choice of t-shirt certainly wasn't. He debated slogans at length and discovered that he couldn't cope with making choices very well. In the end, he went for *Can't Adult Today*, over *I Won't Quit, But I Will Swear a Fricking Lot*. His choice fit the way he felt, but by the end of the meeting with Henry, he wished he'd gone with the other one.

Max founded, owned and had run MJ Properties for two years when it got too big for him as the only director. MJP took Henry on six years ago to manage the groundwork and civil engineering side of the business. The company had grown to employ forty people.

Henry excelled as his Ground Manager, and after proving himself, Max brought him onto the board as a partner. They were fifty-one to forty-nine per cent split partners, with Max being the majority shareholder.

Being twenty years Max's senior, they'd never been friends or socialised outside work and fought over company issues every time they got together. Henry was old and rundown like the renovation contracts they took on, and he made no secret of the fact that he thought Max skimmed too many of the profits and made rash decisions. Max flew by the seat of his pants, and Henry was still an old fart.

The meeting was scheduled, which meant it was going to be a bore with Henry laying bare all Max's failings. Henry's PA, Linda, would be taking minutes because Henry always made sure to cover his arse. If ever litigation was involved or things got heated, the transcript could be used as evidence in court, and it was every man for himself.

Henry was a twat.

Max picked a stem of honeysuckle from the creeper growing outside the main entrance. When he designed the building, he'd insisted on honeysuckle around the door because it was a scent from his childhood and Nanny Clare's favourite. As he swept passed Linda's desk, he presented her with it along with his sweetest smile. It was a ploy to allay the telling off she was going to give him for being late, but it didn't come. He'd have preferred it to the dripping sympathy.

'Oh, Max. I'm so sorry to hear your terrible news.'

It travelled fast. Thanks for that, Gob Almighty Melissa.

'I know, Linda. Isn't it awful? I couldn't believe it myself. It was supposed to be a non-stick frying pan too. The yolk broke on both of my eggs this morning. Tragic.'

'You know what I'm talking about—your thing. You know? Your Diagnosis.'

'Oh, that thing. That's nothing—just an irritating bout of death. I'll be over it soon. Let's say no more about it. Is his lordship seething?'

She nodded and dabbed her eyes with a tissue.

Max tapped on the boardroom window and used his finger to motion Henry to follow him. That was one motion of many he could have chosen for the digit. He would've preferred another one.

The meeting was for Max and Henry, with Linda taking notes. It didn't warrant the twenty-four-seat boardroom. He went into his office, curled his nose and swept last night's McDonald's boxes off the desk. He sat on the leather sofa that was an integral part of the burgundy-grey interior décor. He'd designed it himself, right down to the last staple. Eat that shit, Henry weasel-face. The office was a confusing mix of contemporary designer space to show the company in a good light and a thirteen-year-old boy's bedroom. His desk had a Newton's cradle and an assortment of electronic games. A broken drone was in the corner, and a dartboard on the wall with a picture of Henry's face pinned to it. Max slumped onto the sofa and put his feet on the lacquered coffee table.

'Really, Max?' Henry came in, made a show of choking on the smell and sat on a chair, moving a stuffed monkey with a name tag that said, Henry. Linda opened the window a crack and sat on the edge of another chair with her notepad perched on her knee.

'Henry, you old goose. To what do I owe the pleasure of this impromptu meeting? Would you like a gumdrop? Personally, I find them a bit tasteless. Put it in the minutes, Linda. We should debate it.' He offered Henry a crumpled bag of sweets, and he stared at it as if Max was offering a warm turd on a serviette.

'We need to talk about the way things are going, Max.'

'I figured you didn't want to take me to the movies when you called the meeting—which, I hope you notice, I remembered to attend, aided by the three texts from the delightful Linda, of course.'

'Do you want to tell me what happened with Owen Richards the other day?'

'Not really.'

'Max?'

'I might have told him I'd shagged his ugly mother and to go screw himself.'

'That was a six-apartment build. Have you any idea how much that would have brought in?'

'Haven't a clue, mate. That's why I have you, but I'm guessing it's somewhere near the same as the other builds we've done. He's no loss. We've got people biting our hands off for new builds. There's more of the damned things in the pipeline than we've got time or men to build. And what about the land? Do you remember what this town was like twenty years ago? Green fields for miles, I grew up with places to play. Now, all we've got is housing estates. And not good old council housing that can help people that need it. I'd be all for that. No, the boxes we build all look the same. Where's the architecture? It's clone housing for moronic middle-class robots. Another one's gone up at Pennington, and the environmental insult is that they've had to build a huge roundabout to accommodate the anticipated traffic. Another country road that's been raped and scarred. He made conducting motions with his hands and sang, '*Little boxes, on a hillside. little boxes made of ticky-tacky. Little boxes on a hillside, and they all look just the same.* I pointed this out to that Richards fella and called him a fake fascist fanny, but only because it was alliterative and sounded good. I asked him what his stance was on capitalism, and he didn't like it. Did he?'

'Are you trying to ruin us?' Henry screamed. 'Is it some kind of ploy to get me out? Have you gone mad?'

Max grinned and embellished his derision. 'Apparently so, old boy. That's exactly what I've done. I've gone stark raving mad. If you want, I can get a sick note to say I'm not pulling a sickie. You know how many times I've skived off work to go to a bar and get away from your incessant nagging? And now I don't need to. Kind of takes the fun out of it, but isn't it delicious? And you can't hold anything I say against me. Because I'm dying, and that's discrimination. I can even call you a crispy crap-face, and you can't do anything about it.'

'It's like talking to a belligerent child. In your own interests and the good of the company, I've taken power of attorney, and I'm having you removed from the business. You'll still get your dividends and an additional financial incentive to step aside, but the papers will be drawn up for you to sign immediately.'

'Blah, blah, blah. Is that it? Can I go now? Guess what? Pompey pompous arse? I was leaving today anyway. And you've just paid me a fortune to do it. I think that rests the joke squarely on your shoulders, old boy. I have a boat to charter to Croatia, and from there, I'm going to Asia for some Chinese pussy. Write this down, Linda. Bollocks to you and the horse you rode in on.'

Max felt his mood drop as he left the glass and chrome building designed by himself to resemble a Rubik's Cube. Arguing with people had been fun at first, but it was boring now. His condition had made him more outspoken, and he'd taken liberties with his manners. He wondered if this meant that everything would only have a short shelf life before he tired of it. He didn't want to be a bad person.

Croatia and China had fled his mind by the time he got to the corner. He was onto his next big thing. He was going to grow his hair, buy a camper van and be a hippy.

But first, he had to see Jonathan. He tried telling himself that he was going to be kind and sweet and wouldn't offend Jon or his fit wife, Emily, but that was ridiculous. He always insulted him. That's why his friend was put on earth.

He tapped on the window and walked in without waiting for the door to be answered and was almost knocked over by Lucy, aged five, who screamed and flung herself into his arms.

'Uncle Max,' she squealed again. 'Have you brought me a present?'

He patted his pockets down, hoping for something to magically appear in them and felt the sweets that he'd previously offered to Henry. 'Maybe I have. Maybe I haven't.'

'Uncle Max, you know that means that you have. Is it a kitten?'

'No, your mother would kill me.'

Lucy put her hands on her hips and scolded him in a voice that was way too much like her mother's. 'Stop being silly. What have you brought me?' She tried to put her hands in his pocket.

'Share them with your brother.' Caught off guard, he handed over the half kilo of sugar in the form of gumdrops that he'd been carrying around for days. 'Hey, are you old enough to marry me yet?'

'I'm five, uncle Max.'

'Five, eh? Not quite then, and you know what? I prefer my girls with front teeth, anyway. You'll keep.'

'Maxwell,' the warning tone came from Emily, propped against the door with a tea towel over her shoulder. 'Stop winding her up. And just so you know, my daughter will have more sense than to marry somebody like you.' Max noticed she looked tired, and he hoped she wasn't working too hard. He always joked about it, but Emily was the one that got away. Two years older than him, he'd fancied her when he was sixteen. He slept around, but Emily was better than that. She was more than a grope around the back of the garages. And besides, he had to grow some balls and facial hair before he dared approach her. While he was waiting for his follicles to sprout, Jonathan swooped in at a rave, and that was that. Game over, chances lost.

Jonathan's son, Carter, came in from the garden with a football under his arm. He was ten and shaping up to be a keen player.

'Hey, Max. Game?'

'Sure, Cart, prepare for a thrashing, but let me talk to your Dad first, okay?' They punched each other a few times the way kids do.

Emily pushed a beer into Max's hand and one for her husband. 'He's in the office.'

'Thanks, Em.'

He walked into Jonathan's office without knocking and was gratified to see his friend shut his laptop too fast for it to be casual.

'Don't you ever knock?'

'Let me think about that, wank-boy. No. Do I need to? And is that gorgeous wife of yours ready to run away with me yet? I could show her things you've only seen on the internet. And today, I've got just the thing that might tempt her. Guess what I'm getting?'

'Go on, what?'

'An old camper van. I've found one I like the look of. Here. Feast your eyes on this baby.' He handed Jonathan his phone with the camper's details. 'Fancy a road trip? All the places you've always wanted to see but are too boring to go?'

'Why do you have to be such an arsehole all the time? Since your illness started, you've changed. You're turning into a real dick, and it's my job as your best mate to tell you.'

'And you have been a dullard since the day I met you. You've never amounted to anything and never will. And if you're going to start beating me with bibles and lectures, I've bailed you out more times than I can count.'

'Thanks for that, Max. Didn't miss an opportunity to throw that back in my face, did you? Can't forget who's the big man.'

'Yeah, sorry, Jon. Low blow. I am a dick. You're right. And I'll always give you a hand when you need it. No questions asked, mate. I'm sorry. It's because I love you, Emily and the kids. You're the only ones that have ever put up with me, and I suppose today's a good day to tell you I appreciate that.'

'Maybe just think about the way you talk to people. I've been there for you right through your illness and been your punchbag more than once. But I still have feelings, you know?'

'All right, I said I'm sorry. Don't make me get the violin out.'

'Anyway, If you're buying a campervan, I take it you had good news at the hospital? That's brilliant.' Jonathan went to clink beers with him.

'That's why I'm here. You might want to hold off on the celebrations for a while. You, my friend, have a wake to attend.' He watched as the cogs turned, and Jonathan caught up with the words.

'What the hell?' Jonathan said.

'I've done the "Why me?" I even tried the "Why not me?" That's bullshit. Who actually thinks, "Why not me," and believes it? I tried it once. Won't be doing that martyr shit again.'

'What are you telling me?'

Max drew a finger across his throat.

'No. Shit, Max. I'm sorry. What's the outcome? How long have they said?'

'People always ask how long. Never how wide or how deep my coffin will be, or even how permanent, just how long. Not enough room for a party in there, that's for sure. I'm looking at six months, maximum. And I mean, max with a small M.' He laughed at his bad joke to break the tension.

'Jesus Christ, man,' Jon stood up and hugged Max.

'I need a favour.'

'Right, no beating around the bush then.'

'Not really. In fact, I couldn't give a shit, but it'll get Mel off my back.'

'What is it, mate? Anything. Just name it.'

Max pulled two salmon pink envelopes out of his inside pocket. His jacket had rumpled on a girl's floor the night before, and he was surprised the envelopes didn't tell the tale. Buying good stationery paid off, after all. He would have passed it off as a life rule to his kids if he'd had any. Always buy good stationery. It comes in handy when you're writing your final words.

'I need you to get these to my parents when the time comes. For God's sake, don't send them until after I'm dead. The last thing I need is all the false platitudes and fake tears.'

'Aren't you going to see them?'

'Bloody hell, don't you start. Have you and Mel been drinking the same water? No, I am not going to see them. No need. I'm sparing both them and me the hassle.'

'Come on, Max. They're your folks. They have a right to know.'

Max tapped the envelopes. 'And they will. Are you going to do it?'

'Of course.'

'Thank you. So what have you been doing? I've been calling.'

'No, you haven't.'

'Okay, I haven't, but I've thought about calling. Didn't you get it?'

Jonathan laughed. 'Talking of memos, telepathic or otherwise, did you hear that Dave's finished with Trina? He found her shacked up with that bloke from the garage down the road. He's invited us all out on Saturday night. I don't want to be insensitive. What do we do in this situation? Do you want to do normal, or are we done with going out and stuff? I've got you, whatever this new normal is. But if you're up for it, I'm good either way.'

'Yeah, I'm in, as long as I don't get a better offer.'

'While you're feeling so public-spirited, everyone's gathering at the Abbey tonight at six for a search party. Two lads have gone missing. Not much older than Carter. They were last seen messing about on the abbey grounds, so that's where the police want the public search to start. It's been over twenty-four hours now, and not looking good.'

'Man, that's awful.'

'Haven't you heard about it? It's been all over the news.'

'No, I don't watch much TV. The news only ever tells us bad stuff.'

'It's four o'clock, you might as well stay here for your tea, and we'll go together. I know you've got your own shit to deal with, but it's kids. The community's pulling together.'

'Little sods have probably just run away. They'll be back when they're hungry,' Max said.

'Yeah, probably.'

Carter exploded into the office and threw his football at Max's face.

'Come on, then.'

Max caught the ball and laughed.

Chapter Seven

Chapter Seven

Max was tied up for the rest of the afternoon and made the phone call the next morning. He hoped he wasn't too late. 'Hi, mate. I'm calling about the campervan. Is it still available?'

'Somebody came out to have a look at it yesterday. They took it for a test drive and said they wanted it. They were supposed to come back last night, but there's been no word. So, yes, the first one to come up with the money can take her away.'

'Cheers, mate. Text me your address, and I'll set off now.'

Max had considered a brand new hundred and fifty grand mobile home with beds that came down from the ceiling at the touch of a button and other switches that did incredible things. But those models weren't for speeding down the motorway on a whim and having fun. They were so long and heavy that they'd be lucky to make the speed limit. Max didn't want luxury. He wanted freedom and the hippie dream.

An hour after his enquiry, he drove home in his brand new, five-year-old VWT5 camper van. It was fully equipped with everything he needed for weeks on the road and was big enough for him and the occasional conquest along the way. In some places, it was tatty and needed some loving, but he got it for a song—no time like the present. On the way home, he called at Barrow Market. The bloke on the carpet stall was a wide boy and tried to sell him a carpet of quality, 'Qual-i-ty, man. A hundred and twenty quid, and it's yours to take away today.'

'Look, mate. I don't need Axminster shag or whatever the hell that is. I just want something to shag on. It's for the back of my van. got it?'

'Got it.' He winked at Max. 'Little bit of sunshine right here should fit in your van, me old son, with a bit left over to put down by your feet in the front. How does fifty quid grab you?'

'It doesn't. Twenty, or I'm walking away.'

'Thirty-five, and you've got a deal.'

'Twenty, and I won't shag your missus in my campervan. Final offer.'

'Steady on, old son. She's a diamond in the rough my old lady is. Okay. Twenty, and you're starving my poor children.'

Mel was waiting for him in the drive when he got home. God, that woman could nag. She'd got it into her head that with Max dying, their mother needed help with her finances and investments. Mel had persuaded their mum to let her take out Power of Attorney in case anything happened to her. Mel always had a nose for the crisp aroma of money. 'I know it's a delicate subject, Max, but Laurence and I have been talking.'

'Of course, you have.'

'Now, don't start. There's no need. I want to have an adult conversation. Mum's getting older.'

'She's sixty-three.'

'Yes, and I've got osteoporosis, so she must have it too.'

Mel, you've got a brittle mind. There's sod all wrong with your bones.'

'One day, somebody is going to give you everything you deserve, Max. You nasty little man. What's this thing anyway, and what are you doing?'

'This, my dear sister, is a campervan. It looks like a van, see, and you camp in it. And this is a piece of carpet. Yours are all bigger and more expensive. Bloody awful patterns, too, come to think of it—but you've seen carpet before. It's the stuff your cleaner vacuums to get rid of all the crap. And talking about useless fluff, how is dear Sebastian? Has he moved further than the sofa this week? Do record it for me if he does .'

'Frig off, Max. Will you sign over your share of Mother's assets or not?'

'Jesus, talk about going straight for the jugular. Will I what?'

'Will you sign over your share of the inheritance? You don't need it, Max. You don't need any of it? I'm also hoping that you will look generously on your nephew and me when your time comes.'

Max had been in the van fitting the piece of carpet throughout the exchange. He sprayed the last edge down with glue before he backed out of the van and answered.'

'Melissa darling?'

'Yes?'

'Go pleasure yourself.'

He packed a rucksack that hadn't been used since his college days. The musty smell gave it provenance. There was no time like the present for a drive. Maybe he'd spend his first night in the van with the roof open, looking at the stars. He had the image of a girl in his head with two-tone hair, half blonde, half brown. She'd made an impression last week, and maybe he could take her for a drink when she finished work.

He told Jonathan he'd keep an eye out for those two missing boys as well. The search the night before hadn't given the police any new leads. They were still treating it as a missing person case, but in the press conference, their faces were grim, and the mothers were behind the table sobbing and saying all the usual things about them not being in trouble if they just came home. It ended with a personal note to any individual that might have taken them, to keep them safe and bring them home to the families who loved them. It was poignant stuff, but two thirteen-year-old boys? Max told the police at the search the night before that it was probably a couple of young lads on their first big adventure. They'd be home by the weekend in time for Mum's Sunday roast.

When he got to Morecambe in his van, there was a line of seventeen campervans parked along the road just up from The Midland Hotel. There wasn't one worth less than a hundred grand. What was this? Some rich camping swingers club? He didn't want to park at the end of the row and be conspicuous. He'd much rather have got himself into the middle of the gang—been one of the boys—but you couldn't get a Rizla paper between them. He slid into the last place and made his first cup of hippy green tea in his new home-from-home. It was disgusting. The previous owner had left everything in the van, and he even had a little tin kettle. It whistled like the olden days.

Soon, it rang out like a siren, and the campervan next to his opened its door.

'You can't park here,' a man in khaki shorts said. He seemed unnecessarily angry.

'Why not? You have.'

'We're organised.'

'What like organised crime?'

'We are the north county sect of the Lakeland Camp.'

'Are all your awnings pink then?'

'Look, just move your van, or we'll have you removed.'

Lesson one in the *Campers' Guide to Hippy Living*. The natives aren't always hippies, and they aren't always friendly.

'You know what, you old glamper-faced moron. Keep your Northern Sector Camp Lakeland thing. My van and I have certain standards when it comes to the vehicles we associate with. I won't be offering you a green tea any time soon.' He slammed the door shut, leaving the older man with his mouth agape in protest.

Feeling like the Ulgy Duckling being chased away by the beautiful swans, he drove off and was sure his camper's headlights were facing towards the ground. The van needed a name, and as he drove around looking for a layby to park up, he contemplated a name befitting of his queen. Even the name Barista Paige was considered and discounted. He laughed at himself for sounding like a lovesick teenager. The girl was a decade younger than him and had served him coffee once.

He settled on Diana as the van's name and the sound of his laughter rattled around in the stillness of the late afternoon calm. It was that time of day when the families had gone to the hotels to roost, the dealers, beggars and buskers had shut up shop, and the night owls were just waking from the evening before. There was the hint of an early sunset, and he determined that he would have the bloody brew that he never got to drink. He'd lost his sea view and only had a sign to look at saying *No Fly Tipping*, but he drank his tea in the campervan, *The Good Lady Diana*, and today life was great. He contemplated what kind of person would want to tip flies, and wouldn't a can of fly spray do the job? The café where Paige worked was just around the corner. They'd be closing after the tea-time crowd, and he might get to take her for a drink. He hoped it wasn't her day off. Max got out of his van, locked up and went to the café.

The bell jangled. Damn, that was annoying. Every customer's head in the café turned to look at him—there were only five. With nothing-to-see-here vibes, they turned back to their fish and chips. Max stamped on his urge to launch into a chorus of *All that Jazz* with fluttering jazz hands—Paige worked here, and while he wanted to stand out and woo her with his boyish charm, he didn't want to come across as the town idiot.

Max was disappointed when she wasn't behind the counter. A young lad, who looked to be about seven feet tall, smiled and Max was greeted with a set of braces that reminded him of a railway track. 'Joe' had a name badge, and he didn't look like the type to be leading the revolution.

'Cappuccino, please. No Paige today?'

It was a simple question, but the kid clattered the mug he'd picked up against the counter.

'No, not today.'

Something had rattled him. He looked around as if he expected a manager to appear at his shoulder and fire him on the spot. 'We're not allowed to talk about it.'

'Talk about what?' Come on. He'd set it up like a red ball over a pocket. What else was Max going to say?

'Can't say. She just doesn't work here anymore.'

'I see.'

He didn't see. The best guess was that she'd been caught creaming the till. He chuckled at that, creaming in a café. After her first greeting last time, she'd barely made eye contact with him under his intense appraisal, and yet she'd disappointed him. He didn't like to think of her as a thief.

Joe turned to the coffee machine, and Max glanced at the tabard uniforms on a stand behind the counter, some with nametags attached and some without. It made him sad. On the counter was a silver plate with a couple of name badges on it. The one on the top said, Paige. He kept his eye on Joe, who was elbows deep in steam and reached over the counter to grab it. He wanted to get out quickly in case Joe noticed the tag was missing. He turned to leave the café and almost bumped into a pensioner with a face like a disgruntled Shih Tzu. She had something that he assumed was mayonnaise at the corner of her mouth. Either that or she'd had a nice time with Old Jim in the men's toilets. She didn't say a word but raised one eyebrow. It was a clever thing on two counts. Max had never been able to raise just one eyebrow. Nope, couldn't do it. And, the old bat made one expression, both a question and a reprimand.

He put his finger to his lips in the universal sign for shush and winked at her. The bell jangled again as he left the café. He could live without coffee anyway.

Walking back to the van, he considered his actions. He had no idea why he'd stolen the girl's name badge. Because he could? Because the tumour in his head was making him do irrational things? He almost threw it into the hedge at the side of the road, but it felt warm in his pocket as though it was an invisible thread from her to him. He was getting sentimental. There were a million girls with two-tone hair and green eyes. He needed to get laid. He could find a girl with shocking pink hair and accommodating thighs if he wanted.

He thought about making a bacon sandwich on his new stove in his new van. But that was taking this camping gig way too far. Besides, there was a burger van in the next layby and Morrisons just across the road. He opted for a dirty cheeseburger and took it back to The Good Lady Diana.

This was his first time on the road, and he ate his dinner sitting on the bench seat, with coffee in a tin mug made on his gas stove with his tiny little kettle. It was a fun romantic novelty.

It would have been so much better if Paige was sitting opposite him. He thought about all the questions he wanted to ask her and wondered where she saw her life taking her. He even had a crazy notion about offering her a job in the company, something in sales, maybe, with training that would lead to a decent career. His disappointment was profound. She was like a gift he'd had for a fleeting second and then lost. The prettiest shell on the beach that would be there until the turn of the tide, and then she'd be washed away on the ebb. Like his life being drawn in the sand so briefly that it too would be washed away. He would look out for her in the pubs that night. If luck was with him, she'd be there without a boyfriend, and they could talk.

But other than giving her a life that he could never share, to what end would that be? Even if she liked him, it would be wrong to start a relationship with her or anybody else for that matter. He wondered if this was what love at first sight felt like and decided it would be best for them both if he never saw her again. She would be a good memory when the time came for him to need them.

The image he had of himself as the wayward traveller soon came to a crashing head. It wasn't so good when he wanted to get cleaned up for a night out on the pull. He hadn't considered for one second that he didn't have a shower. He poured some cold water from his white plastic drum into a sink made for Tom Thumb and added a splash of hot water from the kettle. He bumped his head on the cupboard as he bent over to wash his bits with a handful of Fairy Liquid that had been left in the van when he bought it. Anticipating taking Paige for a drink, he'd thrown cologne, a clean shirt, a toothbrush and toothpaste into his musty bag but had forgotten everything else.

His body was covered in washing-up liquid, and he didn't have enough water to rinse it properly. He had no razor for a shave and no towel to dry himself. He used the t-shirt he'd just taken off and was probably going to put on again in the morning. He hadn't been able to wash his hair, and how the hell was he going to pull a bird if his shoulder-length crowning glory wasn't shining like a halo? Camping was losing its appeal.

It was too early to go out. Barely seven o'clock. Time moved slowly when you were camping. He had no idea what people do without television. He was off-grid and, therefore, not hooked up to an electricity supply. He had his three-way leisure battery and even solar panels on the roof, but he'd never used them before. He didn't understand them and wanted to make sure he'd have electricity for the morning. He had his phone but didn't want to be out of touch if that died. But Jesus, he was stuck in a tin can with nobody to talk to. If he went out this early, he'd be hammered by ten o'clock.

Max scrolled through social media and liked a few meaningless posts. His thumb moved through the single-second snapshots of life, and his brain went into chewing gum mode as he passed talking parrots, clever dogs, and a poll on whether he'd prefer to eat frogs' legs or kiss a toad. Neither, at this moment, thank you very much. Ask me again when I'm pissed. Though he'd eaten the *Cuisses de Grenouille* many times.

He almost scrolled past Henry Watson's photo. The first one was just his picture, and he only hesitated because it was so out of place seeing Henry Watson on Facebook. The post below it had the inscription *RIP Henry* above the same picture. He'd only spoken to him four hours earlier.

Thirty-four messages of condolence said he was dead.

He rang Henry's number, hoping that his wife would answer. He had to grope in his mind for the mousey woman's name. Despite being his partner, Henry had rarely mentioned her. Maureen. He'd need to remember that for the funeral.

Their phone went to voicemail. Max scrolled, looking for Linda's number and realised he didn't have Henry's PA in his phone. He should go home. But if Henry was dead, what good could he do? His partner's death was going to be a massive upheaval. Max definitely needed to get laid.

He went into a small dark pub called The Chieftain and battled through the punters to go straight to the bathroom. He used the toilet, and after two cups of coffee in the van while he waited to come out, that was a matter of urgency. While he was in the bathroom, he swilled his face. He appraised himself sans hair products. It wasn't his normal look, but he had to admit he was one good-looking dude, and some lady was going to get lucky tonight. He went to the bar, bought a whiskey and raised it in a silent toast to his business partner. He didn't know what he was going to do now. He supposed he'd have to go back to work. It was a damned, inconvenient mess.

He wandered the pubs ending up in The King's Head which seemed to be this town's best excuse for a nightclub. The women were more than happy to be bought drinks, but when he brought out his brand new chat-up line, 'I've got a campervan with a double bed, would you like to see it?' they all made a hasty retreat.

By the end of the night, only women that he would call the scrag ends of life were left. He watched the last chance saloon men vying for their company and had enough dignity not to join them. He felt guilty for his opinion of the ladies. Most of them were probably very nice people, and he was a bastard, but he wasn't taking any of them back to meet Diana.

Max sat at the bar with his back to the dancefloor and finished his last whiskey.

'Hey, Casanova, on the house.'

The barmaid slid another whiskey down the bar to him. And okay, it wasn't the whole length of the bar, it was only a few inches, but it was enough to impress him. She didn't have pink hair. It was brown, standard, not two-tone. Not Paige.

Despite his earlier thoughts about never seeing her again being for the best, he'd hoped to run into Paige all night. He didn't know if she had a boyfriend. A girl like her probably did.

This girl had a lot of tattoos, a whole world map of them. He travelled from Morecambe to Mozambique in the blink of an eye. She came from behind the bar to sit on the next stool and held out her glass to cheers, and Max clinked half-heartedly. She was older than Paige but without the class. More streetwise and not the type he'd offer a job to.

'So, about this caravan,' she said.

'Campervan.'

'Campervan, then.'

'Eavesdropper.'

'I pick up a lot behind this bar. For instance, I know you're pants at hitting on girls.'

'I'm sure there's a joke there about pants and getting a girl's panties off.' Max couldn't be bothered. It was late, and whereas getting laid was important three hours ago, now he was looking forward to his night under the stars as a solo flight. She was kind enough to laugh, and it had a nice sound to it. Maybe it wouldn't be such a bad thing to come onto this creature of many tattoos. 'Is your name Lydia?'

'*Lydia, oh Lydia, the tattooed lady.* A song about the harshness and poverty in Victorian England in the times of the travelling circus, if I'm not mistaken.'

She was smart.

'As the song says, you can learn a lot from Lydia. My name isn't as romantic. It's just plain old Zoe. But I'm good company. We can hang out, and maybe I can take your mind away from your troubles for an hour or two. It looks as though you have a world of them.'

What the hell, in for a penny. 'Come on then, and I'll show you the night sky through my campervan roof.'

Zoe shouted to the man behind the bar. 'Night, Billy. I'm off. Just make sure you lock up properly.'

Billy waved and opened the door for them, and Max heard the bolt sliding into place as they left.

***

Zoe was great. The girl was funny, one of those quick wits that didn't have you rolling on the ground holding your belly, but she was funny without trying. He liked her, and it was a shame that he'd shagged her because she'd have made a great mate. That was buggered now because he'd had sex with her—twice—and he couldn't get her out of the van fast enough to be on the road.

She looked ethereal as she sprawled out fast asleep on her side. Her hair fell over the pillow like a renaissance Botticelli. He scrambled around to find his phone and took a photo of her because the artistry in her sleeping form struck him. He'd never done anything like that in his life. He wasn't a creepy pervert, and he'd delete it in shame when he got home.

The picture looked peaceful, with the swell of her breast, the valley as her waist dipped into her hips and the rounding of her buttock and thigh as the contour flowed out again. Her whole body was partially wrapped in his white bedding. It was wrong to photograph a sleeping woman without her consent, he knew that, but it was done with innocent intentions. Like when your dog does something goofy, and you wait all night to get him to do it again on camera. But he keeps licking his arse just as you're about to click the button. It was that kind of photograph, but without her trying to lick her backside. He'd show it to her when she woke up if he remembered. His thoughts lapsed into suggestions of dogs. He regretted that he didn't get a dog before he started dying in earnest. A dog and a camper van went together, but it was too late now.

He made coffee, and he stirred as she stirred—good timing.

'Morning, handsome.'

'Thought you were going to sleep all day. I could have been on a ferry with you by now.' He handed her a mug of coffee without asking if she took sugar. He didn't have any.

'Would running away be a bad thing?'

'A brief tarry never gets in the way of a man's roaming soul, and I'm sure you have things to do today.'

'Message received and understood. Do I have time to get dressed before my walk of shame, or are you throwing me out in my knickers?'

'Now, don't be like that. We both know the score.'

'Sure. I'm not going to give you the "I don't usually sleep with strangers" spiel, but you're the only interesting man that's walked into that pub as long as I've been there.' She finished doing up her jeans, rooted for a pen in her bag and scribbled her number on a Wrigley's wrapper after putting the gum in her mouth.

'Anyway, thanks for the brew. Good to go. Listen, man. I'm not being heavy. It's not like I want to marry you or anything. I don't even want to tattoo your name on my arm, but a couple of days by a Scottish Loch would be nice. You, me, the van. Just to escape it all, you know? We could look for Nessie. That's if you wanted to give me a bell sometime.'

And that was that. Not too awkward. He'd had worse morning afters. Max started the engine, crumpled her number and threw the paper out of the window as she walked away. When he passed her on the road, he gave her a friendly toot but no offer of a lift home.

There was nothing to indicate that anything was wrong when he pulled up to the front of his house. And yet, Max knew. It was an inner sense that harked back to primitive man. From the front, everything was just as he'd left it, but he sensed that something was off.

As he put the key in the lock, he moved with caution. He heard his cat crying and scratching on the downstairs bathroom door where he'd been locked in. He left him in there in case the intruder was still in the house. Moving cautiously through the downstairs, he checked each room for trouble and found plenty, but it was all of the static kind. Every room had been turned over. He had a good eye for detail and took in what had been moved or taken. His laptop was gone from the living room with only its orange charging cable left dangling empty, like a fishhook without a fish. He expected that. In the kitchen, a knife was missing from the block, and his Bluetooth speaker was gone. The glass from the panel in the back door had shattered inwards. Both rooms had been picked over rather than ransacked, and he had the feeling that it was staging more than intent. Upstairs, all the drawers had been pulled out in his bedroom. A gold watch and two pairs of c-ufflinks were missing from his top drawer—but nobody wore watches and cufflinks these days. They didn't hold any particular sentimental value. He'd lost some monetary items, but nothing that couldn't be replaced.

Once he was sure that the house was clear, he let Dexter out. The cat screamed his indignation at him, and Max calmed him. But there was nobody to calm Max, and he was white hot with anger. He swore that if he found who'd done this, they'd pay a lot more than the value of the goods. Max didn't like somebody coming into his home uninvited. He didn't like his things being taken. And he didn't like his cat being locked up. He wasn't cool with this. Max wanted to kill the bastard.

He put his house back in order, and his feeling that it was all for show was reinforced. There wasn't much damage apart from the back door, a couple of plates, and a vase in the hall that he never liked much anyway. He decided that there was no point in reporting the break-in. It was more trouble than it was worth having to give a statement.

But damn, he was angry.

Chapter Eight

The next morning, Max went into the office to sort out what was going to happen now that Henry was dead. It was bloody inconvenient and a blight on Max's day.

He picked a sprig of honeysuckle from the creeper around the main entrance. It was the single overriding scent of his childhood. His best mate Jon's house was his escape, and Jon's mum had honeysuckle in the garden. It was always there, that beautiful cloying smell synonymous with parental love, even if he wasn't loved himself. Jon's mum was never keen on him and thought he was a bad influence on Jonathan. Perfectly true, but it didn't stop him from loving the smell of honeysuckle.

He called a meeting and promoted his sales manager to take on Henry's role in Groundworks and Civil Engineering, despite him not knowing the first thing about planning and all the red tape needed to jump through hoops to get permission to build. Never mind anything else that went with the role. It cost him another eight grand a year on Barry's salary.

'You'll be fine, Barry. Just wing it, mate. You've got this.'

'But, I don't know what I'm doing.'

'Who really knows anything these days? I couldn't give a shit. I'm dying soon and way beyond caring. Just rearrange your pencils or something for now, and you'll get the hang of it. There'll be a tutorial on the internet.'

He had to promote a lower sales team member to fill Barry's position, which cost another three grand and two lower-still salespeople because they moaned that everybody was being promoted. It made him realise how much Henry did and, as a direct consequence, how little his own role mattered. He was like the expensive wallpaper he'd chosen at six hundred pounds a roll and about as useful. Henry had carried the business for years. If the staff wanted funds for a team-building day at the races, they went to Max. If they needed help with anything important, they went to Henry.

Max had more than enough money to see out his days, and he couldn't care less about the company. He had no kids to pass it on to. As a legacy, it was useless. He was the boy who took up Judo and got tired of it within a week, so moved on to bassoon lessons and then football club. He didn't need money where he was going—and MJP was just a bunch of money and buildings. What Max needed was the elixir of eternal life or at least a greatly extended one.

He'd never replaced his last PA after she'd quit in frustration. But there was still Linda. Thank God for Linda. And she was there. At her desk, just like always. He dropped the sprig of honeysuckle in front of her with a smile. 'For you.' He didn't think Linda had ever taken a day off. Her eyes were red and puffy, but her makeup was still immaculately applied with no smudging or coal-dusted eyes. If you were into efficiency, her sex appeal was boundless. She was probably around the same age as Max but seemed twenty years older. Her idea of fun was probably doing *The Times* crossword before an evening of arguing for governmental taxation increases on social media, a proper keyboard warrior. He knew her—before—but didn't like thinking about that, and they'd never spoken about it, thank God.

'Good morning, Max. I emailed you and am waiting for an update on company flowers.'

'What?'

'Flowers. For Henry's funeral.'

'I don't like flowers. It's ripping a thing of beauty out of the earth to die.'

Linda looked at her wilting honeysuckle.

'We should send some,' she said.

'Okay, they need to be big then. Bigger than anybody else's, so they stand out. A big wreath in the shape of a golf ball.'

'You're joking, right?'

Max looked confused. He didn't get the intricacies of social niceties and couldn't give a shit about the flowers until they became an issue. He saw Linda's horrified face, and now it was a contest that he had to win.

'No. Linda. I couldn't joke at a time like this. My business partner has just died, and I want him to have the biggest and best wreath we can get him. He was the heart of MJP, and we must show our respect.'

'But a golf ball?'

'A big one in blue. I've seen him with blue golf balls.'

'Max, he died on the golf course.'

'There we go, then. He liked golf.'

Max had had enough of this shit. 'Blah, flipping blah. Let me out of here.' His days of being shut in this place were over. He'd done his time and was happy to let the monkeys run the zoo until he put the company on the market. He got a coffee and went to the chill-out area.

And that's where the two police officers found him. They were already flashing their badges as they manoeuvred around the giant bean bags. The police had a nerve coming here and disrupting the office for a heart attack victim. It took very little for the office staff to down tools and gossip.

'Mr Jones? DCI Nash and DI Molly Brown. May we ask you a few questions, please?'

Max motioned them to two bean bags.

'Perhaps we might sit over here at the table, sir,' Molly said, and Max was disappointed that he didn't get to see her getting in and out of the bean bag. They were like huge primary-coloured vaginas that swallowed people. She held herself in a manner that suggested she didn't shit like the rest of us, and that got up Max's nose. The bean bag would have been fun. They took seats at the bright red table, the colour of anger, with the detectives on one side and Max on the other. They hadn't said anything yet, but it already felt like an interrogation.

'Do you mind if we record this? It isn't an official taped interview, but it helps us with the transcript later.' Nash put his device on the table between them and pressed the record button. He didn't wait for an answer. 'What can you tell us about Mr Watson's activities yesterday? We tried to get hold of you earlier, but you weren't available. Mrs Evans said it's your custom to arrive late. We've spoken to her and have Mr Watson's laptop and physical diary, but we wondered if you could shed any additional light on his day.'

'Why are you here? Didn't he just have a heart attack? I don't see how this necessitates police involvement. I saw him here at eleven yesterday morning. Our meeting lasted no more than fifteen minutes, and that's the last I saw of him. Though I understand he was found on the golf course, so the old bugger must have squeezed a round in at some point. Who can blame him? Shame if he didn't make that eighteenth hole.'

'We'll answer all of your questions in due course, sir, but indeed, he didn't make the eighteenth. He was found in a bunker where it's partially shaded by trees in both directions. Mr Jones, we are unable to release much information, but we can confirm that Mr Watson was murdered.'

'Jesus. Really? I thought it was a heart attack. Who'd want to murder old Watson? He was as dull as dishwater.'

It took Max a couple of minutes to regain his composure. His relationship with Henry was like that of an overbearing uncle that he loved to taunt. And he couldn't imagine life without him. It was a good job he didn't have to live without him for long. Dying took the meaning out of everything. He wouldn't be around to grieve Henry this time next year on the anniversary of his death. And Max would never raise a glass to him because he'd be dead too. Dr Death took massive things, like his partner's passing, and made them small. Insignificant even.

'Can you think of anybody with a grudge against Mr Watson?' DI Brown asked.

'I suppose he got a few backs up with business contracts, but to be honest, he was more used to putting out my fires than causing them himself.'

'What was your relationship with the deceased like?'

'I couldn't stand the pompous old bastard. He was always telling me what to do. But that doesn't mean I'd wished him dead. Murdered. Wow. How?'

'From what we can ascertain, he was attacked from behind. Further information regarding the murder is being withheld.'

'Poor old bastard.'

'You keep calling him old. He can't have been much older than you at forty-eight.'

'Did you ever meet him? If you had, you'd get it.'

'I'm afraid not. Can you tell us anything at all that might help?'

'Nothing springs to mind, and if there's nothing else, Inspector, I have a meeting in five minutes, and then I have to buy flowers. Lovely talking to you. Do you have anything planned for the rest of the day? Here, would you like an MJP baseball cap? It's just your colour.' Nash put his business card on the table between them.

'This isn't a TV drama. Your partner has been murdered and subjected to the most heinous brutality. I believe there was a bitter argument between you and Mr Watson yesterday.'

'I see Linda's been talking out of school.'

'No, several members of staff heard the altercation. Worse than an argument, they've told us that Mr Watson was going to have you legally removed from the business.'

'Yes, but that suited both of us. He didn't have to remove me, as you put it. Funny, that's what he called it, too. I was going anyway. I can see what you're insinuating, Inspector, and if being given a shitload of money for doing absolutely nothing is a motive for murder, then take me away. I don't know if the gossip mill has told you this too, but I'm dying, so couldn't really care less about working anymore. I've hired a new interim Henry, and I'll leave him to run the business as he sees fi t.'

'Yes, we've heard. We're sorry to hear about your illness, Mr Jones. We have one more question, and this is purely to eliminate you from our enquiries, you understand. Where were you between the hours of three-fifteen and five P.M. yesterday?'

***

Max hadn't brought his car to work, and sometimes he liked the five-minute walk to the office, especially since his diagnosis. Time was limited, and he wanted to enjoy the sunshine and birds and trees as much as he could. He laughed as he walked home. The thought that he might have murdered Henry was ridiculous. Or was it? He felt that he could account for every second of yesterday, but after their argument, what if he'd snuck onto the golf course to bump him off? There was no telling what the tumour could make him do, and he couldn't see anybody wanting to kill Henry. You couldn't even call him vanilla. He was just grey. Max made a mental list of people he would murder before he ever got around to Henry. There were a few. Not least, some of his old teachers and kids at school sadistic bastards that they were.

He heard the pitiful screaming before he turned the corner. He hadn't seen the first kick but was in time to see a lowlife piece of scum booting a dog. The terrified animal was on a lead, so couldn't run away. It cowered into the wall of a house and trembled. Its head was low, with its tail between its legs, and it howled and urinated in fear. Max saw a small yellow river roll from between the dog's legs to the edge of the pavement. He would have died right then to save hearing that awful cry again. It was wretched.

The owner, in his late teens or early twenties, had pulled back his leg to kick again.

'Hey. Stop. What the hell do you think you're doing?'

The boy lowered his leg and turned on Max.

'What's it got to do with you?'

'Nothing at all, but I'll tell you now, you're not going to kick that dog again.'

Max had him by the throat and lifted him off the ground before the boy realised what was happening. He squeezed, and it felt good to feel the vocal cords and sinews close in against his palm. He squeezed harder, and the boy wheezed. The dog was still crying, and the sound of the kid choking was sweet music to Max. As the boy let go of the dog's lead, the animal was so traumatised that it didn't try to move. Max caught the lead with his spare hand so that it didn't make a run for it and get onto the road. A few cars went past, but nobody cared enough to stop and see what the violence was about.

He felt the boy weakening. All he had to do was keep squeezing. It wasn't even that hard. He'd never wanted to hurt anything so badly in his life, but if he didn't stop, the boy was going to lose consciousness, and permanent damage may be done to his throat. He could do without the aggravation.

Max let him drop, and the boy fell onto his knees, holding his throat and making the same wheezing noise even though Max's hand wasn't there. Max hunkered, too. He came down to the same level and pulled the terrified mongrel into him. It was skin and bone. He could feel every rib, and the hip bones rose like twin fists. He saw that it was a girl, and she was so scared that she peed some more and screamed as Max held her.

He'd never been one to think things through and made a snap decision.

'Right. This is what's going to happen. I'm taking this dog.'

The boy could barely speak but managed to rasp out the word, 'No.'

'No? And whose going to stop me from taking her?'

'Police.'

'Please call them, and let's show them the state of this poor thing. But you're right. It would be wrong of me to steal a lad's dog. No more Lassie moments together. So, I'm going to buy her from you. It's a legitimate transaction. I'll give you some money. You'll sell me your dog. Deal?'

'No.'

Max ignored him and took out his wallet. He watched the boy's eyes widen as he saw the wad of notes. Max had no idea how much he had, somewhere between three and five hundred. He threw the money on the floor by the boy and watched him scrabble in the gutter for it before the breeze took it from him. Max saw the tracks on the boy's arm and the sores on his face, and his hatred hardened. He felt no pity for this lad who had a miserable life when he wasn't high. His thoughts were all about what the poor dog's life must have been like.

'Are we good?'

'Drop dead.'

Max stood up and talked softly to the terrified dog to encourage her to walk with him.

'How old is she?' he flung back over his shoulder at the boy who was sitting in the dirt counting his money.

'About two,' His voice was coming back.

'And what's she called?'

'Anthrax—and I'm keeping this money, but me and my boys are coming for you, dickhead. I'm gonna get my dog back.' Max made a lunge toward him, and the man cowered against the wall as his dog had done.

'Yeah? I'll have the kettle on, sweetheart.'

Anthrax. He laughed—bloody Anthrax.

Max checked that he wasn't being followed all the way home. The immediate problem when he got in was Dexter, who wasn't impressed with the new arrival in the home. He hissed and spat and had to be forced out and have his cat flap locked while Max saw to the dog. He decided to call her Mia without thinking about it. It suited her and was a pretty name, he thought. The poor dog couldn't take anymore. She was terrified from the beating—and from a lifetime of other beatings.

She was scared of Max, about being in a strange place and the angry cat that wanted to relieve her of an eye.

She was a sweet girl, and though she cried out in fear when he picked her up, she allowed her body to push against him as he lifted her onto the sofa and stroked her. She put her silky head in the crook of his arm and flinched every time he moved in expectation of the next blow. Max couldn't ever remember being this angry at another human being. How could the bastard do this to her? He worried that Mia would sense his anger and concentrated on calming his breathing as they adjusted to this new together. When he stopped stoking her, she put her head under his hand and nudged him, bold enough to ask for more.

This was the first time Max had a second to think about what he'd done. He'd stolen a dog that would outlive him by at least fifteen years. What kind of crazy stunt was that? She was medium-sized, part lurcher, part collie, part something else—a mixed-up special brew. Mia was brown and black and tan, with a bit of beige and a hint of rust. Her eyes were amber ponds of liquid chocolate and gold that swallowed him when he looked at her.

And for now—at least—she belonged to him.

Chapter Nine

Chapter Nine

Dogs shouldn't be on beds. Tell that to Mia, who, in the space of hours, captivated Max. If he could give her a good home for the rest of her life, he'd have been in love. He hardened his heart and knew he had to give her up. She cuddled into him and made his bedding stink, but he didn't care. She was in need of a bath and a flea and worm treatment, too, not to mention vaccinations—although, with what she'd been through, she probably had one of the strongest immune systems in the country. True to Anthrax, her former name, laboratories could have taken blood samples from her to make vaccines for a multitude of diseases. However, Max told himself she was the best woman that had ever been in his bed. Women let you down, but dogs don't. And it was with a heavy heart that he made the decision to rehome her—and there was only one home that was good enough for this little girl. He was ready for a fight when he reached for his phone.

'Jon, my old cocker who never lets me down. I need a favour. It's a big one, and I'm dying, so you can't say no.'

'Max? It's seven in the morning. What the hell?'

'Tell you when I get there.'

'Have you any idea how impossible you are?'

'I know. See you. And tell the kids I've got a present for them.'

The night before, Mia had eaten him out of pocket. And with no idea how much dogs eat, he'd given her five digestive biscuits, half a packet of sliced ham and a bowl of cornflakes. He figured that as a responsible dog owner, he should probably get her something with a picture of a dog on the can. He left her in the house alone in case they ran into her former owner and bought her some awful tinned stuff. He was only gone five minutes because the shop was on the corner, but when he got back, he could hear her howling halfway down the street. Mia greeted him like the owner she'd never had.

He came to regret the canned food, or maybe it was the cornflakes, but through the night, he was physically assaulted by the most noxious farts he'd ever smelt. In a toxicity competition, they would have outshone Chernobyl. She didn't seem in the least embarrassed when he called her out on them. Jesus, who knew a lady could smell like that? She just stretched and rolled on her back for him to stroke her belly. She'd become used to being loved pretty damn quickly. He was amazed at her resilience.

Mia didn't want to leave the house when he put her lead on. Maybe she thought he was taking her back to Wankstain. He talked to her as they drove to Jon's house and told her what a great life she'd have. Mia wasn't convinced.

'Hey, kids. Come see what I've got.' Max knocked on the door and walked in. He stood at the bottom of the stairs with Mia, who looked inquisitive and less scared than the day before but still very timid regarding the unknown.

Carter took the stairs two at a time, and Lucy clattered down behind him.

'No way.' Carter said, 'A dog? For us? Wait till Dad finds out.'

Lucy opened her mouth to squeal, and Max shushed her before she made a sound. He stopped her charging up to Mia and smothering her with love. A Lucy squeal could make dolphins cover their ears in the South Pacific.

'She's had a pretty tough life, kids, and the thing she needs most now is calm, quiet and love. Go into the lounge, and let's introduce you properly.'

He made them sit down and released Mia from her lead. She clung to Max's leg until curiosity got the better of her, and she was in rapture, getting stroked by two kind human beings.

He heard Emily shouting before he saw her, and there were some colourful swear words in there. 'I'm not having it, Jonathan. You tell him, or I will.'

Max got up and left the room, closing the door behind him, but not before he made sure Jon saw how happy his kids were.

'Before you say anything, think about it. Are you really going to break your children's hearts?'

'Not happening, mate. Not this time. You're not going to do this to me. You brought it in here. You go and tell the kids you made a mistake.'

'Can't. Jon, I'm saying it this time without bullshit or messing with you. I've only got a few months left, and that dog needs a home more than any other poor animal you've ever seen. She's my legacy, and you are my best friends.'

Emily had joined them in the kitchen. 'I don't know if I should give you this coffee or throw it at you. We can't have a dog. We work all day for one thing, and for another, Jon is allergic.'

'Hah, no, he isn't. Got you. He had a Saturday job in the local kennels when he was fourteen. Try again, love. And as for everything else, I've thought of that. I'm going to set you up for her entire life. I'm paying for a dog walker for her. An hour a day, allowing for inflation, I've provided enough to cover it.'

'Max?' Jon said.

'Vaccinations, insurance, and everything else, all sorted. Check your bank account I've already transferred the money. Emily, if you'd seen this bloke booting the hell out of her, you'd have done the same. Don't tell me you wouldn't. And she's the sweetest little thing, no trouble at all. You might want to give her a bath, though.'

'You're a dick, Maxwell Jones,' Emily said, but at least she was smiling.

'And you wouldn't have me any other way.'

'We can't take her. It's too much to ask.'

'You have to. There's nobody else, and the kids already love her. Please say you'll do it.'

'And in which world, other than Maxville, do you think it's all right to put us in this position and bring the dog into our home without asking us first?'

'In Maxville, friends will do anything to help an animal who's out of options and a mate that's begging you.'

'A trial,' Emily said. 'Okay, we'll take her on a trial, and if it doesn't work, you're going to have to rethink.'

'Deal. You'll love her.'

Jonathan knew he was beaten, but it didn't stop him from sulking.

'I've never wanted to punch you in the face more than I do right now.'

'And you think you could?'

'No, I wouldn't stand a chance. I'm still that ginger kid you had to protect. But it doesn't stop me from wanting to. You're a bastard, you know.'

'Yeah, tell it to the choir.'

They'd met when they were eight. Max and his mate, Bobby, were collecting conkers in Barrow Park and argued about who had the most, the best, and the one that would win in a match. By the lake, they heard shouting and saw some kids throwing another lad into the water. Max and Bobby grabbed sticks, yelled their heads off in a Barrovian war cry as they ran down the bank, and they saw the kids off. They helped a ginger kid out of the lake and pretended not to notice that he was crying. From there, for the next few years, the three were inseparable during the holidays whilst Jon's little sister, Fiona, was desperate to join them, and they systematically excluded her from their club. He remembered one occasion when they'd said she could play with them. They tied her to a tree and ran around it with air tomahawks, and they patted their mouth to make whoop-whoop noises. It was okay to play that game then, encouraged, in fact. It was good exercise in the fresh air, though, maybe tying a little girl to a tree was going too far. And they were called Red Indians back then, not Native Americans. The name indicating colour sounded so much better to a child playing out their heroes. Max had taken a course on discrimination and another on inclusion—but not back then. In that time and age, people were just people, and they were fun to emulate. It wouldn't be allowed now.

When they'd stopped running around the tree and were breathless, Max was the first to speak. 'Now, we're going to make the fire at your feet and burn you up. Let's gather the wood, men.'

Fiona wailed. And then she screamed.

'Stop, Max. You're frightening her.' Jon liked winding his softie sister up, but he was still a protective older brother. Max gathered wood from the copse behind them, and as he bent over to pick up a twig, Jon piled into him and punched him in the nose. Max turned, and they rolled and tumbled on the grass. There was blood loss to both member states and two bust noses. Max sauntered out of it, and Jon cried with a bust nose and two black eyes. They cut Fiona loose, and they all went home for tea. Happy days.

It was tough for Max to make friends when he was boarding at a private school. Jon and Bobby still called him a posh git at every opportunity, but they were all good mates.

Then Max went off to university, Jon did a plumbing course at college and dropped out after the first term, and Bobby went off the rails. He did some time with youth offenders and dropped off the grid after that. They kept in touch for a while, but Max hadn't seen him in years. Jonathan was done with plumbing, took a job as a packer in the candle factory and had been there ever since. Max went on to build his empire, and while it was an unbalanced friendship, what Max had in brains and finance, Jon and Emily made up for in love and always being there for him.

'We don't know anything about this animal. We'll need her medical records for a start.'

'I very much doubt she has any, Jon. There's a squat near where I saw her owner. There's a good chance he's sleeping there. I'll see what I can do, but don't expect much background. Seriously, Jon, I'd keep her if I could. Her name's Mia. She loves scratches behind the ear and ham, and she farts like a nuclear weapon. Enjoy her.'

***

Max wasn't looking forward to seeing Mia's previous owner again. If that dog had ever been to a vet, he'd be amazed, but Jonathan was a stickler for doing things properly and wouldn't let up. He was worried in case the dog had been microchipped, considering how Max came about her. It was ludicrous, but Jon had insisted that Max track the man down and get a receipt. A bloody receipt. The guy probably couldn't write his name. But to shut Jon up, he agreed to try and track the man down and see if they could at least have a grown-up conversation. It was a fool's errand. You couldn't reason with people like him. But he would have one walk past the squat to see if the lad was around. He figured that covered his promise. He couldn't get a receipt if Max didn't see him, could he?

When he got to the house where Mia was being beaten in the street, he saw something glinting in the gutter. It was a dog tag in the shape of a bone, and it had the single word *Anthrax*. No address or phone number, so defeating the purpose of a tag, but there it was.

He should have left it to the filth of her former life, but it was a symbol of who Mia had been. He slipped it into his pocket. He seemed to be collecting names. First Paige and now Anthrax. It could be his new hobby, name collecting.

Max jumped out of his pondering when he heard sirens on the next street. He rounded the corner and saw an ambulance and two police cars outside the old building that had once been Bar Continental. When the bar shut down, it was empty for some years—home to the rats and the spiders. Nobody seemed to be taking ownership of it, or doing anything to restore it, so squatters had moved in, and the council didn't seem to be bothered. Better to have them contained than sleeping in shop doorways.

Somebody was taking photographs, and a policeman was putting yellow tape around the area. There was something slumped in the doorway, but Max couldn't get close enough to see.

'Hi, I was going in there. Well, not going in, not if I could help it, but I wanted to see somebody that—er—lives there. What's going on?' he asked one of the policemen who had been at the community search. They'd had a chat over wellington boots and hot soup.

'Who were you coming to see?'

'I don't know, some lad. I didn't get his name. Just wanted to ask him about his dog?'

'His dog?'

'Yeah, it's nothing, really.' Max craned his neck to see what was going on. He saw the object slumped in the doorway and followed a pair of brand-new trainers along the legs of filthy jeans to a face that was instantly recognisable.

'That's him. Shit. That's the bloke I saw kicking his dog.'

'You need to move back. This is a crime scene, and we have to keep it clear. When did you see him?'

'Yesterday.' Max gave his details and told the young police officer everything he knew while the policeman wrote it down.

'We may need to speak to you again. I expect we'll want to interview you. You may be one of the last people to see him alive.'

'No problem, officer. You know where to find me.'

First Henry, now this no-hoper, it was time to get out of Dodge. Men were dying all over the place. He felt everything closing in on him. The town was depressing. He'd pack a bag properly this time and get away in the van for a few days. If anybody wanted to speak to him, it would have to wait until he got back. He couldn't decide between Scotland, Ireland or Wales.

That night he booked into a proper campsite just over the Welsh border and into North Wales. The view over Colwyn Bay was stunning, and it made him glad to be alive. He spent an hour setting up camp, and he pitched his awning alongside the van. It gave him shelter and as much space as he could need for his gear. Having the awning up made all the difference. Now, he had somewhere to put up an external table and chairs, and it was big enough to stand up and walk around in. He even had a separate bedroom area to get changed.

Once he had his obligatory cup of tea, he dragged his chair outside to watch the last of the sun dropping like a mirage into the bay. A flock of Barker geese flew in murmuration over the sands as the tide went out before the birds reached their evening roost. Being able to get away in his van gave him a sense of calm that he hadn't felt before. Time didn't matter, and he was away from everybody and everything he knew.

He chatted to some other campers as they passed but wasn't put out when they didn't want to stick around for a beer. Each to their own. They weren't the friendliest people and seemed in a hurry to get away from him. He watched as they went to speak to the farmer who owned the site. They stopped to speak to another couple halfway across the field, and they went with them to the camp office, where the farmer was outside. He saw one of the women pointing towards his van but was oblivious to the fact that he'd done anything wrong. He'd only just got there and hadn't had time to be bad yet.

It didn't even seem odd to him when the farmer knocked on the door of the van next to him and then went across the field with the family next door. Both of the adults had a sleepy child in their arms, and they were taken into the office. He watched as the lights went on. He should have sensed something wasn't right but was one of those people who thought the whole world loved him. There are people persons, and there are non-people persons. Max was one of the first.

Somebody ran across the field and passed his van.

'Bastard, you'll get yours. You're all over Facebook, you monster. There's a call out for your van and everything. How did you expect to get away with it?'

Max went inside for his phone and loaded it up. He saw the news-feed. His van. His numberplate. And the heading *Have You Seen This Van?* It had been shared with him four times in the last hour. The van wasn't registered to him yet. Damn, something else he'd forgotten. If the police came at him, he'd blame it on his condition.

He didn't have time to read the police statement underneath the picture of his van. But he saw the words *Do not approach this van. It could be dangerous.* Four police vans screeched into the campsite and surrounded his campervan. Somebody was shouting at him on a loudhailer.

'Step out of the van with your hands in the air.' He repeated it three times. 'Do as we say, and you won't be harmed.'

What the Hell?

Max came out of the van and into the darkening field to be blinded by spotlights pointed at his face. He was battled to the ground and cuffed.

'What's your name?' A man had stepped forward, but he could only see his boots. They were still shiny despite the grass on the field.

'What's going on? I haven't done anything.'

'Your name, Sir.'

'Maxwell Jones.'

'Maxwell Jones. We are arresting you on suspicion of murder You do not have to say anything. But, it may harm your defence if you do not mention when questioned something which you later rely on in court. Anything you do say may be given in evidence. Do you understand what I've just said to you?'

'Yes, but this is messed up, man.' Before he could say anymore. Two uniformed police officers pulled him up and threw him in the back of one of the vans.

He heard them congratulating themselves. He had been arrested on suspicion of murder, but that's all he'd been told. Who was he supposed to have killed? Henry, obviously. Max was in the back of a black Mariah, not even a regular van. This one had no windows and was reinforced with a wire cage and a black steel shutter between him and the front seats. Minutes later, he was driven at speed down the A-roads, and he felt the difference in road surface when that changed to the smoother Tarmac of the Motorway. It was amazing how much he could tell from the darkness inside the van. He banged on the separating wall and shouted until his voice was hoarse.

He was being taken back North. But why?

Chapter Ten

Jessica showed her security pass to start her shift at BAE Systems Barrow. She was proud to be a tiny part of the history that was responsible for building the country's biggest nuclear submarines. BAE, formerly Vickers Shipbuilding, had made and forged part of the country's history. The order for HMS Vengeance in 1887 by the Royal Navy saw Barrow become the first shipyard in Britain that could build a battleship. They have built 373 merchant ships, 312 submarines, and 148 naval surface ships in Barrow since, and Jessica was responsible in part for the smooth operations of the HR department. True, she had only been inside a submarine once and found it claustrophobic, but it pleased her to think that she was doing her bit for national defence—even if most of her day was spent in the photocopying room and making coffee for people more in the know than her.

As usual, she fought to get a parking space. And she ended up miles from the building and might as well have walked from home anyway. She watched the office staff lining up at another security point to get clearance for their eight A.M. shift. She joined the back of the queue and hoped she'd have time to grab a cup of tea to take to her desk before the pressure piled up with the tasks expected of her.

She showed her pass, and Jake, the security guard, smiled at her. He was a friendly guy and didn't seem to fit the role of a security man. He was too nice. But it was his job, and he gave an apologetic grin like he did every morning as he checked her bag. She had long since got over the embarrassment of him shuffling through the tampons and feminine wipes. She got as far as the locker room, where she had to leave her bag. She had five minutes to get a drink and call her sister before she had to put her phone away. They weren't allowed past this point. She put in a quick call, but it went straight to voicemail. She left a message.

Jess and Paige were going to their parent's house that night for their anniversary dinner. They had been married for forty-six years. Not quite a milestone, but that many years were worth celebrating. Her parents were the shining role models of marriage that she aspired to. They still kissed every time one of them left the house. After being together for fifty-one years through dating and marriage, they couldn't nip to the shop for a box of tea bags without a proper goodbye. It was both sickly and inspiring.

At twenty-three, Jess had only had two proper relationships. She was back on the dating scene after the last one cheated on her. She longed to meet, fall in love, marry, and have kids. The whole nine yards and all in the correct order. Her biological clock was ticking, and she couldn't wait. She had an irrational and stupid idea of wanting to be married longer than her parents—but they had a hell of a head start. They were only in their seventies and could be married for another twenty years before one of them popped off. And the likelihood of either finding joy in somebody else's bed was less every year. Jess needed to get moving and find a husband.

Her sister was supposed to be taking care of the flowers while she said she'd do the actual present buying. Jess took the time to research what she should buy, and while there was no traditional gift for the forty-sixth wedding anniversary, the modern gift was poetry. The traditional gemstone was the pearl, and the flower was the daffodil.

Jess had scoured booksellers and found a first-edition copy of *Daffodils and Other Poems* in Grange-over-sands, the place where pensioners went to die. She remembered Wordsworth wrote *Daffodils*, which was appropriate. Her dad would say, 'What the bloody hell have you bought me that rubbish for? Couldn't you find a decent bottle of whiskey?'

And her mother would say, 'How lovely.' She'd turn the first two pages over without reading a word, and that would be the one and only time the book would ever be opened. Being the eldest, Jess would inherit the God-awful thing when they died. She also bought them a printed anniversary plaque—she'd gone for twee and sickeningly sweet. It said, *If everybody in the world were as happy as you, we'd all be laughing and smiling, too.* It was presented with two freshwater pearls in a matchbox that cost her a fortune. She patted herself on the back for finding the most useless and ridiculous presents she could imagine. Her mum and dad had everything, and buying for them, either collectively or individually, was a nightmare.

If she felt she had problems, she smiled at the thought of her sister trying to find daffodils in September. Jess had insisted on them, a big glorious bouquet and expected the best her sister-of-no-patience could manage would be artificial silk ones.

The cake was ordered from a local bakery. Three tiers to put any wedding cake to shame, with two old people on the top. They looked like sugar representations of the *Elderly People Crossing* sign. The man had a walking stick, and her dad would go ballistic.

Her dress for the occasion was hanging on the back of the wardrobe door, and everything was organised—she hoped.

By four-thirty, when she clocked out, the last thing she felt like doing was driving to Morecambe. She was picking her sister up at seven-thirty and then going to Heysham, where their parents lived. With the hour's drive to get there, it didn't give her long to get ready.

She made good time along the A590 and only got held up behind a tractor once. She'd tried calling three times in the car—but still, there was no answer. She'd better not have forgotten to sort those flowers. Jess reasoned that she must have been in the bathroom getting ready and didn't hear the phone. The fact that her sister was getting ready was a good thing. From her birth onwards, she was traditionally late for everything. Jess smiled and pulled up outside the house.

Going to the flat on the ground floor, she knocked on the door. There was no answer, so she knocked again and then peered through the window. Although the living room looked okay, it was empty, and she felt a bubble of apprehension when she saw a mug overturned on the coffee table. It wasn't much to alarm her, but it hadn't been picked up.

She knocked again.

Then rang her phone.

Then shouted through the letterbox.

'Paige. It's me. Where the hell are you?'

Chapter Eleven

Chapter Eleven

Max was manhandled from the van with a semi-circle of policemen in riot gear around him. This was like some kind of surreal dream. He expected a clown to step out from behind them and squish a custard pie into his face.

'Don't underestimate him, people.'

'I'm about as dangerous as a puppy with a ball of wool. Stop. Listen to me. There's been a mistake. Whatever you think I've done. You're wrong.'

They didn't listen and bent him over so that his head was near his knees.

'Has the reception been cleared of civilians?' an officer asked.

'Yes, Ma'am.'

They took him by force into the police station. At the front desk, he was released from the hold, and his handcuffs were removed. He noticed the guards were armed with truncheons, and although he'd never seen one, some of the men had what he thought were tasers.

The desk sergeant was behind a sheet of plexiglass. 'Michael Jones, you have been arrested on suspicion of murder. Have you been read your rights?'

'Yes, but it's Maxwell. Max Jones.'

'I do apologise. Have you been read your rights?' He corrected the name on the screen in front of him.

'Yes.'

'And do you understand those rights?'

'Yes, but what's this all about?'

'Under the Police and Criminal Evidence Act 1984, you will be restrained using reasonable force. Some of our specially trained officers are carrying and are permitted to use tasers as per the Home Secretary's ruling of September 2004. Spitting at an officer is seen as a risk to physical health and will be treated as a common assault. Do you understand?'

'Yes, but you don't need tasers. And I've never spat at anybody in my life.'

'As you have been arrested under a recordable offence and under the Police and Criminal Evidence Act 1984, we have the right to take fingerprints, DNA and other samples with or without your consent. This is only permitted under the authority of an officer of at least the rank of inspector, in this case, Inspector DI Brown. Police are permitted to take an impression of a suspect's footwear without consent, a DNA sample from a mouth swab as well as swabs from the skin surface of their hands and arms.'

Max was struggling to take in what was being said to him. They must have better things to do than make impressions of his shoes. The desk sergeant was an automaton, reading what they could and couldn't do from a list in a monotone voice that made understanding it difficult. The only word swarming around his head since the campsite was murder. He didn't need to know any more than that. These people thought he'd killed Henry, and he'd seen the television documentaries—they would do anything they could to come up with evidence, however flimsy or circumstantial, to substantiate that.

'I'd like to call my solicitor, please.' Jeremy Stillman dealt with MJP paperwork and legislation. Max had no idea if he knew the first thing about murder law. He didn't know if murder law was even a thing. It must have a name, but it eluded him.

'Once we have finished processing, you will be searched. This is for your own and public safety. Relevant samples will be taken, and then you'll have the opportunity to call your representation.' He continued reading from his sheet like a car insurance telesales person as though nobody had spoken and the sergeant hadn't taken time to inhale.

'Intimate samples include blood, urine, pubic hair, tissue fluid, and dental impression, swabs taken from the person's genitals or from any bodily orifice except the mouth. PACE dictates that taking an intimate sample must be authorised by a senior officer, and in this case, the suspect must consent. Do you consent to any or all intimate samples being taken?'

'Yes, I think so. Of course. Anything to get this cleared up.' Max didn't have a clue what he should be saying. 'But is that in my best interests? Shouldn't I ask my solicitor first?'

'Of course, you can wait. We'll put you in a holding cell until then and halt all proceedings. In this case, you won't be given any comforts until after processing is complete. It is the inspector's responsibility to inform you that if you refuse to give consent, it could lead to adverse inferences being made against you in a court of law.'

'Okay. No problem. Look, I've got nothing to hide. Do what you have to do. What about my van?'

'That has been seized and is being brought back to be impounded as evidence.'

'Evidence of what? Will you please talk to me like a human being?'

'Like you talked to your victims,' another officer piped up, and the sergeant glared at him.

'Our priority is getting the samples we need and making sure that you and all of our officers are safe. Then you can make any requests you like.'

'If you're taking requests, do you know *Telephone* by Lady Gaga?'

'I've told you, you'll get your phone call when we're done with processing.'

Max wasn't in a condition to be embarrassed by the personal and intimate subjection that screening put him through. They'd driven him back to Barrow from Wales. It was after two in the morning, and he hadn't eaten dinner yet. He was refused a cup of tea or anything to eat until after the screening was complete, "As per procedure," but was promised that he could have a meal and as much tea and toast as he wanted when it was done.

He'd seen his share of police dramas and thought that was probably bullshit. The screening, photographing, and sample-taking process took forever, and the officers conducting it refused to talk to him or answer any questions about his arrest. He supposed that made sense. He expected to be taken from screening straight into an interview room for a thorough grilling—with or without police violence, depending on which scenario his imagination was taking him down.

When they were done with him, he found the experience quite humbling. These people—and whatever he thought of them, they were people, just like him, ordinary men and women with lives outside being an officer—thought he'd killed somebody. Presumably in cold blood and for personal gain, and yet they treated him like a person. After the screening was complete, he was taken to a cell where he was allowed to get out of the paper jumpsuit and into a pair of grey jogging bottoms and a matching top. They gave him underwear and socks and even a pair of black plimsolls. All the clothing was individually packaged in see-through bags that were taken away after the paper suit had been bagged. The Duty Care officers seemed nice, and while they couldn't—wouldn't—tell him anything about the charges or what he'd supposedly done, they chatted about nothing and were keen to make him comfortable. The cell was small, a box. It had a stainless steel toilet with a sink built into the top of it.

'We can withhold toilet paper if we think you're going to use it to choke yourself. You aren't going to try anything silly like that, are you?' The lady officer asked him.

'No.' Any other time he'd produce an off-the-cuff quip and dial up the sarcasm, but he was so tired he only had a single word to offer. His bed was a wooden slat built into the wall with a piece of foam covered in heavy-duty washable blue plastic. He wasn't given a pillow, and a single thin blanket was waiting for him on the end of the cot in a sealed bag that was also taken away.

'Have you been with us before, love?' the lady asked. She was the chatty one. The warmth in her voice made him want to cry. Given the guard's presence at the door, she must know what he'd been arrested for. At all times while she was with him, half a dozen people in riot gear waited outside in helmets and with plastic shields, poised and ready to bring him down.

'No, first-time flyer.'

He was in the holding suite with all the other suspected offenders of the town. He couldn't grasp what was going on. All this snowflake society talk was crazy.

'The noise will drive you mad. They always say that's the worst part. My advice is to have a nice brew and something to eat and then get your head down and try to get some sleep.' He'd never been in a police cell before. It was too much for him, and she must have seen the tears in his eyes threatening to spill over and drown them all—more murder on his hands. 'It'll all look better in the morning.' She sounded like his mum, and he expected her to pat his hand and say, "There, there." Well, not his mum but somebody's mum, a loving one.

'So, sweetheart. Let's get to the nicer bit. What can I get you, tea, coffee or a nice cup of hot chocolate?'

'Tea, please.'

'Couple of rounds of toast with that?'

'That would be nice, thank you.'

'And what would you like for a meal? We've got chicken curry, all-day breakfast or bangers and mash. I'll bring you one along in an hour or so. It's only ready meals, but they're not bad, and I'm guessing you're ready for something.'

He sat on the cot and put his head in his hands.

'I know. It's emotional. I'll bring you a sausage and mash. Mashed potato always makes me feel better when I'm upset. See that button on the wall? That's the intercom. If you want anything, just give us a buzz. You can have tea and toast, meals on tap, and we can bring you books to read.'

This was like the Costa Del Nick.

'I dare say they'll interview you first thing. Do you need us to let anyone know you're here?'

'My cat?'

'You want us to ring your cat?'

'No, I mean my cat's on his own. He's all right for now, but will I be here long?'

***

'First thing' turned out to be after ten o'clock. Gathering information, they said. He hadn't slept. Somebody was singing Billy Bragg's *New England* on a loop. It got marginally better as the drunk sobered up, and then he puked. He banged on the door and shouted for hours. And the buzzers—those bloody intercom buzzers. Max was driven mad after one night. The duty care staff must have been demented.

He heard another inmate buzz for three meals in the space of an hour. Max was amazed that he got them. He was going to put in a complaint about taxpayer's money—but wouldn't. He felt guilty the next morning when Glenda—that was the lady who came to check on everybody before the changeover to the day staff—told him that man was homeless. She said that if he couldn't get a hostel, he'd do something to get arrested just to have a warm place to stay and something to eat. Glenda said it might be the only food he got for the day, and they didn't mind.

'Don't the buzzers drive you mad?'

'Like you wouldn't believe.'

He wanted to say more, but his own predicament was too big, and he couldn't be bothered to make small talk.

***

Max rang his solicitor, Jeremy Stillman, but as he feared, he couldn't help. There was a big difference between corporate law and criminal. Max disagreed and said they were both dealing with thieves and liars, but his observation fell on stony ground. Stillman said he knew somebody that was brilliant.

Jane Pearson called within the hour, and he was handed the phone to speak to her. She agreed to represent him but would need initial payment upfront. Max assured her that money wouldn't be a problem. However, she was tied up in court all day, and the earliest she'd get to him was late that night or the next day. The first piece of advice she gave him was free. She told him to say nothing until she got there and was brought up to speed.

Nash said, 'This interview is being recorded on video and cassette. For the tape, present are Detective Chief Inspector Nash and—'

'Detective Sergeant Phillip Renshaw.' Nash's inferior officer kept his voice steady and even.

'For the tape, please state your name.' Nash said.

'No comment.'

'I don't blame you with a name like yours, lad. State your name, and we can move on. It'll make it a lot easier for both of us to make headway, and if we get no further, we can at least lay out the allegations against you. I'm sure your solicitor didn't mean for you not to tell us your name.'

'You know my name.'

'State your name.'

'Maxwell Edward Bartholomew Tyler Jones, but the cat calls me Max.'

'If you leave the comedy to me, lad, we'll get along just fine.'

Max looked at the detectives. Sometime between him being brought in and now, they must have decided that he wasn't going to leap across a table and bite their heads off Ozzy Osbourne style. The riot police had all been called off, and it seemed to be just the two officers and him. He looked at the two-way mirror and wondered how many people were watching behind it. Barrow hadn't had a murder for a while. How many spectators did the slaying of one boring old bastard warrant? One? Twenty? He grinned at the mirror and dropped them a wink.

'Do you think antics like that are going to do you any favours?' Renshaw's tone was like ice.

'No, probably not. I'm sorry.'

'You scare us, Jones.' Nash was talking again.

'I do? I scare myself sometimes too. And you should see me first thing in the morning after a night on the piss.' Max was nervous and couldn't help himself.

'Shut up,' Nash barked at him, and a drop of spittle flew from the corner of his mouth.

Max focused on it and saw the tiny wet dot on the interview table as a being trying to survive just like him. He fancied that if it dried up and died and it was no more, he might die too.

'This bravado isn't working.' Nash motioned to Renshaw, who opened a brown folder and took out some A4 sheets of glossy paper. He slid them across the desk facedown.

'If I find the lady, do I get to keep the tenner?'

'Your mouth is really going to get you into trouble, Jones. For the tape, I am showing Mr Jones exhibit 1A.'

Max wondered if he'd developed Tourette's Syndrome in the last half hour. He had to physically stop himself from saying, "For the tape, he isn't showing it to me. It's face down," by hiding behind a cough. Nash was right. His mouth wasn't doing him any favours, but his nerves brought a shitload of smart remarks, and he had to suppress them to keep them in. He knew that when Renshaw turned the pictures over, he was going to see the mangled body of Henry Watson. Maybe not mangled. His imagination was working as fast as his mouth, but it would certainly be gruesome, and he wasn't ready for that. It was hot. He felt as though he was suffocating and pulled the neckline of his sweatshirt away from his throat. Nash's eyes followed Max's hand. He knew that every word he said and every nuance and gesture was being scrutinised. They probably had a psychologist watching him from behind the mirror.

Nash turned over the first photo, and Max's hands flattened on the table, his body pulled up straight in his seat, and he stared at Nash. He didn't expect that. They watched him and let Max be the first to speak.

'What the hell?'

'Do you know this man, Max?'

It wasn't Henry. It was some old dude with wispy white hair and blue-grey dead skin.

'No. Honestly, I've never seen him before in my life. You have to believe me. I thought it was Henry.' Max couldn't stop himself, and any advice given by Jane Pearson went out of the window.

'Henry, who?'

'My partner, Henry Watson. The one you told me was murdered.'

'Why did you think it was going to be Henry?'

'He's the only person I know that has died.'

'We'll come to that in due course. Look closely, Maxwell. Take your time. No rush. We've got all day. Do you know this man?'

Max didn't want to look again. Nash turned the second and third pictures over. 'For the tape, I'm showing Mr Jones Exhibit 1B and 1C.' They were of the same man. One was a full-view image, and the other was a shot in closer detail. Naked. Max could see he was probably well into his seventies or eighties. His skin was liver-spotted in places and wrinkled. Max noticed that his feet were thick with dead skin that had died years before the rest of him. The body was covered in holes, and there was so much blood. He was lying in a sultry pose on top of an old upright piano. A single-stem flower vase was on the end of the piano's cabinet with a sprig of honeysuckle. The victim was facedown with his empty old-man buttocks uppermost. One leg was bent behind him and kept in position with a cable tie attached to his wrist. His other hand was under his head, holding it up in profile for the camera. The old man had a red rose between his teeth. Blood ran over the upright of the piano and onto the keys. White was black with gunge, and black was wet and looked sticky. There was so much blood, but his eyes were drawn to the piece of music on the stand. At the top of the page, it was titled. *Minuet in G major, BWV anh. 114.* Max hadn't seen a piece of sheet music in twenty years, but he followed it, and the notes played in his head as his eyes read the line. It was by Christian Petzold, and Max had played this piece for his grade three exam every night until his fingers bled. The same bastard piece. He'd hated it and was transported back to those times sitting at the piano with a musty old tutor scrunched on the stool next to him. It was 2001, and sometimes, his hands touched Max's hands as he guided him over the keys. He heard his voice, "Let my knowledge flow through your fingers and play." The tutor lived for music and wanted Max to be the best he could be. Max was good, but at his exam recital, he flunked the piece on purpose. He hated playing the piano when his mates were out playing with girls. He couldn't remember the tutor's name.

'Oh my God. I know him.'

'Who is it, Max?' Nash pressed him.

'I can't remember his name. He came to my house when I was a young kid and taught me piano.'

'What did he do to you, Max?'

'What?'

'What did he do when it was just you and him alone playing the piano? Look at the picture and the staging. The piano is as important as the man on it. You hated that piano, didn't you, Max?'

'Yes, every terrible second of it. But hang on. You're way off-beam. He was just a boring old man. He rapped my knuckles with a baton sometimes if I didn't get it right.' The memories flooded back. 'But he never once touched me. He talked to me when nobody else did. He told me I could be somebody. He was a nice old man, you know. How did he end up like this? I liked him and would never wish him dead. '

Max remembered being eight. He was a lonely child. He had his two best friends and his sister but lived the life of a boarding school child with parents that wanted him to be a high achiever.

The best thing about piano lessons was Mr Armstrong. Sometimes he'd stay well over the allotted hour, and he listened to Max when nobody else did. The man, who was old to Max even back then, taught him to play chess, and they talked. Mr Armstrong never spoke down to him and let him have opinions, even if they were the silly fancy of a young boy. He'd stared with wide eyes when Mr Armstrong agreed that aliens probably do exist. No grown-up had ever said that to him before. 'There are more things in heaven and earth, Max, than are dreamt of in your head.'

One day Max had been punished for some childish misdemeanour and said how much he hated his parents. 'No, Max, you must honour thy father and thy mother because no matter what you do, they will never hate you.' Max wasn't so sure about that.

Mr Armstrong used to come with an old-fashioned satchel. It was brown leather with two pull-over strap buckles. Max laughed and called him a sissy when he said he liked baking. 'In that case, you won't be interested in what I've brought in my satchel.' After that, every time he came, he brought cake or homemade biscuits. There was always a slice for Mel too. But she spoiled it like she spoiled everything. Mel was jealous because Max had a friend and shot herself in the foot. She told their parents how long Mr Armstrong stayed over his allotted time, and then there were no treats for either of them. Max could see now that untrue things were suspected, and Mr Armstrong didn't come again. It was only a week or two until his grade three exam, and that was part of the reason he sabotaged it. He never saw his tutor again. The old man shouldn't have died like that. So lacking in dignity. Max thought back and realised that Mr Armstrong was probably gay and how much harder it was for minorities back then. It was twenty years ago, and yet he could remember the man saying to him, 'There is nothing worse than loneliness.' Being alone doesn't care about age or class segregation. It can hit anybody at any time.' Max and Mr Armstrong had bonded over their loneliness as equals. He was brought back to the present when Nash clicked his fingers in Max's face. Mr Armstrong would never have been that rude. He was a gentleman.

'William Armstrong. That's his name. Is it coming back to you now, Max? Let's be clear about this. Before today we had no connection between this man's murder and you. Now the evidence is piling up like a snowdrift at the cabin door. Did you kill Mr William Armstrong, Max?'

Max was terrified.

'This was your first one, wasn't it? We can tell that from the body. The autopsy showed that you were very wary. You made a lot of practice attempts before breaking the skin very much. They just caused bruising. Then, the next lot of wounds, the ones we are counting from, weren't as deep as later ones. It was as though you didn't have a lot of strength and had to perfect your technique.'

'This is grotesque. Please shut up,' Max said.

There was still a photograph on the desk. What the hell was on it? He felt tears welling up in his eyes. 'No. He was a nice man. I liked him. I did not kill him, Inspector.'

'Are you saying you had nothing to do with this man's murder?'

'I am.'

'We've done a full autopsy. The poor bastard died a painful death. It wasn't fast, and he bled out for a long time. Either this animal knew what he was doing, or he was very bloody lucky. Sixty-eight stab wounds, some of them deep, made with the double tines of a tuning fork. But it was no ordinary tuning fork. The tines had two mathematical compass points attached with electrical tape. We've had an expert analyse the body and tell us exactly how much pressure was put on the handle of the fork to pierce the flesh and make those wounds. It was a lot. The man suffered. And yet, until the last thrust, the final two wounds, not one of them touched any major organs. The coroner said the wounds were time-staged. From the clotting, he was able to tell that Mr Armstrong was stabbed every few minutes. Now, this was a shot in the dark, but we figured that he might have stabbed him once every 2 minutes and 66 seconds. Why do you think that was?'

'It's a short piece. It wasn't the length of time it took to play the Minuet. But he could have played it twice. He was playing the piano in between stabbing him.'

'Him? or you, Max?'

'I never touched him.'

'As I said, this was a shot in the dark until we pieced things together. When we took the witness statements after the body was found, neighbours complained about him playing "One song," their words, not ours, repeatedly on the piano. They knocked on the walls, but the killer held his nerve, raised the volume and carried on playing. When they couldn't stand it any longer, they hammered on the door and shouted for him to keep the noise down. This guy's cool, Max. He raised the volume again until it was deafening and played *Fortissimo*. I'm sure an old hand like you knows what that means. We played the piece to them, and they said that was the tune, and they never wanted to hear it again.'

'It wasn't me.'

'And now we have our link to you. Did you kill him?'

The fourth photo was making him sweat.

'No comment.'

Chapter Twelve

'See, Max? Everything we have is circumstantial. So, he was your old tutor. So what? That doesn't mean you took compass-loaded tines to the man and stabbed him into a colander. But this is where it gets interesting.' Nash looked at the fourth photograph face down on the desk, and Max's eyes followed him like a trained dog.

'We had all we were going to get from the body, so we were given permission to release it for a pauper's funeral. This poor old man didn't have a soul in the world, not even a goldfish to grieve him. He lived alone with no family or close friends to send him off. Before we turned him over to the council to cremate, one of our WPCs went back into the house to get him something to wear for his final day out. Guess what she found in the pocket of his best white shirt?'

Max was dying to say, 'A Morrison's pork pie and a packet of condoms.' He didn't, but he must have smirked.

'Do you find this funny, Jones? A man is dead, and all you can do is make wisecracks or be smug?'

'No, sir. I'm feeling more nervous now. I know it's a childish response, but it is borne of fear and nerves, not from trying to be clever.'

'I wonder if Mr Armstrong made any wisecracks or smirked at you before you stabbed him sixty-eight times?'

'Technically, he was only stabbed thirty-four times because it was one fork with two tines. Sorry, just trying to be helpful. Again it was nothing to do with me. But please, can you put me out of my misery and tell me what was in the pocket.'

'I don't like you, Jones.' He motioned to Renshaw to turn the fourth photograph over, and Max visibly jerked in his chair.

'For the tape, we are showing Mr Jones exhibit 4C,' Renshaw said.

'Those are my cufflinks.'

'We thought as much. The gold MJ monogram kind of gives it away. They were found in the breast pocket of Mr Armstrong's shirt. Here's another funny thing. You weren't as clever as you think, leaving your calling card and expecting us to believe they were left there at the time of the murder. That room was forensically searched when the body was found. The cufflinks were not in that wardrobe at that time. Damn, that was either one enormous cry to be caught, or you have a hell of an ego. To think you'd get away with leaving something so blatant and not be found is ridiculous. I know. You figured there was nothing to tie you to the dead man. Would you care to explain, then, how they got there? Because they sure as hell didn't walk into that shirt.'

'They are my links, I can't deny that, but I emphatically deny putting them there, inspector. They were stolen from my house last week, along with some other stuff.'

'Did you report this theft? Was it a break-in?'

'Yes, but it was just some electrical stuff and my laptop, a bit of jewellery and less than a hundred quid in cash, nothing that couldn't be easily replaced. I've been burgled before, and I figured it wasn't worth reporting. I went online to locate my devices and was able to erase them. Things never seem to get found and given back, anyway. Obviously, I wish I had now.'

'How the other half live, eh? I'm damned sure if I lost a hundred quid and my laptop, I'd be less cavalier about it. Weren't you bothered about your data falling into the wrong hands?'

'Not at the time, and everything on there was backed up before I erased it. I just ordered a new one.'

'You just ordered a new one. Wow.' They went back to the beginning and asked him the questions again—and again. Every time, they were phrased differently to see if he would give the same answer.

'When you brought me in, I thought this was going to be about Henry.'

'We'll get to him. One body at a time, Mr Jones.' Nash was playing with him. There was no good cop, bad cop routine. Renshaw was there as a second officer only and said very little. This was Nash's shit show, and he was running it. He nodded to Renshaw, and he produced another photograph, but this time he put it face up.

'Oh, my God, that's Chelsea. Chelsea Green.' Max stared at the image as though his eyes were showing him the wrong face. The body was hanging and interwoven with an ornate chandelier. A single-flower vase was on the marble mantlepiece below with a single sprig of honeysuckle. It was staged like living art—only this lady was no longer living, and she hung in the pose of a circus performer doing rhythmic gymnastics with two ribbons. A cord around her neck looked like the method of death and had cut in to partially garotte her. Post mortem, presumably, her legs and arms had been pulled back and secured to the light fitting with what looked like black satin ribbon, pushing her body forward, face front. Her skin was blue-tinged with broken blood vessels over her face. The lividity was grotesque. Where gravity had pooled the blood in her face, her neck had formed deep puffy detritus-filled jowls on the former slender face.

Chelsea was a freelancer that Max had worked with several times until he'd slept with her, and it all went pear-shaped.

The body was dressed in a black lace wedding gown with a cascading train. A long veil was folded back to reveal her face. Max recoiled from the image and retched. He looked away, covered his mouth, gagged again and held it in.

'Please take it away.'

'Bravo on your performance, Max. Will you be needing a bucket? We'd hate for you to scream that we'd breached your human rights later.'

'Enough. Please. Can we stop now? I need a break. Where's my solicitor?'

'The minute she arrives, we'll suspend the interview so that you can meet with her.'

'Like Mr Armstrong, until just now, we didn't have a connection from you to Chelsea Green. Would you like to tell us how you know the victim?' Max felt that he shouldn't be saying anything until Jane got there, but he'd already said enough to put him away for a long time. Sod it.

'I commissioned her to work on some projects for me. If I'm not mistaken, this is the chandelier we put in at Ocean Boulevard on Walney Island. She's an interior designer with a great eye for detail, and her work compliments my buildings. She's a good fit. He hanged her, so it was quick, wasn't it? She won't have suffered much, would she ?'

'I should imagine she suffered a great deal. How long did you know her?'

'About three years.'

'Do you draw much?'

'Draw?'

'Draw, paint, make pictures.'

'Yes, of course. I design buildings, and I draw images of things to go inside buildings.'

'And what was your relationship with Miss Green?'

'I told you, I hired her professional services.'

'And that's all? Nothing more? Nothing personal?'

Max sighed and rubbed his eyes. His hand shook, and the adrenalin that the interview was pumping around his body took its toll. He was tired and just wanted to lie down. 'Yes, that's all, Inspector. We had a fling, but that was a long time ago, and I promise you it didn't leave enough messy residue to make me want to kill her.' Nash and Renshaw looked at each other, and Max felt that he was doomed.

'Would you say you were the man she loved but could never have? The one that got away?'

'That's a bit dramatic, but yes, she was upset when we split up. We weren't even together. Not really. We had too much to drink one night after celebrating a deal closure and ended up in bed together.'

'You accidentally fell into bed together? Repeatedly? For the night?'

'Well, it was more like ten minutes, but you know how it goes. That was it for me, really, but she pushed for more. Calls, texts, that kind of thing. Nothing I couldn't handle diplomatically, with tact and without resorting to murdering her. Anyway, I saw her a few times, but it all got heavy. She wanted me to go away with her for a weekend, and her folks were going to be there. I'm not really a meet-the-parents type of man, so I called it off. That was over a year ago, and because she didn't take it well, I haven't seen her since.'

'I see. You asked if she suffered. She did. You left us a surprise under that outfit, didn't you? The dress was stuck to her back with the ooze of fresh blood, but it didn't do anything to spoil the artwork.'

'What artwork?'

'Why don't you tell me? Come on, Max, it was stunning. You must want to brag.'

'I have no idea what you're talking about.'

'You tied her face down. Bound her ankles and wrists and gagged her. And then you tattooed her entire back. It's quite the piece. We've had a tattoo artist examine it, and he said it was a stunning design and well-drawn. The artistry was excellent, but he could tell that the tattooist wasn't used to working on the skin. He estimates that there were close to fifty hours of work in it. Allowing for sleeping, it means you had her tied to that bench for three or four days. Maybe even five. Imagine how much she suffered during that time.'

Renshaw threw another photograph on the table. And Nash watched Jones' reaction. If his shock was an act, he was good. It showed Max's previous bedpartner on the autopsy table. Her back was a mass of oozed and clotted sores from a recent tattoo. From the neck to the crease of her buttocks, there wasn't a millimetre of exposed skin. And the scene was exquisite in its floral beauty and grotesque in nature. It was an English garden scene. It was bordered with climbing honeysuckle. There was so much of it, with the arch leading from the lawn to the flowerbeds heavy with delicate purple and pink honeysuckle flowers and clematis.

'I know this garden. It's Jon's. I grew up there.'

'Jon, who?'

'Jonathan Finch, a childhood friend. But Jonathan is as innocent as I am. There's no way he had anything to do with this.'

In the centre was the tyre swing they used to play on. And a picnic blanket laid with a feast. Two boys lay around the blanket with their heads cut off. The tattoo showed a grassy bank to the right-hand side, and the two boy's heads were depicted rolling down it. Honey, Jon's golden retriever, was hanging dead from a branch of the overlooking oak tree.

Max remembered the day, the swing, the picnic, lying on their sides and rolling down the bank to the stream at the bottom of the garden. Their mate, Bobby, had fallen in. He was in there now, in ink—drowned and headless. The focal point was a paper scroll with rolls on top and bottom designed to look aged.

Some words for the love that could never be mine
The man who always hurt me the most
He took me to bed after drinking cheap wine
And death will turn me into his ghost.

He couldn't look.

His solicitor had told him to say nothing—but he wanted to talk. He needed to purge himself of those images and needed to tell them everything he knew.

Renshaw put another picture down, and Max guessed the formula. It was going to be something personal to him taken from the burglary at his house.

It was a picture of his old appointment diary from a couple of years ago, open on a particular week. He hadn't even noticed it was missing. It was stored in a box in case the tax man ever came sniffing around. The dates he assumed he'd slept with Chelsea had been scourged through with a red pen, and the words *I used Chelsea for sex. I'm a sub-human Bastard*, were written across them. After the last date, it said, *Revenge will come where you least expect it.*

'That's not my handwriting.'

'We'll be taking samples today to determine that,' Nash said.

'I swear, I didn't do this. I can't write neatly, for one thing, never mind creating tattoos like that. You should see my signature.'

'When she was found, there was a speaker set to play the same piece of music on a loop. Can you guess what it was, Max?'

'Minuet in G?'

'The very same. Where were you on the sixteenth of August? We need a full rundown of your day.'

'I can't remember what I was doing yesterday, never mind over a month ago. I can have a look at my computer and check the dates on that.'

'And how do you propose to do that when your laptop was stolen?'

'When I get out of here, I can go straight to the office and email you anything I find.'

'We have your office computer in lockup. And I don't think you're going to be leaving here for some time, sunshine. Moving on,' Nash said.

They'd done away with the theatrics, and Renshaw passed the next image straight to him. 'Do you know this man?'

'Oh, Jesus. I don't believe it. That's Bobby. I've known him since we were kids. Robert Dean.'

'And when was the last time you saw Robert Dean? Alive.'

It took Max a moment to answer. 'Years. I haven't seen him for several years. I heard he did some stuff, robbed some corner shops and got sent down. I saw him a couple of times when he came out, but he was different. Harder. He had a chip on his shoulder. The last I heard of him, he asked me to say he'd been in for an interview so that he could get his benefits. I offered him an interview for real, and we'd see if we could find him something. I wanted to help him, you know? We used to be close. But he said no, he only wanted the dole money. Not Bobby. Not him. Not murdered, surely.'

'Looks peaceful, doesn't he? All tucked up nicely in the hotel bed like that.'

'How did he die?'

'This one's different, Max. If it hadn't been for the same flower in a vase, we might not have connected it at first. You see, this death wasn't gruesome. It wasn't a murder committed in a rage. It was as though the murderer wanted to bring the victim some peace. The same section of music was playing in the room. The flower was beside him. We have a lot of questions about how this one was carried out. There was no doubt by now that we had a serial killer. Is that killer you, Maxwell Jones?'

'No. Jesus Christ, I'm innocent. You can't pin all this on me. I didn't kill anybody.'

Nash showed him the photographs of Henry Watson. 'He was found with a sprig of honeysuckle pinned to the diamond-patterned tank top he wore on the golf course. This murder was done with more speed and less precision. The killer was bold enough to do what he came to do but realised he didn't have time for extracted embellishment. So he made the scene horrific in a much shorter time frame.

'As you can see, the body was found with a golf ball in his mouth. The right side of the skull is shattered, and most of the blood is caused by having his head stoved with the rock that you can see to the left of the picture. No prints.'

Max looked shocked. 'Damn, even now, I can't believe it. Poor Henry.'

'Three more golf balls were inserted into his anal cavity. We believe this was done when he was stunned but conscious, barely but still awake. The killer was going for maximum humiliation again.'

'I didn't kill anybody.'

'My question, Max, is why go from the almost gentle murder of Mr Dean back to the brutality and hatred here with Mr Watson?'

'I didn't kill anybody.'

'But everything leads to you. You see our predicament?'

The questioning continued until Nash abruptly changed the subject.

'Apparently, you were quite the good citizen the other night.'

'I'm sorry?'

'You joined the search for the two missing boys. A very public-spirited thing to do.'

'No. Oh, no, you don't. Not a chance. You have no reason to assume that those kids are dead. I've said all along that they've probably jumped a train to Manchester for an adventure or something.'

'An authority on missing children, are you? Do you know, there's an interesting fact. A killer often returns to the scene of the crime. And often, they involve themselves in the investigation to be up to their necks in the drama of it, so to speak. Was it fun for you, out searching for them like a concerned member of society? What have you done with the boys, Jones?' Nash was goading him. His theory was only that, and he had to keep pushing the boundaries to see if he was right and if Jones would crack.

'Their parents are missing them. Do you know what one of the mothers said to me today? She said that not knowing is worse than knowing that he's dead. Put her out of her misery, Jones. Tell us what you've done with them.' Nash hounded the suspect for another half hour until Jones was screaming at him.

'I don't know where the boys are. I didn't touch them.' Nash watched him sag. He'd pushed him far enough.

'We've run out of our allotted time today, Mr Jones. The snowflakes say you have to have regular breaks. Good job it's not their kids out there, missing. Trust me, if this was twenty years ago, neither of us would be leaving this room until you'd told me what you'd done. And they call this progress. We can keep you for ninety-six hours, so get some rest, and we'll talk again later. This interview is suspended at 13:31.'

Nash cuffed Max and opened the interview room door. Two officers, one on either side, walked him back to his cell.

He was embarrassed when they came out of the interview room into the main reception. It wasn't a police station built to house hardened criminals, and everything apart from the holding cells was built on top of each other. Two men sat on the plastic chairs, presumably waiting to be interviewed, and a lady was at the reception counter. She was talking to the duty officer, and Max felt sorry for her distress. He hung his head as they marched him to his cell.

'It's my sister. She's been missing for two days, and nobody's heard from her,' the woman said.

Chapter Thirteen

Chapter Thirteen

Nash's third interview with Max had just started, this time with his solicitor, Jane Pearson, present. The second interview the night before was stopped after ten minutes when Max refused to speak without his solicitor. She told Nash that she'd been held up in court when the trial she was working on took an unexpected turn with a new witness for the prosecution. She and Max didn't get off on good terms, but Max looked like he softened when she said she would never leave court serving an existing client to help a new one. And he would get the same courtesy too. She'd sent word the day before to say she was sending her junior to represent Max in the initial interviews and she would have copies of the tapes to catch up on, but Max had declined. He said on tape that he felt let down by his representation.

Nash was rushing to get the interview underway. He didn't say anything, but he was conscious of the time. They'd had Max in for thirty hours now and could only keep him for a total of ninety-six before they had to shit or get off the pot.

There was a tap on the door, and Detective Inspector Molly Brown stuck her head in. She motioned for Nash to excuse himself.

'Interview suspended 08:05.'

He knew what was coming before Molly said anything. 'We've got another one. A young girl, unidentified at this time. This one's in Morecambe. The connection is the honeysuckle found on her body. The Lancashire lot have taken it, but I've halted all operations until you get there.'

'Sexual?'

'No intel on that as yet.'

'I'll leave you to see what you can pull out of Jones,' Nash said. 'Watch him. He's slippery. I'm on my way.'

Nash drove to Morecambe with his blues and twos on. The desk had forwarded what information they had and an address on Albany Road. Out of habit, he turned the sirens off before he pulled into the road, though by now, the police presence would be enough to draw a crowd. Sure enough, he didn't need the GPS to guide him to the house.

The honeysuckle link was too strong for it to be a coincidence—but what the hell had brought our perp to Morecambe? The investigation had only opened, but it was a possibility that he thought the police had enough on him to be closing in. So, he'd panicked and widened his field. A man on the edge is likely to slip up and make mistakes. Or it could have been a crime of circumstance. That he was there for an unrelated reason, and the victim was in the wrong place at the wrong time.

Nash walked up the path to her room in the middle of Bedsit Land. It was a big sandstone house, double-fronted. There were no gardens in these builds to speak of, but outside the windows, there was a walkway a couple of feet wide around to the back of the property. The lower left-hand side, as he looked at it, was neglected. It had a filthy net curtain at the window and weeds forcing their way through the little crazy-paving path. However, on the victim's side of the house, two neat flower boxes had been put beneath the clean windows. One of them had been knocked out of place and might as well have been an arrowhead pointing to the window as the means of entrance. He was brazen. This was a busy street. The Scenes of Crime team had already processed the area for footprints.

He went in the front door that had a bedsit to either side and two more at the back of the house. Three floors and a large attic and cellar, each with four accommodations, equated to a lot of money in the landlord's pocket. Nash wrinkled his nose. The distinct smell of cheese was coming from the door to his left—and he didn't mean cheddar. Cheese was the name of the strong version of chemical marijuana with a heroin element. If he had to, he'd use it to his advantage and lean on the drug users to get any information they had. The door had the letters CH gouged into the wood. The markings were fresh. Somebody had picked up most of the splinters, but a little cloud of sawdust lay on the filthy carpet in the hall. A marketing strategy, get you r *Cheese Here*, Nash mused, but the fact that it was a recent tag made him curious.

'Hey, get a photo of this door, he told one of the Scenes of Crime officers. Has anybody interviewed him yet?'

'No answer, sir.'

'Okay, keep on it.'

He put gloves on and paper slippers over his shoes before going into the victim's room. The window was closed. He saw that it had been forced open and then closed again. The perp had left through the front door, brazen as you like. The strong aroma of coffee and the more subtle smell of honeysuckle danced over to greet him and mixed with the clean scent of the victim's room. It took away the stink of the drugs from across the hall.

The body was bagged and ready for taking to the morgue. Nash went forward and unzipped the bag to the girl's waist. He winced when he saw the ragged neck and zipped it up fast.

'DCI Nash,' he said, introducing himself to the Morecambe task force. When he was working Scenes of Crime, he didn't shake hands to avoid cross-contamination, so he nodded hello to the coroner, who was a long-standing and trusted colleague. 'Jesus, it's hot in here.'

Bill Robinson laughed. 'You took your time getting here. Couldn't you authorise a private jet? The heating had been turned up full. We've turned it off. But it's still warm. I don't usually sweat like this.' He grinned at Nash.

'Time of death?'

'Can't be sure yet. Rough estimate—not time but the day of death, about a week ago.'

Nash had thought the same when he saw the body and did a double take around the room.

'Exactly. I expected that reaction from you. What's missing?' Robinson said.

'The smell?'

'Correct. Give that man a fiver. She wasn't killed here. Brought roughly four hours ago, I'd say, making it about daybreak. He's been in before to set the stage, so he came straight in the front door using her keys this time. Bedsit Land, where everybody is invisible.' He pointed to the bathroom. 'In there.'

Nash went to the door. The bath was filled with black coffee, long since gone cold. Robinson showed him some photos of the immediate scene on a tablet. They didn't have the size to give clarity of detail that they would when printed out, but he saw enough to turn his stomach. The top one was easy enough. It was a photo of the girl's ID card: Paige Hunter, aged 18.

'Pretty girl. She was somebody's daughter, the poor bastards. There's a photo on the living room mantlepiece that looks like her parents. No details yet, but they'll need to be contacted before that lot out there get to them first.' Robinson referred to the media, who flocked like vultures waiting for rotting carrion.

The second image showed Paige lying, presumably naked, in the bath of coffee, but it was impossible to tell through the dense liquid. Her head had been severed and put on one corner of the bath to watch herself bathing. The single-flower vase with a sprig of honeysuckle was on the opposite corner. There was more of the creeper all over the room, with vines draped over the three pieces of the shelving unit and even across the toilet. The smell was thick and cloying as it mingled with the coffee. The victim had one leg raised and held in place with a cable tie. She had a yellow sponge in her hand, and it looked like a giant piece of honeycomb toffee.

'Raped?' Nash asked.

'Too early to tell.'

'Was there music playing, a classical piano piece?'

'No. Did the others have music?'

'The first three, yeah. Then he seems to have done away with it. Guess he didn't feel the need, but he's kept his honeysuckle calling card.'

'I've seen a lot of RTA victims, but never anything like this. It's horrific, and I'm going to need a tot of whiskey in my Horlicks tonight to take this lot away.'

Lawson came up to Nash and interrupted them. 'You should see this, sir.'

Nash went into the living room, where everything had been bagged and tagged.

'We almost missed this because it was stuck in the bag of the waste bin when we upturned it. It's only a crumpled receipt but look at this drawing on the back.' Lawson held the bag containing a receipt up with a pair of tweezers to view the evidence properly. It was a childishly drawn stick with two arms and legs, but the head was at the man's feet.

'Test it.'

'Already ordered, sir.' Lawson sealed the bag and attached a label. 'Another thing worth noting is we found a clump of what looks like dog hair, but there's no sign of a dog living here. Could have been visiting, might be nothing.'

'Looking around the place, she's clean. The type of girl that would have got the vacuum out if a friend's dog had left hair in her living room. Well spotted.'

There was wilted honeysuckle everywhere, and the scent felt as though it was crawling down his throat and sticking to every organ on the way down. He imagined his lungs were contaminated with it like a smoker's organs blackened with tar. It made Nash feel sick.

Molly had just arrived from Barrow, and she came with news. 'You have to see this, boss.'

'Another one? Where?'

'Just down the road. Layby near Morrisons. It's another two young women.'

'Jesus Christ. Every time you walk into a room, you bring death with you,' Nash said.

'Well, thank you for that. I'll add it to my CV.'

'Sorry, Molly, one of those days.'

'Morecambe women would agree with you. Looks like three in one day. He's accelerating.'

'Not necessarily. Paige Hunter was killed at least five days ago.' Once he knew it, Nash always referred to the victims by name. It kept them human to him and set an example for the task force. 'We'll take my car. Come on.'

When they got there, the media was already swooping down. Several members of the public had their phones taken off them and posts deleted from social media, but once they were out, it was too late. The police had worked on shutting off the layby at both ends to prevent the public and media from getting in. Nash called Renshaw at the base to troubleshoot and get initial posts removed from the internet. It wasn't easy as the servers and app owners had to be contacted with the relevant court orders and the poster's account located. What was devastating leakage for the police was like all their birthdays come at once for the apps hosting the posts. It was heavy traffic—and traffic was money. It took time to have them removed.

'It's fortunate that the layby is a drive-on, drive-off island with a treeline between us and the roadside,' Nash said.

'Like a RORO,' Molly was trying to lighten the tension, but some tension is too tense to be altered.

'Quite.'

Even though she was virtually falling out of her seat, holding it back, Nash had asked Molly not to tell him anything about this scene in the car. He wanted to be able to see it and read it with clean eyes. Bad enough that the other teams had already been in. Robinson pulled up a few minutes behind them. He'd had to wash and change his forensic suit between scenes. Nash and Brown only had to change their paper slippers and gloves.

'What've we got?' Nash did the talking, and he took in the scene with Robinson.

The first young woman was probably in her early twenties. She was slim, with brown hair, and had been attractive. She was sitting in a camping chair naked, apart from a hat and a coral-coloured crop top that left little to the imagination. However, her private region wasn't exposed.

'This bastard loves his staging,' Nash said.

'Sir?' Molly admonished.

'Okay, this bastard of indiscriminate gender that might come from the planet Nanook likes their staging. Better?'

Beside the chair, the killer had put a bottle of Prosecco and a half-filled old tin mug. Nash watched a fruit fly drowning in drunken bliss. This victim wore a green floppy hat with the slogan *Happy Camper* and a picture of a VWT5 campervan. Her eyes were blown with the pupils fixed and dilated. Some blood vessels had ruptured, and the whites were bloodshot. There were several tracks of blood coming from beneath the hat and some staining at the rim, but it was congealed and not flowing. She put Nash in mind of Sissy Spacek at the end of *Carrie*.

'We're going to need time and cause of death, Robinson. An estimate will do for now.'

'No need on the cause, sir.' One of the Scenes of Crime officers lifted the hat by the middle avoiding the rim, even though he wore gloves. A paring knife had been driven through the victim's skull and into her brain.

Robinson stepped closer and drew in a breath through his teeth. 'Nasty and final, but it wasn't immediate. She suffered. I'd say she was restrained while she thrashed prior to her death. There are ligature marks on both wrists and ankles, and the bodies were posed after death.'

'Which brings us to the next one. What do we think the story is?' Nash turned to the officer in temporary charge of the scene before he turned up.

'Woman, mid to late thirties. No ID. Her role seems to be to finish the picture.'

The second woman was naked apart from a print top and was positioned on her knees beside the chair with her head between the first victim's legs.

'There's a spot of blood on her top that might give us some ID,' the officer said. Nash noticed her long hair had been released from a ponytail. It was brushed and still had the kink where a scrunchie had held it in place. 'The body and clothing have retained the smell of cannabis. It's fainter now than it would have been, but it's still there if you get your nose close enough.' Nash thought about the overpowering smell of drugs coming from the neighbour's bedsit at Paige Hunter's house. There could be a connection.

The intimate area of the first victim was entirely covered by the second woman's face and hair.

'Cause of death?'

'We'll need it to be confirmed by Dr Robinson, but it looks like a knife wound through the heart.'

'Any honeysuckle or music?'

'No music.' The officer picked up the woman's head by grabbing a handful of her hair, and Nash grimaced. She was somebody's daughter, and even after death, she shouldn't be treated like that. Nash glared at the SOCO officer. He was going to admonish him but was taken back to the job when he saw the knife sticking out of her chest. It was much larger than the paring knife.

'This one was fast. Death was instant,' Robinson said.

The kneeling woman had a sprig of honeysuckle in her mouth, and as her head was lifted, the other end slid out of the first victim's vagina.

'This woman doesn't look as important to him. She's a prop. She was dispatched quickly so that she could serve her purpose. The first victim was the star of the show,' Nash said. The word cannabis niggled at him. It had come up twice in one day. The first time at Paige Hunter's bedsit. A coincidence? Maybe. It seemed to Nash that half of today's youth smoked the foul stuff.

'Do you think they were lovers?' the officer asked.

'From what we know of the perp, I doubt it. There may be no connection at all—just somebody in the wrong place at the wrong time. However, don't count anything out. This case has a habit of throwing us off the scent and then providing enough evidence to convict Jones a hundred times over.'

'You still think it's him, then? He'd have to be working with an accomplice because he's in custody, isn't he?'

'He is indeed, but only a select few know that. And, with the amount of circumstantial evidence we have on him, I have my theories. Brown, find out who lives in the other bedsits in Paige Hunter's house. Have we found and bagged the hairband?'

'No sign of it, sir. Trophy?'

'Maybe.'

Chapter Fourteen

Chapter Fourteen

Nash got back to Barrow by early afternoon. Three bodies for an autopsy would take time, but Robinson promised to fast-track them and get the results to him as each one was complete.

He wanted to get Jones in the interview room. It was time to get this guy processed and out of his hair, but until he'd gathered everything, there was little point, even though there was plenty to go on before today's findings. He hadn't presented all the evidence against Jones from Henry Watson—but didn't want to do this piecemeal. He needed time to present the whole picture. Nash knew two things. They were dealing with a serial Killer—and Jones wasn't him.

Nash checked every piece of evidence, and throughout the afternoon, more was presented as fast-tracked test results came back and witnesses were interviewed. Nash stayed until six and said he was going to work from home. Since the pandemic, detectives had been allowed to do certain work in their own homes despite rising crime rates. He couldn't take physical evidence out of the station, but he was free to take as many photographs and photocopies as he wished on the proviso that they were carried in a locked briefcase and kept in a safe in a locked room at his home. He didn't travel by train, so there was no chance of him leaving official and case-sensitive documents behind.

When he got home, he was irritated to see that Sandy hadn't cleared up. They'd spent the night together, and as he walked around the house, he found a diary trail of the morning's events. Sandy's dirty clothes were left by the bed, not even put in the washer, just dropped on the floor in the bedroom. Three towels were dropped on the bathroom floor, and another one was slung over the bath. Nash didn't see how one human being could use four towels in a single session. The bath was dirty, and the shower head dripped a steady refrain into the tub where the tap hadn't been turned off properly. The bed was unmade, and the note Nash had left was still on the empty pillow.

You were sleeping, and I didn't want to disturb you.

Make sure you lock up.

Love you xxx

However, the fifty-pound loan was gone. Sandy had a fondness for the slots—something Nash strongly disapproved of. Almost every time they saw each other, money changed hands, and it was always out of Nash's account, never the other way around. Sandy was irresponsible. Nash knew that before they ever got together. He'd promised not to try and change his partner and had to accept things the way they were. Downstairs, the carnage on Nash's spotless life continued. The remains of breakfast pancakes were smeared on a plate, and a smudge of maple syrup lay in a viscous mess across his breakfast counter. There was a dirty cup in the sink—the hot tea Nash had left beside the bed that morning. And the lazy devil had even taken a second one from the cupboard for coffee, and a glass of orange juice, both with dregs in them left beside the dirty plate. Sandy had brewed a whole pot of filter coffee for one cup and left the rest cooling on the coffee plate.

Nash sighed as he cleaned his house. It was an unequal relationship, and, at some point, he had to stop making allowances and admit he was being used. Sandy was fifty-three, not a child. And as far as lovers went, Nash had experienced better and certainly with less selfishness both in the bedroom and out of it.

He picked up, tidied, wiped, polished and hoovered before it felt like his house again and less like a crime scene. He took his briefcase and unlocked his office. It was almost a replica of the incident room at work. An entire wall had been turned into a whiteboard. One-third was given over to maps of the areas he was working, and two-thirds for gathered intel. Every night, he updated his work with new evidence. Different coloured markers connected pieces of information, and drawing pins with coloured heads marked locations.

That afternoon he'd been called into Lewis's office. More stories had leaked to the press and social media. His boss tore him a new arsehole, and it stung. 'We've got a leak in your division—sort it. There's no doubt it was an inside job because vital information that was being held back has been spilt to the newspapers this morning,' Lewis said. Nash had been asked for a press conference by the media, but up to now, they'd managed to put it off—but the papers had been given chapter and verse. *The Sun* ran a four-page spread, and it was the shitty icing on his shitty day. Among other things, they knew about the honeysuckle left at each of the murder scenes.

'Another reason that leads us to believe it's an inside leak is that only certain information has been divulged. It says the police are looking for a person of interest, but as yet, it hasn't come out that we have Jones in custody. Everybody in the team knows that would blow their case wide open.' Lewis smacked her fist on the table.

Nash was hurt. He wasn't angry, sad or disappointed. He was gutted that one of his team would do this, and he took it personally. The news was out that Barrow-in-Furness had its first-ever serial killer, and he even had a name. The Florist.

Nash's storyboard told the full tale to date of The Florist's history.

At six o'clock, Nash made a sandwich and took it back to the office. By nine-thirty, when the doorbell rang, he has assimilated all the evidence and poured over every witness statement looking for anything he might have missed. The doorbell put him on edge. He saw Sandy last night, so it would be at least a week before he could expect another visit. Or until the money runs out, Nash thought, and then berated himself because Sandy was good fun and put a lot into their relationship. It didn't all come down to money. All the same, when he opened the door, Sandy was the last person he expected to see.

'Hi. What is it? Is everything okay?'

'If I'm not welcome, I'll turn around and go right back. I have lots of friends I can hang out with, you know,' Sandy said.

'No, I'm delighted to see you. Just surprised, that's all. Come in, let me take your coat, and you might want to fix your face a bit. The wind's had your mascara.' As Sandy flounced into the downstairs bathroom in a huff, though Nash didn't see what he'd done wrong, he realised that he still greeted his partner of eight months like an acquaintance. Maybe it was time to take the relationship to the next level and have another key cut. He poured two glasses of wine.

'Can we start again, love? Hello, sweetheart. I'm delighted that you're here.'

Sandy wilted as he handed the glass of wine over. They settled on the sofa, and their hands found each other. It felt good, as though they belonged. 'How've you been, Si? Good day?'

'Tough one,' Nash said, 'but it's better now you're here. Listen, let me just close the office, and then I can put work behind me and relax.' He didn't like to say, 'Lock the office,' in front of Sandy. It sounded as though there was no trust between them, but every civilian should understand the importance of keeping sensitive information safe, and that was his responsibility. Sandy tugged Nash's fly down, and he was loath to move. There was an audible sigh from Sandy as Nash got up to go to the office—and it wasn't a sigh of pleasure.

'Tell you what, give me two minutes, and I'll meet you in the bedroom. I'll bring the wine with me.'

'You've killed the mood now. All you ever talk about is work.'

This was far from the truth. Nash made a point of not talking about his job—it was another strict rule that had to be followed.

'I have ice cream. The extra creamy one you like. Can I tempt you?'

'I like that idea.'

'Fine wine, ice cream, a good film, and you. I'm a lucky man.'

'And don't you forget it. I can't stay all night, though, babe.'

'Oh. Why?'

'Just some stuff I have to do, so let's not waste time. Come on, make the most of me.'

Nash didn't need to be told twice.

Afterwards, they lay in the afterglow, smiling and sweaty. They cuddled close, safe and warm in Nash's protective arms. He felt that if they could just stay like that forever, everything would be all right. 'Don't go.'

'Don't get heavy on me again, Si. I have to.'

'It's turned eleven. What on God's great earth can you possibly have to do that can't wait until tomorrow?'

'Do I have to account for my movements now? Shall we put a tag on my ankle? Is this my boyfriend talking or Mister Detective Super Inspector Chief Policeman?'

'Don't be like that. I'm just concerned about you, that's all. Are you okay? You're not in any trouble?'

'No, I'm not in trouble. Why the hell would you think that? Not everybody in the world is a criminal. If you must know, I said I'd meet the staff after their shift for a lock-in at the bar, and I'm already late.'

'Can't you give me five minutes? We have sex, and you're almost straight out of bed and putting your clothes on. Aren't you even going to wash?'

'Told you. I'm late, and I like the feeling of your stuff in me. The scent will keep all the predators away.'

Nash turned on his side and felt deeply hurt, but there were no words to change the situation.

'Oh, I almost forgot to ask. Look, Si. The reason I came around tonight is I could really do with a bit of cash. I'm broke and just need enough to get me through to payday. You know what it's like, Babe. The landlord's screaming at me, and what with the price of electricity, a couple of hundred will see me right. I'll pay you straight back. Is that okay?'

There was a lot to process there. Sandy said, 'Almost forgot.' Not for a second was there any forgetting. Sandy had sweetened him up with sex and then went straight in for the kill. Nash had handed over fifty pounds last night, and now it was another two hundred. There had to be an end. Sandy had no money for bills but was meeting friends to go out late-night drinking rather than stay the night with Nash. And the big one, the one that really laid the boot in. 'The reason I came tonight.' Not to see Nash or wanting to surprise him with a visit, but just to get more money out of him. This cash cow was going to slaughter.

'I'm not giving you any more money.'

'Fine. I'll go then and have the debt collectors on my doorstep by morning. Sandy made a grab for the faux-fur jacket Nash had hung on the back of the door. It was a gaudy number with pink fluff that

Nash had paid for after giving in to Sandy's two-hour sulk a couple of months earlier.

'Will you still have a cocktail in your hand when these debt collectors arrive? Perhaps you could offer them one as a partial payment.'

'Damn you to hell, old man.'

'If you walk out of that door, don't bother coming back.'

'What?'

'You heard me. I mean it, Sandy. If you leave now, that's it. We're done.'

'Are you fricking joking me? You shag me and then throw me out.'

'Don't twist my words. I'm giving you a clear choice.'

'An ultimatum, you mean. Don't make me choose between you and my friends. You won't like the answer.'

'Do they give you more money than me, then?'

'What's that supposed to mean?'

'Nothing, I'm sorry. Look, forget it. Come back to bed, and I'm sorry for shouting at you.'

'And you'll give me the money?'

In that second, Nash felt old and dirty and tired. He could get a prostitute to service him once a week for less. And that's what their relationship came down to. They had no mutual friends. He suspected that Sandy was taking recreational drugs—probably cocaine—and he was paying for it. They rarely went anywhere, and when they did, it was a fancy restaurant, and Nash always footed the bill—every penny of it. A sweet word out of Sandy's lips cost him roughly a fiver. He lived for the once-a-week visit, though lately, it was less than that until Sandy needed money. It was a relationship he could do without. But damn, it felt like taking his arm off at the shoulder. This thought led him back to The Florist. He had work to get back to. Tomorrow he had to spend hours interviewing Jones, which was a complete waste of time. The sooner they let him go, the better. Nash was itching to get back to building a case or destroying one in this instance. Work was his other love, one that didn't let him down.

'The bank's closed, and this teller is very tired. You're welcome to slam the door on your way out.'

'I don't understand why you're being like this, babe. A hundred, then. I can manage on a hundred.'

'Get out, Sandy.'

'You can't do this to me. You think I'll suck your wrinkly old cock, and then you can just throw me away as if I'm nothing. Nobody treats this bitch that way. You won't get away with this. I promise you'll be sorry.'

He already was.

Chapter Fifteen

Chapter Fifteen

Max was fifty-four hours into the ninety-six that they were allowed to keep him before charging him or letting him go.

They went through the same procedure as on the last interview with some changes. Molly Brown had replaced Phillip Renshaw, and Jane Pearson, Max's solicitor, was present. Max had been given a ten-minute consultation with his solicitor in the room before the interview. She seemed flustered and unprepared and had to leave him to make a phone call to have some additional notes brought in. Max spent five of his ten minutes alone with his thoughts.

They led him to think about the days of his youth. Bobby, Jon and Max were always together. The three wise monkeys, though there was hardly an ounce of wisdom between them. Jon's Mum called them that, and when they got into trouble, she'd laugh and say, 'Leaves of three, let it be.' Max asked her what it meant one day, and she said the phrase related to leaves with three points. ' Never touch them because they might be poison ivy.'

'Charming, thanks,' Max had replied, 'But what about three times a charm? That's supposed to be good luck.'

'You always have an answer for everything, Max. Too smart for your own good. You need to be more like my Jon and just take things at face value.' They'd laughed, and Jon had gone off in a sulk. He said his mum had called him stupid when he couldn't do his maths homework, and she held Max up as a shining example of somebody that would get on in life. His mum said Max was brighter than him and that he should do better. Later that night, Jon tried to cause an argument between Max and Bobby. Bobby misplaced his wallet, and Jon accused Max of taking it, but it didn't work. They fell out sometimes, but it never lasted for long. Mostly they were the proverbial three peas in a pod. Max wished they were with him now—and preferably their eleven-year-old selves because they'd have dealt with all this so much better than Max's adult self. They'd have devised a foolproof escape plan by now and would have smuggled in tools to get them out. At the very least, one of them would have had a Swiss Army knife that they'd ingeniously got through the strip search to pick their way out of jail and stab a few guards with on the way.

He knew his solicitor's name was Jane Pearson, but she had struggled to remember his name two minutes after they shook hands. What was the problem with his name? Max Jones. It wasn't difficult, but people kept forgetting it. Any confidence he'd had in her was leaking away under the door. This woman was his hope of getting out of there. She only seemed to have one piece of advice. Don't say anything. Isn't that something she would say to a guilty man? She must have as little confidence in him as he had in her.

It wasn't Max's job to read people, not like the police had to, but he'd secured some big contracts in his time by appraising a mood. He summed her up in four words. Not that he liked the C-word, but his acronym summed her up well. Caustic, Ugly, Narcissistic,

Treacherous. It was why he was so good at winding people up and getting a rise out of them.

Nash looked tired. His shirt was fine. It wasn't as though it looked as if he'd slept in it, but Max could see that it hadn't been ironed. His shoes weren't freshly shined, and he wore the same tie from two days earlier. A man like Nash would have enough shirts and ties to complement them pre-picked at the beginning of the week. The detective wouldn't work Monday to Friday, but he'd always have his clothes ready. A tic was playing Whac-a-Mole at the side of his right eye, but there was nobody ready with a mallet to whack Nash. He had nothing against the guy. He was doing his job and could be an arse at times, but for the most part, he was polite and treated him well. He seemed like a likeable guy. The kind of man Max would buy a pint—if he frequented that kind of bar.

The woman, Brown, was a ballbreaker. She interested Max. She was in her thirties, trying to get ahead. Making an inspector wasn't bad, but Max thought it wasn't enough for her. Molly Brown was the type that wanted to run the joint. She had the urge to climb, and Max had the feeling that she was being held back. Maybe she just wasn't as good at her job as her attitude implied. Crisp. That's how he'd describe her, from her sharp blue skirt suit to her three-inch heels. She took the time to put on a full face every day. Max saw the tell-tale sign of exhaustion beneath the Copper Glo bronzer. She'd had a late night, too—but the detectives hadn't worked together last night. There was something about their greeting as they walked through the door and the way Nash pointed some documents out to her that said they needed a catch-up on the case. Max suppressed a smile because he noticed that Brown wound him up. The female officer suppressed a yawn. Max deduced that Nash would rather work with Renshaw. He was right, and Nash offered her a coffee. He asked Max if he wanted one as well, and then Jane Pearson—we're all on the same team here. Max accepted. It was nice to be included.

'Interview resumed at 08:16.' Nash motioned to each of them in turn to state their names.

'Good morning Max. I trust you slept well.'

'I've had better nights. You lot should have to spend a night in here once a year as part of your training.'

'Not a bad idea. I'll suggest it to the Prime Minister next time I go for tea.'

'I'm not complaining. The duty team are really nice.'

'Good. Right. Let's get on with it. We have to go through the motions, Max. Every piece of evidence, everything said about you or the victims. But here's the thing. We've got enough evidence against you, both circumstantial and direct—the kind that does stand up in court—to put you away for the rest of your life.'

Max turned to Pearson. 'Is this the bit where I get to say, "No comment"?'

Jane Pearson stopped him from saying more with a look. 'Intimidation, DCI Nash. I will not have my client intimidated. Please stick to questions and make them direct.'

Nash held his hands up in supplication. 'Forgive me.'

'That's it, then? You've decided it's me, and I'm done for. You would be making a big mistake putting me away, Inspector. I'm going to be dead soon, but you'll be letting a bloody monster go free. What if he keeps killing after I'm gone? That's direct blood on your hands.'

Pearson gave him a warning look to stop him from talking. 'I'm very busy. If you have something new, I suggest you get on with it so that I can get out of here,' she said.

'Don't let me keep you. In fact, you can go now if you like,' Max said. The solicitor was getting on his nerves. She didn't seem to care one way or the other about his innocence. She never once asked him if he did the murders, and Max didn't like that. He wanted somebody that believed in him on his side.

Nash nodded at Brown, who took some photographs out of the folder and gave them to him. It was the same folder from the other day because he recognised the doodle of a cat on the corner. Same shit, different murder.

Nash didn't put the photos down but held them against his body as though they mattered very much, literally holding his cards close to his chest.

'There's been another murder, Max.'

'The dog bloke? I know. I was there soon after it happened.'

'The dog bloke? Care to elaborate?'

'The man I took the dog off. He was kicking it. So I took it away from him and gave it to my friend, Jonathan Finch.'

'That would be Ryan Beck. I take it? Formerly residing at what was the Continental Bar.'

'I don't know his name.'

Nash glanced at the photos he was holding. 'These are out of order, Brown. Give me victim number five, please.'

'Sir.'

Nash took the new pictures and put them in front of the ones he already had. Max had a glimpse of the file, and there seemed to be a stack of photos still in there. Jesus Christ, how many was he supposed to have killed? They must think he was a one-man plague.

'Victim five?' Max said. 'What? Victim five of twenty-five? You're not sloppy, Inspector Nash. You're playing games to wear me down. I know what you're doing. Those photos weren't out of order. You're just trying to unnerve me. And let me tell you. It's working.'

'Intimidation, Inspector. This is your final warning.' Pearson was as much use as botulism. She seemed to be up to her eyes in other cases and hadn't prepared for his.

'I'm not stupid, Nash. I bet the rest of the paper in that folder is blank—just a big stack of white noise to frighten me. I've told you about all the dead people I know of. I didn't know anything about the three you hit me with last time that had been murdered. All I knew was Henry and this dog-man. I didn't have anything to do with either of them, so you can take your victim number five shit and shove it.'

Nash laid the first photograph of Ryan Beck.

'You know the drill, Jones. We've been here a few times before. Do you know this man? For the tape, I'm showing the victim evidence 23A.'

'No. I don't know this person.'

'You just said you did.'

'No, I'm being careful what I say.'

Jane Pearson glared at Max and then Nash and Brown. 'My client has said he doesn't know this person. Move on.'

'That doesn't mean I haven't had dealings with him. I want to help you, DCI Nash.'

'I strongly advise that you don't say anymore,' Pearson said.

'Is that all you can say? Look, love, I'm not being funny, but when you came in two days late, you didn't even know my name. You might be good, and I've little reason to doubt Jeremy Stillman, but I don't think you're good for me. I'm sorry, but I don't need your representation anymore. Send the rest of your bill to my office.'

'Mr Jones, I can't advise you strongly enough that this is a huge mistake.'

Nash interrupted. 'We would also advise that you keep your legal representation, Mr Jones. It keeps us all out of trouble.'

'Guys, I've got nothing to hide. I'll answer anything you want and take any tests you need. This place is driving me nuts now. I haven't got long left to enjoy, and want to get this mess cleared up and get out of here. I'm an innocent man, and I'll find a way to prove it—no offence to Ms Pearson. I'm sure she's very nice. But I'm going to represent myself from now on.'

'Please, Mr Jones. Think about what you're doing,' Pearson said.

'I am Ms Pearson. Thank you for coming, I appreciate your time, but you can go now. I'll be okay, and if I'm not, I only have myself to blame. Thank you.'

He realised he'd humiliated the lady and tried his best to spare her feelings. He had to go with his gut, and his intestines were telling him she wasn't the one for him. She was putting her things back into her designer briefcase that could probably buy the Continental Bar. Max hated anybody being annoyed with him, so he touched the back of her hand as if that would make amends, and when she looked up, he smiled at her and thanked her again. She snatched her fingers out from under his.

'You're a fool, Jones.'

Jane Pearson grabbed her briefcase, picked up her phone and stormed out of the interview room, banging the door behind her.

Nash sighed. 'Would you like us to suspend the interview while you hire new representation, Mr Jones?'

'I won't be needing that, but I would like five minutes with my new client, myself and I, please.' Max stood up and looked at the clock, 'Interview suspended at 08:38.'

Nash shook his head, 'Always the joker, Jones.' He picked up his things and left the room with Brown. When they returned, they did the preamble for the tape again.

'It's my duty to inform you that it's in your best interests to have a solicitor to speak for you. Would you like us to appoint a duty solicitor?'

'I'm good, thanks.'

'You are either very confident or very stupid, Max, and I can't for the life of me decide which it is. Going back to Mr Ryan Beck.' Nash tapped the photograph.

'What can you tell us about him?'

'Literally, not much. I saw him in the street kicking the shit out of his dog, so I threw some money at him and took the pup. I don't know if that's classed as stealing, and if it is, I'll take it.' Max was pale, his hands were shaking, and it had been hours since they'd brought him his medication and more hours before it was due again. Nash had told him that he'd sought medical advice regarding Max's condition. If he needed to stop at any time, the interview could be suspended for him to rest. But Max didn't want to stop. He wanted to go home. He clasped his hands together to stop them from shaking and realised he was about to make things worse.

'Look, I'm going to get myself into a world of crap here, but you'll find out anyway, so I suppose you ought to know. I roughed him up a bit as well. Assaulted him, I guess.'

'Was this at the same time?'

'Yes.'

'Did anybody see this assault, as you call it?'

'No. Yes. Some cars went by. They must have seen, but they didn't stop. I didn't kill him. He was alive and well when I left.'

'What did you do to him?'

'I choked him until he was almost unconscious. And then he slumped to the ground. He coughed a bit, but he was okay.'

'And you're a doctor who knows this for a fact. I take it. Showing the suspect item 23C.' It was a close-up of the man's face and torso. He was badly beaten, with two black eyes, swollen lips and a face caked in cuts, bruises and dried blood. His body was black and blue. There was also considerable bruising around the neck and a thin line where something had been used as a garrotte.

'Hell, no. Before you ask, I didn't do any of that. Well, maybe some of the bruisings around his neck, but that's all. I know it looks bad, but I swear, all I did was choke him. Christ, I wish I hadn't let that Pearson woman go now.'

'You and me both. Was the choking in self-defence or to stop him from hurting his dog again?'

'Neither. It was because I wanted to hurt him.'

Nash said, 'At this point, we should remind you that this interview is being taped and video recorded, Mr Jones and anything you say can be used at trial.'

Max reminded them that he wouldn't live to make it to trial. 'Was he beaten to death?' He asked Nash. He felt a second of pity for Beck and then remembered the state Mia was in when he first saw her. He was glad this piece of human waste was dead.

'The beating didn't help, that's for sure, but the cause of death was strangulation. We believe a wire was used. In particular, a string that had been removed from Mr Armstrong's upright piano linked the two crimes. The bloody piano string was found inside the old pub. It was an effective weapon. Do you know anything about it?'

'I cared more about Mr Armstrong than I did about my own mother. I didn't kill him, and I certainly didn't touch his piano strings. But going back to dog-man, I'd like to shake the hand of the person that murdered that piece of scum.'

'Your feelings are clear. Are you sure you didn't go too far? Maybe you just intended to give him a little dig to teach him a lesson when the red mist came down, and you couldn't stop?'

'No. I didn't kill him.'

'But you returned to the scene the next day?'

Max laughed at the ridiculous nature of the situation. 'I did. I don't know how to explain it without digging a bloody big hole for myself, so I'm just going to tell you how it is. My mate Jon and his wife, Emily. They've never so much as had a parking ticket. If Emily did, she'd pay it the second it arrived, not leave it until it's doubled like the rest of us. And she'd still cry for a week because her copybook had been blotted.' He smiled and spoke about them with a fondness that warmed the room.

'Go on. What's this got to do with a man getting beaten to a pulp and then garrotted?'

'I laid a massive poor me. I'm dying, guilt trip on them and pretty much forced them to take the dog off me. The stupidest thing is, you can't tell Jon about the kind of guy this was. He wouldn't get it. They agreed to take Mia, but only if I went back to get a dumb receipt and her microchip records, for god's sake. As if that poor bugger was ever chipped.'

'Go on. I'm sure this story is fascinating.'

'I tried to talk them out of it, and I said the bloke wouldn't be calling the police, but they wouldn't have it and insisted I went to talk to him to get some kind of paperwork and medical records. I figured I'd walk past the building once. Hell, I didn't even know if he was one of the squatters there, judging a book and all that. One walk past would fulfil my promise, and I could go back and tell them I didn't find him. I didn't expect him to be lying dead in the doorway.'

'You realise how far-fetched this sounds?'

'Oh yeah. I wouldn't believe me either.'

'Okay, let's get the rest of the evidence out of the way so we can move on.'

Brown took a plastic bag out of the evidence pack and slid it across the desk. Max's shoulders slumped in defeat. 'Showing suspect item 23D. Do you recognise this?'

'Yes. It's Mia's old dog tag. I found it in the street.'

'Was this before or after you killed Mr Beck?' Brown said.

'It was the day after I took his dog when I was on my way to the squat. It must have flown off her collar when he was kicking her. It was in the same place, and I don't know why, but I picked it up.'

'You picked it up?' Brown was still in the driving seat, and if anything, Nash seemed disinterested.

'Yes. It was just there. And it made me sad. It was a part of Mia, and I felt that she should have it. I don't know how to explain it. Like, when a mother abandons a baby on the church steps, and they keep the blanket she was wrapped in. The same as that. Even though it was a bad past, horrible, horrendous—it was still hers. I picked it up to give to Jon.'

'You like shiny things, it seems.'

'What's that meant to mean?'

'Nothing Mr Jones,' Nash said.

'Please notice the honeysuckle beside the body. Any comments?' Brown asked.

'No, but I can give you a couple of observations if you like. Nice choice. Lilies would have been too obvious. And, your job would be a lot easier if you wore trousers and flat shoes.'

Nash covered his lower face with his hand and coughed.

'And your life would be a lot easier if you weren't a murderer, eh?'

Chapter Sixteen

'Didn't somebody come to our borough asking about a missing sister in Morecambe?' Nash asked. He'd come out of the interview two days earlier and heard a girl at the front desk. He'd meant to follow it up then, but Sandy had called to cancel their date that night, and Nash had to let the table he'd booked go. He was tired, and it slipped his mind.

'I don't know, boss. I haven't heard anything,' Renshaw said.

Nash did a search for the recent reports using the term Missing and Morecambe with the relevant date.

'Here it is. Jessica Hunter. Paige Hunter's sister. Why the hell wasn't this cross-referenced to the Morecambe unit? Jessica lives in Barrow, and the rest of the family in Morecambe and Heysham. This wasn't just reported once. It was done twice. Tracey Davis was on the desk the first time and bloody Jenkins the second. This should have been done and tracked. Who knows? That young girl might still be alive now if we'd been on it.'

'That's not fair, sir. She'd been dead for days when she was found.'

'Even so, it's sloppy work. Cutting cross-referencing corners could have cost us vital evidence.' He went to a different screen. 'The family have already been informed about the death and have been interviewed. I'm sending Brown over there today to see if there's anything they can add. There may have been somebody hanging around, and Ms Hunter might even have mentioned dodgy customers in the café where she worked. I want you on it with Brown.'

'What? You're sending me to Morecambe again? Can't Bowes or Lawson go? It's only going over old ground. They already told the Morecambe lot everything they know.'

Nash gave him a withering look, and Renshaw went to find Molly Brown.

***

Jessica Hunter was fuming when she left Barrow police station for the second time three days before. She hadn't spoken to Paige for five days, and there was no answer at her flat. That knocked-over cup on the coffee table bothered her. Paige should have picked it up by now.

The policeman had been nice enough, but he spouted one platitude after another. No, she wasn't with her boyfriend. No, she hadn't been to an all-night party that turned into three days. They didn't understand Paige. Jess knew something was wrong.

Paige would never have missed their parent's anniversary last night. Not for anything. She was scatty sometimes, but she wasn't that kind of girl. She loved their parents and would never do anything to hurt them.

Jess had covered for her and said that Paige had the flu, and because of their parents' ages, she didn't want to risk them catching it. Mum called Paige, and when she didn't answer, Jess suggested she might be asleep. One lie led to another, and her mum flapped about going to the doctor so they could all get their flu jabs before the meal that night. She wanted Jess to drive her to Paige's with homemade chicken soup, and Jess had to lie again by saying that Paige wasn't that ill. It was just a flu-like sniffle. But it was a necessary precaution to keep them safe.

When Paige didn't turn up for the meal, and seven thirty turned into eight o'clock, Jess was frantic—but kept chewing and smiling. Aunty Maureen and Uncle Fred were there, and she laughed at Fred's jokes and made small talk from sitting down for prawn cocktails through to Raspberry Pavlova at the end. At every opportunity, she excused herself and rang Paige's phone again. It went direct to voice-mail. Wherever her sister was, her phone was dead, or she was on the longest phone call in the world. The word dead struck a chord in her, and she pushed it aside like a drooping cobweb on her face.

She got away as soon as she could and was at the police station by midnight to report Paige missing. She was glad they were quiet, even though it was Friday night. Maybe they'd get people straight out and find Paige by morning.

The desk sergeant made a basic report, and the only thing she seemed to be interested in was her sister's age. When Jess told her Paige was eighteen and, therefore, legally old enough to look after herself, the lady said she'd put a call out for all the drivers to look out for her.

'Is that it?'

'For now, yes. You've only just discovered her missing. We usually find that young girls turn up eventually. If she hasn't come back after the weekend, give us a call, and we'll see what we can do.'

And that was it. She was tossed into the night.

The next morning she was at Paige's flat by seven o'clock. She hadn't been back. The mug was still overturned, and the flat screamed unoccupied. Paige's phone was still dead. Jess listened to her instincts and knew that her sister couldn't come home. She was held, hurt or dead, and Jess was terrified. The Lancaster Royal Infirmary was the most likely choice for her to be taken to if she'd been in an accident, so she rang them first.

Nothing.

'Please check again.'

'I don't need to, miss. I have a log of every patient that has come into this hospital, and I'm very sorry. I know you must be worried sick, but unless she's here as a Jane Doe, she isn't listed on my database.'

That wasn't good enough, and she wasn't going to be fobbed off by some receptionist with a bad attitude. She drove to Lancaster with a recent photograph and arrived an hour later.

'I'd have been here sooner, but I've driven from Barrow. This is my sister. Have you seen her come in? Maybe she's unconscious, and somebody's stolen her ID. Or, maybe she's using a false name, though I couldn't imagine that.'

'I'm sorry, but you've had a wasted journey. She isn't here.'

She drove to Westmorland Hospital and went through the same scenario there. And even though it was the most unlikely of the three, when she got back to Barrow, she went to Furness General and asked about Paige there. Maybe she'd overturned her car on her way to see Jess for some reason and had amnesia. She was thinking of every possibility before she went back to the police station and said she thought her sister was dead.

Furness General drew a blank. And it was with new resolve that she went back to the police station armed with Paige's photograph, and this time she wasn't going anywhere until they did something. It was five days since she'd spoken to her sister. People should understand the seriousness of that. They spoke every day. She was being treated like an idiot with an overactive imagination. The desk sergeant took her details again and said he'd highlight that this was her second visit and that she still hadn't made contact with Paige. He said he'd issue an APB to all cars to keep an eye out for her.

'What if she's dead?'

He laughed. 'It's only been a few days. We have no reason to imagine anything like that at this stage. You say you've checked all the local hospitals?'

'Yes.'

'Well then, if she isn't there and nobody's reported an accident between Morecambe and here, there's nothing to worry about, is there?'

'But you don't know my sister.'

She left the station feeling unheard.

***

This morning, after Paige's body had been found, Nash was there to ask more questions. They must be sick of the same things asked by a stream of officers. Paige Hunter. Another daughter. Somebody else's child. Nash rang the doorbell and saw a figure coming towards him through the opaque glass. It was fragmented in the light and put him in mind of somebody stepping out of deep water.

A young woman opened the door. She was in loungewear with a logo on the breast and had grey slippers on her feet. Her long hair was tied back in a ponytail, and she had no makeup. Her eyes were red with crying. She slammed the door behind him.

'More police,' she said as he showed his badge. 'I suppose you'd better come in. I dare say Mother will make more tea and ply you with digestives.'

She led him into the lounge, where a grey lady sat with a grey man. He'd never seen this couple before, apart from a photograph on Paige's dresser, but he could see at a glance that grief had torn them apart. He motioned for them to stay seated as he shook hands and introduced himself.

'Before you ask your pointless questions, Inspector, and we answer them for the hundredth time, I have some for you,' Jessica said.

Nash nodded. He'd seen this anger before. It came from feelings of uselessness and hopelessness. The slim young woman seemed heavier with grief and rage as she slammed her body into a chair and faced him.

'Where were all these police who are so interested in my dead sister's killer? Where were they when she was missing? And they don't care about her now. They still don't bother to ask about my sister, not really—only about finding who killed her.'

She reached for a framed photograph that was next to her on the end table and held it out to him. He suspected it had been held a lot during the last hours. 'Look at this. Look at it properly, damn you.' Nash went to take it from her, and she snatched it away from him as though to have somebody else's hands on it would obliterate more of Paige.

'This is Paige Hunter, my beautiful sister, Inspector. She was eighteen. She isn't anymore. She loved animals and worked in a café. She was always kind, and I won every argument we ever had.'

'I'm so sorry for your loss.' Nash had said it, and he so didn't intend to offer meaningless platitudes. She snorted at him and knew his words couldn't change a damn thing.

'She supported Morecambe FC and went to some of their games, but only if it wasn't too cold. And she made the most perfect scrambled eggs for me when I was sick last year. Small stuff, inspector, nothing ground-breaking about her—but she was nice, you know?

She wanted to be sassy, and she was but couldn't see it. She'll never be sassy, clever, or beautiful again.'

Nash let her speak, and when she finished, she was crying. She'd done a lot of that. He could tell. The grey couple didn't move after the lady had asked if he'd like tea, and Nash had declined. They had nothing to say, but he saw Colin stroking the back of Hilary's hand as though he was trying to absorb her pain. Nash looked towards them, and Jess carried on.

'Look at my parents. They are too distraught to even speak to you. They're so confused by what's happened that they are working on lifelong routines like automatons. They waited so long to have us, and there's no way they should have lost a daughter at this time in their lives. They were dancing on Friday night. It was their forty-sixth wedding anniversary. Dad had a bit too much to drink and literally danced on a table.'

'Shush your mouth. This gentleman doesn't need to know all that,' Dad said.

'When they danced together, they spun, Inspector, round and round like nothing could hurt them. But it did. You should have heard my mum laugh on Friday night. She runs every day and does yoga. Dad plays tennis in the summer. They're still in love, you know. And Paige worked in a café, and she'd perfected scrambled eggs. They were amazing. Tiny things, Inspector.'

The lady moved her hand in a dismissive gesture but couldn't manage any words.

'I'm not going to tell you I'm sorry for your loss. I'm going to tell you that I do care about Paige. I'm sorry I never met her or sampled her scrambled eggs. I'd have liked that. I care so much about Paige that I will remember her face until the day I die. I understand how angry you are.'

'Do you?'

'Yes. And I'm angry too. We failed you. We need to see that this never happens again. Would that twenty-four hours have made any difference? We'll never know. But, I'm telling you now, on the record with no hidden agenda or platitudes, we should have listened to you sooner.'

'Thank you.'

'Are you sure you wouldn't like tea? It's no trouble.' Mrs Hunter stood up and hovered.

'Actually, yes, a cup of tea would be lovely, thank you.'

'I've got some Digestive biscuits, Inspector.'

Jessica smiled at him, and Nash saw how lovely she was when grief wasn't pulling her into a dark place that she couldn't escape.

'I had to identify her. It was too much for Mum and Dad. I'll never forget that final image of my sister. It's in my head every minute of every bloody day.'

'Jessica.'

'Sorry, Dad.'

'I can't be here. I'm going to go and water the plants.'

'Okay, Dad.' Mr Hunter got up, and where Nash had seen an old man, now he had a glimpse of him as he'd been twenty-four hours earlier. They were a similar age—but Nash hadn't just lost a daughter.

'How can thirty years catch up with you overnight? They were like a pair of forty-year-olds,' Jess said.

'I hope their youth will come back to them. With time.'

'They don't have time. But Paige did.'

'We're going to find him.'

'You say that as if it matters. What good will that do me? Or my parents?'

'It will stop him from doing this to anybody else.'

'He probably already has. He might be doing it now. This minute. He's not going to stop.'

Nash took her through the last time she saw Paige. Was there anything, anything at all, the smallest irrelevant detail that could give them any clues?

'Nothing, Inspector.' She looked at the open door. 'Not a bloody thing. Sorry, Dad.'

Chapter Seventeen

The boys were found within three hours of each other. On both occasions, it was the scent of honeysuckle that made the parents investigate and find their sons. Nash would never forget the image of Annie Wilson rocking her decaying son and singing to him.

After two and a half weeks of being frantic and worrying, her baby was home where he belonged. The boys were left in their own bedrooms. Gareth Wilson was twelve and an only child. He was brought home while his parents ate dinner in the dining room at the back of the house.

His mum noticed the scent of the flowers as she went to the bathroom. She knew it was The Florist the second she inhaled it and realised it was coming from Gareth's room.

The sob was already in her throat as she turned the handle, but she was bathed in golden hope when she saw Gareth kneeling beside his bed. They'd never been a religious family, but he knelt in prayer, and she didn't question why he hadn't called for her or what he'd been through to make praying the first thing he did. She felt such a fierce love as any mother would. She shouted for Jim and ran to her son, sobbing in earnest. Annie gathered her little boy in her arms and said his name as she rocked him.

After the horror came to her, she continued to cradle him, and her husband wasn't strong enough to prise her away. 'Don't you bloody touch me. Get away.' He'd never heard his wife swear before, but he was so deeply immersed in the shock that came over him so fast that he barely registered that his wife was elsewhere. She was back in time to a day when her son was alive in her arms. He had to leave her there rocking with Gareth when he called the police. He gave a full account of what had happened before taking the police into Gareth's bedroom.

And that's how Nash and Brown found her. Jim was talking again. 'She didn't turn the light on when she saw him, and the smell was masked by the scent of the flowers, but only until he was moved.'

Gareth wore pyjamas, but they weren't his jammies. They were new and didn't smell of him, but then, he didn't smell of him anymore, either. His hair had been cut. It was jagged and dirty. The soles of his feet were black.

'He was kneeling by his bed with his hands pressed together in prayer. A rosary was wrapped around his fingers. My boy's throat was cut, Inspector, and his face was dirty and pale.'

Nash looked at the body in his mother's arms. There was no blood. He'd been exsanguinated, and from his colour, it looked as though he didn't have a drop of blood left in his body. 'There was a teddy bear sitting beside him on the bed, but it wasn't his teddy.'

And his mother held him.

Nash called the coroner, and when Robinson came, he had to give the mother a strong sedative. Mr Wilson stood in the doorway like a statue frozen in a rictus of horror. He only spoke once more. 'Please take my precious son away from her. My little boy. My poor Annie.'

But they wouldn't prize the horror of the dead child from her arms. Nash talked to her and got her to agree to have something to take the edge off. He spent time with her and got down next to her on the bedroom floor, and asked her to give her son to them when she was ready. He promised they'd look after him and that he wasn't in any pain now. Mrs Wilson gripped the body of the child tighter, and Molly Brown talked to her in a soothing voice and gave her the time she needed until she was ready to offer Gareth up to Nash. He lifted the child from her arms and lowered him when his mother screamed that he hadn't had a goodnight kiss.

Bill Robinson helped Mr Wilson get her into bed, where she'd sleep for a while, but nowhere near long enough. Not for the million years she'd need for the pain to ease.

***

Jamie Little was only eleven and had never been away from home. Mr Little had been out all day searching for his son with their dog. The number of volunteer searchers had gone down as every day passed. On day one, it had been almost every man, woman, child and dog in the town. Day two was half that amount, and when almost three weeks had gone by, only six people had turned up to search the dunes at Roan Head. Paul Little didn't know who made the decision to search there, but they thought it would be the ideal place for a killer to drop a body after dark. Paul told Nash that he'd overheard somebody say that, but he couldn't remember who it was. That would have been great if they were searching for a body, but they weren't. They were searching for Jamie and his mate. That's all. No bodies.

Nash had patted his shoulder and felt the weight of his hopelessness. Little had come home at seven. They'd had dinner—homemade cheese pie, chips and beans, the boys' favourite. Only Adrian, Jamie's younger brother, had seconds. He was ten and hungry. They watched TV for a bit, and Eileen had nagged Adrian about his homework, but only a little bit, not like before, and only to be normal. Adrian said he didn't want to do it, and Eileen said he didn't have to.

'I bet he was chuffed about that,' Nash said. 'But normal is good, you know. He won't break.'

'He might, Inspector, and where would we be then? The little bugger smirked and then played me for ice cream. And he got it, too.' Mr Little looked at the closed bedroom door and turned away from the slaughter waiting for them inside.

They put Adrian to bed at nine o'clock. He'd never had the room to himself until Jamie went missing, and he'd been unsettled since then. They had to leave the hall light on for him and the door open, and he was allowed to have his tablet in bed with him.

Mr and Mrs Little were thinking about going to bed and said it was about eleven when Paul heard a noise outside. He ran to the front door in time to see a figure running down the street, it was a fleeting glimpse before they turned the corner, and he couldn't give Nash much of a description. All he saw was somebody running away in the dark. Eileen heard her husband shouting. She panicked and went to check on Adrian. Paul told her to ring the police, but she was already halfway up the stairs. They both smelt it as they ran up to their son's room, the sickly smell of flowers.

They ran into the room. Their son, Jamie, was home, but they knew straight away that he was dead. He wore pyjamas, but they weren't his. They were new and didn't smell of him. His hair had been cut. It was jagged and dirty. The soles of his feet were black. He knelt by his bed with his hands pressed together in prayer. A rosary was wrapped around his fingers. His throat was cut, and his face was dirty and pale. There was no blood. He'd been exsanguinated and didn't have a drop of blood left in his body. There was a teddy bear sitting beside him on the bed, but it wasn't his teddy. It was new and smelt of a supermarket.

Mr Little told Nash he'd covered his ears, but he didn't think it was to drown out his wife's screaming, 'Just the sound of my own inadequacy,' he'd said. 'I couldn't do anything.'

'I know. We'll find him,' Nash said, but he wasn't talking about the murderer. There was a new and equal horror. When his mother saw it, she screamed for her eldest son, who had taken his last breath and then she screamed again for her kidnapped youngest son.

Adrian's bed was empty.

Nash rang the Coroner. Bill Robinson was in the mortuary. He said he'd hardly scrubbed in for Gareth's autopsy when he was called out again. 'The other one?'

'Jamie Little,' Nash said. 'I'm going to need anything you've got on Gareth Wilson in the few minutes you've looked at him. Anything at all. Our perp brought the body of Jamie home but took his brother.'

They put out a countywide APB. When it comes to kidnapping, the beauty of Barrow-in-Furness is that it's one road in and one road out. The A590 had been closed from Ulverston, and just in case he got through, as a precaution, it was closed again at the motorway in both directions. The road into Askam was shut, and higher up at the junction for Broughton and Millom, there were roadblocks. All the little dogleg roads like Soutergate and Kirkby were shut down. Everywhere he could escape had roadblocks and a police presence within ten minutes of him having left the Little's household. Every vehicle on the roads was stopped and searched, and by the time the South of the county was closed, they had police helicopters up and searching woodland and farm tracks.

He'd gone to ground.

***

The last train pulled out of Barrow towards Ulverston at 21:46. The first train the next morning came into Askam at 04:49. Station attendant June Alder was the first person on the platform that morning. She found the little boy in his pyjamas and barefoot. He was frozen, and at first, she thought he was dead.

Nash hadn't been to bed. He was there ten minutes after the first responders. He knew he wouldn't sleep and hadn't gone home. He was waiting for the sunrise outside the police station when the call came in. The road was empty, and he didn't give a shit about traffic lights.

He wanted to be the one to tell the parents their second child was alive.

It was a game. The killer was playing with them. One in, one out. What fun. They took Adrian to the hospital to be checked. Nash insisted on talking to him when he'd been given the all-clear and had Mum and Dad beside him. He promised to be gentle. For a single hour beside their son's hospital bed, that one on its own, they put their grief over Jamie to one side and gave in to the joy of having Adrian safe.

Nash said, 'Hi, Adrian. You had quite an adventure, didn't you, buddy? Look at you with a drip bag and everything. I'm going to ask you to turn on your Spidey-sense for me. Do you think you can do that?'

Adrian was still groggy after being drugged by The Florist, but every second was important. The little boy nodded with large frightened eyes.

'Do you remember what happened last night after you went to bed?'

He shook his head and began to cry.

'It's okay, son. Don't get upset. You're doing great. Just tell me what you can remember.'

'Nothing. I was playing Roblox, and then I went to sleep, and then I woke up at the trains, and the men put me in the ambulance.'

The doctor confirmed that he'd been drugged with a sedative. They'd found a hypodermic spot on his thigh, and it was likely that Adrian never woke up through his ordeal.

'That's fine, Adrian. You did great, matey. Good lad.'

Chapter Eighteen

Chapter Eighteen

It was getting harder to keep a lid on things—stories leaked from the incident room every day, things that only the team had access to. Paranoia was rife. Nobody knew who was passing information to the press. The latest story gave vital information that Nash had wanted to keep closed. The tests proved that the woman found between Zoe Conley's legs was Catherine Howard, who was also the woman who lived in the bedsit adjacent to Paige Hunter. The sick bastard had taken her to Zoe's death scene to link her to Paige. It also showed that the top she was wearing belonged to Paige and had splashes of her blood on it. Internal Affairs was on the case and were monitoring every person going in and out of the incident room. Each member of the team had been interviewed and accused of selling intel to the press, which was denied by everybody. Morale was low. What Nash couldn't understand was that the person was selective. Some of the most newsworthy and spectacular information wasn't shared. Why would they take some details, enough to keep the press sniffing, and yet leave most of the really juicy stuff untouched?

The Florist Strikes Again. Girl Found in Bath of Coffee.

They released that but left the fact that she'd been dead for nearly a week. They didn't mention that her head had been removed and left on the side of the bath. Or the fact that they'd had a suspect in custody for three days. The leak was taking just enough—but just enough for what?

All devices and note-taking materials were banned from the incident room, and a log-in sheet had to be signed at entry and exit. Only senior management—Lewis and Nash—were allowed to take anything home.

'We need to throw the book at Max Jones, Boss. I know what I'd like to do to him,' PC Bowes said. 'And the person he's working with.'

***

'For the tape, the interview is resumed at 09:00 a.m.'

Seventy-two hours had passed, and they only had one more day to make a decision regarding Max.

Nash had already made up his mind. From the time they had him in custody, despite the killer escalating to record numbers in quick succession, there hadn't been any more deaths or people reported missing. The three women had been dead for days, and the two boys had been killed long before they were found. Max could have killed them all, but he was in custody when the boys from last night were staged on return to their bedrooms.

Either Max was working with an accomplice, or he was innocent, and the real killer was still out there.

'Tell us about the girl in Morecambe.'

'What, girl? I can't believe what's happening to me. Why is somebody doing this? It was nothing, just a one-night shag that didn't mean anything. I took her back to my camper. We had sex and said goodbye the next morning.'

'You had sex with Paige Hunter?'

'Paige Hunter? Paige is dead? No.'

There was no evidence of recent intercourse with the Hunter girl. It was information that hadn't come to light during the autopsy when swabs were taken. Nash was surprised by the admission.

However, this victim meant more to him than he was admitting. Jones was on the verge of tears, and Nash pushed a box of tissues in front of him.

'How? When? Oh, my God. This is my fault. I led him to her, didn't I?'

If this was an act, he was bloody good. But then, psychopaths are masters of deception. 'Paige Hunter's death is important to you. Why is that?'

'I had nothing to do with any of it.'

'So, why her? How did you meet her?'

'I didn't meet her. She was just a barista in a coffee shop that I blundered into.'

'But she matters enough to make you cry? That smacks of overkill.'

'She seemed nice. I only saw her once. We never even spoke. Not really. But I liked her. She had so much life, you know?'

'And you decided to take it from her?'

'No. That came out wrong. What I mean is that she was so alive and seemed happy. It was as if she had more life in her soul than the rest of us. She served me a coffee—once. And that was it. I never saw her again.'

'We'll come back to Miss Hunter. But when I said tell us about the girl in Morecambe, I meant Zoe Conley and, indeed, her friend Catherine Howard.'

'Catherine Howard?'

'That's right. Talk.'

'The name strikes me as ironic, that's all.'

'Ironic how?'

'I die a queen but would rather die the wife of Culpepper.'

Nash bristled. 'What the hell are you talking about, Jones? You want to be a queen? I have no idea what you're saying.'

'Catherine Howard was the fifth wife of Henry VIII. She was murdered too, and they were her dying words.'

'What?' Nash slammed his fist on the desk. 'From the way Zoe and Catherine were staged, we reckon you don't like lesbians, do you? They offend you.'

'No, I'm not homophobic at all. I'm perfectly happy in my own skin. What about you, Inspector?'

'I have no idea what you're babbling on about, and as far as I know, Henry VIII isn't responsible for these two girls being killed. This is a serious interview, and you're going to smart-mouth yourself into nothing but more trouble. Stick to the facts and just answer the questions. Otherwise, I'll take you back to your cell, and you can quote Wordsworth until your entitled, rich-boy heart's content.'

'Shakespeare, but near enough. Careful, Inspector. Your class discrimination is leaking into your interviewing technique.' Max grinned at him, and Nash wanted to smash his smug face in.

'Are you homophobic, Max?' Molly Brown asked.

'Sorry. Who? What? Why are you going on about gay stuff?'

'We have evidence to suggest that Catherine Howard and or Zoe Conley may have been lesbians. Does this bother you?'

'Not at all. I've had the company of lesbians more than once, if you get my drift. Only on a TV screen, though.'

'Trust me. You wouldn't appeal to many straight women, never mind gay ones,' she said, and Nash gave her a look.

'I am sorry, Mr Jones. For the sake of the tape, I retract that comment.'

'It always comes back to you, doesn't it?' Nash said. 'Every time, every lead, every piece of evidence and witness statement. They all bring us right back to you. What do you know about Zoe Conley and Catherine Howard?'

'Is Zoe dead too?'

'Body number seven as they were found in chronological order.'

Max looked shocked. It was as though his fingers transferred the touch of death. Everybody he came into contact with was being killed around him. It was terrifying, and, if Jones was a superstitious man, Nash could forgive him for thinking that he was inflicting people with his own terrible condition.

'Zoe was nice.'

'Nice?'

'Yeah, a good kid.'

'Your DNA was all over her like a snail trail.'

'She's the one I meant before. The one I had sex with.'

'And where was Catherine Howard while this was going on?'

'I don't know what you're talking about. I never met a Catherine.'

'We found your semen in Zoe's vaginal passage, and then she winds up dead?'

'I told you we had sex. I'm not denying that. What am I being questioned about here? A murder, or the fact that I had a one-night stand with a girl I met in a bar. Has that never happened to you, inspector—a girl in a bar?'

Nash imagined standing and wrapping his hands around Jones' neck. Suspects rarely got under his skin like this one.

Brown slid pictures of all three women across the desk, and Nash announced them for the tape.

Max looked shocked and turned his face away after a glance. 'This is sick. The guy wants locking up in a straitjacket. A beach scene? It's horrible.'

'Actually, I think it was a dig at your camping. Keep talking.' Nash noticed that he looked again and touched the photo of Paige in the bath of coffee and moved it away from the other two. 'He cut her head off?'

'Yes. How do you feel about that?'

'Why is the water black? Is that blood?'

'Coffee.'

'Coffee. Why?'

'You said you never went back to Paige's place of work, but that's not true, is it?' Nash had his mind set, but he wanted a last-ditch attempt to get Max to slip up. He had to be certain. His gambit was to fire quick questions at him, swapping between all the victims to see if his story changed.

Jones shook his head.

'Going back to Zoe Conley. We found a green cigarette lighter in your camper with her prints on it.'

'I took her back to my van. We had sex. She left.'

'And we found a screwed-up phone number on a scrap of paper at the scene where the bodies were found. That had your prints all over it. It turned out to be her phone number. How do you explain that?'

'I took her back to my van. We had sex. She gave me her number. She left.'

'You didn't like this girl? You wanted to screw her up and throw her away like her number?'

'Are you asking me or telling me? I liked Zoe, she was cool, but I didn't want to marry her. You've got nothing on me except a load of circumstantial evidence that I have explained.'

'Oh, there's more, Mr Jones.' Nash threw a phone in a clear evidence bag across the table and announced it for the tape. 'Is this your phone?'

'It looks like it, yes, but I'm sure they made several of that model.'

'And still, you're being smart. You look worried, Jones. Anything you want to confess?'

'No.'

'Passing item 43A to suspect. Photograph of Zoe Conley sleeping.' Jones gasped and touched the photo.

'This is an image extracted from your phone showing the seventh victim Zoe Conley asleep in what looks like a campervan bed. Did you take this photograph, Mr Jones?'

'Yes.'

'Make a habit of taking pictures of young women when they're vulnerable, do you?'

'No, I met her in a bar. I took her back to my van. We had sex. She left.'

'You can see how it looks bad for you, though.' Nash left the statement hanging, and Jones didn't respond.

'Isn't it true that you recently called a potential client, quote, a "fake fascist faggot?" Unquote'

'No. Never. That's a lie. I called him a fake fascist fanny, but only because it was three words that began with F. I could just as easily have called him a crusty, cock-sucking cu—could we stop now?'

'Here are three words for you, Jones. How does bang-to-rights sound?'

Max had his head in his hands. He was shaking and looked pale. 'Are you okay? You look unwell.'

'No, I'm fine. A touch of nausea, that's all. It'll pass in a minute.'

'Are you okay to continue?'

'Yes.'

They went back to Paige.

'You say you never saw Paige again, but you did go back looking for her, didn't you? Did you find her? This girl very much your junior.'

'No. Like I said, I never saw her again. But I did go back to the coffee shop.'

'Really? Why was that?' Max blushed, and to an old man like Nash, it made him seem vulnerable.

'I told you. I liked her. Yes, she was younger than me, but does that really matter? It was only ten years. While I was there, I listened to her talking to the pensioners. No, not like that. I'm not a bloody stalker before you start. She was great with them, you know? I wanted to help her. I thought about offering her a job with training.'

'Isn't that, in itself, a bit creepy? A psychologist would call that grooming.'

'No, you're twisting it all out of shape. It was a good thing. I genuinely wanted her to make something of herself. I volunteer at a youth group to help young people find direction in their lives. I saw something good in Paige and wanted to give her a start.'

'So that she'd sleep with you?'

'No. I mean, I fancied her. And I wanted to sleep with her, but it wasn't grooming. If she didn't want to go for a drink with me, that would have been fine, and my job offer would still have been there. I'd have got to know her first. Natural, you know. Look, it was nothing. Just an idea I had, and then I went back to ask her out for a drink, and she wasn't there.'

'We have some witnesses that put you back in the café on the eighteenth. One of them said you stole a badge from behind the counter. And the assistant on that afternoon said you were shifty and acting strange. You made him uncomfortable. Why did you take her name badge?'

'I didn't.'

'But you were seen taking it.'

'No, the stupid old cow's lying. She looked half-blind anyway.'

'I didn't say who saw you.'

'You didn't have to. There was only a load of old people in there. I didn't steal anything.'

Nash slid the name badge in an evidence bag across the table.

'Guess where we found this, Max?'

'I don't know.'

'It was in your van.'

'Okay, so I admit I took it, but I don't know why.'

'Why did you lie?'

'Wouldn't you, in my situation? You've made me feel as guilty as hell, even though I haven't done anything.'

'Fair point.'

An hour later and every murder had been laid out in front of him. The three murders prior to his arrest, as well as Henry Watson, Ryan Beck, the dog owner, the three young women in Morecambe and the two boys. Ten people were dead, and Nash was at a crossroads.

'We need some answers, Max.'

'I've told you everything I know.'

'So let's go through some stuff. We found dog hair at the scenes of all three girls and both boys. The hair matches the dog hair in your house. How do you explain that?'

'It must be from Mia. But she was only in my house for one night. He must have been fast and got in while I took Mia to Jon's because I vacuumed when I got home. I have no idea how it got to the murder scenes.' Nash could see that Max was weary of the questions. Nash had gone in on him hard over the last hour and let him think that there was no doubt in the police's mind that he killed ten people.

'You have the dog tag from Ryan Beck, who was beaten to death. And a name tag from the bit of stuff you took a shine to. Do you know what we call that?'

'Messed up?'

'No, we call it taking trophies. How many other trophies do you have?'

'None.'

They put another evidence bag on the table. It contained a silver locket.

'That belonged to Chelsea Green. Are you saying it was in the bottom of your wardrobe for two years?'

'No.'

'Well, how did it get there?'

'Get where?'

'In your wardrobe.'

'He must have put it there when he collected the dog hair.'

'We have a problem with that because you've already told us that when you got back that day, you said that nothing had been disturbed in the bedroom.'

'It must have been when they broke in and stole my laptop, then. They put the locket in my wardrobe to frame me and stole my stuff, again to frame me.'

'And you never saw the locket there.'

'When I go in my closet, Inspector, I keep my eyes at suit level. Where are your eyes when you're in the closet?'

Nash sat up straighter, and Renshaw's head came up to see why Nash had reacted.

'One chance to change your answer before I throw the book at you, Jones.'

'Go on, what have you got? It's obviously something big. I'm going down anyway, so you might as well hit me with the lot. I can understand why criminals confess to things they haven't done.'

Nash slammed the last evidence bag across the desk at him. This time he did it in anger.

'What is it?'

'Just a pair of red lace underwear belonging to Catherine Howard. Are you sure you never met her?'

'Never. Not that I'm aware of.'

'You replaced the carpet in your campervan the day you got it, didn't you?'

'No. There was no carpet. It has insulated flooring. It was stained in places. So I put a new piece of carpet down on top of it to make it look nice.'

'Guess where we found these?'

'Under the carpet?'

'Worse. They were under the insulated flooring.'

'That proves I didn't put them there. Don't you see? I'd just bought the van, had it an hour and went round the market for an offcut of carpet. I pulled up in the van, and my sister was in the drive, so I showed it to her. She stayed chatting—took every opportunity to look down her big bloody nose at me, as usual.' Nash could see that Max was sweating. A thin line of perspiration appeared on his forehead, and he wiped it away with his sleeve. He was talking too much. 'She's had a nose job, but it's still like an Alpine ski slope. Melissa was there when I put the carpet down. It only took me five minutes, and I sealed it with carpet glue. I never went near the floorboard, and if I had lifted it later, you'd be able to tell because of the glued edges of the piece of carpet.'

'All verifiable, of course?'

'Absolutely. I got the carpet from a bloke in a green flat cap, and he charged me twenty quid. That day, my sister wanted me to sign some papers that she needed for my mother's Power of Attorney. She'll tell you. And there was another witness, Linda Evans from the office, who came to drop some things off that she'd cleared from Henry's desk. I said I'd give them to his wife.'

'They've told us they were there. And Melissa says you argued.'

'We bantered.'

'She says that you threatened her.'

'Bullshit.'

Nash wrote some notes and stared hard at Jones.

'Hey. Here's something else you can check. When I went to pick up the van, the man said somebody else had been there before me. The man took it for a test drive and said they definitely wanted it. They made arrangements to make payment and pick it up, but they never turned up. It must have been him.'

'And this can all be verified?'

'Yes, everything.'

Nash was sure. He'd been pretty sure for several days. Because some of the bodies turned up while Jones was in custody, the word in the station was that Jones had an accomplice—but Nash didn't believe that for a second.

Bronwyn Lewis took some convincing, but with the evidence in front of her, she was willing to go with his plan.

Lewis came into the interview room and introduced herself. The tape had been switched off, and Nash saw Jones take a double take at the recorder.

'Mr Jones, thank you for your cooperation in this investigation,' Bronwyn said.

'I didn't kill anybody.'

'Mr Jones. We'd like you to take a polygraph test. How would you feel about that?'

He didn't pause or take time to consider his options, and that only solidified Nash's belief that Maxwell Jones was innocent.

'No problem. Yes. Hell yes. Yes, please, even. I want to do it.'

'I must warn you that the results are inadmissible in court and won't be used in your trial. They have been the catalyst of doom in many cases. I've seen a lot of guilty men who've thought they could beat the test, Mr Jones, and if you fail this test, we will move heaven and earth to put you away. Do you still want to do it?'

'Yes.'

'You must rest. The conditions have to be right, and we don't want you saying that you were under duress from lack of sleep, do we? So I'll arrange it for eight hours' time,' Nash said.

'Rest, Mr Jones,' Lewis said.

Chapter Nineteen

Max was as nervous as hell, and the man attaching all kinds of wires to him didn't help. He wondered if being nervous would make him fail when he should pass. And then it led him to worry about doubting himself. Maybe that could also cause a failure.

'My name is Derek Tipp. Can you confirm that you are here to undertake a polygraph test of your own free will?'

'Yes, I am.'

'And nobody has coerced you or forced you to take it?'

'That's correct.'

'We will begin in a moment. Are you sure you want to go ahead?'

'Do I get a best of three?'

'Excuse me?'

'Sorry, I'm nervous. Will that affect the outcome?'

'All that is taken into consideration as it reads your body's responses. Do you want to go ahead with this polygraph test, Mr Jones?'

'Yes, please.'

Max felt his hands sweating and his heart beating to the rhythm of *In the Jailhouse Now.*

'Can you tell us your name, please?'

'Maxwell Jones.' He heard Tipp breathing and the mouse clicking as the laptop recorded his results. He hoped Maxwell Jones was still his name and that wasn't showing as a lie.

'Now, can you give us a false name?'

'Mickey Mouse. Hardly original, but there you go.'

'Just answer the questions, please, no embellishments.'

'What is your age?'

'Twenty-eight.'

'And a false age?'

'A hundred and fifty-three.'

'Did you murder William Armstrong?'

'No, I did not.'

'Did you have anything to do with the murder or disposal of Mr Armstrong?'

'No.'

'Were you present at either the murder or disposal of Mr Armstrong?'

'No.'

'Do you know anything about the murder or disposal of Mr Armstrong?'

'No.'

Derek Tipp went through every murder and asked the same questions. Max gave the same answers to each of them. He was aware of his results coming up on the laptop screen and heard their progression with the click of the mouse. Even he could tell that he had a greater emotional response to both Henry and Paige.

'How am I doing?'

'I can't discuss the test results with you, Mr Jones. Please just answer the questions, and if you interrupt the flow of the test, we will have to mark it as null and void.'

By the time the polygraph was finished, he felt sick with worry. He wished he hadn't said he'd do it. He didn't have to. If this was another nail in his coffin, he'd done it to himself. He imagined what Jane Pearson would have said and was almost certain that she wouldn't have allowed it. And then he heard another voice in his head. 'If you've nothing to hide, Barty, you tell the truth, and you tell it with conviction, boy.' It's exactly what Nanny Clare would have said, and it calmed him.

It was done, and he felt as though he'd run ten marathons. There was nothing he could do now. At least they'd done away with hanging. He felt sweaty and could smell the fear from his armpits. He'd managed to get through the test, and it wasn't until after it finished that he found he didn't have the strength to stand up and had to ask for a waste bin to vomit in. He'd ask for a shower when they took him back to his cell. And that was always fun because he had to have a guard with him at all times. He was given a tiny bottle of shampoo and body wash that they have in hotels and was watched in case he drank them. 'Mind,' he was told by a guard the first morning, 'All it'll do is give you the pukes and the shits. We wouldn't take you to the hospital for it.' He wasn't allowed to have a razor while he was in custody. That was something to work up to when he started his ten life sentences for crimes he didn't commit. The stubble was driving him mad.

He felt better after a shower and lay on his bed reading some rubbish about a Martian invasion in one of the donated books. PC Bowes came to his cell. He knew them all by name now. 'Come on, Jones. The governor wants you. Face to the wall and hands behind your back. You know the drill.' Max did as he was told, and Bowes put the handcuffs on his wrists.

'Not again. Haven't you lot had your pound of flesh for one day? You have to let me out tomorrow, don't you? Does that mean you're going to grill me all night until I crack?'

'You've been watching too much TV, mate. And anyway, it's not an interview this time.'

'What is it?'

'I don't know. They don't tell me anything. I just do as I'm told.'

He was taken to Bronwyn Lewis's office, and Bowes knocked on the door.

'Come in.'

'Jones, Ma'am.'

'Thank you, Bowes. You can take the cuffs off, and that will be all.'

'Are you sure, Ma'am?'

'Quite sure. Please take a seat, Mr Jones.' Bowes took off the cuffs, and Max realised that he'd been using the officer for balance. When Bowes moved away, so did the earth. Max was hit with a fit of vertigo that made the room spin, and he heard a noise in his head that made him cover his ears with his hands. It was like a discordant Jazz band playing the most grating arrangement in their repertoire. The tinnitus caused by the tumour pressing on his trigeminal nerve was getting worse. But thank God it only came in quick blasts.

Bowes rushed to grab him and helped him into the seat. Lewis gave him a moment before speaking. 'Do you need a doctor? Are you all right, Mr Jones?'

'No, I'm dying, but I guess I'm okay. Thanks for asking.'

'Please let us know if you require any assistance. And Bowes?'

'Yes, Ma'am?'

'This meeting never happened. Do you understand you were given this task on trust? This didn't happen.'

'Ma'am.'

Bowes left, and Lewis asked Max if he'd like a coffee. This wasn't unusual, but in the interview room, it was served warm and in Styrofoam cups. This time he was given a mug. There was no recording equipment, and this wasn't running like any other interview he'd had.

'I'm confused. What's happening? I don't think I like this.'

'Mr Nash will be joining us in a moment.'

'I've seen my share of nature programmes, and sharks smile like that. No offence.'

There was a tap at the door, and Nash came in. He neither sat on Lewis's side of the desk nor Max's, but he took a place at the end.

'Who are you, Switzerland?' Max said.

Lewis nodded at Max.

'Let me tell you about your test results first, Max, and then DCS Lewis wants to talk to you.'

Max had no idea what was going on. What he did know was that they had enough on him to put him away for a hundred and fifty years or more. Max felt that a murderer should serve a full human life sentence to death, and he estimated that it should be eighty years a person, not thirty. In fact, forget softie sentencing. He believed in the death penalty and would have no qualms about pulling the plug on the bad guys. This had to be a trick, but he couldn't work out what their game was.

'I've got the results of your polygraph here. I'm sure you're curious.' Nash was smiling, and Max didn't like that one bit.

'Go on. I'm equally sure that you're dying to tell me.'

'You passed every question. It's ninety-nine per cent certain that you're innocent on all counts.'

'Go me.' Max was still confused and didn't know where this was leading.

'However,' Nash said. 'That still leaves one per cent that says you might have killed at least ten people.'

'I didn't, but okay, I'm playing along. So what now?'

'You have two other aces up your sleeve.' Max badly wanted to make a smart remark but didn't. 'The first is that when the last five bodies were found and staged, you were locked up in here. Very few people knew that. Including, presumably, our killer. Of course, the guys on the task force are all saying you've got an accomplice.' Nash went quiet. 'But I don't believe that. You aren't the kind of bloke to share in any glory.'

'And?'

'And?'

'And the other ace—the other thing in my favour?'

'I believe it's not you.'

'Why?'

'Too much evidence against you. Cry for help? Wanting to be caught? Okay, but if that were the case, it's too sloppy—no nuance or subtlety. I've watched you for the last four days, and it's not your style. If it was you, you're a lone wolf, Jones. You wouldn't be working with somebody else. We know it's not you. However, it is somebody with an axe to grind against you.'

'You don't say. But thanks for the vote of confidence.'

'I'm not a fan, Mr Jones. I don't like you very much, and I have to ask one last time for the record. Did you kill ten people? What about the kids? Those two dead little boys. Did I tell you the bodies of Jamie Little and Gareth Wilson have been released? Adrian hasn't got over being abducted. That's the kind of trick you'd play, isn't it? It was victimless. Nobody got hurt, taking a kid from his bed who was back with his folks before he even woke up properly. Adrian is on sedatives. He's terrified to go to sleep in case he doesn't wake up in his bed. Two families are arranging funerals for their children this week. What about that Maxwell Jones?'

'It's terrible. I can't imagine anything worse. Not even my own death is anything compared to what those parents are going through. I feel so sorry for them.'

'With your condition, is this a retribution on the world kind of thing? Going out in a blaze of glory with a mass killing spree to remember you by?'

'Nice analogy, but no. I'm dying, and that means my time is limited, and if I've thought about it at all, pretty much the opposite of your picture is true. First and foremost, I want to enjoy what time I have left, and that's not by killing people.'

'Not even for the posthumous fame it would bring? You must admit, you like the attention.'

'No. Sorry to disappoint you, but it would be too messy, too much planning and too much like hard work. I don't like work, Inspector. I have things to do. People to see and say goodbye to in my own dispassionate way and new memories to make now that they're so damned important. I know I can be a dick, but I want to make people happy before I go.'

'It hasn't worked so far. I find you an obnoxious little toerag. The thought of having to spend any time with you makes me want to go back into my retirement—which bored me even more than you do.'

'That's enough, DCI Nash,' Lewis said, and Nash rubbed his eyes where the strain was showing. He looked as though he was about to say sorry, but Max didn't need to hear him humbled and wanted to give him a break, so he spoke again to fill the chasm.

'Okay. Hellfire. Don't pull any punches, will you? What do you mean about spending time together?' Max could hardly breathe. Was Nash saying they were going to let him go? He said he believed him, but what did that mean in real terms?

'DCS Lewis will take it from here, Jones.'

'Thank you, Nash.' She smiled, and Max didn't trust her. It was warm, and it went all the way up to her eyes and seemed sincere, but if there was one thing Max didn't trust, it was a powerful woman.

'Mr Jones. Do you care that there's a maniac in our town, killing innocent people?'

'What kind of dumb question is that? Of course, I do. I care even more now that I'm not the patsy on the receiving end of the maniac tag.'

'Don't get too complacent, Mr Jones. DCI Nash has persuaded me to ask for your help. I think it's the most stupid thing I've ever heard, and it could cost us all our careers if he's wrong. But we're going to let you out tonight.'

'I can go home? Without charge? I'm free?'

'That's right.'

'What are you waiting for? Get whatever I've got to sign, and let me out.'

'We need your help.'

'You said. What can I do, a donation to the Policeman's Ball? You got it. I'll give you a raffle prize for your next summer fete. Name your cruise. I'll buy the tickets. It's yours. But please let me get the hell out of here.'

'The killer doesn't know you're here.'

'No. You've already told me that.'

'We can use that to our advantage.'

'I already don't like this. How?'

'Against every fibre of my being and my better judgement, we'd like you to help us catch him, Mr Jones.'

'You know what, Ms Lewis? I was kind of getting to like my cell. I think I'll go back in there until I die. The décor's a bit vanilla, but hey-ho, with a nice print for the walls and maybe a bookcase, I'll be fine. Hell no. Are you mad? I'm not getting all tangled up with a crazed killer.'

'You already are, Mr Jones. Where do you think this is going to end? There's only one end-of-the-line target that I can see.'

'Me? You think he's going to kill me?'

'Don't you?' Max looked at Nash for backup, and he was grinning. Nash was enjoying his discomfort. 'Helping us catch this man before he gets to you could be your only chance.'

'Am I next?'

'Maybe, but probably not. He's having too much fun,' Nash said.

Max had seen the awful photographs. He didn't want to die like that. And he didn't want anybody else that he was close to being killed.

'What do you want me to do?'

Chapter Twenty

Jessica was sick of answering the door. And that was only when she was sure it wasn't the press. She despised them. They were devious and would do anything to get a picture inside her parents' house. When they couldn't, images of the family grief would do, or the garden shed through the window, though who would be interested in her father's potting she had no idea. They photographed the contents of her parent's dustbin, and one unscrupulous reporter came carrying an empty casserole dish to gain entry.

'You must want the world to hear your story,' the reporter said when she'd conned her way in.

'Would you like a cup of tea, dear? I'm just waiting for my daughter to come home with milk,' her mum had said to the reporter.

Jess had come back from the shop—they'd been drinking black tea for hours because it was preferable to trying to get through the reporters—and she couldn't stand it any longer and decided to run the gauntlet in a black hoodie pulled down over her face.

'Get out of my parents' house. Now. This is intrusion and harassment, and if you aren't out of this house in five seconds, I'm calling the police.'

The woman left, and Jess screamed down the path, 'Parasite,' to a strobe of camera flashes. Her parents were getting older now, and they were less able to cope with all this drama on top of their grief than younger parents might be. They had been GPs and waited for years until both careers were well established before having children. Since retirement, Jess said they were Those People that had no idea what to do with themselves. And she'd seen her mum's intellect dimming every day like a printer running out of ink. Losing Paige had changed them into old people overnight, and it seemed all her mum was good for was making tea and her dad drinking it.

Somebody else was coming to the door. A smart lady in her forties who made her look dowdy in her two-day-worn lounge wear. But smart or not, Jess was ready for her. The fact that they still had the audacity to bother them appalled her.

She knocked.

'Go away.'

'I'm not the press.'

'I don't care. Our lives are not for sale.'

The lady posted a piece of paper through the letterbox and waited. *Give me five minutes of your time. If you want me to go, I will, and I'll have done my duty and won't bother you again. I need you to listen. Yesterday morning you sat on Paige's bed. You held her crystal pendant and asked her to give you the answers. She has given me the evidence you need. Speak to Silas. Ask him about Paige's name badge. He has it.*

'Go away. I don't know anybody called Silas.'

'He was there when Paige was found.'

'There were only policemen, and I don't think any of them were called Silas.'

'My number's on the bottom. I know you're grieving. Call me if you want answers.'

'Who are you?'

'Amanda Keys.'

'If you aren't the press, are you the police?'

'No, but I can help you find Paige's murderer. I'll wait to hear from you.'

'You can piss off with the rest of the parasites.'

Jess saw Keys turn away in the frosted glass that made her look like one of the aliens out of *Close Encounters*. She opened the door, and the cameras outside the gate went wild.

She was right. Jess had been sitting on Paige's bed. She had spoken those exact words to her. Nobody could have known that. The curtains were closed, and it was between her and her sister.

'Wait. You'd better come in, but if this is a trick like the last one, I'll call the police.'

Amanda Keys followed her inside, and Jess showed her to one end of the sofa. Hilary went to make tea. 'Don't fuss, Mum,' Jess said, but she wanted her out of the way while she spoke to the woman. 'You make a start on dinner, and then I'll come and join you.'

'Does she know anything about Paige? Please don't shut me out, Jessica. I need to know everything too,' Mum said.

'I know you do, Mum, but let me deal with this. I promise I won't exclude you.' They waited for her to leave the room.

'My parents are fragile. I won't have them upset any more than they already are. They need to be left alone to grieve their daughter.'

'I know they're fragile, love. That's part of the reason why I'm here, but it wasn't something that I could write on a piece of paper and slip through the door.'

'I still don't know who you are. What do you want?'

'I'm a psychic, but please hear me out. I promise I can help you. I don't want anything. I just want to help.'

'This is preposterous. I think you'd better leave.' Jess stood up and spread her arms to indicate that the other woman should get up too.

'It's your dad, Jess. You need to be with him tonight.'

'Don't you come in here spouting your gibberish. How dare you.'

'You mustn't go home tonight, Jess. Your dad's going to have a heart attack, and you being here to help is the difference between him getting through it or not.'

Jess didn't shout at her. She was beyond that. Her anger felt as though it had risen from the tips of her toes and travelled through every nerve ending in her body. It was so strong that it took away her need to shout and curse. She spoke in a voice that she held in chains in case it broke free.

'Get out of this house.'

'Call me. I only mean well.'

She closed the front door behind the woman, and Hilary came along the hall with the tea tray. 'Oh, has she gone, love? What did she want? She had a lovely coat, didn't she? Cashmere. You don't see that so often these days. Quality.' Jess had the uncharitable thought that she got it from ripping off the elderly and the gullible. Thank God she was here to protect her parents.

'It's all right, Mum. It was nothing.'

Jess sat on the sofa and realised that she was shaking. There was no way she could hold a teacup, and over the last week, she was surprised she hadn't drowned in her mother's weak tea. She didn't even like tea that much but drank it for something to do.

'Is Dad upstairs?'

'No. He's in the study, I think. He's been reading a lot this week. He was trying to escape it all. I can't concentrate and end up reading the same line ten times before it sinks in. We all do it differently.' Hilary dabbed her eyes with a tissue.

'Back in a minute.'

Jess had the overwhelming urge to go and check on her dad. Colin was the fittest old man she knew. Damn that bloody woman for scaring her.

She knocked on the study door and went in.

'Hey, Dad. You okay?'

He'd been crying too. It was a house of total sadness. Where before it had been a house of memories, now grief lurked in every corner and clung to every dust node.

'I'm fine, darling. Just catching up on some reading, seeing as I can't get in my garden for the vultures outside. What about you?'

'Listen, will it be okay if I stay here tonight? I can't face the drive back to Barrow and don't want to sit at home by myself.'

'You may be all grown up and tell me off on a daily basis when you're mother hasn't beaten you to it, but you're still my little girl, Jess. This is still your home.' He was about to cry, and Jess knew he was thinking about his other little girl.

'Come on, Dad. Come with me to the kitchen, and we'll see how dinner's getting on.'

'What are we having?'

'Steak pie, mash and green beans.'

'Lovely. I'm starving. Fancy a game of chess afterwards? We haven't played for ages,' Colin said.

'You bet.'

With the psychic's stupid words in her head, Jess watched him throughout dinner. They were all subdued because there was still that empty seat at the table. But he seemed as healthy as usual. He had more pie and a glass of wine. He moaned about the investigation and then about the press and how his garden was suffering because of them being virtually camped on their doorstep. They were all cooped up, and it was getting to them.

'I just want to go for a walk on the cliffs. It's a lovely November evening, and we aren't going to get many more nights like this before it gets too cold.'

'You know what?' Hilary said. 'We haven't been out of this house since we lost her. Let's do it. Let's push past the scoundrels and go, and if they want to follow us, they're welcome. We'll see how we feel, and if we can face the sympathy, we'll even stop in Heysham for a drink before we come back.'

'No.' Jess said. The word was sharp. 'No, let's stay in. I don't want to go out tonight. Maybe tomorrow? Can we just stay in and have a game of chess and then watch *Strictly*? Please, Dad.' That bloody woman had turned Jess into a bag of nerves with her stupidity.

'Of course, we can, but we have to face the neighbours sometime. Chess and dancing it is, but nobody waltzes like your mum and me. Isn't that right, Hill? I might just get you up and show our Jessica what her old fogies are made of.' He winked at Hilary. Jess was hedging her bets and kicked herself for suggesting *Strictly* and giving her dad the idea of dancing. She wondered how long she could make a game of chess last. He couldn't go out walking. They must not dance. Cocoa and bed were what they needed, but most old people die in their sleep. Jess wasn't going to sleep a wink that night, listening for every sound.

This was ridiculous. It was the biggest load of bollocks she'd ever heard, and she was furious with Amanda Keys. But when somebody tells you your parent is going to die, tells you when, and gives you the means to stop it, she had no choice. She knew her dad was going to live to see the morning—but what if he didn't?

At half past ten, Colin stood up from the chessboard. They had played the best of three, one game each and a decider to Colin. He stretched his back and whistled as he went to the kitchen to get a glass of water to take to bed.

Jess was putting the pieces away when she heard the glass break. She ran to the kitchen in time to see her dad hanging onto the unit, clutching his chest. He fell to the floor before Jess got to him.

Hilary was already in bed, or at least in the bathroom, putting her face cream on. Jess had left her phone in the lounge where they'd been playing chess.

'Mum, ring an ambulance. Mother. Mum. Mother help.'

He fell on the floor, clutching his chest and moaning. He was awake, so needed a steady flow of oxygen. A brown paper bag.

Oh god.

Oh god.

A bread bag. It wasn't brown, and it wasn't paper, but it would have to do. Her dad was fourteen stone to her nine. She wrestled him into a sitting position while he moaned.

'Hang on, Dad. It's okay. Just hang on.' Jess was more frightened than she'd ever known, and the bloody bag had anti-suffocation holes, so wouldn't expand when her dad breathed in it.

'Mum.'

Hilary stood in the kitchen doorway and gasped. Her hand went to her mouth, and she had some green gunk over her face. Surely she didn't sleep in that stuff. 'Your phone, Mum. Where's your phone? Get mine from the lounge. It's on the arm of the chair.'

She sobbed, 'I'll go and find it. Is he all right?'

'Call for an ambulance. Now. Mum.'

Hilary went, and Jessica put her hand around the neck of the bag even though it was a useless prop.

'Dad, breathe into this. It'll help. The ambulance is coming.' She heard her mum's voice in the hall. 'Breathe in, Dad. And out. In. And out.'

Colin's eyes rolled into the back of his head until only the whites were showing. He'd lost consciousness.

Jess didn't have time to piss about being gentle. Her Dad was dying in front of her. She pulled him by the legs until he slid down the wall and lay prone on the floor. She winced when she heard his head hit the laminate, but it wasn't as bad as she'd expected.

She knelt beside him and rammed two fingers into his mouth, sweeping them over his tongue and pushing it down to check that his airway was clear. It was. She put her ear to his chest. There was no rise and fall. She held her cheek to his mouth and desperately wanted him to kiss her cheek the way he had a million times before. There was no breath and no kiss.

'Come on, Dad. Breathe, damn you.'

Nothing. Her Dad wasn't breathing. He was dead.

She put one hand on the back of his head and the other under his chin and tilted his neck back, pointing his chin forward to open his airway.

'Dad, people are coming to help you. You can't leave me now. We need you.'

Jess interlaced her fingers, felt the V of his sternum where his ribcage joined and moved to the soft area two fingers down. She put the heel of her hand into that hollow and knelt up straight so that her wrist, elbows and shoulders were in a straight line with her upper body directly over her arms. And then she pressed, with short, intense movements, as she filled his lungs with air.

She'd recently retaken her first aid certificate and remembered that you don't have to do respirations and all modern CPR requires is the compressions. She hoped modern CPR was as effective as the old-fashioned kind. It was thirty compressions to two respirations, but she used the respiration time to pause before the next thirty. She wasn't going to think about the song, but she heard herself singing, ah, ah, ah, ah, staying alive, staying alive, in her head, and if nothing else, it helped to calm her. It was tiring, and she knew she had to keep it up until the first responders brought a defibrillator. She didn't know if she had the stamina to keep going.

And then she saw her mum knitting her hands and crying in the doorway, and she knew that she did.

'Make a cup of tea, Mum,' she managed to rasp, and Hilary ran down the corridor for the want of something to do.

It felt like forever, but in reality, the ambulance arrived within five minutes. A lady in a green jumpsuit came in, waited for the pause and then put her hands where Jess's had been while the other paramedic set up the defibrillator.

'Good job. You might have just saved your father's life.

Jess slumped in a heap into her mother's arms and sobbed.

Mum was good for making tea—and for making everything better.

'He's back. We're going to get him into the ambulance, and we'll have him at the hospital in no time.'

'Thank God,' Hilary said.

Jess's mum went in the ambulance with them, and as only one person was allowed, Jess said she'd follow in her car. She'd rather have travelled with her dad because she was worried that he might have another attack and die on the way. Her mum would crumble and couldn't take any more grief. As she grabbed her coat, she realised that if grief was coming, he was going to get her, and she wasn't big enough to protect Hilary from that. As an afterthought, she picked up the piece of crumpled paper that Amanda Keys had put through the letterbox with her phone number on it.

'Poorly but stable,' the cardiologist said. That was what they always said. To Jess, poorly was having a second bowl of Tiramisu and making yourself feel sick—that was poorly. Her dad was in intensive care, and a tube was breathing for him. They'd put him into a temporary coma to give his body a rest, they said. Jess equated a coma with being one step away from death. Sitting up in bed and eating the disgusting hospital jelly was stable but poorly.

She just wanted her dad.

When he was settled, and there was nothing else they could do but sit, she excused herself and told Hilary she was going to get them a coffee.

She straightened out the paper and rang the number. She didn't know if she should blame this woman for what had happened to her dad. That was ridiculous, but it was as though by predicting it, she'd willed it to happen. Jess was furious. She didn't ask who she was talking to or give her name. She went straight in with the only part of this craziness that she had any interest in. Amanda Keys could play voodoo dolls all she liked, but not with Jess's family.

'Is he going to die?'

'No. He'll be fine.'

Jess hung up before the psychic could say any more.

Bitch.

Chapter
Twenty-One

Chapter
Twenty-one

'Go on. Tell me again what you want me to do.'

'This man is targeting you. Therefore it stands to reason that you either know him or you've had dealings with him that haven't worked in his favour. We need to get close to him, although he leaves enough clues—they all lead back to you. And he hasn't left a shred of evidence pointing at him. Obvious question. Who do you think it is?'

Max was tired. He'd been up half the night throwing up and couldn't decide if it was the meds killing him, the tumour, or the bogeyman. He'd spent the other half of the night thinking about everything he knew.

'Steve Hill.'

'Who the hell is Steve Hill?'

'My tenant's boyfriend. And, inspector, I swear I have no reason for this other than that he complained about the decorating not being done in the dining room. I've wracked my brains, and that's the best I've got.'

Nash scribbled on his pad. 'Okay, we'll look into it.'

'So I've gone from being the killer to being the top cop on the case. Do I get a badge and a gun?'

Max saw Lewis cover a smile, and for some reason, she enjoyed Max winding Nash up so easily.

'You do not,' Nash said. 'And it's no laughing matter. You'll be alongside me. Don't think you're off the hook, Jones. I'm going to be like the smell from your backside. I'm going to follow you everywhere you go.'

'And with such a beautiful and enticing metaphor. Do I have any choice in this?'

'Yes, you can wait for him to get bored of his games and kill you.'

'Eeny, meeny—that would be you Inspector—miny, moe. Okay, I'll do it, and I'll make my own badge out of a Ready Brek box and some sticky back plastic.'

Lewis interrupted their pissing competition. 'I warn you, it's dangerous. But as DCI Nash has said, you aren't in a great position, Mr Jones, but you will have all the protection of the law.'

'In real terms, what does that mean? As in, if some crazy lunatic comes flying at me in the shower, Norman Bates style, where are you r officers going to be?'

'We'll be right in the shower with you, Jones,' Nash said.

'There will be twenty-four-seven surveillance on your house, front and back. And if you wish, you can have an officer inside with you.'

'Can I have DI Brown for the shower scenes?'

'You will have whichever officer is assigned the duty,' Nash snarled.

'And I'm going to be working with Nash here, who always seems five seconds away from wanting to rip my head off. He won't be armed, will he? Or sitting next to my bed at night.'

'For God's sake. Must you be so childish all the time?'

'It is a bit of a default mechanism, Nasher. It's the way I'm wired.'

'The correct title is, Sir,' Nash said.

'No, Nasher. You don't have to call me sir all the time. Boss will do, and when it's just me and you, all cosy like, you can call me Maxwell.'

'You will address me as Sir at all times. Do you understand?'

'How about Doc, like in Bugs Bunny? Nah, what's up, Doc? It has a ring to it and suits you. It can be my special name for you.'

'You will do as you're told when you're told to do it, and it will be exactly as I say. Your smart mouth will get you and my officers killed, and I'm not prepared to risk good people to save your skinny neck.'

'See? I get the impression he doesn't like me, Missus Lewis. We aren't a good fit. He can't accept our working relationship. Can I have somebody younger and maybe with better legs? He doesn't want this.'

'On the contrary,' Chief Superintendent Lewis said, 'it was DCI Nash's idea to bring you in. And, for the record, I'm against it. But, you're our best hope of catching this man. So you're going to have to find a way to work together.'

'Help me, Obi-Wan Kenobi. You're my only hope. Okay, but as long as I can be the little spoon.'

'I've had enough of this,' Nash said.

'Serious question. Where will I be staying? Do I get a safehouse?'

'No, you'll be in your own house. You'll go about your business exactly as you would under normal circumstances. It's apparent that the killer doesn't realise you've been with us for the last four days. He probably assumes you've been away in your van, which is a good smoke screen for us and could work to our advantage. We have already fitted all of your vehicles with a tracker. Your house is installed with hidden cameras and audio equipment. Please bear that in mind.'

'Got it. No shagging on the dining room table.'

'We'd also like you to wear a bracelet monitor with audio and tracker. It will look like an unobtrusive watch.'

Max said, 'You don't know me, do you? Do I look as if I do unobtrusive?'

'As it happens, yes. We've studied your wardrobe, and the watch is modelled on your normal dress watch.'

'Ah, but can it tell the time?'

'Should you be in a situation where you wouldn't ordinarily wear it, we've put the same tech into your phone. Do not rely on this alone, as it's the first thing you'll be separated from if you're apprehended. This person likes to play, and when it comes to you, he will have his ultimate toy. The initial jump might be fast, but after taking you, he'll want to toy with you.' Nash seemed to take pleasure from this.

'I realised straight off that you're dangling me as bait, but Jesus, I didn't expect it to be so blatant.'

'We have studied your movements prior to your arrest from CCTV, and on most occasions, you wear a watch. Details are everything, and this won't seem odd to the killer. He's been watching you. He knows your movements and your habits. Don't do anything out of the norm. And this is important. I mean anything. This guy isn't stupid, and he's going to notice anything unusual.'

'Presumably, he knows about my diagnosis and that I'm going to get very sick very soon, and then I'm going to die. I think he'll expect things out of the norm, as you put it.'

'We think your illness and the fact that you aren't going to live long is what trigged all this.'

'It's great to talk to people that can mention my illness without bawling or squeezing out every trite epitaph written before I'm even dead. You're told you're dying, and suddenly everybody wants to spout the verses from sympathy cards and inspirational verses at you. *Live each moment as if it's your last, and dance like nobody's watching.* As you can see, guys, that's working out very well for me. I'm suspected of being a sodding serial killer. But there's a flaw in your thinking because the first three people were killed before I even received my prognosis.'

'True,' Nash said, 'but you already had the diagnosis. Are we right in thinking you were told the outcome of your tests three weeks before your appointment on the second of September?'

'Yes. Pretty much. The doctors didn't want to put a date on it, but they more or less said I was dog meat.'

'So the last appointment was just for confirmation, and you were given a more realistic timeline?'

'Exactly. But I didn't tell many people. Mel knew I was ill, and Jon and Henry. That's about it.'

'And did you ask them to keep it confidential?'

'Not exactly, but they aren't the type of people to take an ad out in the paper. Oh, hang on. Yes, actually, Mel is. In fact, she probably stopped the postman to tell him that her beloved brother was going to croak. Good point.'

'With the exception of Henry Watson, everybody that knows is a current suspect. And that's exactly what happened. Melissa broadcast it in the bakery, according to Mrs Thomas, the owner. Several people we interviewed in your sister's social sphere knew prior to the confirmation.'

'That's my sister. All mouth and no knickers. I have one last question.'

'Go on.' If Nash was expecting a smart remark, he'd have been surprised. Max just wanted to get out of here now.

'If I'm being watched and have to be a Normal Norman, how are you going to fit into this? Won't we be seen getting together for our cosy, candlelit dinners?'

'Up to now, he doesn't know where you've been for the last half a week. We're blowing it out there. We'll be issuing a press report that a man has been arrested and released on tag pending further investigation. That man will have to report to the station, and it won't be unreasonable for us to be seen together out of the office for evidence-gathering and further questioning. '

'What? I've got to be cast in the role of a murdering social pariah and have one of those ankle things, as well?'

'Just in the short term. A few months, that's all.' Nash grinned.

'Touché, DCI Nash. That is a very admirable point to you, I believe. You're getting the hang of this.'

***

At home, he touched things as though he'd been away for a year. He touched his bookcase in the hall and brushed his hand over some of the books. He'd never been in jail before, and it was a big deal to be free. It had only been four days, but it felt like four years. He called for Dexter, but the cat didn't come. When he went into the kitchen, he saw that his bowls had been washed and put on the draining board. Max unlocked the back door and called for his cat. Panic set in, and he called again. It felt as though Dex was the only friend he had in the world. As he called the cat, he heard the front door closing and somebody in the hall. He swore and thought about hiding in the downstairs toilet.

He looked for a weapon. The nearest thing to hand was an eight-page junk mail supplement, and he rolled it up and brandished it in front of him like a foil.

His relief was palpable when he saw it was only Hayley Mooney, his tenant from the cottage he owned across the road. She held a casserole dish wrapped in a tea towel.

'Hayley. Hi. What are you doing here? Can I help you?'

'Hi, Max. I didn't know you were home. I hope you don't mind. I used the spare key you gave me for emergencies. Oh, heck, this is awkward. I've got Dexter, by the way. He's fine. I'll bring him over now.' She held out the dish. 'This is for you. We didn't know if you'd be back home today, but I've called around every day on the off chance. Steve and I thought you might be hungry. It's still warm, but two minutes in the microwave will see it right.'

'Right. Thank you. That's very kind.' They made an awkward exchange as she handed over the food, and he remembered handing her boyfriend, Steve, to Nash on a plate. What the Hell? People brought hot food and cakes when somebody died. He wondered how many times she'd been in the house that he didn't know about, and then there was Steve too. Cufflinks, he thought. Hayley looked at him in confusion.

When they stared at each other too long for it to be bearable, Hayley was the first to break the silence. 'It's Irish stew. Nanna's recipe, so it should be good. She's gone now, but the stew lives on.'

'Crikey, how long ago did she make it?'

'No. I made it, but it's handed down through the generations.' Max could tell she was on the point of babbling as the tension between them rose. 'Very thick gravy and a whole bulb of garlic. The police have been up here a lot, going through your stuff. They brought lots of things out of the house—your computer and whatnot. A woman came, and she said she was taking Dexter to a rescue centre until you came home. So I said I'd take him.'

'That's very kind. I hope he's been no trouble.'

'No trouble at all. He misses you, though, I can tell.'

This woman was the cat whisperer. He wondered if he smelled. Once they told him he could go, he just needed to get out of that place and hadn't asked for a shower, preferring the privacy of his own. It used to be private, but now he wasn't so sure.

The place looked bugged.

It even smelt bugged.

'The food smells delicious. Thank you.' The lid was on the small cast iron casserole dish, and Max couldn't smell anything apart from all the little pieces of recording equipment that he knew were behind every curtain pleat and even hidden in the toilet brush holder. Paranoia was winning over common sense. He wasn't even near the bathroom. He was holding his impatience. The self-induced Tourettes was threatening again. He wanted to scream at her to go but had to be polite, they were lovely people, and he'd hate to offend them. But one of them could potentially be the killer. 'Hayley, this is a little bit delicate, but would you mind leaving your key, please? You know—strangers. I mean recent events and what have you. I hope you understand. I don't mean to be rude.'

'Of course. And I'll go and get Dexter, now. He'll be happy to see Daddy.' She put her key on the corner of the counter, which left Max holding the dish.

'I've got some important things to take care of in the office.' The same office that didn't have a computer to do important things in, but he couldn't face her again. 'Can you leave the front door open while you're gone and just put him in the kitchen, please? Give the door a good slam afterwards. And Hayley?'

'Yes?'

'Thank you. You're a real sweetheart.' He was going to ask her to force the cat in through the kitchen cat flap so that she wouldn't have to come back in, but that was a bit much, even for him.

She blushed and tucked her chin into her chest to avoid looking at him. 'I said to Steve that you won't have done anything wrong. Those children and everything. Little boys, some of them, and all those girls. Not you. It couldn't be you.' Max had the awful urge to rush at her with his hands over his head, moaning like a Scooby-do monster, and the thought almost made him laugh out loud. He suppressed it and choked.

'No. Not me. I didn't do anything. You'd think I was Paedo Paddy from Pennington.'

'Max, one day, that inappropriate sense of humour is going to get you into trouble and then—bang—it'll be too late. I'll go get your cat now.'

He wondered what she meant. That sounded like a threat. He was jumping at shadows. These people were his friends. He was going to quiz her on it, but she turned her back and flounced out in a haze of floral perfume that Max had only just noticed.

In the office, he picked things up and put them down again, just to make his lie a truth as if she could see him through walls, a road and two garden hedges.

He had a spare flat in Barrow and wondered if he should be there instead. The area was more populated than here, but it had that air of impersonal couldn't-give-a-shit-about-anybody flat living. It was more of a bedsit, really, but this was his home in Ulverston.

He owned the whole house in Barrow but kept the top floor of the last house on the street for himself. The other five flats in the house were filled with the no-hopers, the no-chancers and the useless. There was no lift, and he said those eighty stairs were his best friend. He liked being higher than the trees and looking down on Wetherspoons across the road. At Christmas, the council put a tree at the bottom of the pedestrianised part of the high street, and it was just across the road. He loved looking at the tree and all the lights and decorations. It was as though they went to all that effort just for him.

Most of the time, he lived here in the Ulverston house. The loneliness made him feel like Heathcliff, and he loved the clean air and the isolation. It felt like the end of the world. You got to the King's Arms—the big Kings, not to be confused with the little Kings—and walked up the hill until all the houses, all the people, and all the life had petered out, and then you kept walking up the fell road, which was a killer feat of endurance, for another mile. Max owned the big house on the right. It was built out of old stone for an old house and held no history for him but history for some family somewhere.

He'd bought it from a school teacher who'd terrorised the children at Ulverston Victoria High School. His days of screaming and bawling at frightened children and whacking canes around were over, and he was old. He'd mouldered away in the big house until he couldn't look after himself anymore. Max bought it for a song and didn't feel guilty about knocking the price down to rock bottom—the owner hadn't been very kind to children, apparently. And then he'd died years ago in a nursing home.

Max had bought the cottage, too. It was a sweet little two-in-one deal. Maybe the whole thing was born of nostalgia for that little old stone shack. He remembered it when he left school and had a fondness for it. Twenty years ago, while the boys were all still living at home with their mammies, Fiona, Jonathan's sister, had struck out for independence pretty much as soon as she left school. She got a job at Ashley's Accessories, a factory making plug sockets, and had just enough money left at the end of the week to pay her rent and bills. She rented that little cottage. It didn't last long, only a year or so, and then she got herself into trouble and went home to her mum, who didn't know the half of it.

The cottage was upside down in that the bedrooms and bathroom were downstairs, and the living room and kitchen were at ground level. It was built into the hill and had a ramshackle green porch over the front door where Fiona always seemed to have washing hanging on a wooden clothes horse. The first thing to greet you when you knocked on the door was Fiona's knickers. And yes, he had to admit that he had pocketed a pair once for his own dirty deeds.

Fi did this weird thing—she grew up. Man, did that scrawny kid grow up. She bought a racer and cycled to work every day. She had some tiny Jeans that she'd long grown out of, but she cut them down to make the world's smallest shorts. Her arse fell out of them at either side, and when she rode that bike standing forward over the bars to get up Soutergate Hill, Max wanted to do things that he never expected to do to his best friend's sister.

Jon's little sister had her own place, and that was an opportunity not to be missed. Jon, Bobby and Max partied there a few times, but old man Collins lived across the road and went ballistic if he heard so much as a mouse squeak. It killed the fun. And then Max partied there a few times on his own. Fi had muscles where he didn't know a girl could have muscles. Riding that bike made her one hell of a ride. But she was serious. She was all about overtime and making her rent, and all Max wanted was to have fun. She got pregnant. Max asked if the baby was his, and she said no. And that was that. Max had already moved on several times before Fi had a quiet abortion and moved back home to Mummy. He grinned as he remembered those times in that cottage. He thought he might have gone from Fi to one of her school friends, but he couldn't even remember that one's name. The girls fell out for a while, and he remembered a lot of high-pitched yelling. Way too heavy and bitchy for Max. He was out of there.

It wasn't like that now. The cottage had a new extension on an extension by an extension behind an extension before he bought it. You could still see the shell of what it had been, but it was insulated and had solar panels and was very different from its humble origins.

Hayley reminded him a bit of Fiona back in those days. She had long brown hair and a sweet smile. He flirted in the early days and even tried a direct come-on but was firmly put back in his box before he even got the lid open. Hayley and Steve were a blended family, and Steve wasn't there all the time. She'd been in the cottage for over three years now, and Max had received the message. He looked out for her, though. It was isolated up there, and she was alone sometimes with two young kids. Isla and William were great, and Max liked talking to them.

They were at the age where William wanted to be an astronaut and Isla a great ballerina. Max said he wanted to be a rock star and would do some singing with his air guitar while the kids laughed and covered their ears. Steve's kids, Theo and Ellis, came to stay every other weekend, and Max loved sitting in his living room and hearing all the noise and laughter from the cottage across the road. It was a happy home, and they were some of the nicest people Max had ever known. Max couldn't understand why he'd blamed Steve so readily to Nash. Now he even wondered if Hayley could have something to do with it too. He didn't know what was wrong with him.

But lovely though they were, today he couldn't face anybody, and the intrusion into his home had hit him like a bullet. He'd make it up to her with a bottle of wine one night. He couldn't wait for the front door to shut again. He realised he missed Dexter a lot more than the cat probably missed him. He just wanted to cuddle him. He heard the door close and then her checking it to make sure it was shut properly, and he forced himself to wait a minute before opening the office door.

Max was in for a serious telling-off. Dex wasn't proud enough not to twine between his legs until his dad picked him up and made a huge fuss of him, but he made it clear that Max's recent behaviour was unacceptable.

Max was starving. Dexter, on the other hand, turned his nose up at the bowl of Nanna's Irish Stew that Max put down for him.

He took the lid off the dish, and it smelt delicious, but if the cat turned his nose up at it, maybe it was poisoned. Max was so hungry that he decided it didn't matter. He was a dying man. He was supposed to be living each day in the moment and all that shite. In custody, he'd had as much toast and as many ready meals as he liked, but at three times a day, you can only eat so many frozen individual fish pies.

The house was left in a mess from the police being in and out, and every flat surface was black with fingerprint dusting powder. He put the dish in the microwave and hunted his office for a pen and paper. The damned things bred when he didn't want one, and he had pens all over the place. When he needed one, he had to wade through his desk drawer for—socks. What were they doing there? Post-it notes that would do to write a note on. There were paper clips, cigarettes and a lighter. He hadn't smoked for six years. And at the bottom of the drawer, an old Playboy, very old. It showed a black-haired girl with black boots sitting in a cocktail glass—classy. He found a pen.

If I turn up dead, I've been poisoned by Nanna's Irish Stew, kindly donated by Hayley Mooney. I suspect her Boyfriend, Steve Hill. I'm a mess. I suspect everybody. These are lovely people. I'm a bad man. Please look after the Playboy Magazine in my top drawer. It's iconic. It will be worth something in a few years.

Maxwell Edward Bartholomew Tyler Jones

He looked at the bookcases in the office. He had a lot of books and a lot of bookcases. He wondered which one the police would shake out first and went for Winnie-the-Pooh.

The microwave pinged, and he decided he was being ridiculous. They were his friends, or was he just their landlord and, therefore, dispensable? He took the note out of Winnie, scrunched it up, and threw it in the bin. He was being ridiculous. Of course his tenants weren't psycho killers, not even with a *Qu'est-ce que c'est?*

As he straightened, the world span in a fast vortex of dizziness. Geometric floaters the size of spaceships appeared across his vision, and he had to hold on to the counter to stay upright. He watched the shapes dance, and they looked as if they were made of chrome. It was like being drunk when the room went around, and as one shape appeared, he had to follow it across his field of vision otherwise, he'd have thrown up. He couldn't keep it up for long, and despite taking deep breaths—in through his nose, out through his mouth, he had to stumble across the kitchen to the sink to vomit. He was glad there was no week-old washing up in it, and that was something else he had Hayley to thank for. Max did domestic chores once a day. He saw little point in doing them more than that as they only needed to be done again the following day.

He squirted a sheen of disinfectant spray and washed the sink out. It was coming—he—death. He was coming to get him.

A couple of hours after being ill, he was starving. Nanna's stew should have been the best he'd ever tasted. He heated it in the microwave, and the smell permeated throughout the room. Max brought the spoon up to his lips but couldn't force himself to open his mouth. The thought that Nanna's stew might be poisoned prevailed, and with a huge and regretful sigh, he opened the pedal bin lid and scraped the

whole delicious-looking lot into it. He could have sworn the cat was
laughing at him.

Chapter Twenty-two

'We should talk.'

'Of course. Shall I come to you?'

Jessica sounded repulsed. 'No. Text me your address, please, and I'll come to you.'

With the arrangements made, she pulled up outside Amanda Key's house. There were no skulls or broomsticks. That was a good start. Amanda met her at the door with a warm smile that Jess had no intention of reciprocating. 'Let's just get this shit show over with, shall we? How did you know my dad was going to have a heart attack?'

'Are you going to shout at me on the doorstep, or would you rather come inside and do it?' The smile was still there, and in other circumstances, it would appear genuine and interested.

Amanda led them to a bright kitchen that was as welcoming as its host. There were no black and purple throws used as wall hangings and no crystal balls in the middle of the dining room table or burning incense.

'Shall we sit, and I'll answer all your questions.' Amanda brought a teapot and cups over on a tray. She laughed.

'What's so funny?' Jess wasn't amused, even if her hostess was.

'I'm sorry. I was just given your last thought. My guide told me you'd rather throw the chair at my head than sit in this crazy house. Do I need a protective helmet?'

Jess almost laughed with her but stopped as the sound formed on her lips. That was exactly what she'd thought, word for word. Not close enough, not in the ballpark to take a punt on. She thought that exact phrase and needed to sit down. She accepted the cup of tea with gratitude.

'How do you do it? Is it a trick?'

'No, love. No tricks. Just something that's been around as long as time. We all have these abilities and a spirit guide when we're born, and most of us lose them as we get past the age of five. Our guides see us through early life, and then when the time's right and we don't need their help anymore, they leave us to help somebody else. Occasionally, as in my case, we retain the ability and carry it through our lives. I don't know why I was chosen.'

Jess's expression must have shown her opinion, or maybe the witch read her mind again—but either way, what she picked up wasn't very pleasant. 'Talk to me about my dad, specifically. How did you know? What did you do to him? Why?'

'First, let's get one thing straight, or I'll show you out with no hard feelings on my part, and that will be the end of it. I did not make your dad ill.'

'How could you possibly know he was going to be, then?'

'Sven, my spirit guide told me.'

'Sven? Okay, stop right there. I've had enough. If you're going to insult my intelligence, I'm out of here. Thank you for the tea.' She stood up and collected her bag.

'I know you've put your phone on to record, and it's in your bag under a pink scarf. You were worried that the sound wouldn't carry through.'

Jess sat down.

'This morning, you threw your kitchen clock out because it wasn't keeping good time. And yes, I know you live on Rapier Street. I could have taken some of that from social media, I suppose. So how about this? You've been thinking of coming out of the shipyard and have been offered a job in marketing in Chester. You haven't spoken to anybody about it because you feel that the timing couldn't be worse—because of your sister.'

Jess took a gulp of the tea, and it was too strong and still too hot.

'What do you know about my sister?'

'That's why you're here, love.'

'Go on.'

'I realised that I had to make you believe me and only had a very short window of opportunity to do that before you wrote me off as a quack or a charlatan. Believe me. I've had both. You build a thick skin fast in my job.'

'I'm listening. What do you know about my sister?'

'I'm so sorry for your loss, and I know she was murdered.'

'It was in the papers.'

'I've just been shown the bathroom and how she was left. I can describe it if you'd like me to, but I'd prefer to spare you from going through it again. I'm sure it haunts you. I know she was killed else-where and brought home to be found. She wasn't breathing when she was put in the bath. I've been told to tell you that it was quick in the end.'

'You've just been shown? I suppose Sven showed you that.'

'Yes.'

'Are you sure it wasn't Casper? Is Sven a doctor as well now, then? He seems to know a lot.'

'Ask me anything you like, and I'll do my best for you. It might be more productive for both of us if we can lower the aggressive stance you're taking, but as long as you're here and listening, I don't care how we get it done. If that's how you need to be before we talk properly, I understand. I've just seen how she was left, and I'm struggling to be professional.'

'Yes, awful the way he pushed her face underwater like that.'

Amanda sat back and appraised the other woman. 'I don't want to say it, love, but we both know her face wasn't submerged in the bath of coffee.'

Jess gasped. Nobody knew the details. And then she cried. 'The bastard cut my sister's head off and left it on the corner of the bath.'

'I know, love. It's horrible. Just to give you further proof, she had long hair, and it was loose and flowing into the bath. Sven wants you to know her hair was tied up when she was killed. It was in a messy bun, and the killer took a plain black scrunchie.'

'I haven't been told that. If that's the truth, the police haven't released it to me. Do you have a source there?'

'The police won't have realised. Do you need a moment to process?'

Jess shook her head and managed a weak smile. If this woman was full of crap, she was damned good at it. She was good, Jess had to give her that, but logic and reason were dominant traits in her mind and personality. They won over fancy and mysticism every time. However, Jess couldn't argue with the facts of what she was saying. Jess felt that she was a fact-over-fate kind of person—but in this instance, the fact was that Amanda was telling her things she couldn't know. 'I still don't get it. If you're as straight as you say you are, why won't the police let you work with them? Do you know Conrad Snow? He does what you do, and I saw a programme on the TV about him. He lives in Cumbria now, but he said he'd worked with the police when he lived in London.'

'I don't know why they won't let me help them. Maybe the police in big inner-city forces are more progressive than up here. And yes, I know Conrad. We've worked together a couple of times. He's highly respected.'

'I'm sorry. I didn't mean to have a go at you. I'm finding it hard to take all of this in. I used to have a sister, and now she's dead, and I'm talking to a psychic. It's all new to me.'

Amanda patted her hand, 'Do you want me to go on?'

'Yes, please. I'm confused and struggling, but I'm intrigued by what you have to say, too.'

'I'm being shown another image. The killer is walking through the bedroom. Pink, there's a lot of pinks. He opens a drawer and takes out a square pink gift box. He takes the lid off. Inside there's a butterfly broach with coloured jewels. It's costume jewellery, and there's no real value to it. He—I'm assuming it's a man, but I can only see the hand. I'm looking through his eyes, and he's wearing black gloves—he returns the lid and puts the box in his pocket. Sven wants you to know that the killer has the box and the broach.'

Jess covered her mouth with her hand and let out a sound that was somewhere between a gasp and a moan.

'I didn't know it was missing. Yes, the butterfly broach. Mum and Dad bought it for her as a stocking filler a few years ago. I had an identical one, but I broke the clasp on a night out and lost it soon after.

It's a standing joke that I only get cheap jewellery because I either break or lose any good stuff. Who killed her?'

'I wish I could tell you. It doesn't work like that.'

Jess had been thawing, but she got angry again. 'If you can look through his eyes, why can't you look in a mirror? You can tell me about pink bedrooms and shit butterflies, but when it comes to the stuff that matters, like a name or even an idea of what he looks like, good old Sven is as silent as a Victorian ghoul spewing ectoplasm like a snow machine.'

'Let me try to explain. Sometimes we get different things in different orders. It can be a name. I hear information that's spoken and see images. Sometimes it can be a jumble of images and noises, smells and other attacks on the senses that I have to try to decipher. Sometimes, we get cryptic fragments, and the information can be wrong. I don't know why Sven can get some information but can't cut straight to the chase. All I can do is take what I'm given and try to make it work.'

'Not an exact science, then? Have you thought of introducing Sven to Wikipedia?'

'I'm trying to get you on side. So I don't want to go into Sven's age. This time what he's got is a walk-through. So he's taking me through the house—sorry flat, and I'm seeing it through the killer's eyes.'

Jess understood what Amanda was saying and was animated. 'The mirror. you're rummaging through Paige's dressing table drawer, and there's a mirror above it.'

'He had his head down the whole time.'

'You must be able to see something.'

'Nothing helpful. The one glance I had in the mirror only showed a black ski mask. There's no hair visible, no facial features. He's wearing black gloves. They don't have a label, no skin showing, and no visible tattoos, I'm afraid. It's not like the movies. I'm sorry. He seems to be quite small, below average height, I think, but he's crouched, so I can't even be sure about that.'

'If you want me to believe you, can you give me anything? Anything else at all that's something I can go to the police with. You need credence. And speaking of which, if you're so good, why aren't you working with the police on this? Sorry, but it is a point.'

'No offence taken. Your first question. I can get more. I know I can. I've had flickering images at night, and we can go through them together and see what's relevant. And for your second point, the police won't have anything to do with me. They are aware of my work. They think I'm a charlatan and in this for the fame. I don't take any payments, so they can't accuse me of that. I won't lie to you. I'm here to help, and that means being honest. If I can't give you anything more than the bits and pieces I'm getting, it's been a waste of both of our time—but surely it's worth a try, isn't it?'

'If it helps me get this bastard put away for my Paige, then I'll try anything. It—you—are against everything I believe in. I don't think you're for real, and I don't particularly like you, but I'm drowning here, and I'll do anything to get justice for my sister.

'Exactly. I have a question, and it might seem odd because I don't think it's correct. I'm getting an image of a boy of about twelve playing in a hotel corridor. And yet, I'm not getting a brother vibe. Do you have a younger brother, Jess? No, you don't, do you?'

'No, it's just Paige and me. It was.'

'I'm still seeing a little boy. Maybe he's the killer's next victim?'

'Really?' Jess tried to be polite, but she couldn't keep the scepticism out of her voice.

'Sometimes we get crossed wires, and things that are unrelated to the person I'm working with come through. This child could be from my last appointment or even my next one. It makes it difficult to be believed and to have things fit. Did either of you have a blue Mini?'

'No.'

'I'm sorry, I don't think it's anything to do with you. Can I take a moment to focus, please?'

'Would it help if I told you more about Paige?'

'No. Absolutely not. I like to work blind. You might tell me something that influences my reading, and it can cloud the input.' Amanda took a pen and paper from her bag and sat up straight with her eyes closed, drawing circles. Within seconds the paper looked like a child's Spirograph drawing with circles interconnecting circles into other circles.

'Grandma passed away. When?' she asked Sven. 'Okay, yes, about three years ago.'

'Yes.'

'Background, just background, give me something specific. He's showing me grandma's garden. I'm walking through an arch. There are flowers. Lots of summer flowers.'

'The killer's in Grandma's garden?' Jess sounded horrified.

'No. No, love. This is just images. He's not here. But there's something about the flowers. I'm led to the arch with the flowers. What? Give me more.'

'I understand the reference. But I'm not allowed to talk about some specific points from the case.'

'Okay, good. If you understand it, that's all that matters, and I don't need to.' She went back to drawing circles. 'They are linked. Sven won't let me come away from the flowers until I see what I'm meant to. In the flat. In the bathroom, the same flowers are everywhere. Flowers with long purple stamens—honeysuckle, maybe? I'm no botanist, but does the killer leave these flowers at the scene? Is that his thing?'

'Yes. They call him The Florist in the papers and on social media.'

'Okay, yes, I've seen all that. But I try to avoid the news; occupational hazard in this game. I get bombarded with stuff. I'm being shown a picture. Lots of pictures. Pictures on walls, hundreds of them all blanked out. The frames. Frame? Does a picture frame mean anything to you?'

'We have them. Everybody has picture frames. But no, not especially.'

'Okay, I'd like to try something else. Do you understand what psychometry is?'

'Kind of.'

'Okay, it's using something belonging to the victim to build a bridge between them and us. I warn you that things can come thick and fast, and it can be overwhelming. Or we might not get anything. Are you willing to give it a go?'

'Yes.'

Chapter
Twenty-Three

Chapter
Twenty-three

'I need to speak to Inspector Nash,' somebody said.

'He's very busy, miss, and can't come to the desk. If you tell me what it's about, I can give him a message.'

Nash wasn't in the incident room. He heard the insistent request after making a cup of coffee.

Something about the urgency in the woman's voice made him poke his head around the door. He'd been at the receiving end of Jessica Hunter's pique before and considered poking it back again like a tortoise in retreat. Jessica had been on the phone at least three times a day asking for updates on the case despite Nash telling her that he'd keep her informed and share any information that they deemed safe to divulge.

'DCI Nash, there you are. I need to speak to you, please.'

'Ms Hunter, take a seat, and I'll be with you in a moment.' He needed a few minutes to find something to keep her happy but nothing that would jeopardise either the case or her safety. Not that they had much. Like all roads leading to Rome, all leads brought them back to Maxwell Jones, and he'd been eliminated from enquiries—for now.

'Who is Silas, Inspector? Is it the killer?'

Nash stopped in his tracks. 'How do you know that name?'

Jess gasped at his reaction. 'You know him, don't you? You know who Silas is?'

He put a hand on her shoulder and led her through the public areas to his office. They passed the reception and the row of interview rooms. Nash took her into the back area of the building where the incident room and upper-rank offices were. She was still talking, damn her.

'Who is it? Who is Silas? He's got Paige's name badge, hasn't he? He must be her killer. Have you caught him yet?'

Every head looked up as they walked to his office.

Jessica stopped and put her hand on one of the privy screens by a desk with one of the officers craning his neck to see what was going on. 'Inspector, it's clear from your reaction that you know who Silas is. I'm not moving until you tell me if you have him in custody or not.'

'This way, please, Miss Hunter.'

'Who is he?'

Everybody had stopped working, and DI Brown had moved forward to make note of this new piece of information and an unfamiliar name being thrown into the mix.

'Who is Silas?' Jessica looked as though she was going to start throwing things around the room if she didn't get an answer.

Nash moved a stapler out of her way. 'I am,' he said. 'I'm Silas Nash. Now, if we can just go into my office, you can tell me what this is all about.'

His tone was still conciliatory, but inside, he was fuming. A victim's relative was digging into his personal information, and he wanted to know why. Nash motioned for Brown to join him and slammed the door on the outside childishness behind them. He heard their laughter even though his door was closed.

They took seats on either side of the desk, with Brown next to Nash. Jessica tried to shout over him, but he was leading this conversation from now on. 'Right. Start talking. Why have you been delving into my personal life, and which part of "leave the investigation to us" didn't you understand?'

'You're Silas? I don't understand. And you have Paige's name badge from the café where she worked? Why?'

'Not me personally, no. The badge is with all the other evidence in the case and has been filed properly, ready for presenting at court should we have the perpetrator.'

'Killer, Inspector. The person that killed my sister is a cold-blooded murderer. Let's not diminish him to the rank of a perpetrator. He didn't steal a Milky Way from the local shop.'

Nash wasn't coping very well with leading the conversation. 'You still haven't answered my question, Ms Hunter. Why have you been poking around in my personal life?'

'I didn't know it was you. I thought we'd found the killer?'

'We?'

'Look, I don't know why you're shouting at me. A lady came to my door, told me my dad was going to have a heart attack, which he did, and said I had to ask for Silas and that he had Paige's badge.'

'And that lady would be?'

'Amanda Keys.'

'Amanda Keys, the bloody psychic? Sorry.'

'Yes, but you're still shouting at me.'

'Because I had you pegged for an intelligent woman, but if you believe a word that comes out of that harridan's mouth, you're as crazy and deluded as she is. We've had many dealings with Miss Keys, and none of them has been productive.'

'Have you ever taken her seriously and listened to her?'

'Are you serious? "Inspector, my seven hundred-year-old ghost has instructed me to tell you to look under the sofa for your missing comb." The woman's a crank. Look in the phone book for my name, did she?'

'Is it listed in the phone book?'

'Of course not. I was making a point.'

'Well, it wasn't a very valid one if you aren't listed. And nobody uses a phone book these days. She told me my father was going to have a heart attack, and two hours later, he did. How do you explain that?'

'Just bloody lucky, I guess. Or she put something in his tea.'

The rest of the conversation didn't go well, and Nash felt incompetent and as though he was letting all of the victims down, not just Paige Hunter.

That afternoon they had a break in the case, but it made no sense at all. A spot of blood had been found on Robert Dean's body. And while they hadn't been able to source its owner from DNA sampling due to the number of proteins in the blood, Nash wrote up his report and added the new information to the whiteboard. It wasn't Dean's.

He was at the house in Ulverston when they returned Jones' camper van to him. The idiot was like a kid at Christmas.

'I can go away for a few days, right?'

'Do everything you would normally do. However, you've had a couple of episodes while you've been in custody. I think it would be my civic duty to take your licence and put it out to the cars that you're to be pulled and charged if you're seen driving in your condition.' Nash must have been going soft in his old age because he felt pity as Jones pleaded his case.

'It's my medication. I promise you. I didn't get all of my meds in there. Now that I'm out, I can regulate it so that I don't get dizzy spells and nausea. Please. I can feel when it's coming on and have time to pull over. I swear, I'm not a danger. I'm begging you. I don't have long. Don't take my licence away.'

Nash handed Max his keys. 'Don't drive under any circumstances, and if you do, I'll have to report you— of course, my memory's not as good as it used to be, and I believe things are backed up for a few months. I can only do my best. Do not bloody kill anyone.'

Max grinned, 'Never have, never will, boss.'

Nash grunted and turned to his paperwork. They concluded what they had to do, and Nash left without trying to hide his presence.

He went home and turned the television on. He sat through half an hour of University Challenge and didn't understand many of the questions, let alone answer them. It made a decent analogy for this case. In the TV quiz, some of the maths questions had their origins based in Latin, and the whole question might as well have been read in the ancient language for all the sense it made to him. The case was the same. If you have no understanding of the evidence, it might as well be in a foreign language. Nash worked by logic, reasoning, patterns, and elimination. He would disseminate every piece of information until it formed a conclusion, but in this case, once they took Max Jones out of the equation, they had nothing in the way of suspects.

There were, however, plenty of clues, and one of them was turning into a furry beast.

He thought about the dog. It kept cropping up. Hairs from the same dog had been found at all of the more recent staging sites. That afternoon they'd confirmed that all of the dog hair found on the victims came from one animal. It was the dog that Jones had taken from the thug, Ryan Beck. Only the four sites before Max took the dog from him were clear of any dog hairs. Ryan Beck had a clump of hair in his hand. This was planted, but he had owned the dog, so it's not impossible that it would have been there. It was unlikely during the violence of the murder, but not impossible. The two boys had hair from the same dog in their praying hands, and Paige and Zoe both had fur on them as well. With Paige, it was found during the post-mortem in the mouth of her severed head.

Nash worked on the whiteboard in his home office and added information as he tried to make sense of it. DNA testing showed that the semen found in Zoe Conley's vaginal cavity belonged to Maxwell Jones. That wasn't surprising. He openly admitted to having intercourse with her. If anything, it helped because it pinned another piece of evidence to the timeline. They'd had sex soon after three in the morning. That meant that Zoe was murdered sometime within twelve to eighteen hours of that. It was another stable time element.

There was no dog fur at the sites of the first four bodies because, in Max Jones' world, the dog didn't exist yet. It was planted at the later sites as an afterthought when the victims were killed. The killer had had access to that dog, even if it was only long enough to pull a few hairs from it.

And then there was the blood spot evidence to think about and log—it was there but may have nothing to do with Robert Dean's murder. If it wasn't Dean's, where did it come from?

He erased the blood spot finding from its place on the whiteboard and put it on the far right-hand side under incidentals. Now the picture was clear, and a new name jumped out at Nash. It had to be.

Bingo.

Pleased with his findings, this one would keep. The new suspect was secure in his lack of detection and must have felt invincible at this point. It wouldn't last long with surveillance on him. Nash wanted to track his movements for now. He locked doors, checked windows, shut down the house and called it a night. There was nothing to stay up for.

Nash sorted out his bag for the next morning and left it by the front door. He took his mug to the kitchen and washed it, and then he climbed the stairs and fell into bed.

Sleep didn't come. He missed Sandy and couldn't stop thinking about all the times they'd shared this bed together. As he drifted off, thoughts of Sandy intermingled with pieces of the case and thrashed around in his head. Maybe he'd made a mistake ending their relationship, and he'd ring tomorrow just to see how the land lay.

He told himself he'd be a fool if he did.

Chapter
Twenty-Four

Chapter
Twenty-four

Nash had a bad night. Loneliness was always worse when it was dark and he was in the house on his own. It was crippling. Having a selfish, narcissistic lover was better than having no lover at all. After a dream about being left on a crowded train platform when he was four, watching everybody walk away from him, he'd woken with sweat on his brow. He felt that he deserved to be loved as much as the next person. However, all thoughts of getting in touch with Sandy were banished with the dawn and the birdsong.

He got up with no enthusiasm for the day. He sorted his emotions into one compartment and his mood for working on a murder case into another. At the start of the investigation, all the officers were fuelled by rage. Nash had experienced it twice now, once with the Johnstone case twenty years ago and now with The Florist. In the first week, he woke with determination carrying his feet out of bed before the alarm sounded. In the office, the collective demeanour was one of cool professionalism, but at home, his rage was overwhelming. He was going to get this bastard, and Nash would look him in the eye and grin as they sent him down for an eternity. A new mood insinuated itself as the investigation wore on with no result. This was the feeling of helplessness that always hit in the slump of a case. It was shrouded in a thick coat of despair, and when you lose hope, you lose motivation. Nash couldn't let that happen. He had to keep his own and his team's emotions snapping with synapses of positivity and belief.

This morning he showered and dressed in a grey plaid suit. It was Thursday, so he wore a blue shirt and a navy-and-grey striped tie. He made coffee and toast. Most days, that was enough, but damn, he wanted something sweet. There was nothing in the fridge. Sandy liked dessert. There had always been something ridiculous like tiramisu or black forest gateau in the fridge back then, and he remembered eating cake from sandy's navel.'

There wasn't even a half-empty tub of cookie dough ice cream in the freezer. It was six-thirty in the morning, and he was angry because there was no dessert. He opened the cupboard where he kept two spare jars of coffee, always two in hand, so he never ran out, and a giant box of tea bags. He was annoyed again because he'd agreed to go back to work. He moved cooking oil and gravy granules and reached to the back for an old jar of runny honey that had been there for years. He'd read somewhere that honey was the only food item that never went off. He hoped it was true because there was nothing runny about this stuff. It had crystalised and didn't look very appetising. There was a crusty brown rim of stickiness around the neck of the jar, and he almost threw it in the bin. But then he wouldn't have it for his toast that was sitting by his coffee going cold. He wiped the messy rim with a wet cloth and went in search of the honey dipper at the back of one of the drawers. What the hell was he doing? He slammed the drawer shut and used his knife. He was angry because his life was such a terrible mess.

He put his head in his hands. He was in a position of power over everybody at work except Bronwyn Lewis. And yet he felt so small. They looked up to him and waited for him to give them answers. He had none to give. Over forty years in the force and with a few courses under his belt, he had a special knack for reading people and scenes. It was at his insistence that they let Jones go without charge. Every fibre of his being told him that Jones was innocent. His belief was corroborated by the fact that Jones was locked up when most of the bodies were brought to the crime scene and again by the lie detector. It was all irrelevant because Nash knew they had the wrong man, and that was the only indicator he needed. The rest was just fluff.

He should be happy that they had a new suspect, but he wasn't. Forty years of giving the worst news in the world to grieving families had broken him. He wasn't whole anymore, and parts of him were missing. He'd stopped puking at crime scenes a long time ago. And the day you don't puke at horror is the day you stop feeling.

That was probably why nobody loved him. He didn't feel enough. In his head, he thought he was giving everything a partner should. He thought he gave enough love, but perhaps he didn't—couldn't. He held so much of himself back from pain.

He felt it now, and his body ached. It gnawed at his brain like a tooth abscess, and the feeling was remarkable. But there was nobody there to remark about it too. If only there was one person in the world that wanted him. He had nobody. No relatives, no friends, only work. Lola felt his anguish when it came from somewhere deep inside him and jumped on his knee. He offered her toast and honey, and she had a tentative lick but didn't like it. He held her close to him and nuzzled into her fur. She understood and let it happen.

Silas Nash was a very different person from DCI Nash. He hadn't been late for work in forty years, and today wasn't that day. A splash of cold water to his face did the trick.

Nash was back.

***

'Listen up, people.'

The team were slouching at their desks. With so little evidence pushing them forward, the lack of enthusiasm showed. The keenness in their eyes a few days earlier had turned to frustration.

'Item number one on today's agenda. Brown, let Jones know that the joint funerals are taking place for the two little lads tomorrow. I want him there. He may see something worthwhile. And I want a good police presence for Wilson and Little. As many of you as possible will be around the perimeter at all times.'

'Sir,' Brown responded.

'Little Wilson and little Little, eh?' Lawson said.

'Can it, you idiot. There's a time for gallows humour, and this isn't it. It's a kiddie's service.'

'Sir.'

'With respect, sir, I think you were mad to let Jones go. We should have thrown the book at him.' Bowes was turning into a good cop. He was prepared to stand up for what he believed, even if what he believed was bollocks.

'Is that right, Bowes?'

'Yes, when the next one shows up, that's blood on us.' What he was saying was that the blood would fall on Nash's head entirely like the pig's blood in Carrie. The rest of the team didn't agree with his decision either, but Bowes was the only one with the balls to say it.

Nash spent the next twenty minutes filling them in on the new intel and brought the board up to date with test results that had come in after most of them had left the day before. They straightened in their seats when he brought a new name into prevalence on the board.

'Max's best mate, Jonathan Finch.'

'No way. It can't be,' Renshaw said.

'What's the motive? I can't see one.' Brown tapped her pen against her teeth and then scribbled like lightning on her pad. Nash knew she was using her shrewd brain to try and work a timeline and an entirely new process for the suspect.

'None that I can see yet, Brown. That's what we're working on today. I want a rundown of the suspect's movements to cover every second of the day. If this is our guy, we're going to get him.' Nash was glad to see some enthusiasm igniting and spreading a small flame through the team. They were hanging onto Jones' coattails and were reluctant to let go—but he was all they'd had up to now, and having somebody new to work around shifted the dynamic.

'Why don't we just haul Finch in and throw everything we've got at him? Hey, he could be Jones' accomplice. That makes much more sense. I think we've got them, boss, both of them.' PC Lawson looked pleased with himself.

'Jones having an accomplice is a line that we haven't ruled out, but I don't want you to focus on that for now. I've spent a lot of time with this man, and I know he's not the type to work with a partner.' Nash groaned at the thought of being lumbered with him for the duration in just that capacity. 'You have to keep an open mind, Lawson—all of you. I've got the tandem florists working together on a backburner, but it's not something I'm on board with. Let's open our eyes and look at the case with a fresh perspective.'

'Jones' jizz was found in one of the victims. That seems pretty conclusive to me,' Lawson said.

'Then God help you, son, the next time you pull a random one-nighter in The Robin Hood. I hope it doesn't come back to haunt you. That's all I can say.' Everyone laughed, and Lawson played to their humour by standing and giving a pelvic thrust.

'Brown and Bowes, you will relieve Jackson and Miller at eleven and take surveillance outside the suspects' house. If he moves, you stick to him like a cheap, wet toilet roll. Renshaw and Lawson, you're on a split shift.' They both groaned. 'Go and get some rest now, Lawson. Get laid and come back concentrating. I want you on the next turnaround on the seven to three shift. Jackson and Miller are back on after that until eleven tomorrow morning. We'll rotate this shift pattern until something breaks. Overtime is available for anybody that wants floating patrol. Any questions?' Nash said.

'Where will you be, sir?'

'Me, Brown? I'm going to see a woman about a ghost.'

Chapter Twenty-Five

Chapter Twenty-five

Nash tapped the desk as he listened to the ringing on the end of the line. He didn't think Jones was going to answer.

'Jesus, can't a man pleasure himself in the shower now without being disturbed?'

'Meet me outside at two. Be ready.' Nash hung up.

Getting called into Lewis's office was rarely a good thing. He knocked and heard her shouting at somebody on the phone from the other side of the thick door. 'I'm telling you now—come in, Nash—I want it pulled from all social media. Have you got it? I want it gone. Now. Otherwise, my legal team are going to come down on you so hard you'll wonder which hole your arse is.'

She slammed her phone down so hard on her walnut desk that she winced and picked it up again to check the screen. 'Police property, damn. There's been another leak. Nothing we can do about the newspapers, it's out there, but I'm getting it pulled from socials.'

'What is it this time?'

'Apparently, you've brought a medium onto the case. What the hell are you playing at, Nash? Have you lost your mind?'

'That's not true. I'm going out to see Jessica Hunter this afternoon. She's been taken in by this woman. I'm going to quash it and get Jessica to drop it.'

'It was all over the war room yesterday. Are you losing control of your team?'

'No, Ma'am. There was a bit of frivolity concerning the information, that's all. The guys thought my name was hilarious.'

There was the merest hint of a smile as she said, 'So I believe, Silas.' But it was gone a second later as though somebody had slapped it off her face. 'Any idea who the leak is, yet?'

'It's not my team.'

'It's one of them.'

'I trust them implicitly.'

'Lawson's got a mouth on him.'

'He's a good man. And if it was him, do you think he'd hold back? Lawson would spill chapter and verse. It's not him. Whoever it is, they are drip-feeding the press to keep the story running. They love it because they're getting a new headline every day.'

There was a knock on the door.

'Come in.' Bronwyn Lewis was furious, and it showed in every muscle of her body. Her posture was always strong and upright, but she looked as though somebody had stuck a poker up her backside.

DI Brown came in with a tablet and put it in front of her. 'There's been another leak, Ma'am. The news editor didn't mention he was running a different story in the lunchtime edition. He says they are about to name the man whose semen was found in Zoe Conley. Either the leak is keeping the name back, or the press already knows it but are teasing the public and holding out. Either way, it's going to be trouble. It needs shutting down before it goes to print, Ma'am.'

'I'm on it. Ross Kirk, the editor, won't answer if I ring from my office line. I've suppressed his stories so many times this week that I've got him on speed dial.' She rooted through her bag and pulled out her personal phone. She rang the newsdesk and put the phone on speaker. 'Put the editor-in-chief on the phone. Now.'

'As I told you earlier, DCS Lewis, he's in a meeting.'

'Listen, Marvin.'

'Marcus.'

'Whatever the hell your name is. Get him on the phone in the next thirty seconds, or I'm coming down there, in person, to arrest the lot of you.' She put the phone down on her desk after Marcus had put her on hold. 'Better not smash this one up. It was a Christmas present from Grant. He'd go mad.' She managed a half-hearted grin. 'Ross, how good of you to speak to me. It seems like ages. Get it taken down.'

Ross sighed and said in a Scottish accent. 'Immediately, Chief Superintendent Lewis, it's coming down as we speak. There's just a little problem with the server, so it might take a few minutes to action but trust me, we're on it, and my reporters will be told about buying sensitive material. You have my sincere apology—again.'

'And print?'

'Off the press.'

'It had better be. I suggest you sort out your little server problem, or you may find yourself with a little freedom problem. You've got two minutes.'

'Done.'

It was a game. The ultimate win was to get a story online because once it was up, it couldn't be stopped. It only took one person to share before it was pulled, and it could still go viral. Every second it was online, there were additional shares creating global reach, leading to more advertising and revenue for the media group. This story had been up over ten minutes before Brown brought it in. It would be nearer twenty before it came down—that was a good hit for the newspaper and Ross Kirk.

Nash had to call in at home to get some papers before he picked up Jones and went to Morecambe. His bladder played its usual trick on him as he got out of the car and danced while he slipped his key into the front door. Because he was in a hurry to get to the loo, of course, the key stuck, and it took him three jiggles to get the door open.

As he flung it wider than necessary. It banged off the wall, and all thoughts of his bladder were forgotten. Somebody had been in his house. He looked at his hall and cried out at the mess. Red spray paint in two-foot-high letters had been graffitied on both sides. The first said *Let's play*, and its opposing wall said, *Coming, ready or not.* Nash picked up a bronze candlestick from the occasional table and ran into the living room. He flung the door wide. Lola wound around his legs and told him about the intruder. She was vocal, and her tail stuck straight up from her body, her back end quivering because her dad was home. The feature wall above his Victorian mantelpiece said, *I know what you are.* In his bedroom, all the walls were defaced. One wall said *I'm going to tell your secret...Silas.* His closet doors at the end of the room were sprayed with, *Come OUT, come OUT ...* And the far wall said, *Wherever you are. I know you're a friend of Dorothy.* The space above his bed was sprayed with the outline of an ejaculating penis.

'Bastard.'

Nash thought back to the interviews. The snide remarks and comments. The little digs were aimed personally at Nash and meant only for him.

'Bloody Jones.'

He'd been going to have a sandwich before he set off, but any appetite had left him. In the kitchen, Lola's bowl had been filled with her kibble—Nash picked it up in case it had been poisoned. He went to his office, unlocked it and got an evidence bag. Without contaminating the contents, he took a sample of the cat food for testing and threw the rest in the bin. As an afterthought, he threw the rest of the opened box away. He went to his spare supplies, opened a new box for her, and filled a clean dish. Using his tweezers, he dropped the contaminated dish into another evidence bag for fingerprinting. For obvious reasons, he wouldn't call his colleagues out to the crime scene, so this would have to do. He'd deal with this on his own.

Jones may not have been a murderer, and Nash was still convinced that he wasn't—but it didn't stop him from being a cruel, vindictive bastard.

He couldn't face eating in his defaced home, but it wasn't his custom to miss lunch. He was a breakfast, lunch, and dinner man and always had been. Sandy was one of those people who graze all day long, and Nash disapproved and tried to enhance his ex-partner's diet by cooking nutritious meals and introducing more vegetables into everything. Sometimes it was like feeding a child, and he had to do it on the sly. He'd blend broccoli into his omelettes and add pureed parsnip to his shepherd's pie. He'd leave bowls of fruit around the house and throw them out five days later before they were overripe or, God forbid, rotten. He had nobody to feed now, and it made him sad.

He thought back over the interviews with Maxwell Jones. He was a cocky little shit—that was a given—but Nash had never thought he was vindictive enough to do this. He thought Jones had been hard done by. He was certain he wasn't a killer—almost. *Come out, come out wherever you are.* Maybe it was somebody else and not even connected to this case. He'd made enemies over the years. Nash had put a lot of people away, and getting backs up was always going to be part of the job.

He wondered if Jones had eaten. Even if he was a blackmailing bastard, he was still a man in the end stage of life. And Nash was stuck with him. As much as it galled him, the narcissistic fool was his responsibility. There was nothing he could do about the state of his house right now. The thought of being late for anything went against the grain. The phone calls to tradesmen would have to wait until he got back, and then, he'd open his own investigation into who was threatening him.

Sod it. He'd make a sandwich.

The kitchen hadn't been defaced, but he still didn't want to be in there. His house felt dirty for having had a stranger in it, but he had to eat.

He buttered wholemeal bread. Then added a bed of iceberg lettuce, with Emmental cheese and honey-glazed ham. He sliced thinly cut tomato and cucumber, added salt and pepper, and just a dribble of mayonnaise before cutting the two sandwiches, one for him and one for Jones. He wrapped them carefully in tin foil, put them into a plastic food container and dropped them into his bag. Before leaving, He picked up two red apples from the bowl by the door.

His briefcase didn't have anything sensitive in it, just their lunch, so he threw it in the footwell of the passenger seat. On the drive to Ulverston, he contemplated his beautiful house. He'd hired people to decorate it less than a year before and hadn't skimped on the wallpaper. It had cost him sixty-five pounds per roll. He was furious. He doubted this was anything more than a scare tactic from Jones. He was pissing up the wall to show his dominance over Nash to get his own way. Or it was a sick game to amuse him. He wondered if his life could be in very real danger, but only for a second before he discounted it. It had to be

Jones. The more he thought about the home invasion, the angrier he got. To hell with him.

When he got to Jones' house, he slammed hard on his horn and didn't take his hand off until Jones came out, banging the door behind him.

'All right. All right. Keep your hair on.'

Nash got out of his car, leaving the door open in the narrow country road, and he rammed Jones up against the wall of the opposite house. He had both hands on his rugby top and used it for momentum to repeatedly bring him forward and slam him back onto the wall with every statement.

'You bastard. Enjoy that did you? Have you any idea what it's going to cost to have my house redecorated? You sick sonofabitch.'

'What? What have I done?'

Nash was running out of steam. 'Why do you have to be such an arsehole?'

'If you tell me what you think I've done this time, I might be able to answer you.'

A man ran down the steps of the cottage in his boxers with a towelling dressing gown flying loose behind him. He was in his socks, and his feet weren't accustomed to running on stony ground. He let out a grunt when he came off the bottom step.

'What the hell's going on here? Get off him, or I'll call the police.'

'I am the police.' Nash took his hand off Jones to flash his warrant card, and Jones didn't bother to move. Nash's initial anger was spent, and he was glad of a reason to stop. He realised that being his age wasn't conducive to slamming scumbags against walls. He was a fit man, but he'd still exerted himself.

'Steve,' Jones said as though they'd met getting in their respective cars in the morning.

'Max.'

'Missus and the kids okay?' He broke into a coughing fit on the last word, and Nash released him.

'What's going on?' Steve asked.

'There's nothing to see here. Please go back into your house, sir.'

Max had one hand against the wall with his head low, coughing. The neighbour went over to him, and Jones held out his hand, palm up, to indicate he was okay.

'This is police brutality. You can't do this.' Steve readied his phone and then held it out, recording the scene for posterity.

'What's your name?' Nash asked.

'I don't have to tell you my name unless you're going to charge me for something. Have I done something wrong, officer?'

'This is my neighbour, Steve. Steve Hill. Thanks for looking out for me, mate. It's all good. You can get back to Hayley.' Steve looked doubtful but went back inside.

'You. Car. Now,' Nash said. They got in the car and drove away.

'Easy, tiger. You'll blow a gasket.' Jones was still wheezing and looked pale.

'Are you okay? Do you need medical attention?' Nash said.

'No, I'm good, Starsky. Let's go.'

'When you're out with me, I want you in suitable clothing. What the hell do you call this?'

'Apparently, it's the perfect attire to be pounded against a brick wall. Are you okay, Nash? Want to talk about it?'

'Lose the rugby shirt and address me with some respect.'

'Respect has to be earned, my friend. I know you don't like me, but I know that you're the one that has my back as an innocent man. Or at least you did until today. I haven't thanked you properly. I realised I could have been charged with murder and would have died on remand. I'm grateful to you for believing in me.'

Nash gave him the side eye as he negotiated the little roundabout outside the big Kings pub. He was waiting for the punchline and a snarky remark.

'Thank you, Nash.'

Nash grunted.

'So about my Ayckbourn, Harlequin rugby shirt? You said act naturally, so I figured that meant dressing as usual.'

'I can hardly pass you off as a copper looking like that, can I? Bloody red and navy stripes, what were you thinking, man?'

'You're going to lie and say I'm a cop?'

'No, I was just going to introduce you and hope they'd assume, but that's hardly going to work now, is it? Even undercover guys don't go out looking like circus clowns.'

'This shirt cost me a fortune.'

'Jesus Christ.' Nash turned Radio 4 on.

Jones leaned forward and switched to *The Bay* radio station. Rod Stewart's *Maggie May* blasted into the car.

Nash leaned forward and turned the radio off.

'Good music, man. How can you not like a bit of the old *Maggie May*? And, come to think of it, if we're going to be hanging out, we're going to have to talk about your wheels. Starsky and Hutch did not drive a boring old man's car.'

'We're more like the Laurel and Hardy of Homicide, and I will not be made a fool of.'

'No, I can see how you don't need me for that, but honey, without Stan, there is no Oliver.'

'Shut up, Jones.'

They drove in silence apart from the odd remark from Jones until they turned left at Bolton-le-Sands, and the first glimpse of Morecambe Bay came into view.

'It never gets old, does it?'

'What doesn't?' Nash asked.

'This view. The sea is a beautiful lady when she's calm, but she's a stunning goddess when she's angry.'

'It is a beautiful part of the world.'

'First place I came to when I found out I only had a few months left. The sea and the cliffs at Heysham calm me. It's restorative, you know. Not that anything can restore me. I'm past that. So what's the info on tomorrow? I don't get why you want me at the kid's funeral. I didn't know them.'

Nash noticed that there was no self-pity in his voice when he talked, and he showed a genuine passion for the Bay. Nash admired his outlook— but he was still an annoying little prick.

'No. But the killer is setting you up for their murder. There's a good chance he'll make an appearance or at least cause some kind of mischief. Half the force is going to be there, and I want you in the middle of it all with eyes on.'

'Is that a police term? Am I part of the handcuffs-and-truncheon crowd now? Anyway, before you shout at me again, are you ready to tell me what got you so riled up this morning?'

'Somebody graffitied some unkind things in my home.'

'Ah.'

'What do you mean, "Ah"? Bloody ah?'

'Were you outted?'

'I don't know what you're talking about.' Nash's hands gripped the steering wheel as though he had them around Jones' neck.

'How did you know?'

'Not, "Is there some crazed, madman killer coming after you?" Or, "What can you do to protect yourself, in my civilian opinion?" Just, "How did you know I'm gay?" I don't know, I just did.'

'Is it obvious? Does everybody know?'

'I don't think anybody does. And even if they do, what does it matter? No, it isn't obvious. It's in the way you click your biro or the way you open your briefcase. I don't know, do I? It's in the way you—breathe. It's just you.'

'Just me?'

'Your team respect you for the job you do. But I don't think any one of them has a clue. You hold yourself very tight. And one day, it'd be cool for you to let that angst go.'

'I'm the DCI of a police force.'

'So bloody what?'

'Quite.'

They were almost there, and Nash asked the next question without taking his eyes from the road.

'I'm asking you in a civil manner. Did you deface my house?'

'No.'

'Good.'

Chapter Twenty-Six

Chapter Twenty-six

When Nash rounded the corner at Happy Mount Park, he swung into a parking bay at the farthest point from the bustle of the busy parts of the prom. Not many people came this far on foot, the occasional dog walker, maybe. It was quiet. He was facing the sea. Nash used to bring Sandy here all the time.

'I'm not that kind of boy, Inspector Romeo.'

'Shut up and pass me my briefcase.'

Nash took out the plastic Tupperware box and two apples. He threw one to Jones, who caught it in one hand. 'Here, I've made you a sandwich.'

'Thank you, Mother, that's very kind of you.'

'Oh, piss off.'

'Hey, seriously, though, that's a nice thing to do. Thanks, Nash. You can put some of that Radio 4 shit back on if you want.'

As they ate, they watched the ocean. The water was grey, and the white tips of the waves frothed and spat backwards as they crashed against the sea breaks. She wasn't angry yet, but she could turn in an instant.

When they'd finished, Nash handed Jones a serviette from the packet that he kept in his door caddy. He used another one to wipe out the container, put the lid on and put it back in his briefcase.

That's when he saw the envelope, and he wouldn't have reacted, but it was unexpected and a shock to see it there. He'd emptied his case in the evidence room when he got to work that morning, as was his custom. All that was in it after nipping home at lunchtime and discovering the graffiti was their lunch.

And now an envelope as well.

He grabbed it as he put the tub in and closed the case. He had a cursory glance at the envelope, trying to keep his face as neutral as possible.

Detective Chief Inspector Silas Nash

He stuffed it into his pocket.

'What's up?'

'Nothing, why?'

'No reason. You just seemed to tense up when you got that letter out. Hey, listen, man. How much are you a copper on duty at this moment?'

'I'm always a copper on duty. Why?'

'If a bloke was caught short and had to go for a pee around those rocks, you wouldn't be evil-minded enough to arrest him, would you? What's the penalty for peeing in public?'

'PND? eighty quid.' He'd have had plenty to say about moral responsibility if his mind wasn't on the letter. He would have refused to be a party to any law-breaking, but right this second, he needed Jones out of the car. 'Just be discrete and don't wave it around like a conductor's baton.' The thought of him getting back into Nash's car and touching things after he'd touched his thing disgusted him, but he let it go.

He waited for Jones to disappear and grabbed the letter from his pocket. His name was printed in a sans-serif font. He tore into it, and his hands shook as he read the words on the paper that had been folded in half.

Twenty grand in cash. I'm not an unreasonable man, Silas. You've got two days to get it ready. And don't get any clever ideas about running tests on the note. I'm sure you don't want the whole world to know your secrets. I've got very friendly with a certain reporter at The Mail. *Mixed with a few juicy details from the case, I'm sure he'd like to know about you, Mr Chief Inspector.*

I'll be in touch with instructions.

Toodle pip.

He refolded the note and put it in his breast pocket. He would give the envelope to the lab later. He wasn't aware of Jones getting back in the car until he slammed the door too hard. Nash didn't react.

'What's up?' Jones asked for the second time.

Nash had another piece of evidence but had to keep it to himself. It wasn't case-related, and he wasn't sure if Jones could have done it. Nash wracked his brain for any second that Jones could have got into his briefcase. And there it was—a second where he'd leaned down and scratched his lower leg inside his sock while Nash had been concentrating on the road. He said the tag bracelet was annoying him. He could have reached over then and put the envelope in Nash's bag.

He didn't know how else it could have got there. It was empty when he went home. He dropped it by the front door when he came in. The kitchen was at the far end of the hall after three open doors. He kept them open through the day, even though it played with his tidy mind, to give Lola the run of the house. The only explanation was that an intruder—the killer—had been in his house the whole time. He was a hardened cop, but the thought that the Florist had been in his home made his blood run cold. It signalled him as the next target. The only piece of useful intel was that the person in his home and the one leaking the information were the same guy.

Was The Florist one of his team? If so, it was somebody close to him that he would trust with his life.

He looked at Jones, who was pressing the seat-warming button like a kid with a new toy. In that instant, he was a harmless buffoon. But, Nash preferred to think it was him, blackmailing him as one of his mind games, rather than a deranged murderer coming to gouge his heart out with a corkscrew.

***

Amanda Keys sat with her eyes closed and rubbed her fingers over Paige's necklace again.

'There was somebody. He was in the café before Paige died—come on, show me, yes, okay, okay—he has brown hair, it's quite long, past his collar. I can see him reaching over the counter. He was stealing from the till, I think. A traveller. I think he may be a gipsy. I can see him living in a caravan.'

'A traveller killed Paige?' Jessica asked.

'I think she tried to stop him from taking the money.'

'Like that other murder twenty-odd years ago. Could it be that gipsy lad Johnston that killed his cousin?'

'No. Maybe. I don't know. It's not clear.'

'We need to tell the police.'

'It's changing. I've got it wrong. He liked her. I'm getting a warm feeling. Lots of red. Red all over. Romance. He wanted to ask her out but was too shy,' Amanda said.

'Maybe the red was blood.'

'I'm seeing something else. That little boy again. He's running down a corridor. Nope. It's gone. I'm sorry.'

'It's okay. Maybe we can try again later?'

'Yes, Nash will be here soon. And he'll be expecting a freak show. Their negative energy doesn't help me get information across clearly. Could you put the kettle on, please? I need five minutes to clear my chakras.'

When the bell rang, Jess went to let Nash and Jones in and led them through to the conservatory where the psychometry reading was taking place.'

***

Nash was impressed. It was a beautiful room with luxurious cane furniture topped with soft, comfortable cushions. The light was perfect and ignited the room with a wash of autumnal colours. The lawn was littered with fallen apples. And as he sat, Nash watched one fall from the tree to be pounced on by an opportunistic squirrel ignoring the other apples all over the lawn. He wanted that one. The incident with the envelope had thrown Nash off his game, and he wasn't paying attention to the introductions.

'I'm sorry, please forgive me. You both know me, and this is Mr Jones.'

'He doesn't look like a policeman. Jess said, eyeing his Converse.

'He isn't.' The colour had left Amanda's face, and her expression was set and grim.

'What?' Jess said.

'It's him. The man I saw in our reading, the one from the café.'

Nash sat forward in his chair. She couldn't know that. It hadn't been released, and no photographs of Max had been leaked to the press.

'I told you this was a bad idea, boss.'

Jess was screaming. 'Did you kill my sister? Was it you?'

'No. Calm down, love. Honestly, I swear. I only saw her once. She was kind and sweet, and I would never hurt her.'

'What the hell's going on, Inspector? Why is he here?' Jessica said.

Amanda put her hand up for silence. 'That chain around your neck—give it to me,' she said to Max.

'No way, not a chance, lady. You look very nice, and I expect you like puppies and kittens, but you aren't pulling any of that voodoo shit on me.'

'Your chain, please.'

Max looked to Nash, who'd said he didn't believe any of this crap, but he nodded for him to do it. Psychometry is what they were there for, if only to get Jessica Hunter off their backs. Max was reluctant as he handed his necklace over. 'If this is some sort of trick, it's not going to work. I'm telling you now. I'm innocent.'

Amanda rested back in her chair with her eyes closed. She rubbed her fingers over the chain and came back to the clasp several times. She shook her head as though speaking to somebody and murmured a few times. There were some hairs trapped in the opening mechanism, and she focused on them. She gasped, and her eyes opened, staring at Max.

'What?' they all said at once.

'What have you seen?' Jessica asked. 'Is it Paige?'

'No. It's bad. I can't say.'

'Oh, for goodness sake, Ms Keys,' Nash said. 'Please, let's cut the theatrics. If you've got something to say about Mr Jones, just say it. And then we can get out of here and do some real police work instead of this ludicrous fiasco. I have no patience for this charade when there's a killer out there.'

Amanda's voice hardened. 'I can't say, Inspector, because we have a code of practice, and there is certain information we will not divulge to a read subject.'

'If you're going to say what I think you are, I already know, honey. I've done all my bawling and wailing so you can spit it out,' Max said.

Amanda smoothed her tailored green trousers and straightened her blouse to buy herself time before she spoke. 'You have been to the hospital recently.'

'Yep, that's me. Guilty as charged. But that's all I've done.'

Amanda leaned forward and touched his hand. 'Sweetheart, I can confirm that your time on this earth is short.'

Jessica gasped.

'Correct.'

Nash was flummoxed. His brain wanted to come up with the word impressed, but there was nothing impressive about some tart with money, preying on the lost, lonely and, in this case, dying.

'Where did you get that information?' he asked.

Amanda sat back and put her hand on the right side of her head above her ear. There is darkness here. It's a large shadow covering the healthy parts of the brain. I can see people waiting. They are here ready to take you home when the time comes.'

'Oh, for Christ's sake.' Nash wanted to end this rubbish and get out of there, but Amanda kept talking.

'Such a sad little boy. You're sitting on a big staircase, in a hall, with mosaic tiles on the floor next to some suitcases. A lady wearing fur is kissing you on the forehead, and another lady takes you away. I'm getting so much love around this woman. No nonsense, so much love. She's singing. *I'm gonna see the folks I dig. I'll even kiss a sunset pig. California, I'm coming home.'*

Max had tears rolling down his cheeks, and Amanda put her hand over his to comfort him.

'What the hell is all this nonsense? Jones, we're leaving.'

'She couldn't have plucked that song out of thin air. It's impossible. Nanny Clare sang it to me in my playroom. Nobody knows that but me.'

'They have ways of finding things out. What about your sister? She might have posted something on Facebook. Fake mediums go back for years on a timeline,' Nash said.

'But you never told her I was coming. This is the first time she's known about me.'

'Okay, we'll play for a little longer, but I warn you, Jones, I'm getting pretty sick of this.' Nash was rattled. If she could reduce Jones to mush in seconds, he was terrified of her starting in on his private life. 'Bring it forward and get to the point, lady. We're only interested in the murders.' He saw Jess flinch. For God's sake, that's all he needed. Was the lovesick puppy going to start stalking the sister now?

'I can only give you what comes through. I can't request an order for specific information. This isn't a Chinese takeaway, Mr Nash.'

Who did she think she was, talking to him like that?

Amanda ignored Nash's scowl as though he wasn't there and went back to talking to Max. 'You have a big name. No, lots of little names, she says. She's laughing. I'm getting Barty and Nanna.'

'Nanny. Nanny Clare.'

'Are you buying this?' Nash asked.

'Shut up. I want to hear this.'

'Oh, bless you, sweetheart. Yes. I'll tell him.'

Nash grunted. Amanda, Max and Jessica glared at him.

'I've got a lovely young man here. He says you know him, Max. His passing was violent. He's showing me the left side of his face, and it's all battered.'

'Oh, God. Not another one,' Max said, and Nash sat forward in his chair again. 'Yes, yes, I'm saying it. He's not part of this case. He passed about ten years ago. He's showing me the numbers. Yes, ten years when he first came to this country, he was beaten and left for dead. He says he came to you for help, Max. But you did nothing.'

'You're wasting police time, Keys,' Nash said, 'and that's a criminal offence. Give us something relevant to today, or I'll arrest you.' They all ignored him.

'I don't know anybody who was beaten to death ten years ago,' Max said.

'He's showing me a small room, lots of shelves and stationery. He says he's sorry for knocking you over, but you frustrated him. He's saying, "Find the man. You find him." He looks very sad.'

Max jumped out of his seat in his excitement. 'Kami, that's Kami. A refugee.'

'He says yes. From a place beginning with I. Come on, give it to me, Iraq? Iran?'

'Kami was dead? But I saw him. That day, when he knocked me over—was he already dead? But he was right in front of me.'

Amanda laughed at something the spirit said. 'He says you're a bit slow. He was trying to get your attention. He wants you to find his murderer.'

'Has this got anything to do with The Florist?' Nash asked.

'Not a thing, Inspector, and you've chased him away now with your negativity.'

'Get him back. Tell him I'll try,' Max said.

'He's gone, love. I need a minute to try and clear the room of negative vibrations. Perhaps you'd prefer to wait outside, DCI Nash?'

'I'm not going anywhere.'

'Okay, but please try not to block me with your damaging energy. I'm trying to help you. There's a girl—but it's not Paige. Tattoos. I'm getting the name Zola. Lola. Zola?'

'Lola is my cat, Ms Keys, and the only crime she's ever committed is being too cute for her own good.'

'I'm sorry. It's a zed. Zara, Zoe.'

'Been in the papers and all over the news.'

'She wasn't a lesbian. She says it would have been cool if she was, but she wasn't that interesting. She says to tell Max she didn't want marriage, but the Scottish loch would have been nice. She says never stop looking for Nessie. Does that make any sense to you?'

Max was choked up, and Nash saw that he was filled with emotion. He just nodded.

'This is all very sweet, but it's not catching a killer,' Nash said.

Amanda was quiet for another couple of minutes. 'I'm getting nothing violent. I can't tell you who the killer is, but I can tell you that it's not the wearer of this chain. This man didn't kill anybody, Inspector. But I am getting a warning from my guide to be careful. They are getting closer?'

'They?' Jessica asked.

'He's gone. I don't know, just an expression, maybe. I can't tell if it has relevance or not. He, they, I'm not sure which he said now. He. He is getting closer.'

'Let me put this very simply, Ms Keys. In your opinion, is there more than one murderer?'

'And let me answer in words of one syllable or less, Inspector. I don't know. That's it for today. I'm exhausted and feel quite weakened.' She stood up and swooned back into the chair. Nash was glad to get the hell out of there.

Max gushed about her all the way home in the car until Nash felt like committing murder himself. The gullible fool.

'Wasn't she amazing? I mean, wasn't she, though? She was fabulous—and the medium woman wasn't bad either.'

She had hit on a few points. Two murderers threw them right back into the land of Max and an accomplice—and then there was that letter.

Chapter Twenty-Seven

Chapter Twenty-seven

Lawson said, 'Boss, they're waiting for you with the suspect in Interview Room Three.'

'Who've we got?'

'No idea, boss.'

Nash felt his heart rate quicken. He wondered who the hell was sitting in that room—Jones or somebody close to him. The real Florist?

The fact remained that Nash was being targeted as well as Jones. He didn't know if extortion and blackmail were just the start. Following the logical line of thought, the next step for Nash would be death. The note he'd found inside his briefcase had disturbed him. His mind was seesawing between it being written by Jones or the real killer. This brought him back to the eternal question of whether they were one and the same and had Nash made a grave error in letting Jones out to walk the streets and kill again. Even he couldn't be that brazen. But he had nothing to lose, a few weeks left to live. That would mess with a man's mind.

Nash went into the observation room and looked at the suspect through the two-way mirror. What the absolute holy hell was going on? Of all the people he might have expected to see sitting at that table—this wasn't it. The next half hour could ruin his career—and his life.

He straightened his posture, rested his files under his arm, and walked into the room with an air of confidence that he didn't feel.

Brown said, 'For the tape, we have been joined by?'

'DCI Nash.' He almost fell into his seat beside her and could hardly speak his name.

'Interview commencing 10:17 AM. DCI Nash, this is Mr Alexander Burns. He was picked up for suspected soliciting when he was caught in a lewd act with a gentleman in the front seat of the other man's car on Anson Street in Barrow. Both men have been detained. The other gentleman's name is Graham Miller, and he's being held in Interview Room One.'

'Why does this concern me? There's no need to waste my time with petty crimes of this nature. Damn you for taking me away from my case, Brown. Process them and have them sent on their way.' To avoid eye contact with the suspect, Nash made a show of rummaging in his folders.

'I'm sorry to have annoyed you, Sir. It was not my intention, and I'd thank you, not to berate me in such a way in front of a member of the public. For the tape, I'm happy for this statement to be deleted later but will not be spoken to like a child.' She glared at Nash, who didn't look up to meet her eyes. 'We brought you in on this for a reason, sir.'

Brown waited until Nash showed some interest. 'Go on.'

'When we did a pat-down search of Mr Burns, we found a photograph relating to The Florist case, folded up in his back pocket.' Brown adjusted her position in the chair, folded her arms, and waited for Nash to respond. Her expression was smug, and he wanted to bring her down a peg or two, but the impact of what she'd said pushed all petty hierarchy to one side.

'What?'

'An incriminating image from our case, sir. And in light of that, the arresting officer asked Mr Burns to unlock his phone, and when he refused, we requested a warrant from Judge Bradbury. We presented the evidence, and he was happy to comply. We pulled over three hundred images relating to the case. There were pictures of all the victims and the crime scenes, but more than that. There were photographs of sensitive documents and pictures of collated evidence.' Her tone was still cold. 'I thought you would want to be brought in, sir.'

'Okay, Brown. Enough. I'm sorry I snapped. Good work.' He glanced up at the suspect and then looked away. 'Carry on.'

'I assumed you would want to conduct the interview, sir.'

She had no idea that Nash knew the suspect. 'No, please, you carry on.'

'Sir.'

Brown looked thrown, but Nash was finding it hard to breathe. There was no way he could conduct this interview. The room was stuffy, and he wondered what a heart attack felt like. 'Continue, Brown, please. We haven't got all day.' His mind was racing for a way out of this. Brown shuffled some papers and straightened her posture, which brought her up another couple of inches. She assumed an air of command which in other circumstances would have made Nash smile. Good on her.

'Mr Burns, please tell us what this photograph was doing on your person at the time of your arrest. For the tape, I am showing the suspect Item One.'

It was a photograph of the Wilson boy kneeling by his bed. Nash shuddered, and for the first time in twenty years, he felt sick in an interview. The photograph was taken from his office at home. He hoped that Brown would assume it had been stolen from evidence lockup.

Burns looked between Nash and Brown and shrugged his shoulders. 'I've never seen it before in my life. I don't know how it got there. Someone must have planted it on me.'

'Come on, Burns, you can do better than that. While we were waiting for DCI Nash to join us, I took the liberty of having our boys run it for prints. Guess what we found?'

Burns shrugged.

'We found your prints all over it. So let's make this quick. I could extend this interview over ninety-six hours, but we've got you right in the middle of the murder case. My men have been busy through the night while we've had you in the cells. You're a lucky man. You have an airtight alibi for all of the murder's bar one. Where were you on September the eighteenth between eight in the evening and one AM?'

Burns looked at Nash, then at Brown, and he shrugged again. 'I don't know. I can't remember.'

'We don't believe you're The Florist. To be honest, you don't seem that clever. So, I ask you again. Where did you get this picture?'

'That man. The one I was with.' He glanced up, then looked back at his hands. 'He must have slipped it into my pocket when I was—you know.'

'But his fingerprints aren't on it. Only yours.'

'Maybe he had gloves on.'

'Was he wearing gloves? You were closer to him than we were.'

'I don't know.'

'Well, you tell us. Was he wearing a glove when he had his fingers wrapped around your penis? Look, Burns. I want to get this over with, so I'm going to throw the book at you. We haven't got enough to charge you with murder—yet—but we can make a damned good start with you being up to your neck in this case. Alexander Brian Burns, I am re-arresting you on suspicion of murder.'

'All right. Stop. I'll tell you everything.'

Nash jerked and leaned forward in his seat, making eye contact with the suspect for the first time. Brown drilled her nails on the desk until Nash wanted to pull every one of them out with a pair of pliers. The sound, meant to intimidate the suspect, was drilling into his brain like a Woodpecker on a pine tree.

'I met a man in the pub.'

'Mr Miller?'

'No, another man, a few weeks ago.'

'Which pub and what was his name?'

'The Tavern, I think, but I don't know his name.'

'Go on.'

'He stopped me in the toilets, and I thought he was after a bit of game, you know, a trick for money, like.' Brown was immobile, and Nash winced. 'But he was different. He gave me some stuff in an envelope and told me to ring Jonas Scott at *The Mail*. He gave me a hundred quid, told me exactly what to say, and said if I did it right, there'd be more.'

'What was in the envelope?'

'I tried to open it, but it started to tear. It was sealed, so I couldn't get into it.

'And it happened again?'

'Yes. About eight times.'

'And you don't know this man's name?'

'No.'

'What does he look like?'

'Big. He was six feet three and had black hair. He wears a long black leather coat. And he's got a spider's web tattooed on his face.'

'Really?'

'Honest.'

'Give him some white face paint like the Joker, and you've just described every DC baddie there ever was. Do you want to try again, Mr Burns?'

'I'm telling you the truth, honest. Ask Jonas Scott at *The Mail*.'

'Rest assured. We will. Did Mr Scott ever see this man?'

'No. He gave me the envelope and told me what to say, and then I rang Scott.'

'Would you be willing to take a polygraph to that effect?'

'No.'

'But you've told us the truth, haven't you? If you've got nothing to hide, why the reluctance?'

Nash had to get out of there. 'Okay, DI Brown, I think that's enough for now. Let's charge him with indecency, and we'll pick this up when we've looked into it further.'

'What? But we need to detain him. This is one of the biggest breaks we've had in the case, boss.'

'No, Brown, only in the leaked material.'

'But sir, even if he didn't do the murders, he could be in cahoots with The Florist. It might be him that leaked the material to Burns.'

Nash shouted, and the papers on the desk fluttered with the force of his breath. 'I said, charge him and let him go, Brown.'

'Sir.'

Nash was the first one out of the room. He had to get Burns' phone out of evidence, but he couldn't do it now. There were too many people around. He wanted to go to the men's room and throw up. But he leaned against the wall to calm his stomach. He watched Burns come out, followed his confident swagger to the front door, and let him get down the steps and around the corner. He watched him walking down the street, and Burns didn't look back once.

When he turned the next corner, Nash broke into a run. He ran with a fury he hadn't felt since his early days on the beat. He caught up to Burns and tackled him from behind, slamming him against the wall.

'What the hell, Sandy?'

'Piss off, Silas.'

'It was you. The leak was you all along?'

Alexander 'Sandy' Burns turned in his arms, but it was far from a loving embrace. 'I'm afraid so, sweet cheeks. I told you, Silas. I warned you not to mess with me.'

'You vindictive bastard.'

'Take your hands off me, or I'll have you done for police brutality. It's a pity you weren't this lively in the bedroom, darling. Let's get down to business. I'm not pissing around. Twenty grand, You've had twenty-four hours, but because today must have been a shock for you, I'll give you another day. Twenty thousand quid by tomorrow, or I sing like Mariah.'

'The graffiti in my house. That was you?'

'Bravo, darling. I must get some brownie points, though. I fed your miserable cat.'

'I threw it out. I thought you'd poisoned her.'

'I like Lola. She was the only good thing about spending time with you.'

'You have a key?'

'You're getting good at this detective stuff.'

'And a key to my office.'

'The question is, what are we going to do about it? You can have me put away, but the consequences for you are equally dire. Criminal, I shouldn't wonder. Having some little queer at large in your house, tampering with evidence, sucking you off at night. Knowing all kinds of things that he shouldn't. Is DI Brown still screwing Sergeant Renshaw, darling?'

'If I meant anything to you, you wouldn't do this to me.'

'You never meant a thing to me. Just one more thing. If you don't do as I say, I'll go for the big one before you can have me picked up again. And you aren't going to march me back in there right now, are you, my love? You haven't got the balls. I'll go to Jonas Scott and tell him chapter and verse, everything—I'll give him every damned detail you've got, pictures and the lot. That's got to be worth twenty little thousand to keep it hush hush, hasn't it?'

Nash let go of Burns and looked at his hands as though he'd been burned. He leaned against the wall and tried to make sense of it.

'Or you can make it all go away. I'll stop selling my stories. You'll give me twenty K, and off I go into the night, never to be heard from again. I'll leave town, darling. It'll be easier for both of us that way. I have something lined up. I can be gone as soon as tomorrow morning. I'll need my phone back. And don't worry. I deleted you from it. Only an in-depth investigation would find any intel on you. Do we have a deal?'

'No. I'm an honest cop.'

'Let's talk about this new suspect you have then. I can have him all over the morning edition.'

Nash's head shot up.

'What's his name? Ah, yes, Jonathan Finch.'

Chapter Twenty-Eight

Chapter Twenty-eight

Max was meeting Nash at the station. He was in time to see the senior officer wrestling somebody further down the street. He heard the bloke asking for twenty grand. He took out his phone, held it up and pressed record.

'Sandy, please.'

The man tried to move away from the wall Nash had pinned him against, and Max watched the detective grab him.

'Get off me, officer, or I'll scream.'

The man tried to run, but Nash refused to let go. 'Why are you doing this? What did I ever do except love you?'

Max had seen enough. He ran down the street and grabbed Sandy by the shirt, slamming him against the wall. 'I'm getting good at this, don't you think, Nash?'

'Is this the new boyfriend? You didn't waste any time, Si.'

'You nasty, unpleasant little worm. I was up the street and might not have caught everything, but the sound on my phone is exceptionally good. I can afford to buy good crap. What I saw was you blackmailing my friend, Nasher, here. Are we friends, Nash? I like to think we are. Semantics. I'm witness number one for the prosecution. My phone is witness two. You've already been in the jailhouse, as far as I could tell. I think you're in trouble, my friend. If this piece of shit plays nice, can you make this go away, Nash?'

Nash nodded his head.

'See? It all turned out nice in the end. Did you say you had a new boyfriend somewhere a long way from here? Give him our love, won't you, knobhead? I think we're done here.' He gave the little snot rag a shake for good measure and let him go.

'I'll have you both done for this.'

'No, you won't,' Nash said.

They watched him disappear. Max leaned against the wall with his hands on his knees, breathing hard.

'I think I'm going to throw up. You are the only person apart from my previous relationships in the world that knows I'm gay,' Nash said.

'I feel truly blessed.'

'If you're just going to take the piss, you can shut up. I won't bore you with my mess in future.'

'No, carry on. My confessional is open for another three minutes until I get my breath back, and then we're going for a pint and will go back to hating each other. Deal?'

'Deal. Damn, why the hell am I confiding in you? Of all people. You. The thought of my ex-boyfriend being a prostitute on any level disgusts me, never mind anything else. I suppose I should be tested for something.'

'Yeah. Suppose. Mate, you should be tested for everything. Bummer for you. Do you want me to come with you?'

'Don't be ridiculous.'

'Did you give him that graze on his cheek?'

'Yes, when he was facing the wall.'

'I'm not taking the rap for that, Hutch. Just so we know.'

And that was it. They were done.

Max moved down the street a few feet to the drain and vomited. 'Sorry.'

'Are you okay?'

'Apart from dying? I'll live.'

He felt better, but Max had to admit that he was getting worse, and ramming the little rat against the wall had taken it out of him.

'We've got two hours until the boys' funeral. Are you well enough for it?'

'If it helps to find the man who killed those innocent kids, I'd rise up from my coffin to be there.'

'Dramatic, Jones.'

***

Max joined the briefing outside the church. For once, he felt pumped rather than sick.

'Right, eyes on. Everybody pay attention. Jones, you worry me. You've had no reconnaissance training. I need you to be aware and scour every face in this pantomime. And that's what it's going to be. Everybody and his monkey will be out. We're expecting most of the town outside the church and lining the streets. I need you to watch the crowd and know what their mood is. Most of all, I want you to do it with your head down and not draw attention to yourself. Reconnaissance takes years of training. Here's your ten-second crash course. Eyes on. See everything. Listen to everything. Be observant, look, listen and find out what you can from clever conversation. Most of all, don't be caught being observant. What I want is to know the person with no place being there. Somebody that's being too helpful at the wake, getting in on the action too much. Saying all the right things but not feeling them. I want that gleam of joy in somebody's eye. Got it?' Nash said.

'Yes, boss.'

'No smart remark, Jones?'

'Not this time.'

'Right, everybody, going in. Please respect the family and those two boys at all times, but remember why you're there. With the television cameras outside, it's not beyond the realms of possibility that our perp might try something today. Be prepared for anything, and if it all goes without incident, that's a win. Team, around the perimeter. Undercover, get yourselves lost in the crowd. Jones, get in with somebody you know. You won't be stuck for a choice. The church is heaving.'

Nash wasn't wrong, and just about everybody Max knew was at the church. As far as he was aware, Mel didn't know either of the families, but she was there, on the end of a pew a third of the way down the aisle. Given her penchant for theatrics, he was surprised she wasn't front and centre. She wore a black pillbox hat—new—and a veil covering her face that made her look like a crazed killer. Her husband had the good grace to look uncomfortable, though that might have been the tie that was choking him, that he kept fiddling with. Max would have laid money on it that Mel had tied it for him. Windsor knot, big, showy. Mel saw Max and made hand gestures to get him over to them. She'd have had no qualms about moving the person next to Lawrence to make room for Max. He ignored her.

But he let out a sigh of relief when he saw a more friendly group to join. Jonathan, his wife, Emily, and Carter were in a pew towards the back of the church. He wanted to be on the end for a quick escape because churches made him uncomfortable, but he was glad when Nash squeezed in next to him. Lucy wasn't with the family, and Max was pleased about that. This was far too heartbreaking for a little girl to attend. Emily explained in a reverent whisper that Lucy went to the same school as the boys. Carter was fidgety, and his dad had to tell him to calm down. It was his first funeral, and Max envied his youth and ability not to see the finality or sheer, miserable sadness of death. Carter asked if he'd be on television, and like any young boy would be, he was excited about seeing himself on the news. He nudged Max and whispered, 'I've never seen a dead body before.'

'Neither have I, mate. Good job, they're in coffins, eh?'

'Do they really go stiff and go blue when they're dead?'

Emily leaned over and told them to shush, she glared at Max, and he grinned. Max loved winding the key in Carter's back and watching him go.

At the other side of the church, Linda Lewis, Henry Watson's personal assistant, sat at one end of the pew, and Max recognised Fiona, Jon's sister, at the other. They looked like a pair of bookends. Max imagined them as painted novelties for sale in a shop. The artist would title the limited piece *Delicious Mourning*, and they would sell for a stupid price in craft shops around Windermere. People would show visitors their unusual bookends and call them charming.

Like Mel, they both wore black coats with hats and a small veil, but they wore them far less obtrusively and not as a fashion statement like Mel was doing. Most of the churchgoers were modern and opted to forego black in favour of clothing that wasn't sombre as a celebration of the boys' lives. Before the service started, Nash was humming a bloody tune, for Christ's sake.

Max was aware of somebody trying to get his attention, and in a pew, on the other side of the church, he saw Hayley Mooney waving her order of service at him. Hayley was always smiling, and it was as though she wanted to now, not from a lack of respect but because it was her default mode. She kept her lips flat and her face closed. One smile from Hayley and the church would have been bathed in golden light over the two white coffins at the railings. Steve nodded at him.

Max risked a quiet look around. Jessica Hunter was there, and that voodoo woman. She was a strange one. He saw a lot of people he recognised. Most were acquaintances and people he knew enough to nod to in the street. Now, he looked at them again. He gave them the face of a child killer. The awful thing was that they all fit the part.

The funeral was the saddest thing that Max had ever been to.

It was sadder than Nanny Clare's funeral. She'd had her life, and it'd been a content one. These little boys had never blown up a science lab or tasted their first beer. He would have donated the last months of his life to give those boys who were strangers to him their lives back.

He wondered how many people would attend his funeral. It would be nothing grand like this in terms of turnout. He made a list of attendees in his head and wanted to punch himself in the face because he'd let himself get distracted when he was supposed to be observant.

When everybody bowed their heads in prayer, Max looked around. He was startled when he turned and saw Jon with his head up looking right at him. Their eyes locked, and Max saw something shifting in his pupils. It looked like hatred. 'Nice suit,' Jon whispered, and Max jerked his head down to stare at his intertwined fingers. Emily shushed them like naughty schoolboys, and Max saw Carter's shoulders shaking with silent laughter.

The wake was better for people-watching, and the finger food was fabulous. Everybody goes to a funeral for the buffet, the beer and the brawl at the end of the night. He saw Nash looking on. 'We need a debrief before you go home tonight.' Max walked past with a half-full plate to get some more of the excellent smoked salmon on crackers and said, 'I can be sad, but I don't have to be hungry.' Nash was humming that bloody song again.

Linda was her usual walking efficiency, gliding around with a plate of vol-au-vents, and he took two on his way to the salmon. Mel was already tanked on sherry. He'd seen her take three over the course of half an hour. It was amazing what you saw once you opened your eyes and looked around. Carter's aunt Fiona was insistent on comforting him, but he didn't look as though he needed any comforting at all.

Max flitted between the grounds and the venue. He stood among hundreds of people, listening to conversations and picking up information that was of no use to the case at all. Jenny Ripley had new curtains in her lounge—maybe she'd used the old curtains for wrapping dead bodies. Colin Hyman had a market stall that sold vegetables from an allotment big enough to bury bodies in. He still had the soil under his fingernails. Fiona had a scratch on her neck and blamed it on Jon's new dog. Peter Green just had an evil face. Everybody had something that stood out to Max if he looked hard enough.

'I said to Jon, that bloody dog's vicious. You should never have taken it in,' Fiona told Molly Crompton.

Max took umbrage. Mia would never hurt anybody on purpose.

Molly said, 'I made banana bread last night, but it had a soggy bottom.' After two glasses of prosecco, how they laughed. Max nearly wet himself with the hilarity.

It was all just crap.

He wanted to sneak away from the mourners who were getting pissed. He wanted to talk to the dead boys. He needed to tell them how sorry he was for what happened to them and that he was a useless fool, but he was trying. He couldn't do that. Both boys had been cremated. He looked at Jon and still couldn't get his head around him being Nash's prime suspect. His mouth was chewing a slice of buttered malt loaf, and Max wondered if their little bodies were burning as he chomped.

At some point, those kids would have been told, 'Don't talk to strangers,' and that's what he was, just a stranger. Max was a nobody. He had one fact to take to Nash, and it wasn't an earth-shattering hypothesis. Nash would have worked it out for himself.

They knew him—Gareth and Jamie knew their killer.

When he saw Nash, he was still humming the same bloody tune. 'What the hell is that?' Max asked him.

'What?'

'That damn song. You keep humming it.'

'Sorry. Wasn't aware that I was. It's a brain worm. It's *Two Black Cadillacs.*'

'Never heard of it.'

'But the women in the two black veils didn't bother to cry. The funeral reminded me of it, that's all.'

Chapter
Twenty-Nine

Chapter
Twenty-nine

The knock at the door was timid, and there was a whirring in Max's head that wouldn't go away. The tinnitus was getting worse, but it wasn't that. It was only ten thirty, and he'd had to pull on a pair of jogging pants and run to the door in his bare feet. Not looking where he was going, his foot squished into a dead field mouse that Dexter had brought in for him. It was soft and hard and wet. He felt the imprint of the mouse's tail along the instep of his foot and cringed. 'Bloody cat.'

He limped to the door on one foot and one heel. As he opened it, he tried for a smile. 'Morning, Hayley. How's it going? You look radiant today. I hope Steve's looking after you.' He ran out of simpering platitudes and shut up. She was such a nice person, and the law of humanity states that you have to be nice to nice people.

'How are you, love?' she asked. 'You looked so poorly—I mean, tired. You looked tired at the funeral yesterday, and the kids wanted to bake you some brownies. Isla said to tell you they're special ones.' She held out a package wrapped in paper with printed unicorns and tied with a red satin bow that reminded him of the black ribbons that Chelsea used in her posthumous circus act. He hadn't had his medication yet. He was going to puke. Hayley was light on her feet. She just managed to skip out of the way, but he threw up all over his doorstep. Unfortunately, he missed the unicorns.

'Sorry.'

'Don't give it another thought. Are you okay?' Hayley looked as though she was going to vomit as well, but she was strong and came here to say what she wanted to say. 'Max, I was wondering.'

'Yes?' He was wheezing and struggled to get his breath. Her words were coming at him in a tangled buzz from the tinnitus in his brain, and he didn't have the energy to separate them from the cacophony.

'I'm sorry to be the bearer of bad news, but while you were away, dealing with the police accusations, the gardener said he hadn't been paid for a while and wouldn't be coming back until he was.' Shit, he'd forgotten to pay Tom again. 'Steve's whizzing over your lawns now, just to keep on top of them.' He had an image of Steve lying on Max's lawn, making a snow angel in the grass, and whizzing his tits off. Max wanted to join him. He laughed.

'Sorry? Are you okay?'

'Oh nothing, just—that's so kind of him. Tell him I'm very grateful.' Please, God, don't make me go out there and thank him myself. I can't do anymore being nice. Not yet. Let me sit down. Just let me sit the hell down before I fall down right here in my puddle of vomit. 'Was there anything else?'

'Yes, I wondered if you'd like me to come in and give you a couple of hours?'

Would I what? Oh, man, would I, but I don't think the knackered old body would manage two hours. If that's what Steve was getting, no wonder he was whistling as he mowed the lawn. 'A couple of hours?'

'Yes. Sorry. Hope you don't mind me saying, but when you were away, I couldn't help but notice that your stairs could do with a good going over with the vacuum. And that hob. Go on, you go and get comfy, and I'll sort this mess.'

'No,' he screamed. 'No, thank you, no. It's okay. I'll get the hoover out. Today. Yes. I'll do it today. Thank you, Hayley. Lovely biscuits, tell the kids. Hugs to Isla, Bye, bye. Yes, bye, bye, bye.' He shut the door and had to run for the bathroom.

***

Max and Nash sat in Amanda Key's psychic reading parlour after Jessica had called them. Nash was dismissive. 'We can't deny that what you've told us has some merit, Ms Keys, but much of what you brought us could have been researched and found in the media or on Facebook.'

'Ignore him. He hasn't had his Sugar Puffs yet. I think you're fabulous.' Max couldn't resist hamming it up to annoy Nash. He had to have some simple pleasures left in life. 'What else can you tell us?'

'I've been getting image fragments for several days. I keep seeing a door.' For effect, her voice went wispy and lacked any substance. 'A green door that's old and scratched. It looks like an internal entrance, but it has a Yale lock on it. It had a word scratched in the paintwork at about eye level. No, not a word. Initials. It's a D and an H. No, that's not right. I'm being shown a big red road sign with a white cross in the middle, which means I've made a mistake somewhere.'

'Let me save you the performance. The initials were CH,' Nash said.

'Close, though,' Max added.

Jessica said, 'Inspector, if you're going to be negative about the reading, perhaps you should wait outside. I'd hate anything to stop Amanda from being able to work.'

'I'm sorry. Please continue.'

'I'm getting a King. No, a King's wife? I'm sorry. This is obviously wrong. I'm just getting a string of garbled messages, somebody saying the word Culpepper. Culpepper? It was spoken about in a police interview recently. I have no idea what it means or if it's even a real word. Does that make any sense?'

'Yeah, it does.' Max couldn't believe what was coming out of this woman's mouth.

'The initials belong to a woman close to Paige and link to a third girl. I'm being told that CH and Paige were close but didn't know each other. I know it doesn't make sense, but I can only pass on what I'm given. They are both connected to Paige. CH is Paige's flatmate? But Paige and the third woman didn't know each other.'

'Good, good. Go on.' Nash was writing relevant points even though the session was being recorded. He'd told Max that writing something makes it real and solidifies it in the writer's head. Nash couldn't argue this one, and that information couldn't be found on good old Facebook.

'I'm seeing some children, a boy and a girl. They're fighting. Is this the little boy that keeps coming back to me every time I try to focus? I'm not sure. Same age. Could be him. The girl is screaming. "I hate you. I hate you. I'm going to kill you." The boy is laughing. Toys, dolls and teddies. A tea party. Something to do with a red teapot.'

Max breathed in hard. 'I've never got on with Mel, but isn't that the same with all brothers and sisters? It's laughable to think she'd kill ten people to set me up for filling her teapot with clay when we were kids. That would be some payback prank.'

'There's a barman. He saw somebody leaving the pub with one of the girls. It's confusing information and not coming in the right order. He's saying it's you, Max. I can see him in an interview pointing at your photograph. He's saying, "That's him there. He was a shifty-looking guy with a crush on Zoe." He locked up after they left together.'

'It's okay. We've tied all that up.'

'And did he say that?' Max asked.

'Yep. Word for word,' Nash said. 'Personally, I think you're full of shit, I'm too old to change my opinion, but maybe there is some merit in this psychic stuff. Who knows.'

'The little boy's back. He's showing me a cut finger. The way he's holding it up to me makes it important. No, he's gone.'

Max saw Nash's entire body posture change. He knew more about this than he was letting on.

'The Florist's going to strike again. Soon. I'm trying to get some information on the next victim. I can see the killer. He's going inside a house. He's dressed in black and holding something in his hand. A knife, maybe. It's dark. I can't make out where he is.' Amanda stared around the room. She threw her hands up and screamed.

Jess was the closest, and she went to her, dropping to her knees to comfort Amanda. 'What is it? What have you seen? Is he coming for Max?'

'No.' Amanda was sobbing and turned into Jessica's embrace.

'What then? Tell us what you saw.'

'He's coming for me.'

Chapter Thirty

Chapter Thirty

Nash knew that look. Jessica might as well have been standing with her hand on her hips, tapping her foot with impatience. She didn't adopt the stance, but it was the message her face was getting across without any possibility of a misunderstanding. Jess had followed Nash and Max to his car when they left.

'What are you going to do about it?'

'Do about what?'

'The death threat, of course.'

'Miss Hunter, nobody has threatened anybody with anything.'

'She's just seen it, clear as day. You need to get her into a safe house. Right now.'

Nash scoffed. 'Are you kidding me? Have you any idea how much that would cost the taxpayer? I'd be laughed out of the accounts department if I put in a safehouse request because a misguided psychic saw her own death.'

'Hang on, though,' Max said. 'You can't ignore this. It's serious.'

'Damn right, I can. Bloody fortune tellers and kooks.' He sighed and came to a compromise. 'Fine. I'll get the lads to drive by a few times through the night, okay?'

'No, Inspector. It's not okay. I need to get back in there because that lady is distraught. I'd stay with her myself, but my parents are still beside themselves, and I have to be with them. But I'm telling you now. You need to put your prejudices aside because if so much as a hair on her head is injured, the blood is on your hands.'

'I agree, Nash,' Max said. 'Come on. You've got to admit she saw things that nobody knew. Personal stuff. You have to do something.'

'Do it now, Inspector. There's no time to waste. while you're trying to pull every stitch of her credibility apart word by word, she's in danger.'

'Okay. You win, but I'm going to have a hell of a job getting this past my Super. I'll arrange guards outside the house.'

'Thank you, Chief Inspector.'

Jones looked pale. He was standing with a daft grin on his face until Jessica turned the corner. Nash had been so involved with the conversation with her that he didn't see the colour drain from Jones' face or the beads of sweat breaking out along his forehead and upper lip.

Before Jess's shadow had disappeared, Jones was trembling. Nash ran to him in time to catch him as he fell. He stopped his head from hitting the floor and used his body as a buffer to lower Jones gently onto the pavement. He was between the next house's garden hedge and the car and was shielded from the other officers and the house. Nash flipped him onto his side and put him in the recovery position. He felt for his pulse, which was strong but erratic, and when he lifted an eyelid, he saw that Jones' eyes had rolled into his head so that only the whites were showing. He loosened his coat from around his neck and undid a couple of buttons on his shirt. Nash was pressing buttons on his phone as Jones' eyes flickered open.

'Gonna be sick.' He lurched over to the base of the hedge and threw up.

Nash knelt down beside him and passed him a wad of tissue from out of the car. 'Lie back down. I'll get help.'

'No ambulance. I'm fine.'

'Yeah, I know, don't say it. You're fine for a dying man.'

'You're catching on, Nasher.'

Nash helped him up and opened the passenger door for him. Jones wilted into it and breathed a sigh of relief. 'I didn't want to do a dying swan in front of the sexy Jess.'

'Yeah, I saw that.'

'Thanks for being there.'

Nash drove him to his Barrow flat because it was closer to the hospital than his house in Ulverston. Nash wasn't happy and nagged him about turning around and going to the hospital the whole journey. Jones wouldn't listen and insisted on going home. Nash made them a drink and found a tin of chicken soup in the cupboard.

'Sick people's food,' Jones said. 'Chicken soup, it's what you give to sick people. Though traditionally, it's supposed to be homemade, so you could have made an effort.'

'Sod off. I've got better things to do than be playing Nurse Ratchet to you.'

Nash saw that he was comfortable, fussed around him and made sure that he had his phone beside him in case he needed to call for an ambulance. By the time he was done, Jones virtually threw him out of the house to get back to work.

At the station, Nash put things in place to have a guard outside Amanda's house. He spent the rest of the day putting together an airtight case against Finch, even though he had doubts about his guilt.

***

Nash and Renshaw avoided contaminating evidence in Amanda Keys'
kitchen. Nash felt ill. This one was on him, and he felt the burden
of guilt pressing down on his breakfast. He was warned but chose to
make light of it. He should have done more.

'The Florist was waiting for her when she got home,' Renshaw said.
'The poor cow didn't stand a chance. I hope you haven't eaten yet. It's
not nice in there.'

'Is Robinson here?'

'Yes, he arrived half an hour ago. Done the preliminaries, and I
think they're ready to bag and tag her.'

'I want a statement from the patrol outside her house. Didn't they
see or hear anything? What's the bloody point of them when they
let a murderer walk in under their nose and kill the person they're
supposed to be guarding?'

'Sir.'

Nash followed the noise into the victim's parlour. While the rest of
Amanda's house was bright and modern, this room was more subdued, with soft lighting and a calm atmosphere. In her line of work, it
was dressed differently, but it's what the rest of us might call an office.
SOCO had finished dusting for fingerprinting and photographing the
body and were filing out when Nash arrived.

'Here we are again,' Robinson said. 'I can talk you through the
scene, but it speaks for itself. Sicko.'

'Time and cause of death?' Nash asked.

'Sometime between ten and two last night. This is corroborated
by the patrol guy outside. It's another slashed throat. Sharp knife.
Smooth blade, no serrated edge. It's a single clean cut. Confident. No
dummy runs to test the blade. Grabbed her hair from behind to pull

her head back and expose her neck. One slice and it was all over. It wouldn't have taken her long to bleed out. A couple of minutes at most. As to all this theatre,' Robinson spread his hands to indicate the staging. 'You can make of that what you will.'

'Thanks, Bill. The Florist likes to get our attention. This took time and effort, and while he had her tied to that chair, our officers were drinking coffee and eating fairy cakes fifty feet away in her drive.'

'You reckon?'

'What do you think? He took her because it was easy, and it shouldn't have been.'

'He's a brazen bastard. If she'd got one scream out, we'd have had him.' Nash shook his head. This one was personal, and he was angry. He'd taken her from underneath Nash's nose. He looked around at the mockery in the form of an elaborate tableau. It had taken hours to create. He worked on it while Amanda was tied to the chair. She must have been terrified.

The action was centred around Amanda Key's séance table. He assumed every good medium should have one. The table was an expensive piece of furniture. He'd seen some on TV with pentagrams and all kinds of devil-worshipping stuff on them, but this one was whittled in good-witch wood. It had carved doves, shaking hands and hearts around the stunning inlaid marquetry. All the fluff ruined what was a beautiful piece of furniture, in Nash's opinion.

Amanda was staged with both hands flat on the table, with her fingers touching the other hands. She was dressed in traditional Gypsy Rosa-Lee garb that was less than original. Nash took a point off the killer for that one. She'd had a long veil covering her face that had been photographed and then pulled back with tweezers for identification. There was a lot of blood, most of it in a spreading stain across the inlay of the table.

Amanda wasn't seated alone. The sick bastard had brought her four guests to make up the séance. Equally distanced around a Ouija board were four shop mannequins. Their hands were on the table and spread to join the people on either side of them, making a circle with Amanda Keys at the centre. They had been dressed to look like certain characters in his sick game. This had taken a lot of planning. The four dummies resembled Paige Hunter, Zoe Connolly, Catherine Howard—and Jessica Hunter, the only one that was still alive. 'Oh shit. The Hunter sister is in danger. He's after Jessica.'

'It could be him playing, sir.' Renshaw didn't look convinced.

'No, I'm telling you this is his calling card and our invitation to the next scene. Get some officers to her house now and check on her. I don't care if she's at work. Bring her into protective custody. Lock her in one of the cells if you have to. I don't care what you do but keep that girl safe. He's not getting this one.'

'Sir.' Renshaw turned to leave the room, and Nash shouted for Brown to come in.

'Sir,' Brown said, averting her eyes from the table.

'Get onto every outlet selling mannequins in a fifty-mile radius, and then see if there have been reports of shop dummies being stolen. Go back six months. No. Go back as far as you have to in order to find this animal. Our clue is in finding out where these dummies came from.'

'I'm on it.'

He motioned to one of the SOCO team with a camera. 'Get a picture of this part of the table. I want to see this writing more clearly.'

'We already have, sir.' He handed Nash the camera showing the high-resolution image.

'When you go to print, make this one a priority. I want a blow-up of this photograph as soon as we can,' Nash said.

'I'll try to get it to you within the hour.'

Robinson stood beside Nash. 'The killer must have left the room before she was dead. How hasn't he seen this if we have?' he said.

'It could be that he did see it and is throwing us a few crumbs. Being a cocky bastard. For all we know, he might have written it himself. We've had Jon Finch under surveillance for days. He's been nowhere near here. According to patrol, every second of every day is accounted for. I don't get it. How have you done it? How've you pulled it off, Jonny boy?'

Nash looked at the photo again. 'I want to see this in better detail back at the office. In the meantime, Bill, we'll have the writing properly tested, but is there any fast way of knowing whether she wrote it or he did?'

'Can't tell and wouldn't like to make a guess. However, if you had my hand tied behind my back and had someone kick me in the bollocks, I'd say probably her. Female, small writing. She either kept it small so that he wouldn't see it or didn't think to make it bigger. That's putting a lot of trust in police forensics.'

'Thanks, Bill. Even if we can't say for sure until we get it tested and get handwriting samples, it's something to go on. If we think Amanda wrote it, I'm more likely to trust it and not think it's just another white-rabbit run-around from The Florist.'

He adjusted his mask to ensure that his breath wouldn't move or contaminate any evidence. Nash put his face close to the writing. The blood almost touched his nose from this angle, and he could smell it. Nash got his head as close to the position that Amanda Keys was in when she died. He wanted to see what she saw. She may have had the foresight to move her head to the left as she'd died to hide the word from her killer.

The last note and her dying testament read:

Jon si

'I failed to protect her, and she wrote her last thought to me. This is a message to help me after I let her down. She's telling me. It's Jon, Silas.'

'Who's Silas?' Robinson asked.

'I am.'

Since Maxwell Jones had been cleared, Jonathan Finch had been the primary suspect. It looked as though they were on the right track, and it was time to bring him in.

Nash flinched as he heard a voice he recognised. And he knew the tone, too.

'What's going on? Is Amanda okay? Let me get in.'

He left the crime scene and headed Jessica off at the pass. Taking her elbow, he guided her away from prying eyes.

'Can we get in my car, please, Ms Hunter, and we can talk?' He was taking his whites off and putting them in a yellow crime scene waste bag.

'Tell me. Is Amanda all right?'

'Not here.'

'She's dead, isn't she?'

'Bloody hell, woman. Will you just get in the car before you announce to the whole world that something's happening?'

'Sorry.'

She had tears in her eyes by the time Nash opened his passenger seat for her and guided her in. He went around the other side and drove away.

'She's gone, isn't she?'

'I'm afraid so. Yes.'

'You bastard. You absolute bastard.'

'I'm so sorry.'

'It's too late to be sorry. This is on you.'

'You think I don't know that?'

'Where are we going?'

'Somewhere quiet where we can talk.'

'You didn't listen to her. You were supposed to protect her.'

Nash stopped the car on the seafront, and they watched the waves breaking on the shore. It was cold, and there was only one dog walker on the sand throwing a ball from a plastic launcher while two golden retrievers chased after it. Jess was still pointing out Nash's failings, and she was crying—albeit quietly, thank God.

'Right,' Nash said with a gentle touch on her coat sleeve. He leaned over her and searched in the glove box for a packet of tissues. 'I want you to tell me everything that was said between you and Amanda. Every word from the beginning.'

'There were a lot of them, Inspector because while I went into it as sceptical as you, I gave her the time of day and listened. I still don't believe in ghosts and the afterlife and all that crap, but I was open-minded about it, unlike you.'

'Stop talking, woman. Can't you hold your flapping mouth for even a second? You could be next.'

That stopped her. Her hand was raised to point at him. No doubt to list another failing on Nash's part, maybe for not inviting the lady in white, the silent monk and the headless horseman to dinner. She stopped dead. He had the conscious thought—alive, not dead. He wanted her to stay that way. This woman was vibrant and young. She had all the answers and opinions that were the right of passage for a person under thirty. He had to keep her alive. Forget the rest of the force. Nash knew her. It was his responsibility.

The killer must know her too. He'd have done his homework. Jessica Hunter was the only living person at the séance table. He doubted he only knew her as Paige Hunter's sister. By the fact that he'd chosen a dummy of her to take that fifth seat, he had to assume he knew about her involvement with Amanda too.

'You're not going to be alone for a second,' Nash said.

'Okay, but keep them outside. Nobody in the house. I can't have strangers parading in and out and upsetting my parents more than they already are.'

'Outside? Like we did for Amanda? If you sneeze, an officer is going to be next to you to hand you a hanky. You will shower with the door open and either talk—you're good at that—or sing Happy Birthday for all I care, but the second they can't hear you, my officers are in there. You will sleep with the bedroom door open and somebody guarding your doorway.'

'You're frightening me, DCI Nash.'

'I'm scared too, kid, and that's a good thing. It's okay to be terrified because that's what keeps us one step ahead. Here's my promise to Paige. I won't lose you too. I won't.'

'Will he come tonight?'

'I don't know, but when he does, we'll be ready for him.'

'You know the best thing about dying would be seeing Paige again.'

'You aren't going to die, and I thought you didn't believe in all that afterlife rubbish.'

'I don't, so the best thing about dying is not dying.'

'Here's to living.'

***

'What have you got?' Bronwyn Lewis asked.

'We're stretched, Ma'am,' Nash said. 'Three teams deployed on around-the-clock surveillance. It'll lighten the load when we bring

Finch in today, but I've still requested another twenty bodies, as agreed.'

'Apt choice of words in this case.'

'Sorry. We've got Finch wherever he goes. We don't think he suspects anything. Jones is Jones. He's a pain in the arse and thinks it's a game to keep losing his shadows. The killer's adapting on the hoof. That is a big leap from his MO, and when a killer drops his form, it means he's either very calculating and calm or he's on the slide and coming apart. Both are equally dangerous.'

'Tell me about Finch.'

'I've got a horrible feeling about him.'

'And when you have a feeling, Nash, we ignore it at our peril. Coffee?' Bronwyn thumbed the intercom and ordered drinks for them. As an aside, she told the person receiving to bring two cakes in as well. Bronwyn Lewis had a great figure but lived her life on a diet. Or, Nash mused, maybe it was a continuous string of diets. When Lewis ate cake, it meant that she was worried. And when Lewis was worried, Nash had to keep his head down even lower than the troops. He was in the direct line of fire. 'Go on,' she said.

'When we knew it couldn't be Jones, everything—and I mean everything—pointed to it being Finch. It had to be him because he's the only person close enough to Jones to have the necessary intel on him.'

'Motive?'

'In a court of law, it would be circumstantial. The motive is well covered, but it's a strong one. It's jealousy and resentment. This guy has watched Jones succeed his whole life, while Finch packs candles in boxes for a living. I've pulled his finances, and the bank balance isn't great. There's more going out than coming in every month. And it shows a big hit of cash from Jones every few quarters. They might be best mates, but I think there's a whole world of resentment there.'

'Is it enough to bring him in and hold him? We only get one shot at this.'

'Are you suggesting that we leave him out there and give him more rope to hang himself or somebody else?'

'Something like that, I think. What I'm saying is if we mess this up, we're stuffed. We'll have blown the element of surprise and lost our options. The second we bring him in, we've got ninety-six hours to charge him or let him go. We have to be sure about this, Silas. It's too big to get wrong.'

'We've had eyes on him for five days, and he's so clean he's squeaking. He does the school run. He goes to work. He comes home. Hell, last night before Keys was murdered, he stopped off at Booths and came out with wine and flowers. The team were betting on it being an affair, but he took them home to his wife. He was there all night as far as our officers could tell, but for all we know, he could have a secret tunnel in and out of his house.'

'Could you be wrong?'

'And here we have the problem. It has to be Finch, but a couple of things aren't lying right with me and here's that feeling I told you about.'

'Hit me.'

'Finch isn't all that bright. He's nowhere near as tuned in as Jones. Our killer is sharp. Look at the scenes. They are intricate and planned. And then, when every detail is in place, he goes in, and his timing and precision are like a surgeon making his first cut. The MO feels all wrong for Finch.'

'Who else have we got?'

'Jones mentioned one of his tenants, a bloke at Ulverston, but I'm not liking him for it. I've been into him with a fine tooth comb—a couple of parking tickets, always paid before they double, and that's it. Not a blemish. Divorced with no problems, it's all amicable enough, and he has regular access to the kids. New partner for a few years. All the children adore him. Doesn't fit the profile. Loads of mates, and everybody seems to like him.'

'Who else?'

'Hell, boss, I haven't got a deck of cards full of suspects. That's it. Steve Hill, the tenant, but he's a rank outsider, and Finch, who's being pegged for it, but he feels wrong too. Nobody else. Nada.'

'So where do we go from here?'

'I have no idea.'

Chapter Thirty-One

Chapter Thirty-one

'You see our predicament, Mr Finch?' Nash said.

Nash and Brown were on their third cup of coffee at their third house that day. The children were fussing around in the kitchen, and Jonathan got up and closed the door to the lounge so they wouldn't be disturbed.

'I can't see why you'd think it was Max. He's not a killer.'

'No. We know because some of The Florists' work was done while we had Max in custody. So, unless he was in two places at once, it couldn't be him.'

'Well, I could have told you that. I did say this in my previous interviews. If Max has proved his innocence now, I really don't see what more help I can be to you, so if you'll excuse me, Detective Nash, I have things to be getting on with.'

'Just a few more questions, if you don't mind, sir.'

'I'm watching the children. At least you haven't come in uniform this time, like the last lot. They frightened my kids. I've told you everything I can think of to further your investigation.'

Nash wasn't coming down hard at this point. He wanted to let Finch talk himself into a trap. 'If you wouldn't mind sitting back down, sir.'

'I've said everything I've got to say. That you're barking up the wrong tree. This is nothing to do with Max Jones, and the mere fact that you'd think anybody around here could be mixed up in something so evil is ridiculous.'

'Where is Mrs Finch?'

'She's in her office upstairs. She's a telesales assistant. Hence the reason I've got the children. Would it be possible for you to call another day?' They heard a yell from the garden. Finch looked through the window to check on the kids, who had left the kitchen to go outside. Carter was winding his sister up, and Finch rapped hard on the window to stop him.

'This can't wait, Mr Finch. We can either do this here or down at the station. It's your choice.'

'You say that? Wow, you really do say that.' He sat down, but every few seconds, his eyes went to the window. 'I need to watch Carter. He's been a bit boisterous lately. It's not like him.' Nash had to stop him before he went as far as getting the baby photos out and loading a slide show to the TV from his phone or whatever they did these days.

'I'd like to take you along our thought process if you can humour us for a second. We've had Mr Jones with us, and we've interviewed him at length. He's passed a polygraph test with flying colours, and we know that he's not The Florist. However, all of the victims, bar the last one, have been people that are or were connected to Mr Jones.'

'Coincidence and bullshit.'

'What makes you say that?'

'Some old man that taught him a million years ago. And two boys that he didn't know? I think your thought process is sketchy at best.'

'We've found out that there was actually a connection between you and the two children.'

'Me?'

'Isn't it true that the two boys were in the same junior football league as your son?'

'Well, yes, that's why we went to the funeral to pay our respects. Emily is friends with Gareth's mum.'

'And you used to take it in weekly turns to carpool the boys to training?'

'Yes, and Emily sometimes, and I think even Max took them for us once when I was held up at work. Bugger me. You can't be using that as a link to Max, surely. It's so tenuous that it borders on the ridiculous.'

'Children have trusted people on less of a connection, believe me. But to be honest, I'm interested in you.'

'Excuse me?'

'You, Mr Finch.'

It took a while, but little bird Finch got there in the end. 'You think I had something to do with this? That I'm this Florist character. That's preposterous. I'm a married man.'

'Most serial killers are.'

'Do I need a solicitor? I haven't got one. What do I do?' He looked frightened and appealed to Brown. 'Do you agree with this rubbish?' Nash was clearly a bad cop in his eyes.

Brown said, 'Don't worry. This is only an initial interview. Tell us the truth, and we'll do everything we can to help you. If you feel you need a solicitor present, you can join us at the station, and we'll get one for you. We just want to eliminate you from our line of enquiries.'

'This is sounding more like a TV detective show by the second. I didn't kill anybody. Hell, If somebody asked me how to murder a man, I wouldn't have a clue. This is surreal, and I can't get my head around it.'

'You're doing fine. Take your time. Did you know that we had Mr Jones in custody last week?'

'What? No. I had no idea. He dumped the damned dog on us and went on a camping trip. There's nothing unusual about that. Max does his own thing. Always has. We thought he'd gone off in that bloody camper van. He gets fads, spends a fortune, and then gets bored with his new hobby as quickly as he jumped on it. It boils my piss, to be honest.'

Nash didn't give him time to think before coming in with this next question. He wished the kids weren't making such a racket in the garden because he needed the suspect's full attention. Throw in a piece of information and hit him straight away with a barrage of questions before he has time to think too much and come up with any alibis.

'We've been watching you, Finch. We've had a team of officers on your back for over a week.' Nash stood up and took a step towards Finch so that he towered above him. It was one of his tactics to tighten the noose around the suspect. Finch leaned back into the sofa. 'There's a lot of resentment when you talk about Jones. He dumped a dog on you. He went off without telling you. He spends a fortune on rubbish when you struggle to pay your bills. Is that how it is?'

'No, of course not. Max is my best mate. We've known each other since we were kids.'

'That's a long time to build up a lot of resentment. Tell me the truth. What was your relationship like?'

'I love him like a brother.' His eyes went to the garden and back to Nash.

'Brothers fight, though, don't they? They don't always get on.'

'Can you sit down, please, Inspector Nash? You're trying to intim-idate me, and I won't have it.'

'Let's go back to when you were kids. There was a lot of rivalry and one-upmanship between you. Always fighting to get the best conker, see who could piss furthest up the wall?' Nash followed Finch's eyes to the window. The little girl was standing against the garage wall, and the boy was kicking a football. One kid in goal, one striking, but he was going in pretty hard with that ball. If it hit her, it would do some damage. Finch flew up from his chair and banged on the window. 'Carter, stop that. If that ball hits Lucy, it'll hurt her. Can't you go and play on your Xbox or something? Sorry, officer. What was the question?' He sat down and watched the window as the children walked away from the garage. Carter had his ball under his arm. 'There you go—a classic example of sibling behaviour. Kids don't think. If that football had hit her in the face, it would have been a hospital job. But kids don't think, do they? And Carter loves his sister like I love Max.'

'But you didn't have that blood bond,' Nash said. 'You were friends, not, in fact, brothers.'

'Can you get to the point, please, Inspector Nash? I don't under-stand what you're driving at.'

'You said you were like brothers, but you didn't have that blood bond. Surely rivalry could turn into resentment very quickly.'

'If I resented Max to the point where I became a crazed murderer, wouldn't I just kill him rather than everybody else?'

'But you wouldn't need to kill Max. He's dying anyway. I've heard that Jones used to stick up for you against the bullies when you were kids. Having somebody to fight your battles must have made you feel very small and weak.'

'No. I was picked on, and I was always grateful to Max for looking out for me.'

'Wouldn't it be good to be the strong one for once, though? We think you found a way to be the clever one. You really socked it to him by setting him up for murder, didn't you?' Nash went for him with the question, and Finch looked terrified.

'I never killed anybody.' He was saying exactly the same things as Jones had the week before, and like Jones, Nash believed that this guy was just as innocent. But that was the way of the true psychopath. They hid in plain sight and lived in normal society with a beautiful wife, two-point-four children and junior football league. Nash had to push him to at least try and make him crack.

'We've heard about the big one, though. The one time you really got one over on Jones. You got the girl, didn't you? Both of you fancied Emily Howell, and the underdog won for the first time in his life. It must be hard watching them year in and year out, knowing that your best made wants to steal your missus. Jones is in love with her, isn't he? Always has been. Do you think they've ever done it? One week in three, you're on the night shift. While you're putting taper candles into boxes, do you think Jones is putting his taper into your wife's box? You've always been punching, haven't you, Finch?'

'That's disgusting, Detective. Not only are you throwing daggers at Max, but you're questioning my wife's morals. Max and Emily would never do that. How dare you speak about my wife like that. I won't stand for it.'

'Are you getting angry? What will you do? Will you come at me in the night with a big knife?'

'Don't be ridiculous. I'll report you to your superiors.'

'He was one for the girls, though, our Max, wasn't he? I suppose it was an unspoken pact not to talk about what happened to Fiona.

Easier not to talk about it because then you'd have to choose a side between your annoying little sister and your best friend. Talk me through it. What was it like for a good catholic family to have a girl in trouble at barely seventeen?'

Finch dropped his head into his hands and ran his fingers through his hair. 'You have no idea. My parents were devastated. We managed to keep it away from most of the parishioners, but people talk, and the word still got around. Mum cried all the time. Fiona told Max once that it wasn't his, and that was it. He believed that Fi had been sleeping around with half the town. In his head, he was exonerated. But Fiona was besotted with the bastard. She'd been in love with him all her life, and there was nobody else in her eyes except Max.'

'And that bastard, as you rightly call him, just side-shifted to one of her friends, leaving your family to clean up his mess, as usual. Strictly between us, I don't like him either, Jon. Too cocky for his own good, if you ask me.'

'Yes,' he shouted. He banged on the arm of his chair, his composure slipping. 'I'm sorry.' He calmed himself before he spoke again. 'That's Max to a tee. Devil may care, love them and leave them, and to hell with anybody's real feelings.'

'And you've sat on all that anger for years. He flings his money about and bails you out when you need a bit extra but holds it over your head like the sword of Damocles. Why should he have everything at his fingertips? He makes you look weak in front of your wife, doesn't he? I'll ask you again, Jonathan. What was your relationship like with Maxwell Jones?'

'I love him and hate him in equal measure.'

'I think this resentment was always going to boil over at some point. And now, damn that bastard to hell. He's dying. So you'd never have your revenge. That's what triggered you, isn't it?'

'No.'

'Why did you kill them, Finch?'

'I couldn't have killed them because, for the last two weeks, when I haven't been at my day job, I've been working as a leaflet distributor in the middle of town. My boss can verify it, not to mention the town centre security cameras.'

It was clear this suspect didn't know a damned thing. Nash didn't have any option but to let him go. But he was glad to release him because the real killer was still out there.

'If that was true, you'd have told us when we arrived,' Brown said.

'I was going to, but you didn't give me a chance. Jesus. The kids.' Finch was out of his seat, and at first, Nash thought he was going to lunge at him, but he ran out of the room. Brown chased him, unclipping the handcuffs from her belt. Nash was slower to his feet. Through the window, he saw Lucy on the swing and Carter pushing her. Higher. And higher. Lucy was squealing with laughter—and then she wasn't. That's when he saw Finch and Brown in the garden.

Nash joined them on the lawn. Lucy was begging her brother to stop the swing and let her off. Carter had his head thrown back and was laughing from the pit of his stomach with every swing. It came back, and he pushed it again. The chains squealed as they reached their zenith and buckled on the way down. And with each thrust, he put more into it—more anger. More rage.

Jonathan tackled Carter and pulled him away from the swing. 'What the hell are you doing?'

'She wanted a push.'

'She's terrified. Look at her.'

'Sorry, Luce.'

Jonathan pulled Lucy into his arms, and she sobbed against his shoulder.

'Get out of my sight, Carter,' Finch shouted at his son.

Brown readied the handcuffs to slap on Finch, despite him comforting his daughter. Nash knew if they had a serial killer on their hands, she wouldn't give a damn that she was taking him in front of his children.

He put a hand on her arm to stop her. 'Put those away, Brown. He's not our man.' He helped Finch to stand with Lucy still sobbing in his arms. 'We'll leave you now, Mr Finch, but we still need to get to the bottom of this.'

Chapter Thirty-two

They drove away, discussing the fact that they were out of options. It wasn't Max, and it wasn't Finch. That left them with nobody. Every time they had a suspect lined up for it, the evidence shot them down in flames and left them a pile of smouldering ash.

'I was sure it was Finch,' Brown said. 'Amanda Keys even wrote his name in her blood. She wanted you to see that. I think Finch is lying, and we must have missed something.'

'It's not him, Brown. We'll check the latest alibi against his previous statement, but he's clean. I'm sure of it.'

Nash indicated and turned onto Abbey Road. It was getting late, and the rest of the afternoon would be taken up with speaking to the managers at both of Finch's jobs. He had to clock in at the candle factory every day, and they already had his recent time clock cards in evidence. They could be cross-checked against his hours at the second job. The rest of Nash's day would be in the town's security control office, where the twelve town centre cameras were monitored twenty-four hours a day. 'We'll take Bowes and Lawson with us,' he said. 'It'll mean going through every one of his shifts and painstakingly tracking his movements.'

'Isn't that the Finch kid?' Brown pointed at a kid on a bicycle.

'Looks like it. He's going hell for leather, and see the way he's glancing around, shifty little bugger. What's in that pillowcase over his shoulder? In a town of fake designer backpacks, it's a strange thing for a young lad to be carrying around. Change of plan, Brown. Let's see what he's up to.'

'Are we going to pull him over?'

'That would be a very stupid thing to do. I'm always telling you, think ahead, Molly. If we stop him now, we won't know where he was going.' Nash slowed the car and maintained a distance where he could keep the boy in sight.

He hadn't heard anything from the officers protecting Jones at his Ulverston house for hours and was waiting to get in the car to check on them. He used the radio to speak to the surveillance team parked outside the house. 'Alpha to Kappa Three. Lawson, how's it going out there? All quiet? Over.'

'Yes, boss. No movement for a couple of hours. We think he's been unwell today, he hasn't invited us in like he usually does, and when he came to the doorstep earlier, he looked sick. We offered medical assistance, and he declined. We think he's gone to bed early.'

'At six o'clock? Have the back-of-property team had any contact?'

'No, he hasn't been near the garden at all.'

'Do me a favour and give him a knock, will you? Just to put my mind at rest. If he gives you any grief, put him on to me.' While Lawson knocked, he rang Jones on his mobile. It went to voicemail.

'Alpha. There's no reply here.'

'Gain entry, Lawson. Repeat. Use the key he's given you and gain entry.' He waited for what seemed like an age. He was keeping the kid in sight but had a bad feeling about Max Jones. Lawson thumbed the mic as he moved through the house looking for Jones, and then he muttered, 'Bastard.' Nash guessed what had happened before Lawson came back on the radio. 'He's gone. The slimy toad's given us the slip. I don't know how because we've never taken our eyes off the house.'

'Save the excuses for your report, Lawson, and just hope he's still alive.'

'He's never going to learn. Doesn't he realise the taxpayer's shelling out thousands to keep him alive, and he treats it like a big game?' Brown said.

If this was Jones playing stupid games again, he'd bang him up in one of the cells overnight to teach the prick a lesson. 'Get boots on the ground. I want everybody looking for Jones. I want to keep an eye on this kid. Look where our little explorer's going.' It looked as though they were heading towards Jones' townhouse in Barrow. Interesting. 'I think we may have hit two birds with one stone. And talking of birds, it looks like our little Finch has had a bollocking from his dad, so he's going for some tea and sympathy at Uncle Max's. Carter must have rung Jones from home, and that's why he left the Ulverston pad. I'll bet he's meeting him here.'

The kid had pulled up outside the Barrow house, and Nash was surprised to see he had a key. He let himself in and pushed his bike into the beautiful old tiled hallway. 'What the hell's going on here?' Nash said.

Nash and Brown pulled up outside, and Nash was glad of his gym sessions when he jumped out of the car to grab the front door of the huge townhouse before Carter had finished putting his bike in the hall and coming back to shut it. The boy tried to hide the pillowcase behind his back.

His face was a picture when they followed him in. 'What are you doing here, Carter? Is your Uncle Max in?'

'I don't know. I was just coming to feed his goldfish.'

'What's in the pillowcase, son?'

'Some food and stuff for a film with Uncle Max. He's meeting me later.'

Nash heard a bang followed by a muffled cry coming from the top of the house. Somebody was in trouble. He listened, but everything had gone quiet upstairs. All he could hear was the low hum of a television set in one of the two ground-floor flats. The kid looked undecided about what to do and glanced at the front door. Nash could tell he was thinking about making a run for it. Carter still had the set of keys in his hand to let himself into the flat at the top.

'Grab the kid,' Nash said.

He snatched the keys as Brown held Carter's arm to stop him from running. Nash charged up the stairs and was aware of Brown guiding Carter up in front of her. By the time he got to the top, he was panting. Brown and Carter were still a floor behind. He took a second to slow his gasping. Something was going on in the flat. Nash had met Jones there during the last week when it was more convenient to meet in Barrow than Ulverston, so he knew the layout. The boy and Brown reached the top landing, and Nash whispered. 'There's a bedroom, last door on the right. Take Carter in there and call for backup. Advise stealth.' It took two attempts to find the right key and slide it into the lock. He wished he'd signed a taser out of the police hold that morning. Nash listened and then opened the door and went in ahead of the other two. He used the flat of his hand to close the door quietly behind them.

Waiting until he heard the soft click of the bedroom door, Nash crept along the hall to the main lounge at the front of the house, where he heard low voices. Jones wasn't alone then. The first person he heard was female, and he wondered if he was making a fuss about nothing. Jones must have been entertaining company.

As he crept to the door, that bloody song came into his head. *They decided then. He'd never get away with doing this to them. Two black Cadillacs waiting for the right time.*

He heard something being poured into glasses. There were two. Just Jones and a woman.

'A toast, I think.' It was the woman's voice, and the ice-cold tone and command it held sent a chill down Nash's back. He tried to place the voice but couldn't.

'To lifelong friendship. What do you think, Max?'

Max muttered something that Nash didn't catch. There was the sound of clinking glasses, and a third voice threw him. Nash's body went on instant high alert when he heard two women laugh. 'What the hell was Jones up to?' He had two choices. He could go in now and hope this was innocent and friendly, or he could wait for backup.

Going for the element of surprise and hoping he wouldn't get an eyeful of a Ménage à trois swansong from Jones, he opened the door and slipped in. He didn't make a sound.

The women had their backs to the door and didn't see him at first. Jones did but was savvy enough not to let on.

Nash was so horrified that he almost alerted them to his presence by making a noise, but what it would have been, he had no idea. He only got in undetected because the women were distracted. He'd never be able to slip out again to wait for backup before they saw him. It was now or never.

'Police! On the ground!'

One woman jumped, but the other was as cold as ice as she turned around. 'Detective Chief Inspector Nash. We've been waiting for you. How lovely to see you again. Would you like a glass of Champagne? It's Maxwell's good stuff.'

'I said get on the ground. Now.'

'I couldn't possibly. I wouldn't expect you to recognise Prada, but have you any idea how unseemly that would be?'

'Actually, I do recognise quality clothing when I see it and trust me, lady, that isn't it.' Prada was just one of the many designer labels he'd bought for Sandy.

'And would you recognise the make of my blade if I ran it through your belly and released your innards?'

Max couldn't lift his head because of the wooden bracket holding him down, but he raised his eyes, 'Run. Get out of here, Nash.'

'DCI Nash would never be so rude. Would you, dear? Max, do shut your mouth, or the next word you speak will be your last. If you spoil this before the verdict is read, then we'll have to continue eliminating other people, won't we? And poor Inspector Nash will likely be our next participant. However, Maxwell, if you're a good little philanderer and keep your big mouth closed for once in your stupid life, this will end with us—and you. Now. What do you say, Maxie? Nothing. Good. You catch on fast.'

'Get down. Now,' Nash said.

He heard a creak on the stairs, still a way off. He estimated it was two floors down, but his shirt would stick to his back less knowing they had backup. The sound in the old house was so quiet it was the merest creak, and neither of the killers gave any indication of having heard it.

'For the last time. Get on the floor with your hands behind your heads.'

They didn't pay any attention, but the woman who hadn't spoken yet put her glass on an occasional table and turned around. They were both wearing their outfits from the funeral and had the veils down. *Two Black Cadillacs.* It was there all along. His subconscious knew who the killers were, but he'd been too stupid to listen to it.

He took in the staging. They'd worked hard on it. The end game was always going to be spectacular. Jones' living room had been turned into a courtroom drama. The dock, however, was far less civilised and had been replaced with a full-sized guillotine. Jones was naked and bleeding from slash marks across his back where he had been whipped, presumably while he was in place. He was on his knees with his hands tied behind his back and had a crown of thorns on his head. In several places, blood trickled in rivulets from his forehead into his eyes and down his face. The letters I N R I had been gouged into the flesh of his forehead, and the scratched wounds were already scabbing in places, showing that he'd been there for some time. His head was resting on the red velvet chin cushion, and the block was in place to secure his head. Three feet above him, the blade gleamed as the bright afternoon sunlight shone through the open curtains in a shaft of beatific light.

'Get him out of there,' Nash said.

'Leave it, Nash. They're insane, and they'll kill you, too.' Jones whispered.

'Do you like our guillotine, Inspector Nash? We borrowed it from a production of *Les Mis* showing in The Lakes. We did laugh when we thought of their faces when they found it missing. A small adaptation to put in a productive blade—and I can assure you, it has been tested, and it is fit for purpose. *Fait Accompli*. Would you like a piece of fruit?' The taller woman offered him a plate with two halves of apple on it.

The lady in charge moved to the device and untied the rope so that only the pressure of her hand was stopping the blade from falling. 'So this is how it's going to work. If anybody comes near me, this blade falls.'

Nash winced as he looked at the bucket, waiting to receive Max Jones' head. 'You've made your point. You can stop now, Ms Evans. Let's talk,' Nash couldn't believe that one of the killers was Linda Evans, Henry Watson's PA. They'd had no idea, and there wasn't a shred of evidence leading them to her. And yet, from the minute he'd seen her in the church, his subconscious mind had joined the dots.

She was laughing, and the shrill sound of it cut through Nash's nerves to grate along his spine. 'Stop? We have no intention of stopping until we've done what we set out to do. After that, yes, we can talk if you insist, Inspector.'

'Nash, get lost, will you? You're surplus to requirements. Go home, mate,' Max said. Blood rolled down his cheek. 'It's better this way.'

Evans made a show of letting the blade fall, and Max screamed. Nash shot forward and shouted, 'No.'

She held up her other hand to stop him. Linda Evans wore leather driving gloves in place of the lace ones she'd worn at the funeral. She'd dropped the blade at a slow and controlled pace, not the velocity it would need to take a man's head off.

She stopped a couple of inches before it reached Jones' neck.

After smiling at them like a benevolent teacher, she pulled the rope back up to the top of the rig. 'I told you to be quiet, Maxwell. Next time you open your big fat mouth, I let go of the rope for real. This production has to play out properly. We need a verdict before the execution.'

Nash appealed to Fiona Finch, the second woman. She was taking a lesser role, and he guessed she did as she was told. The whole time Nash had been in the room, Fiona had kept hold of the cat o' nine tails. He saw that she had blood on her hands, metaphorical and literal. As she moved, she left a half-moon footprint of blood on the oatmeal carpet.

'Fiona. Think about your nephew. We're looking after Carter in the next room. You wouldn't want him to see you like this, would you?'

Fiona Finch was only twenty-five and hadn't married yet, and she had no children of her own.

'We know about the abortion. It must have been awful. We understand how much Max Jones hurt you. We can help. Fiona, you must love your brother's children. You don't want this. I can see you've been forced into it.'

Fiona found Nash's speech funny. She smiled, and the mirth behind it was unpleasant. 'You think we killed all those people, Inspector? Oh, you do make me laugh.' Nash faced the woman in charge. 'Linda, please tie the rope back up. Make it safe, and we can talk about this.'

'Before his trial? That's ridiculous. We have to wait until sentencing has been passed. The jury has listened to all the evidence and has made their deliberations. You came just in time for the best part.' She indicated the twelve polystyrene display heads. They were arranged in two rows as in a courtroom and had white curly wigs and black robes glued to their necks.

'We can stop this,' Nash said. 'It's not too late.'

'We could indeed, but why would we want to? We've waited a long time for this, Fiona and I. Haven't we? Do you realise I've worked with Maxwell Jones for years? He's passed my desk every morning and again every night. He's stared at my breasts and flirted without seeing me—as he flirts with every woman he meets. And despite taking my virginity and having intercourse with me on several occasions, he has never once acknowledged me. He moved on to his next conquest and forgot so fast. All this time, he's known who I am, but to him, I'm just a secretary. He called me that once. Henry's secretary.'

'That's awful for you, Linda. You must have been so angry. I get it.'

'Do you? It's only eight years since he took me to bed. I started at his company for Henry Watson less than a year later, and yet his eyes passed through me. How could he not see me? To him, I was just a girl he'd had his way with, and I didn't matter.'

'He treated you both very badly. I know that. But all this, ten murders and now Max? I know he's scum, but no matter what he's done, no human being deserves this.'

Her voice rose in a rage that Nash knew she'd held in for all those years. She'd sat at her desk while Max Jones walked in front of it and was blind to her. 'Are you saying this isn't justified?'

'No. I'm not saying that. But it's okay to stop now. You can let it all go because we've seen him for what he is. Everybody has.'

She controlled the fire in her voice, and it took on an authoritative quality. 'I know jurors don't wear the fancy garb, but the costumes were just there, hanging up in the theatre, so you have to allow us a little artistic license, Inspector Nash. Each juror has his own expression. As you can see, juror number three looks as though she may be sympathetic to his plight, but I don't fancy Max's chances with the other eleven. They look grumpy, don't they? Should we find out?'

Nash spread his hands, buying time and bringing the SWAT team outside the door up to date. He chose his words carefully. 'Please, Ms Evans, go ahead. You've come this far, and it's not as if I can stop you. One slip of the rope in your hand and the guillotine blade comes down on Jones' head. Who knows, maybe it's all he deserves.' He knew the team was waiting outside the door, listening and assessing the situation.

While the killers were playing out their scenario, and with the rope in her hand, Linda was an unknown entity. Nash knew they'd be waiting for a trained negotiator to be brought in and were biding their time so as not to spook the killers. One slip, and if that blade dropped, Max was dead, and Nash would never sleep at night without the image of Jesus' head dropping into the bucket.

Linda Evans turned to the polystyrene display heads. 'Members of the jury, have you reached a verdict on which you are all agreed?'

Fiona said, 'We have, Your Honour.'

Chapter Thirty-Three

Chapter Thirty-three

Linda banged her gavel on the table. 'On the charge of being a despicable human being who has no right to walk this earth or have the get-out clause of dying a natural death, do you find the defendant guilty or not guilty?'

'Guilty as charged.'

'Fiona Finch, he denied your baby and withheld any responsibility. How do you find the defendant?'

'Guilty as charged.'

'He cast you—and me—aside like rubbish. How do you find the defendant?'

'Guilty as charged.'

'And what say you? What should be his sentence?'

'I'm sorry. I'm so sorry, girls. If I had to do it again, I'd do it differently. I promise.'

'Girls.' Fiona said. 'He still calls us girls as though we are nothing.'

'What about all those innocent people, Fiona? Why?' Nash said.

'We wanted to squeeze every ounce of pain from him that we could. Don't you see? When women can be controlled and treated so badly, it means that life has no worth. A child's life, a woman's life. Even an old man who has served his use to society. It all means nothing. Just so long as the Company Man gets to play with his wealth.'

Max struggled against his bonds and tried to free himself from the stock holding his head in place. 'I've never heard you sound so bitter, Fiona. You were always such a sweet little thing. I'm so sorry for what I did to you.'

'You destroyed our child, and for that, other children have had to die. They were the same age as our baby would have been. I've looked forward to this moment since you left me to deal with the abortion on my own and brought such shame on my family,' Fiona said. She nodded at Linda.

'Foreman of the jury,' Linda said. 'What say you, Fiona Finch? What should be the fate of this fallen son of God?'

'Off with his head.'

'Now,' Nash shouted, and the room filled with officers. He held up his hand to stop them from going near Linda, who still clung to the rope and looked surprised at the room filling with people with rifles aimed at her head.

'Go on, shoot me. My life's as good as over anyway. But let me say this. It was worth it, and by the time your finger moves, the bastard's head will be on the floor.'

'Do it,' Max screamed.

The men circled both women, and Linda tried to regain control of the situation. 'Stop, or I'll drop the rope.'

'But you only have one second of glory, Linda,' Nash said. 'It's not as though you have a submachine gun that can do a lot of damage to a lot of people. You only have one trick. All you get to do is drop a rope, and your second of glory is over. You have to pick your second wisely, you want maximum impact, and now you're surrounded.'

Her hand twitched. She was going to let go. 'Wait,' Nash shouted, and she stopped. He laughed. 'See, Linda? Your decision can be halted with a single word. You have no follow through.'

She screamed, and Nash was in the position of control now. While he'd been talking, the men behind her were closing in, a millimetre at a time. Tiny movements to get them closer to the woman holding the rope that, once let go, would decapitate a man. Fiona was out of her depth. The room was full of people in riot gear. She picked up the champagne bottle, but it was always going to be a useless weapon.

Nash gave the nod. He'd never been so scared for a man's life in his life. Linda Evans held the rope—but symbolically, so did he. If he said one wrong word, he would be killing Jones as much as Linda. His gambit relied on split-second timing, and if he got it wrong, he'd never forgive himself. Linda was confused. The team had swarmed the room out of nowhere, and the reason she hadn't let go of the rope at that moment was ego. Nash knew she wanted everybody's attention when she killed Maxwell Jones, and the place was swarming with the confusion of bodies.

On the nod, two men rugby tackled Linda, and the same happened to Fiona.

Linda let go of the rope.

A third officer was standing by with his hand ready. He caught it at the precise moment that Linda fell to the ground with a piercing scream and let go. He was wearing gloves. It could have gone so wrong. He caught the rope, wrapped it around his hand, and the blade stopped an inch from severing Max's neck.

The men were on top of Linda and Fiona. Nash had his hands on his knees. He had to calm his breathing. That was one call that was too dangerous. He'd hated playing God and having to make it. He was only a humble man. The adrenaline had poured into his body too fast, and he had red spots in front of his eyes.

Jon Si. It made sense now. Amanda Keys didn't try to write, Jon, Silas. She was trying to write, Jon's sister. Why the hell didn't he see it sooner?

They had the women subdued, and it should have been over. Nash took his jacket off and draped it over Max's bloodied body to give him some dignity while they got him out of the contraption. He removed the crown of thorns and winced as he had to pull some of the thorns out of Max's flesh. It was important to him that Nash be the one to do that for him.

But the door opened, and a pre-pubescent voice said, 'Keep walking, bitch.'

Carter shuffled into the room. He was standing on his tiptoes behind Brown and had a butcher's knife to her throat. What the hell was happening? Brown was supposed to be reading the kid *Goldilocks and the Three Bears* or something.

He pushed her forward another step. 'Sorry, boss. He got the blade out of nowhere, and I didn't expect it.'

'Sorry, Boss,' Carter mimicked Brown. 'For God's sake. "He's just a stupid kid, Mr Detective, and he tied my hands with cable ties before I could stop him. I even put my own hands behind my back when he asked me to show him how we get the bad guys." She's so stupid. I'd be a better policeman than her,' Carter said.

'Go on, Carter,' Fiona shouted. 'Slit her throat. Do it and be the most famous boy in your school, honey.'

'Put the knife down and let my officer go, son. You don't want to do this,' Nash said.

'I do, Mr Nash. I'm ten, and it's another example of people being invisible. I'm only a kid, so people don't see me, and I can do anything I like. That's why I was thinking about how to kill my sister when I was pushing her on the swing. You'd take notice of me then, wouldn't you?'

The SWAT team had released Max, and the boy didn't seem to notice. Max hobbled towards his nephew. Carter tightened the knife at Brown's throat, and several points of blood leaked from underneath it like the blood from Max's forehead.

'Get a chair,' Carter said.

Nash nodded, and a chair was brought over. Carter told Brown to sit.

She twisted and tried to kick him. He let out a bellow and moved the knife to her upper arm, going in hard. He sliced through Brown's bicep, and her cry of pain rang through the house. While she grabbed her arm, he moved the knife back to her throat. 'I'll kill her. I will.' His voice was loud and shrill.

There was a knock at the door.

'Hey, lady, are you okay in there?' They heard the officer posted at the door asking the neighbours to go back into their flats and stay there.

'It's our friends from earlier,' Linda said. 'They helped us carry everything upstairs. I told them it was a guillotine to kill Max Jones. And we all laughed. He just saw tits and arse. Maybe if the brain was more visible, we wouldn't be as invisible.'

'Shut up,' Nash said.

'If this wasn't over, we'd take another woman next, and we'd expose her brains to show society that we do have them. And the men, well, we'd go down the predictable route of cutting off their disgusting genitals. I wish I'd thought of it earlier.'

'I said shut up. Take them away.'

A man appeared at the door and was headed off by one of the officers before he saw anything.

'Come on, dude. I'm your uncle Max. What the hell have those two witches got you into? This is beyond crazy. You're a good boy, Carter. This isn't you, buddy. We've always been mates, haven't we? I'm listening to you now.'

'So am I, son. Carter, is it? I'm listening and would love to know how you fit into all this. I'm Silas. It's a silly name, I know—I blame my parents. I'm the Chief Inspector for Cumbria, so I'm a pretty important guy, too. Just like you.'

'Slit her throat, Carter,' Linda screamed.

'Get them the hell out of here,' Nash shouted.

Fiona twisted in her handcuffs and tried to get to him. 'Do it, my beautiful boy.'

The SWAT team had Fiona and Linda cuffed and on their feet. 'I said get rid of them.'

'No, I want them to stay.'

'If they go, Carter, this is all yours, and you won't have them interrupting you all the time.'

'I need them to help me.'

Nash gave the officers the nod to take them. Linda and Fiona were dragged out of the flat and downstairs to waiting vans. There were too many people about for it to be safe. Carter started to cry, and Linda screamed and ranted as they carried her down the stairs to where a crowd would have gathered outside.

'You don't need them to help you kill that lovely lady, do you?'
Nash said. 'You know she's called Ms Brown, don't you? That's a real
person. What has she ever done to you? Carter, it's a very bad thing to
kill somebody, you understand that? Molly has a family that loves her
and wants her to go home tonight. And it's not as easy as you think,
all that sinew and muscle to cut through.'

'I don't want to talk about it no more.'

'Why not, Carter?'

The boy looked at the floor. Nash had to decide how to play it and
whether to go in like a kindly granddad or be harsh. He went for the
middle ground, but his tone wasn't gentle.

'Come on, lad. Answer my question.'

'I don't want to get into trouble.'

'Well, son, I can't lie. You're in a bit of bother. But tell us the truth,
and we'll do everything we can to help you. I can't believe a nice young
lad like you really hurt anybody.'

'I did, and I can prove it, too.'

'I find that hard to believe. Are you trying to be brave and take the
blame for Aunty Linda and Aunty Fiona?'

'No.'

'Tell me what happened.'

'It was me. I killed them all.'

The room went silent, and the only noise was the air moving and
the sound of the traffic a long way below.

'No, you didn't. That's impossible. You're just trying to be good
and take the blame for Aunty Fi.'

'I killed every one of them. I did the killing bit on them all. Aunty
Fiona said I took their lives. She and Linda set up the scenes. I'm not
big enough to do that yet. I'm only little. When I'm older, I will.'

Max was holding Nash's jacket around him, and Nash was shocked at how emaciated his legs looked after just a couple of weeks. He stumbled. 'Mate, you don't know what you're saying.'

'I do, Uncle Max.'

'Put the knife down, Carter, and come and give me a hug. I think we could both do with one.'

'If you keep talking to me as if I'm daft, I'll kill her now, Uncle Max. I'm clever, but only Aunty Fiona and Linda saw that. Everybody else just shouts at me and tells me to get down or go to bed.'

'I'm sorry for that, mate. I'll never shout at you again.'

'No, because that thing in your head will have exploded by then. You'll be dead, and I won't even remember you.'

Nash said, 'Carter. Molly's bleeding a lot, and she's getting very tired. That's because she's in shock, and we need to get her to a hospital. I don't believe you killed anybody, and I don't think you want her to die.' There was no narrative in the room. Even the spiders in the old house had taken to the rafters and weren't coming out. Everything was still. The only movement was the passage of time and the spread of blood from Molly's arm. Her neck was cut, too, but that was just a surface wound. They had to keep it that way and get her out fast.

Blood.

Of course, right at the start of the investigation, a sample of blood had been found on the body in the hotel room. They hadn't realised the connection at the time, but it was a child's blood that they'd dismissed as being irrelevant. One of the tests had come back with blood that proved to be from somebody between the ages of five and twelve. They'd had the result from that tiny droplet of blood on Robert Dean's shirt for days, but the investigation hadn't brought anything into the open.

'I killed the old teacher first. It was scary because I hadn't done it before, but I liked it. It made me feel funny in the tummy. But a good funny. And Aunty Linda said I can remember that feeling next time.'

Nash thought back to the autopsy report and Bill Robinson's words. 'It was as though he didn't have a lot of strength and had to perfect his technique.'

Nash felt sick.

'What will happen to him?' Jones whispered to Nash so that Carter couldn't hear.

'Initially, I should imagine he'll be sent to a secure facility for assessment rather than going to youth offenders.'

'And then?'

'After that? Who knows. He's reached the age of culpability.'

'What? At ten years old?'

'I'm afraid so. It was set during the Bulger trial in the early nineties.'

'He's very sick, isn't he, Nash?'

'Yes, he is.'

'No, I'm not.'

It was as though Jones was working through something and needed confirmation. Nash was a seasoned detective, he should have seen it, but there was so much going on. He was preoccupied. 'It's been an ordeal for you, Max. Let's get this over with and get you to the hospital to be checked out.'

'Sorry. I'm feeling queasy,' Max said. 'Is it okay if I open the window? There are too many guns around to do anything without asking.' Nash nodded, and Jones opened the old-fashioned sash window all the way up. An instant breeze gusted into the room, reminding them that it was winter, but it was as though the cold wind had cleansed the atmosphere. Max was freezing, and he shivered. There was a trail of blood dripping down his leg from beneath the jacket.

'Can somebody find this man's clothes?' Nash said. 'And where the hell are the paramedics?'

Carter was still talking, and his young voice sounded like a nursery rhyme in a horror movie. 'Then I did the lady, but she wasn't up in the air when I killed her. She struggled a lot, and Aunty Fiona had to help me a little bit by holding her still, but I managed to strangle her all by myself.'

It was as though the kid was talking about a science project he was working on. Nash was appalled and fascinated.

'And then there was the man in the hotel. I put the injection into his leg. It was like being a real doctor. And then I got to sneak into the security man's room and stop the cameras. I don't know what I like best, being a doctor or being a security man. When he was in bed, he didn't drink the hot chocolate. I snuck back in and drank it, and it had the works, marshmallows and squirty cream and everything. I put the sticky flower in the room, but I don't like the smell of it.'

Nash remembered Amanda Keys. She'd mentioned a little boy at every reading. She even told them about the blood when he held up his cut finger in her vision. She said he was playing in the hotel corridors. It showed just how invisible a child in a hotel could be. Nash was furious that they missed so much that was right in front of their noses.

An officer came into the room, 'We've just had a call from the station, sir. The boy,' he wagged his head towards Carter, 'has just been reported missing.'

'Right, I'll speak to the parents shortly.'

'Missing. But I'm not missing. I'm with Uncle Max. Will I be in trouble?'

'No, son, it's all right. I'll talk to your folks and tell them we're just clearing something up here. But you can give me the knife, and it'll make everything better.'

'Maybe I should go home now. I don't want Mum and Dad to worry about me. I'll get in trouble when I get in.'

'Good idea. Come on. I'll take you home. Just let Molly go, and we can do that right now.'

The boy was confused, and he was tired. His arm was shaking. Along with the confession, this was what Nash had been waiting for. He gave the nod, and the men took him down.

'Look, before you take him, can I just have a minute with him? Just one minute. I'll get him to be compliant and tell you everything,' Max said.

'One minute, and then we have to go, Max.' Nash couldn't imagine what Max was going through. He expected he was happy to be alive, only to have to go through the lead-up to death again very soon. Life was unfair.

The women were in custody. The boy was cuffed and ready to be taken away. Nash couldn't feel any pity for the child inside the monster who was confused and crying. Was the child inside the monster, or was the monster inside the child?

It was over.

He felt like weeping for all the injustice in the world as Jones bent to his nephew. Everybody relaxed muscles that had been tense for over an hour. Too late, he realised what Jones was going to do.

Jones gave Carter a big hug. Tears were streaming down his face. 'It's going to be okay, little man. Everything's going to be all right. There's nothing to worry about.'

'Am I in trouble when I get home?'

'No mate, you're not in trouble. I'll make it all right.'

He straightened and picked the boy up. The most natural thing in the world for an uncle to lift his nephew up for a cuddle.

And then he was heading for the open window. One step, two, before Nash or anybody else in the room realised his intention.

'The window,' somebody screamed. Jones launched himself through it to the flat roof. He was a dying man who could barely lift the child. Nash guessed it wasn't as easy as he'd imagined clambering out of the window.

There was a felt-roof porch over the window of the flat below. It was old, and part of it gave way. Jones tried to throw himself and the boy off the third-floor roof and was taken down by officers grabbing his leg. He tried to throw the boy off, but Carter caught the edge as his fight-or-flight instinct took over. Jones was dragged back into the room, and the boy was helped in by two other officers. Max threw himself on the floor. 'Let us go. Please just let him go. It will be better for him this way. I love him.'

Nash looked around the room. Only four officers were still there. Molly had been carried down already to the waiting paramedics. It was still a murderous situation and too risky to let them in the flat, so an officer she'd never met before had carried her down with all the tenderness of a lover. Two officers he knew, and two he didn't. Nash put his hand up to speak, but one of the other men stopped him. He was a seasoned officer of about forty, drafted in from another division as an extra body.

'It's okay, sir. Don't say it. We get it. The last three minutes never happened.'

Nash felt a tear brimming in his eye, 'Thank you, men, I appreciate it.'

Chapter Thirty-four

The hospital was too sterile and too quiet, especially at this time of night. 'How is he?' Nash asked.

'It won't be long now.' The nurse was pretty. Max would like that. Nash might always be known by his surname—and with a name like Silas, who could blame him?—but he hadn't thought of Max as Jones for weeks. He'd been visiting the hospice every day, usually in the evening, but not always. It depended on work. Nash had been busy for the last three months since the killers had been put away—but he always made time to come here on his way home. Max said it was the highlight of his death—or he did when he was lucid. They were working on a new case together. Max felt it was time to give everlasting peace to Kami Hakimi, the refugee boy that Amanda Keys told him had been murdered.

When he first went into the hospital and before his treatments, he'd made three donations to the fertility clinic sperm bank. He'd told Nash, 'My juice is going to be in high demand, and, of course, they will be the most gorgeous babies on the planet. Every one of them will look just like his papa Max. So, I expect you to be the best uncle to my many progenies,'

'Assuming they are viable.'

'Of course, they are. It's me we're talking about.' He spoke about the unborn children often, and it gave him comfort to think he'd live on in them. 'See? Even when I'm dead, I'll still be getting my end away.'

'You're impossible. You do know that, don't you?'

'I'm not impossible. I'm impressive.'

Nash brought him back to the subject of Kami. Max wanted to solve the refugee's murder as the last good deed he did before he died. Nash sat by his bed every evening, and they worked on his case to find closure for him.

The hospice was nice—that endless insipid word. The nurses were nice, the food was nice, and the drugs were fricking awesome. The rooms were bright. They'd tried very hard to hit the balance between happy and clinical. The sun seemed to shine brighter in Max's room than anywhere else on earth. Sometimes it hurt his eyes, and they had to close the curtains and once the sunlight made Max scream in agony.

'Are you in pain? Shall I get a nurse?' Nash asked.

'I'm always in pain, Nasher, and only buzz if Natalie's on duty. I reckon she's going to agree to go out with me tonight. She says she likes Mexico so we might catch a nine o'clock flight.' He'd wheezed then and had to stop talking, but he was still in pain.

'Can I do anything for you?'

'I hate closing the curtains. I have so little time left to see the sun.'

'I'm sorry.' Nash got up. 'I'll open them.'

'No, please leave them. It's like a laser into my head. I can't stand it. But when it's shut out, I miss the sun more than I miss Paige.'

'You never even met her, you fool. What about that knackered old van?'

'Are you mad? I don't miss anything more than that, except maybe Dexter. Have you heard how he is?'

'He's fine, mate. Driving Hayley and Steve mad. He loves the kids, and they have bought him more toys than any cat on the planet.'

'As long as he's happy.'

Max had to turn away then, and he brought up blood into the cardboard receptacle next to him. He was weak and lay back on the sheets. Nash was glad because he'd had to turn away, too, because of what happened to Dexter. Hayley and Steve didn't hesitate when he asked them if they'd consider taking Dexter on. And the cat had settled—to a degree. But every time he got out of the house, he crossed the road to sit on Max's windowsill, and he'd wail pitifully for his master.

Max had drifted away again. He did that all the time now, and the lucid moments were fewer than the clouded ones. They kept him medicated, so he was rarely in much pain. When he was, it was unbearable to see. He slept mostly, and Nash sat beside his bed, holding his hand. Just being there.

He'd been in the hospice for three weeks now. Living at home since the case had proved too much for him as his health had deteriorated. And Dexter still went looking for Max every time he got out. Last night he'd crossed the road. They were all in the living room, and the kids were the first to scream when they heard the awful screech of brakes. Dexter had been killed by a car. Hayley and Steve were devastated, the kids heartbroken, but they'd agreed that Max shouldn't be told. Through her tears, Hayley said it happened for a reason. It was so that Dexter would be there first to wait for his master.

Max loved that cat. The tragedy of it made Nash feel sick.

He went to work. He came to the hospital. He went home to an empty house. That was his life. Visiting Max wasn't for his benefit, though he was glad it filled a mutual need.

This time he'd been sitting for four hours, and the times between Max waking up were getting longer. That was a good thing. It showed that the pain medication was working. He was steady, as they said.

Max wanted to send everybody away. But first, his friends and family gathered around his bed. That was after his muscles gave way and his legs stopped working. He'd never stand up again. After that last visit, he wouldn't see anybody. The only person he allowed into his room was Nash.

Steve and Hayley still visited, and every time they came with gifts, but they never got past reception.

Jon was filled with guilt. The sins of the son and all that. Nash thought he was probably glad not to have to watch his best friend die a little bit more every day and then leave to visit his son. Nash was the one given that penance. And he took it gladly, with both hands, every precious moment of it.

Max opened his eyes, and they were sticky. His eyelids were stuck to each other with rheum. Nash was no nurse but could take a warm flannel and wash his face. 'Where's Mum, Dad?' Max asked.

'She'll be along later, son. Don't worry.' His mother had been to visit, but only once, when he was lucid, and they'd argued. Now that he was quiet, she said it was too painful for her and retreated back to Majorca.

'Look. Nanny Clare's bought me a cowboy outfit.'

'So she has.' The nurses said never to argue with him and to go along with anything he said. It lessened his agitation and anxiety. He still had the hallucinations but none of the attitude. Well, mostly.

'Where's my money? You've taken my money.'

Nash showed him the wallet. With the same twenty pounds in it that he always showed him. It had been Nash's best wallet. And on one occasion, when Max accused him of stealing his money, he gave it to him and put a twenty-pound note in it. Max accused the nurses a lot when he wasn't trying to kiss them.

That was his mental state. Horrible to see, but so was the physical. The man he'd met less than five months before was gone, and somebody had put a skeleton in his place. He hadn't eaten for three weeks and was only given saline from a drip with his medication. His eyes had sunken so far into his head that you could rest a marble on the socket if you had such a desire. The worst thing for Nash was looking at the corners of his mouth and the constant build-up of brown, yellow sludge that congealed there.

He wiped it away again now and thought back to one week ago. His decline had been coming for weeks, but the end game was sudden. Last week he was in and out of confusion, anxiety, agitation and hallucination. And then, like sunlight through the trees, there would be that spark of pure, lucid brilliance that had been Maxwell Edward Bartholomew Tyler Jones.

A box ticker had come in to tick some more boxes. Nash was appalled at her condescending manner, but Max was spared her. He was somewhere far away at the time, shagging a woman or drinking a Jack Daniels.

'Now then, Maxwell. How are we today?'

'How are we today?' Max parroted her words back to her.

'Do you know where you are at all?'

'No. Do you know where you are at all?' Max said.

'Yes. I know where I am, but do you?'

'Coming into my house asking all these questions at me all the time. Are you a bailiff? He dribbled, and a line of saliva ran down his chin.

He had the open expressionless smile of nobody at home. Tick-boxer's lip curled in distaste.

'I have to ask you some questions, Maxwell. We want to see how we are, don't we?'

'Do we? How are we?'

'It's not important how I am, Max. Do you know where you are?'

'I'm here. Are you lost? Should I call a policeman?' He wasn't as sick a week ago, and he'd picked up his shoe. Nash felt physical pain in his chest as he watched him put the shoe to his ear. 'Hello? Hello?'

Box-ticker, whose role wasn't apparent, took the shoe away from him. She didn't ask. She just did it. Her exasperation was showing as she threw it on the floor.

'Hey, that was my baby. She stole my baby. A dingo stole my baby.'

The woman wrote faster than her hands could keep up, and Nash intervened. 'He often gets confused like this. Perhaps if you give him more time and are a bit softer in your approach.'

'And you are?'

'Nash. I'm a detective, and I'm Max's friend. Max, not Maxwell, if you don't mind.' The woman scribbled some more, and Nash's heart broke as he remembered a crazy conversation with Max after his interrogation. 'Do I get a badge and a gun?' He had to cough a lump away.

The woman tried a different approach. 'Max?'

'Dr Jones. Jones, calling Dr Jones.' Max sang the song loud.

'Mr Jones, do you prefer that? Should I call you Mr Jones?'

'Hello, Mr Jones,' Max said. He held out his hand for her to shake. She ignored it because ticking boxes was more important than the person in the bed.

'Do you know your date of birth, Mr Jones?'

'Happy Birthday. Happy Birthday. Happy Birthday to me.' He made blowing motions as though he was blowing out candles on a cake. And knowing he'd never see another one tore Nash's heart as well. The woman was like a stone.

'Do you know your date of birth?'

'No. Do you?'

The woman sighed.

'Perhaps if you don't sigh at him, he might be able to answer your questions better,' Nash said.

'I know what I am doing, Mr Nash.'

'Do you? Well done,' Max, said and he gave her a round of applause. If it had been a conscious thought process, the sarcasm would have been beautiful, but even as it was, it was funny, and Nash snorted.

It was clear Tick-Boxer just wanted to get to the end of her form and get out of there. 'Can you remember your last address from when you lived at home?'

'I can remember my address now.'

'You can? Perfect. What is it?'

'What is what?'

'Your address What's your address?'

'Well, I don't have one do I?'

'You don't have an address?'

'No.'

'Why don't you have an address?'

'Because it's cheese pie, beans and chips at school today. I like it here'

'Where, Max?'

'Here?'

'Where's here, Mr Jones?'

'Well, it's the same place as you. Where are you? Have we got ice cream?' Max farted.

'Okay. I think that'll do for now. I might come back another day—when you're feeling a bit better.'

'Bye-bye, baby. Baby, bye-bye.'

She left in a haze of inexpensive perfume. Nash had to look out of the window for a minute. It was the most upsetting display of Max's condition he'd seen to date. When he'd got his wits about him, he sat back down.

'It's okay, mate. I've got you.'

'I've got you.'

'I know you have, mate,' Nash said.

'You're not going to start bawling again, are you?'

'No. It's okay, Max.'

Max was laughing. 'Come on. You weren't taken in by that shit as well, were you?' He reeled off his name, date of birth, and address with postcode and finished with, 'And Silas Nash is a great big gullible prat.'

Nash did cry. He couldn't help it because that was the thing. Max was such a dickhead that you couldn't tell when it was the disease and when he was amusing himself for the hell of it. He laughed, cried, and he might even have snotted a little bit. 'You were putting all that on?'

'Every word of it.'

'You little sod. Don't ever do that to me again.'

'But it's so easy. Pack it in, Nasher. Come on. I like cheese pie, so it's not that sad.' And Nash didn't want to tell him that it was so sad it hurt. Today was great. A memory that would live with Nash for the rest of his life. He felt honoured to have been the one who witnessed it, and his heart was filled with feelings of a strange friendship for the dying man. And it was so sad.

That was only last week.

He was awake less often now. There were fewer times when he was lucid, and Nash was never sure when it was just Max being a dick. He didn't want him to die.

'You're awake.'

'Yes. At least, I think I am. Are you awake?'

'Sod off.' They laughed. 'Hayley and Steve have been.'

'Have they?'

'Yes, they've brought you fruit, Ribena and some chocolates. But as you can't eat anything, I'll have them.' He got a weak grin, and then Max fell asleep.

'You're awake?'

'I need to get something down on paper.'

'Okay, calm down. Don't try to stand. Your legs don't work anymore. What is it? What do you want?'

'Write.'

'Okay, I've got a pen.'

'I want to give Hayley and Steve their house.'

'That's a lovely thing to do.'

'Money and stuff to Melissa and family.'

'Got it.'

'Barrow house, and Nanny Clare's house to Jon and Emily. There's some money for them as well to help with Carter's legal costs. I want the business signing over to Jon. He can sell it if he wants to. I don't care.'

'I've got it all, relax, it's all written down. Lie back and take it easy.' He grinned. 'But hey, what do I get?'

'You get my respect, Nasher. And, in return, I get to call you my friend. But yeah, there's something for you, too.'

'No. Hey. Honestly, Max. I was joking. I'm honoured to have your friendship, and I don't want anything else.'

'Tough. You get the Ulverston house. And, are you ready for this?'

'Max, no. I was joking.'

'I said, are you ready for this? Don't spoil my big moment.'

Nash sighed. 'Go on.'

'I'm leaving Lady Diana to you. I think you're a good fit, and I want you to have some fun. Promise me you'll get out and camp in her at least four times a year.'

Nash was horrified. 'I don't know, Max.'

'Promise me?'

'It's not really my thing.'

Max's voice had risen, and he started wheezing and coughing.

'Okay, I promise. Now relax before you hurt yourself.' Max winked, and Nash knew he'd initiated a promise under false pretences. He seemed more peaceful, and he slept after that. The next time he woke up, his voice was thick, and his words slurred.

'Nash?'

'Yes?'

'Do not ask me if I'm awake.'

Nash laughed.

'I want you to get back out there.'

'What?'

'Don't think I don't know how many hours you're sitting here every damned night. Cockblocking a fella from all those nurses. You need to find somebody.'

'I don't need anybody.'

'But you do. It's me you're talking to. And you're not that ugly. I'd be your boyfriend if I was gay and you weren't like a million years old.'

What was it with Nash and tearing up? He couldn't stop it from happening. He guessed that was the definition of real friendship. 'I wouldn't have you.'

'Get you, sweetheart. Have me? I'm not an object to be adored and pawed over, you know.' He was weakening, and Nash wanted to hear everything he could before he was gone. It didn't matter what they said and if it was complete rubbish. He didn't want Max to die. But he was going to, and they couldn't make friendship memories. Going fishing—as if. Hanging out at the pub, having dinner. So Nash had to get as many individual sentences in, so that he could put them all together later. A week later, Max would be gone.

Tomorrow he'd be gone.

'So why wouldn't you have me as your boyfriend?' Max said.

'You're Far too self-centred and opinionated.'

Max's eyes were closing. 'And you dare to say that to me after the last princess you had.' He was struggling but fought the medication and the sleep. 'Find somebody who loves you, Silas. You deserve it.'

'I will,' he said as he leaned over and kissed Max's cheek.

His breathing deteriorated an hour later.

The next time he woke was the last time. Nash struggled to hear what he was saying. 'Where's my horse? Why is he over there in the corner?'

'It's okay, Max. He's just having something to eat, and then I'll bring him over.'

'Joking, you mug. You fall for it every time. I think this is our last date, Silas.'

It was too big a statement to lie to him. 'Shush, Max. Just relax.'

'We had fun, didn't we?'

'You? Fun? You were a bloody nightmare. Yes, we had fun, my friend.'

'I'll miss you. I think, maybe. Don't know, that bit might be bol-locks.'

'And I'll miss you, but that might be bollocks, too.'

His eyes were closing.

'Enjoy, Lady Diana.'

'I will.'

And then Max's eyes opened again. He clutched Nash's hand with more force than he'd had for days. 'It's coming, Silas. It's happening. Don't leave me. I'm so frightened.'

Nash cried out in pain for him. He got onto the bed beside him and pulled Max's broken body into his arms. 'I'm here. You aren't alone.'

'I can feel you, Silas. Will it hurt?'

'No. I don't think so, but that bit might be bollocks.' He didn't get the joke from earlier. So Nash had to talk fast. 'No, Max. I don't think it will hurt. And if it does, it won't be for long. I'm right here.'

'Thank you, mate.'

'Shush. Let it happen, now.'

'Guess what, Silas.'

'What?'

'It doesn't hurt.'

Chapter Thirty-five

At the Dale View secure mental health facility, Carter Finch had been in isolation for three months. And now he wasn't. He'd behaved so much like a model citizen that they let him out with the other kids. This was his first day on the integrated wing. He wasn't a threat to anybody, and all the terrible things he'd done were committed under coercion.

Nash said, 'No.' He wanted the little bastard kept in manacles and chained to a wall in a dungeon fifty feet underground. Carter Finch was the most dangerous human being he'd ever encountered. At least his accomplices had a reason for killing—he just enjoyed it.

Adam Vance was deemed criminally insane by three doctors. He wasn't put in a youth offenders programme but in the psychiatric ward, on a colourful unit, for assessment. He underwent a barrage of tests and counselling sessions prior to the case of The Florists going to trial. The media went into a frenzy when the story had been released in full, so, for his own protection, Adam Vance was given the alias while he was in the facility.

Again, Nash said no.

Adam Vance liked his new name. He thought it sounded like a superhero alias. He'd told his psychologist—who was lovely—that he'd stopped having bad thoughts about killing his sister. He missed his parents, but they said his mum and dad weren't allowed to visit. That made him sad, and in counselling, when he had to draw his mood onto the blank face, he'd scribbled a sad expression. He wanted to add blood dripping from the eyes, but he didn't.

He said the room where they carried out his counselling was scary, and could he have it in his bedroom? They agreed and were lucky he didn't have a weapon at that point. The inmates weren't animals, he'd been told, so they weren't locked up in cages. In Nash's opinion, the staff were all spare-the-rod snowflakes. When they looked at Vance, they saw a sick child. Nash wanted to show them the photographs. He saw a monster. Since he'd been released from isolation, Vance had a proper bedroom with a single bed, a desk, and a camera on the ceiling.

And a roommate.

He rocked. He rocked all day and often at night, too. He enjoyed reading, and although he wanted to read Stephen King, he didn't. He chose the Percy Jackson books, and while he was reading, he put his chair back onto two legs, and he rocked some more. But otherwise, he was okay, and they told him, 'Very good, Adam. You're doing very well, aren't you, sweetheart?' When the psychologist said, 'A chair has four legs,' he burst into tears, so she didn't try to stop him again. It was a comfort thing, they said and should be ignored for now. After all, he was doing so well.

They put him in with a much bigger boy. Jackson was his role model, and they could see that Adam looked up to him.

It was all going very well.

'What are you in for?' Jackson asked.

'I like killing people too much.'

Jackson laughed and called him a little freak, and Adam went back to his book about Percy and the Olympians.

One day, Adam did something different. It was risky, he knew that, but he had little choice. It was after lights out, and Jackson was already asleep. He dragged the blanket off his bed and pulled it over his head on the floor next to his chair. A guard saw his strange behaviour on camera and flung the door open.

'What's going on, Vance?'

Adam stuck his head out from under the blanket and pretended to be embarrassed. 'Private stuff,' he said, and the guard went red.

'Bloody hell.' He closed the door.

Jackson woke up and laughed, 'You dirty little pervert. You'll go blind doing that.' But this laugh made no difference. The last time Jackson laughed at Adam when he said he was a killer was enough. Adam didn't like being laughed at.

Under the covers, he wasn't doing what the guard and Jackson thought. He had reached his objective, and with all the rocking, he'd managed to get the leg off the chair. It was a wooden seat, and he'd spent days on two legs to weaken the joint. What he could have done in five minutes at home with a saw took five days here. He slipped into bed with the leg.

And waited.

For half an hour.

For light thirteen-year-old snoring.

He knew he didn't have long, so he had to make it good.

Adam Vance roared like a bear and shot out of his bed. He crossed the room to the other boy and figured he had less than a minute if they were on their game and longer if they were playing cards. He knew they sometimes turned the sound off on the monitors.

The first three hits to Jackson's face were hard. Bang.

And fast. Bang.

And bloody. Bang.

The kid was big, and he was probably as hard as nails. Adam didn't give him time to react. There was blood. A lot of blood. More than any of the others, and that's what turned him on.

'Private stuff.'

He kept hitting Jackson's face, using the chair leg with the screws sticking out of it until he heard them at the end of the corridor. They were running. They didn't usually run. He kept hitting his roommate until they used the card reader to open his door. His arms were aching. He'd lost count at fifty-one. But. He. Kept. Hitting. Jackson.

Until they pulled him off the dead body. Nash wasn't surprised. He'd seen the others. Vance was always going to escalate.

Nash would use his dying breath to fight any appeals and see that the kid was never released. God help the world if the day came when Adam Vance breathed the sweet air of freedom.

It was a dirty world.

Also By Katherine Black

About Author

Printed in Great Britain
by Amazon